THE TOKEN : BOOK TWO
SHADOWS OF THE EARTH

NATHAN HYSTAD

Copyright © 2024 Nathan Hystad

All rights reserved.

No part of this publication may be reproduced, distributed, or transmitted in any form or by any means, including photocopying, recording, or other electronic or mechanical methods, without the prior written permission of the publisher, except in the case of brief quotations embodied in critical reviews and certain other non-commercial uses permitted by copyright law.

This is a work of fiction. All of the characters, names, incidents, organizations, and dialogue in this novel are either products of the author's imagination or are used fictitiously.

Cover art: J Caleb Design
Edited by: Christen Hystad
Edited by: Scarlett R Algee
Proofed and Formatted by: BZ Hercules

ISBN: 9798322308546

PROLOGUE

Mare Serenitatis (Sea of Serenity)
December 8th, 1972

Commander Peter Gunn paused to gaze at the blinking lights of their command and service module passing overhead. He'd trained for this, but nothing could have prepared him for being grounded on the Moon. The lunar module, *Pelican*, sat a short distance away, while Colin Swanson assembled the flag nearby.

"*Everything good, Commander?*" Fred Trell's voice held a hint of anxiety. He figured Trell was disappointed to brave the stars, only to stay in orbit. Gunn downplayed the experience while Helios circled them.

"The specimen collection is coming along. We'll secure the next few core samples and pack it up," he told Trell.

Swanson had left the flag upright, but was bounding farther from their position.

"Swanson, where are you going?" he asked.

"*I see something, Commander,*" he said, the voice slightly garbled.

"Don't venture too far. We have work to finish," he warned.

Peter rolled his cart, bringing the carefully selected

rocks, regolith, and core samples toward the lander. He peered at the Earth, a marble-sized beauty in the distance. He thought about his son, daughter, and delightful wife, glad he'd have more time with them after all he'd put them through this past year.

He loved being an astronaut, but they were more important.

Peter spent several minutes loading supplies, and searched for Colin. Swanson was an affable man, with too much curiosity for his own good. Peter knew he'd get them in trouble from the moment he'd first met Colin, and while they were close friends, it was this kind of carelessness he'd cautioned his superiors at NASA about.

"Pelican, this is Helios, requesting updates." Trell was relentless in his communications.

"Helios, I've got you loud and clear. We're loading the cart, and—"

"*...holy...spac...don...ouch.*" Colin's voice crackled through his helmet.

"Helios, did you hear that?" Peter asked, tapping his facemask. "Swanson, come in." He didn't receive a reply. A hissing sound penetrated his ears, but no words. This was typical of Swanson, abandoning his post to explore an unsanctioned region. They'd set direct parameters, and…

Peter spotted his counterpart, two hundred meters north. Colin Swanson was still, his white spacesuit contrasting with the darkness of space beyond. He was perched on a rocky outcropping, staring down.

"Colin?"

"Peter, come here."

Peter took long strides, half-floating to Colin, and slowed his approach, gathering his balance. "What are you doing? We have to—"

Peter spied the glowing triangle in Colin's grip, and had the urge to cuff it free. "Where did you find that?"

Colin pointed with his other hand, which was noticeably shaking.

Peter followed the direction and gasped at the sight. A black oddity hovered above the surface, an impossible fog lifting from the edges before vanishing. "What is this?"

The triangle grew brighter when Colin stepped toward the anomaly. Peter stretched for his crewmate, but Colin was out of reach. *"I have to know ..."*

Peter glanced at the lander, then at the shadowy hole. "Not on my watch. Get to the rendezvous. We're leaving."

Colin disregarded the order. He loomed near the abnormality and crouched, waving an arm through the leaking mist. He gazed at Peter, the reflection of the dark blotch inhibiting his face shield. *"I need to find out."*

"Find out what? Quit messing around and head to the lander."

Colin ignored him and moved closer. Peter rushed him, tackling his friend. He attempted to push Colin past the black fog, but it seemed to stretch, enveloping them.

Day became night, and Peter ceased to exist.

PART ONE
A CHANGE OF PLANS

1

*W*aylen put his cell phone into his pocket and cursed.

"Problem?" Assistant Director Ben asked.

"Nope. No issues," Waylen said. "I'm standing in the laboratory of a weapons manufacturer, whom we've just arrested. I don't have the tokens, and I think the civilians you instructed me to stay clear of are in possession of them."

"Then you shouldn't have any difficulty getting them back." Ben approached the center of the lab, where the hexagonal platform remained behind the clear, shielded walls. "He obviously believed in the Delta's power."

"Don't you?" Waylen asked him.

Assistant Director Ben rubbed his bleary eyes and sighed. "I don't know what the truth is. All I have is my experience with the token. They've ordered me to cut you loose."

"You're firing me?" Waylen blurted.

"Nothing so drastic."

"Then what?"

"That's it, Assistant Director," an unfamiliar voice called from the entrance.

"That's the guy from the meeting in DC," Waylen said

quietly.

"Waylen, I'd like to introduce you to Theodore Belleville."

Waylen watched the man in the expensive suit enter, hands clasped behind him as he examined the laboratory. "It's bigger than I expected." He didn't try to shake with Waylen.

"Theodore works for the Secretary of Defense."

"Indirectly," Belleville said.

"How does one work *indirectly*..." Waylen stopped when the guy motioned at Ben.

"You can leave. Thank you for your time and the FBI's efforts to secure the asset."

Assistant Director Ben made eye contact with Waylen. "Good luck, Brooks. You have my number if you ever need anything." No one spoke while Ben's footsteps echoed through the cavernous lab, and Theodore only acknowledged Waylen when the hatch sealed shut.

Theodore knocked on the clear barrier surrounding the platform. "How much do you know about alien life?"

"Not a lot, sir."

"I understand your reluctance to discuss the topic. Believe me, I've been ridiculed in the upper echelons of our great country's leadership. When I approached Jacob about starting the organization, he was even more resistant."

Waylen thought about Ben's comments, and the fact Theo was talking to him at this very moment. His gut told him it wasn't a good career shift. "Organization?"

"What would happen if aliens set foot on our soil?"

"Hopefully, our pathogens would kill them. Sir," he added.

"The thing I admire most about Leo Monroe is his

confidence that there's another access point for aliens to travel to Earth. While everyone is constantly assuming they'd fly, he warned us there could be an alternate avenue. Leo surmised they might harness wormholes. He assumed they had the ability to create portals. When he heard the astronauts from Helios 15 discovered something on the Moon, he became obsessed."

Waylen listened while Theodore circled the platform, then stopped at the locker containing high-tech spacesuits.

"The entire facility is dedicated to defending our country," Theodore said.

"Not the planet?"

The question got a wry grin. "Leo doesn't come across as overly patriotic, but he sure as hell follows the money. We partnered with him to build a few facilities within the States, and he siphoned some of the cash to construct this under our noses. We didn't even know about it until you were brought here. Shame on us, right?" Theodore hefted a helmet and briefly tried it on, before returning it into the cubby. "Leo called this Operation Delta, and I've been ordered to continue his work, but under the guidelines of the US government, not a private CEO."

"Are you offering me a job?" Waylen asked.

"If you'll accept. You were able to get the tokens," he said.

"Clearly that's not true, since I don't have them."

"Where are they?" Theodore asked. "I mean, it's brilliant that you brought fakes to your meeting with Leo Monroe. I commend you on the move, but I would like to see them. Testing must begin as soon as possible."

"I don't know where the originals are." Waylen

wouldn't give up Rory, Silas, and Cody so easily, not before hearing their side of the story. He was certain one of them had made the swap, and he had to understand why.

Theodore stared at Waylen. "What do you mean?"

"I thought I was in possession of the real tokens."

Theodore clearly fought to keep his composure, but it was obvious he was on the verge of freaking out. "You'll retrace your steps. Contact those civilians and find them."

"What's my title?"

"Title?"

"Who's signing my paycheck? Do I get a badge?" Waylen asked.

"You answer to me, the Director of Operation Delta. You'll maintain your FBI credentials, should someone ask, and your paycheck will come from the same source."

"I want a raise," he said.

"A raise? This is about our national security, Mr. Brooks."

The longer he spoke with the guy, the less Waylen liked him. "I understand, but if I keep getting thrown into dangerous situations, which might eventually involve actual aliens, I should be compensated for it."

"How much do you want?"

"What are they paying you?" Waylen asked.

Theodore's crisp edge crumbled a bit as he laughed. "Wouldn't you like to know? I'm sure the government won't mind you taking an additional salary. How does an extra two hundred thousand sound?"

Waylen considered the sum, and while it was a lot more than he was used to being paid, he figured Theodore wouldn't start at the top. "Four hundred. Half upfront. If I'm going to be removed from my usual job—without a choice, I'll remind you—then I want to ensure

I'm taken care of."

"Waylen, there's always a choice." Theodore pointed at the exit. "Go ahead."

And he disliked his new boss even more. "I can leave?"

"If you do, I'll handle the tokens. I'm sure your friends won't mind a team of Marines dropping in." Theodore walked away.

"I only answer to you, and I get to hire my own team."

Theodore turned and smiled. "Deal. I want the tokens in our possession. Find them, Waylen."

When he was alone in the laboratory, he sat at the largest desk, staring at the computer screen. There was endless data at his disposal, and Waylen couldn't access any of it.

He texted Martina. *You still around?*

In the yard talking to Ben.

Five minutes later, Waylen walked up to Martina Sanchez, who'd betrayed him only days earlier, then redeemed herself a few hours ago. "I need someone on the inside. Can you be that person?"

"You're asking me to feed you information?"

"No, but I might occasionally require some help," he said.

"I owe you that much." Martina waved at the last SWAT truck. "Want a ride?"

The Marines that had come with Theodore and Ben were staying to protect the facility. "Sure. I'm off to DC."

"Why?"

He didn't want to tell Martina that he had a date on Friday night. "To tie up some loose ends."

"We'll bring you to the airport," she said.

"How about the train station?"

"Suit yourself."

Waylen watched the gigantic building as the SWAT truck rumbled away. What had he just agreed to?

"Rory, talk to us," Silas begged. She'd returned through the Delta thirty minutes earlier, and had barely spoken two words.

The spacesuit lay in sections on the hardwood, and Rory's hair was still plastered to her brow. "This is bad," she finally whispered.

"How bad?" Silas checked on Cody. "Where are we with the footage?"

"The camera broke from the cold, but I've almost transferred the data." Cody typed furiously on the laptop, far more concerned with whatever Rory had recorded than the woman's well-being.

Silas touched Rory's wrist, and she flinched, her expression blank. "What did you find up there?"

"Got it!" Cody proclaimed, and plopped down between Silas and Rory, setting his computer on the coffee table. "Let's see what spooked our friend."

The camera was shaky, but the picture remained clear. "That's the lander gear," Cody said, narrating her venture. Rory's eyes were fixed on the screen, but she didn't comment. It showed the Earth, far in the distance, and Rory's voice cracked in the speakers. *"Is this real?"* She sat up straighter after the question, and looked stronger.

The next ten minutes was her wandering through the site, tracking their progress. She paused eventually, the camera angling to the surface. There were footprints, men's boots from the Helios mission. It took Silas a moment to grasp that Rory had actually been on the Moon. This had been filmed only a short time ago, making it difficult to comprehend how Rory was presently sitting beside them on the couch. No wonder she was acting so strange.

Rory let out a whimper, and for a second, Silas wasn't sure if it came from the woman, the speakers, or both.

"What the hell was that?" Cody paused, then rewound the footage.

"I didn't see it."

Cody zoomed, and they all stared at the screen. The imprint differed from the boots. It was longer by a couple of inches, two toes, and another appendage at the rear of the foot. He pictured a talon, but that couldn't be right.

Rory raced to the Shadow, bouncing along the Moon, and the camera cut off.

Cody flipped the computer shut and rested his head in his palms. "What is happening?"

"Rory, you're safe now." Silas took her hand. "You're back in Loon Lake."

She blinked and met his gaze. "Silas, there was something else on the Moon."

They focused on the Delta at the same time, and Rory beat him to it, tearing at the individual tokens until they were all separated. The Shadow lingering in the living room dissipated until there was no sign of the anomaly. The room was instantly heated by a few degrees.

"Now it's obvious why they wanted to keep the Delta quiet," Silas said.

"Maybe the prints came later."

"What?" Rory asked Cody.

"Think about it. What if the aliens showed up after the Delta left? It would make sense that they'd send someone to investigate," Cody said.

Silas had all but forgotten the journal, and hopped to his feet. "I might be able to shed some light."

He rushed down the hall, grabbing the book from the bedside stand. Silas hadn't dived in, not wanting to think about the tokens any longer, but now he didn't have a choice in the matter.

"What's that?" Cody asked.

"Grandpa Gunn's journal."

"Seriously? Why were you holding out on us?"

"I wasn't doing anything of the sort. You showed up unannounced and sent Rory to the Moon. When did you expect me to do any reading?" Silas flipped through the pages, finding entries dating back to a year before takeoff. The handwriting was fluent and coherent, easy to discern, unlike his own. Silas went to a later entry, one after their return to Earth.

"I'll never be the same. Colin either. Fred will recover, because he didn't go. He hasn't seen what we have, and while Colin and I described it, Fred doesn't understand exactly what transpired. We lost two hours. That's what they told us. NASA believes our story about faulty communications, which makes our job much simpler. Whatever this is must stay buried. Forever." Silas ran a finger along the page, noticing the writing seemed more erratic, the penmanship deeper and less curved. It was the first sign of the changes after the Moon trip.

"We can't use this again," Rory said.

"That's not your decision to make." Cody snatched the tokens with a cloth. "They must be able to transport us to somewhere other than the Moon."

"Are you crazy?" Silas shouted. "You saw what Rory

recorded. We're being watched by an unknown enemy."

"Perhaps it was an anomaly," Cody countered. "Who's to say that wasn't random? It didn't look like a footprint to me."

"Not a human one," Silas muttered.

"Gunn and Swanson could have made it by dragging the flag. Come on, guys, we have something incredible here."

Rory stared at the spacesuit.

"Rory, tell him…"

"We shouldn't stop yet," she said.

"All we need to do is carry the Delta across, and that might activate the second Shadow." Cody looked ready to initiate the Delta again, and Silas shot him a glare.

"How do you know you won't be trapped if you do that? What if it's a one-way trip? Maybe the tokens ground you to the location you're traveling to. Even if our grandfathers did leave the Moon, they were returned to the Shadow. You don't have a spaceship to transport you home, Cody. Unless you're secretly a billionaire and haven't told us."

Cody rubbed his chin and set the tokens aside. "You bring up some valid points, Silas."

Silas relaxed slightly, and noticed Rory's color had started to return. His phone buzzed again, and Rory grabbed it before he could. She showed him Waylen's number. "We have to talk to Waylen."

"Cody, any objections?" Silas asked.

He lifted his hands. "Plenty, but clearly, you two won't listen to me."

Silas answered the phone and tapped the speaker. "Are you okay?"

"*I'm fine. Tell me you have the tokens,*" he said.

Shadows of the Earth

"We do. Cody and Rory are here."

"*In New York?*"

"Loon Lake," he said.

"*Good. Whatever you do, don't touch them. We'll use this facility to test the Delta.*"

"Uhm, it's too late for that. Rory's already been to the Moon."

2

Sleep was a distant memory, a state of mind vanquished by her subconscious. Rory tossed in the guest bed, unable to shut her brain off. She slid from the warmth of the covers and moved to the window. There were no clouds, but the Moon wasn't visible on this side of the house. She crept out of the room and into the hall, cognizant of the sound the hardwood made with each step.

Rory borrowed one of Silas' hoodies, hanging near the exit, and unlocked the deadbolt. The air was cool, brought in by a strong wind from the west. It had subsided, but the tops of the large trees surrounding the property continued to sway, temporarily blotting out the constellations.

She glanced at the camera mounted near the entrance, and continued toward the pier. Her feet were freezing, since she'd forgotten shoes, and soon her socks were damp. It must have sprinkled again while she lay dazed in bed for the last two hours.

The Moon was nearly full, and it drew her gaze. Was it possible that she'd just been on the surface of that miraculous celestial body, looking at Earth instead? Surely the Delta had only tricked her senses. But there was the footage, which proved she'd left the living room. Didn't it?

Rory sat in Peter's chair, not caring that the seat was wet. It was no wonder these astronauts had spent their retirement watching the Moon. How could you do anything else, once you realized how mundane your existence on Earth was?

Somehow sleep found her outside in the cold, of all places, and Rory finally forgot the endeavor. She dreamed of blissful things, and pictured herself working on a book. Rory glanced at the shelves, finding copies of various titles she'd never written, with her pen name on the spines. In the vision, the computer screen was fuzzy, so she couldn't read the words dream-Rory had provided. She rose and removed a volume from the bookcase. When she flipped it wide, the pages were blank.

Rory's eyes snapped open to the sound of an engine firing on. Someone was in Cody's van. The brakes depressed, shooting red light across the gravel driveway, and a lamp flicked on in the home.

Even in her groggy condition, Rory knew what was happening. She sped down the dock and dashed over the rocks, ignoring the pain in the soles of her feet, then pounded on the window of the driver's door. Cody gawked back, shock on his face.

"Turn it off!" she shouted.

Cody's hand lingered on the gearshift.

"Cody, don't do this! They'll come for you!" Rory didn't have to look at the seat beside him to know the tokens were in the van, but she did anyway, confirming he was attempting to steal them.

"What's going on?" Silas had a gun, wearing only his boxers and a tank top. His gaze darted around the property.

"Cody was about to check the oil," Rory said. "Weren't you?"

Silas grunted and reached for the handle. Cody finally turned the key and popped the old manual lock. "I don't want to give it to the FBI."

"You heard them. It's not the FBI we're bringing it to," Silas assured him.

"Operation Delta? First off, the name is super cheesy, and second, it's still controlled by the government."

"What do you have against them anyway?" Silas asked.

Cody's jaw dropped. "Everything!"

"Three hours ago, you promised to come with us to New York. What changed?" Rory asked.

"I had a dream."

"Yeah, so did I," she whispered.

"Can we talk about this indoors?" Silas shivered and started away.

"What did you see?" Rory asked Cody as they headed to the front steps.

She noted how closely he held the tokens to his chest. "I was at my day job, drinking from an endless coffee cup. Mindless IT tickets were streaming in, and I couldn't keep up."

"That does sound like a nightmare," Silas agreed while flipping the latch.

Rory's toes tingled as the heat reached them. She felt much better out of the foggy haze she'd been drowning in since returning through the Delta. She wondered if it was an after-effect, or if her mind had shut down to protect herself.

The clock blinked to 3:21 AM. The sun wouldn't rise for some time, but she doubted any of them would be falling asleep tonight. Silas wouldn't let the tokens out of his sight now, not since Cody had proven unstable.

"Let's drive," she said.

"Where?" Silas asked.

"To New York."

"It's kind of far." Cody dangled the keys between two fingers. "If we do this, you guys have to pitch in for gas. That beast isn't the most affordable mode of transportation."

"Rory, can I have a word with you?" Silas smiled, but she could see his glowering mood in the fake gesture.

"Sure." Rory went to the kitchen, where Silas continued to watch Cody.

"Why are we driving to New York? At least we could use my car."

"We should stick together, and think of the leg room. Waylen wants us there by Saturday, so we have a chance to stop by my parents' house," Rory said.

"It'll take two days," he said.

"It'll help us devise a plan." It seemed as good an excuse as any. She really didn't want to be in that place any longer, not after the Shadow had spread across the living room floor.

"Fine." Silas exhaled slowly. "Cody, I'll take the first shift."

"Good by me. I have a cot in the back, so we can rotate." He went to the couch, where he'd set up for the night, and threw a couple of belongings into a duffel bag. Apparently, he'd been willing to abandon his spare pants and sweatshirt when he'd tried to escape with the tokens.

Everyone packed up, and Silas loaded some snacks in a bag and drinks into a cooler before hauling them to the van. As promised, Cody took the tiny cot and was snoring before they reached the highway. It was after four when they started east. Woodstock was over 2200 miles from Loon Lake, and as they drove by the airport exit, Rory regretted suggesting the road trip. The van smelled musty, and she made Silas stop at a rest area to dump the fast-food bags and empty paper soda cups.

They didn't find an open store until after the sun rose, and by then, they were already halfway to Cheyenne. "I had no idea that Wyoming was so big."

"It isn't, but it just so happens that Loon Lake's on the far west side." Silas closed his door after grabbing coffees and breakfast sandwiches. Cody continued to sleep, so Rory stashed his portion behind her and bent the flap on her lid. Steam poured out, filling the van with a much better aroma.

"You want to talk about it?" Silas had them on the highway, and kept the speed right over the limit. The van chugged along, probably unable to go any faster if they wanted it to.

"Not really."

"But you left my house through—"

"Do you think Cody's right?"

"I highly doubt it." Silas laughed and sipped his coffee, muttering under his breath. "Too hot."

"I'm serious. Maybe that wasn't an alien's footprint. No one ever mentioned extraterrestrials, and the journal didn't say they'd encountered them."

"To be fair, it didn't say much," Silas countered. "But there's a chance these beings returned to the Moon after the Delta was taken. We'll show Waylen the footage and ask what he thinks."

"What are they going to do with the tokens?" Rory viewed the road as traffic grew congested. A construction sign advised her they were twinning the section, and that was causing the holdup. How many areas would they be delayed at during the two-thousand-plus-mile journey?

"That's none of our business. I just want to deliver them and be done."

Rory nodded absently, but wasn't sure if she was actually agreeing or not. "We have to watch Cody. I still believe he's a flight risk."

"We will." Silas hit the brakes, and they stopped on the highway while a large truck backed out of the ditch, then pulled away.

Rory checked behind her, almost feeling like Cody might have silently slipped out. But he remained on the bed, snoring at random. "I was on the Moon," she said when they started forward.

"And?"

Rory let the fear-based part of the experience slip to the side for a second, and smiled as she recalled the sensation of walking the surface. The near-weightlessness and realization that she'd traveled somewhere around two hundred and forty thousand miles. Suddenly, the drive to Vermont wasn't so daunting. "It was incredible, Silas. But I don't think we should be involved."

Silas blew on his coffee and took a drink. "I'm not sure I would if they asked me to."

"You're willing to give the Delta to Waylen and scram?"

"You have another idea?"

"I don't know what I want anymore." Rory pressed the radio on, finding a single station playing music. It was Top Forty, which really wasn't her thing, not since high school, but she left it on low, preferring it to the constant noise of the struggling engine.

"You going to write again? That's what you should focus on, instead of the Delta. The government is aware of it, and Waylen has a facility, along with a team, to figure out what it is and how it operates. They don't need us. Plus, why would they send you or me to the Moon when they have qualified people with years of experience and training?"

"You're right, Silas. I get that, but it'll be difficult to let go," she said.

"You could come to Loon Lake with me. Stay for a while and finish your project."

"We just left there," she reminded him.

"So what? We'll go back… but on a plane."

"Can I think about it?" Rory asked.

"Of course." Silas turned his attention to the road as the traffic found normal speeds once they passed the construction zone.

The beckoning of sleep evaporated a little more with each sip of coffee, and by the time she finished it, the cobwebs from her trek to the Moon were vanquished. The entire experience seemed like a bad dream encompassing two weeks, basically from the moment she'd arrived in Woodstock. Perhaps the last decade could have been part of the nightmare. Ever since meeting Kevin.

Rory was determined to get her life on track, and that meant agreeing with Silas. They needed to get as far from the tokens as possible. She reached over the console separating her from the driver's seat and took Silas' right hand while he steered with the left. They sat in silence while they continued east.

3

*W*aylen woke in the Capitol Hill hotel and stretched. The bed was extremely comfortable, and he realized he'd slept for twelve hours. His phone had a handful of messages, one from Ben, two from Martina, and a couple of texts from Darren Jones, the UFO expert. He'd forgotten and left Darren in Washington.

After a few minutes of scrolling, Waylen walked into the suite's living room wearing a white fluffy robe, and dialed Darren.

"*Finally,*" Darren said. "*Where are you? Can we talk about what you found?*"

"I'm in DC."

"*I have my speaking engagement tomorrow. Has your office booked my return flight?*"

"Let's have lunch." Waylen checked the time, learning it would be in an hour.

With a sigh and brief pause, Darren relented. "*Sure, but I'd like the ticket home before we get to the restaurant.*"

"What are you in the mood for?"

"*Thai?*"

"I know just the spot," Waylen said.

"*Shoot me the details. I can't wait to hear what happened,*" Darren admitted.

"See you soon." Waylen texted him their meeting place and moved through the methodical process of preparing for a big day. He operated slowly, not wanting to rush his thoughts as he relived the last week over and over. Technically, he was no longer employed by the FBI. He looped his tie and wondered what dress code was proper. Did he need a suit? He'd grown so used to them, it would be strange to wear anything but.

Waylen loved his run with the Bureau, and suddenly regretted accepting the new role with Operation Delta. It was unclear what his official title was, or what his day-to-day would consist of. But if they could utilize the Delta to reach other worlds, someone had to protect their planet from a possible attack. But why him? Waylen was a numbers guy, an expert on criminal financial fraud, not aliens or military matters.

And then there was his new director, Theodore Belleville. The man had made a horrible first impression, and Waylen doubted he'd ever like the guy, but did he have to? Waylen had been lucky to report to Assistant Director Ben, but many in the field weren't so fortunate.

He considered messaging Charlotte, but decided against it. They'd made plans, and he'd show up as promised. The new endeavor might have put a halt to any future dates, but that didn't stop the fact he was drawn to her. In their past, he'd abandoned her on countless occasions for work, and he wouldn't do that again.

The lunch spot wasn't far from the hotel, so Waylen pressed outside, choosing to walk. The streets were busy, as they usually were in this district. It was a hectic political capital, so he couldn't expect anything else.

Charlotte worked a few blocks away, in the big white building, and he smiled at the thought of her. Waylen had never been into politics. His father had enjoyed discussing stances on issues at the dinner table, much to his mother's chagrin. But unlike most people, Waylen's dad had been educated on the subject. He'd told Waylen from a young age to only contribute when he had something constructive to say, and since Waylen didn't focus his energy on the state of the country, he rarely spoke about the topic.

There was still something special about being in the heart of American politics. Lives were changed because of the daily actions of the men and women in DC. It didn't hurt that he was technically employed by the government, and had been for years.

He cut through a stretch of fancy townhouses, with perfectly crafted hedges and large trees overhanging the narrow streets. Cars were parked so tightly that nearly all of their bumpers touched, and Waylen watched as a young courier in the bike lane almost got sideswiped by a speeding truck.

He liked the area, with the low buildings and big blue skies. Could he see himself settling down in DC? Now that he was no longer connected to the Atlanta field office, why even keep the house? He never used it. As he crossed the road, Waylen decided to sell. That didn't mean moving to Washington, or Arlington, or Alexandria, but it represented a change, and he guessed that was probably overdue in his life.

Darren loitered outside of the restaurant, wearing a golf shirt and shorts. He removed his sunglasses, tucked them into his pocket, and shook Waylen's hand when he approached. "You have the plane ticket?"

"They should be sent by now."

Darren checked his phone, and a smile crept onto his face. "Harvard is waiting."

"You might want to listen to my story before jumping on that plane," Waylen said.

Darren held the door for him, and the scent of Thai food hit them from the kitchen. "I doubt there's anything you can say to keep me from my commitment. I've been waiting for the invite from the department for years. Someone in my position requires proof of concept, and with establishments like Harvard under my belt, booking a speaking tour becomes a lot easier."

Waylen held up a pair of fingers to the older woman at the hostess table, and she nodded, grabbing a pair of plastic menus. They sat in a cramped booth, and Darren was almost too big for the seat. He didn't complain, and slid in, eyeing the food options.

Waylen was about to mention what happened in New York when the server showed up with water. "We'll need a minute." He tapped the menu, and she proceeded to the next table, clearing plates.

"Enlighten me," Darren murmured.

Waylen did, starting with the car crash and successive kidnapping by helicopter. Somewhere in the discussion, they ordered lunch and coffees, and Darren almost knocked over his water glass when Waylen mentioned the facility north of the city.

"Operation Delta," Darren said. "Sounds made up."

"Well, technically, it is."

"You know what I mean." Darren adjusted his coffee cup when the meals came, and Waylen's stomach growled at the sight of his pad Thai. He'd eaten it all over the country, but this place made the best. He'd never tried whatever it was Darren had ordered, but it was a curry dish with ample chunks of pineapple. Darren scooped a forkful and smiled. "It's good."

Shadows of the Earth

Waylen finished the story, ending with Leo Monroe's attempt to connect the Delta using the fake tokens. Darren leaned in and listened with rapt attention, absorbing every detail.

"And he let you go?"

"I forgot that part. My ex-partner in the field dropped by with FBI SWAT, and we have Monroe in custody now. Well, the military does. I'm not certain where he was taken."

"Interesting," Darren said.

"Why?"

"A weapons manufacturer with active contracts with the US government is arrested, and you haven't been told where they brought him."

"Do you believe it was a show for me and the assistant director?" Waylen wouldn't put it past them.

"He's probably in a fancy facility, being asked politely to continue his work under a more clandestine banner," Darren said.

"It's a fascinating theory." Waylen set his fork down. "They've given me permission to create a team."

Darren lifted his eyebrows and stopped eating. "Is that so?"

"I'd like you on it."

"Me?" He pointed to himself. "I'm not sure I have the credentials…"

"You're a lawyer, right?"

"Ages ago."

"If anyone asks, I wanted legal counsel on the team." Waylen laughed. "And you're the only authority I have on alien life. You'll come in very handy as we proceed with the testing."

"Testing?"

Waylen saw that he had Darren. All he had to do was reel him in. "I know where the tokens are, and Monroe's facility is set up for testing the Delta. We're going to travel to the Moon, and possibly other planets."

"There's no way," Darren said.

Waylen didn't bother trying to explain. He removed his cell phone, made sure no one was watching, and showed Darren the brief clip from Rory's video. He paused it prior to the ending, not wanting to chance someone from another table catching sight of an alien footprint on the Moon.

"What's this?"

"It's from last night," he said.

Darren dropped his napkin and gawked at Waylen. "You're telling me this footage was taken yesterday?"

"Yes."

"Impossible."

"That's what I'm saying… it's not. And we have the means to use the Delta."

Darren laughed nervously, and stuck a hand over his mouth when he received stares from nearby patrons. "What about the control mechanism I mentioned? Have you found it yet?"

"No, but Silas agrees there probably is one. That's where you come in," Waylen said.

Darren appeared to consider his options, but it didn't take long. "You knew I wouldn't decline, didn't you?"

"I had an inkling."

"When do I start?"

"Monday. Let's give it a weekend, since I'm waiting for the tokens to be delivered anyhow." Waylen realized he had very little information on the man across from him, and decided to remedy that. "Darren, this isn't a job interview, because you're already hired, but tell me about yourself. Are you married?"

Usually, he'd know every last detail about Darren, but he was under a time crunch leading up to this moment. Waylen glanced around the inside of the restaurant, struggling to believe he'd been dragged to New York in a helicopter just twenty-four hours earlier.

"Married? Not presently." Darren looked wistful. "It didn't work out. We got together too young, in our hometown east of Boston. One of those small, upper middle-class towns with a private school that catered to the county's elite. I was lucky to enter the program, since my mom taught there and had some pull. We met in senior year, when she transferred from another school. We both enrolled in the same university, living off campus after getting married. Our families hated it, but they loved Belinda. They really did. All their advice was one hundred percent accurate, but when you're twenty-one, you don't see it that way. I stopped talking to my parents, and as expected, we divorced after eight years, with two little ones caught in our wake."

Waylen listened carefully for what wasn't said. That was how you truly understood a person.

"I'd always had a fascination with aliens, and took the messy divorce, filled with greedy lawyers and angry custody battles, as a sign that I should find a new profession. So, at thirty, I hung up my courtroom jacket and changed trajectories."

Waylen offered a wry grin. "How does someone shift into… aliens?"

"They do it with no plan and no income, and a dash of court-appointed alimony," he said. "But seriously, I started a podcast, and was one of the earlier to market. In those days, it was a micro-trend, and we never expected to grow like we did."

"We?"

"My former partner. Her name's Lucy."

"What happened to Lucy?" Waylen asked.

"She's doing true crime now. More lucrative," Darren said.

"You still talk?"

"We did, in the first couple of years, but as usual, time separated us even more."

Waylen thought about Martina Sanchez, and assumed the same would happen to them. She'd betrayed his trust, accepting money from Leo Monroe, but in the end, Martina had saved him. The deception was enough to create an invisible barrier he wasn't certain could be repaired.

They talked more. Waylen picked up the check, wondering if the FBI would still cover the charges, and they stepped outside into the warm day. "Your flight's in three hours. You'd better run."

Darren extended his hand. "You've distracted me from my speech tomorrow." They shook, and Darren grinned at him. "How long will I be in New York? Do we have accommodations on site?"

Waylen shrugged, knowing none of the pertinent details.

"What about a salary?"

"Tell you what. Let me spend the next day working on it. I'll be in touch Saturday, after your big afternoon at Harvard," he said.

"Deal."

Waylen escorted Darren to the hotel, and waited in the lobby while the UFO expert returned and checked out. He watched the taxi leave for the airport, and felt a small sense of accomplishment. With the tokens en route across the states, Darren on board, and Monroe behind bars, they might finally discover what the Delta was capable of.

4

Silas stretched in the passenger seat, and Cody slowed as they entered the municipality. They'd driven for nearly sixteen straight hours, and still had a long way to go. None of them were in a place to continue, so Silas made the decision. "We should stop."

"The van needs fuel," Cody said.

"I mean for the night." Silas glanced at Rory in the row behind, and she reluctantly nodded.

"I think Waylen would…" Cody started, but Silas shook his head.

"Waylen won't be in New York until Saturday. We have time. Plus, this van sounds like it's about to explode. We should get an oil change."

"I did that."

"When?" he asked.

"A couple of years ago," Cody replied.

"Why am I not surprised?" They were in a small town, about two hours from Chicago. It fringed the Iowa and Illinois border, with a river separating the two states.

"Fine. Let's check if there's any hotels we can afford," Cody said.

"I'll pay." Silas had his phone out, searching the area for somewhere to stay. "This is strange."

Shadows of the Earth

"What?" Rory peered from behind him, resting her elbows on the center console.

"There's no availability anywhere!" He scrolled through, finding zero vacancies listed on the sites.

Cody pulled over and grabbed his own cell. "That's why. There's a big festival. Cool, I love some of these headliners."

"I guess we continue." Cody put the van into gear, and a noise clunked from ahead. Silas waved at the noxious scent filing in from the vents. He slid the lever, trying to close them, and reached to the steering column, turning the key.

They hopped out, with Cody popping the front. More vapors rose, and for a second, it reminded Silas of the Shadow, until he caught the stench of burning chemicals.

"Great, just perfect," Cody said, and let the hood fall, loudly slamming into place.

"What should we do?" Rory asked.

The sun began to set, but since it was the middle of summer and they were farther north than Silas was used to, there was a solid hour before it was all the way down. He checked his phone again, changing the parameters of his search, and found a log cabin for rent on the other side of town, nestled up to the Mississippi. Once his companions gave their stamp of approval, Silas confirmed his reservation, and searched for a rideshare.

"Of course they don't have that out here," he complained. He was so used to the constant availability in the city, he'd forgotten that not all towns offered the service. After waiting on hold for ten minutes, Silas got through to the local taxicab company and ordered a car.

"*We're running behind because of the festival,*" the woman croaked. Silas recognized the inhale of a cigarette while she waited for a response.

"That's fine. How long?"

"*An hour.*"

Cody tapped his shoulder. "Get them to bring a van."

"Do you have a van?"

"*That'll cost more,*" she said.

"Whatever. There's an extra twenty if they get here sooner," Silas told her, knowing it would fall on deaf ears. Why would the dispatcher care if the driver scored a bonus?

Rory was already sitting on the curb, staring at the pale silhouette of the Moon. She looked small, her posture almost inverted. He noticed Rory's hands recessed into her sleeves as she rested her arms on her knees. Cody was behind the van, rifling through his possessions, and he dragged the crate from the back, calling to Silas to help.

"What do you think you're doing?" Silas asked, rushing to catch it before the trunk smashed into the road.

"I can't very well leave a spacesuit in my vehicle unattended. Do you have any clue how valuable these things are?"

"No."

"Fred told me he could have offloaded this for around a million bucks. More, if he had the one that he'd actually used on the mission. Commander Gunn's would probably sell for closer to three."

"Seriously?"

"Yeah. People pay top dollar for the lunar samples alone," Cody said.

"You're saying we can snatch rocks with the Delta and sell them?"

"Not really. It's kind of that whole supply and demand thing," Cody said. "And ours wouldn't be authenticated by NASA. If a steady stream of auction samples suddenly appeared, there would be questions."

Silas understood economics, since he'd taken enough classes on it to last a lifetime. "Okay, we'll bring the suit to the cabin." He sat on the trunk while they waited. Cody reached into the back, grabbing warm sodas, and handed them out. They were on an industrial street, with all the businesses closed for the evening. It was the usual. Tire shop. Welding outfit. Gemstone supply warehouse.

"We should reach my parents' house tomorrow," Rory said out of the blue.

Silas guessed she wasn't coming to New York, but didn't express it, because he honestly wasn't ready to part ways with her. They were connected by their relationship to the Helios 15 crew members, but also with the Delta. He'd been shot trying to save her in the hurricane, and then there was that night at Loon Lake…

Silas tried not to be obvious as he watched Rory. She wasn't the same after her experience yesterday on the Moon. Her movements were calculated, and she jumped with every noise. It would be selfish for him to ask her to meet with Waylen, yet he couldn't imagine her absence.

She glanced up from the curb and caught him staring. Rory had the decency to smile, and he glided from the trunk, sliding to the sidewalk next to her. Saying nothing, she leaned on his shoulder and rested her head.

To Silas' shock, the taxi arrived twenty minutes earlier than expected, and the driver rolled his window down. "You Miles?"

"Silas."

He shrugged and gazed at the large piece of furniture. "Bringing that?"

"Yes."

"I got a bad back," the guy said. "You load it."

Cody popped the van's rear door, and the pair of them hefted the weight. It fit, but barely. They tossed their bags on top and slammed it shut.

"Are you here for the festival?" the driver asked. Rory took the seat behind the driver, with Cody occupying the front. They'd already voted before he came, making Cody the designated talker.

"Oh yeah, the van broke down, but we're pumped to see my favorite band," Cody said. "They're on tomorrow night at nine. Should be a killer show." He'd suggested they have a cover story, because another three visitors in town for the festival would be extremely forgettable.

The driver crossed a few four-way stops without braking, and merged to what passed for a freeway. "I've never understood that rock and roll stuff. Too loud. I'm more of a crooner." He began humming a song from the Sixties, and Rory stifled a laugh. Silas liked to see her in a better mood.

The cabins looked packed, and Silas wondered how they'd lucked out in securing one at all. It was a party zone, with hundreds of twenty-somethings lingering at fire pits, drinking from red cups, and cranking music from Bluetooth speakers. The entire place had congregated in one area, a communal party central for the complex. He almost told the driver to turn around and take them somewhere else, but there was nowhere to go.

"This is it." He stopped at the edge of the lot, where a cabin stood with an OPEN sign lit up.

Silas paid in cash, relinquishing the extra twenty, and once the trunk was clear, the cab took off with a few new patrons, talking loudly about heading to the bars. Silas imagined they'd have quite the headache in the morning.

"Give me a minute," he said to Rory, and strode into the office.

"Yeah?" The woman didn't peer up from her crossword book. A small TV played a game show, where the contestants spun a wheel. The volume was low and, at the moment, was being drowned out by the outdoor activities.

"I'm Silas. I rented the…"

"Lucky you." She finally set the book aside and flipped her glasses onto her nose. "We had a last-minute cancellation."

Silas gestured to the firepit. "Quite the event out there."

"It's the same crap every year. Usually, we're a delightful spot, but the festival drags 'em in like moths to a flame. I fought it at first, but now it's one of my best weekends, so I let 'em do their thing for a night." She scrunched her face and slid a piece of paper to him. "Sign this. I'll need a credit card and ID, please."

"Can I pay cash?" Silas was intent on discretion.

She pointed at the sign above the desk. "There are rules, son." Then she leaned in. "But you look like a decent man. I can make an exception." She smiled like she was doing him a big favor, and Silas understood she'd be pocketing the cash.

"I appreciate it. Any idea what time the party will be over?"

"Quiet time is at eleven. So they'll probably settle around three in the morning," she said, and gave Silas a key. "Number twelve."

Silas snatched it. "Thanks." He ventured outside, where Cody was nodding his head to the music.

They found the unit, and he was grateful it was separated from the action. He dragged the heavy trunk, brushing the narrow doorframe, and let it fall to the scratched floors. The living space had a fireplace, a couch, two worn leather chairs, and a flat screen with a slight fracture in the bottom corner.

"Home sweet home," Silas whispered, and turned on the lights.

"There's only two bedrooms," Rory said.

"I'll take the couch," Silas offered.

"I don't mind…" Cody started.

"Not this again. I won't let you steal the tokens. Speaking of which, where are they?"

Cody offered them to Silas. "Where would I bring them? Do you expect me to throw on a spacesuit and crash a party tonight?"

"Stranger things have happened," Rory answered with a grin.

"I'm going straight to the firepit. We passed a couple of cute girls earlier, and I would love a beer. You guys wanna come?"

Silas couldn't imagine trying to talk to those people outside. "Not even a little."

"Same." Rory pointed to Cody's hair. "You should…"

Cody took his bag into the bathroom, and after a few minutes of running water, emerged with a fresh shirt and styled hair. "Better?"

Rory motioned her hand back and forth. "Kind of…"

"Funny," he said. "I'll be back. Eventually."

The door shut, and Silas glanced around. "Want something to eat?"

"Let me. You get the fire on. It's freezing in here." Rory lifted a box out of her bag.

Shadows of the Earth

The night was cooling with the set sun, so Silas moved through the process of prepping the hearth. He guessed the chimney had seen better days, but he still made it, using paper, then kindling, before stacking a couple of narrow logs. They caught quickly, while Rory worked on boiling water for mac and cheese in the kitchen. They ate with the flames flickering behind the chain-link barrier.

Music vibrated on the outer walls, but the main noise from the party remained muted. Silas cleaned up, and Rory poked at the logs, adding more. "I can't return to Loon Lake with you."

Silas washed the bowls, watching her from behind. "I thought so."

"I care about you…"

"We have lives," he said.

"Right."

"And yours is in Woodstock?"

"Not for long." Rory faced him from a different room. "You'll stay in Loon Lake, all alone?"

"I'm actually undecided," he admitted.

"We shouldn't be involved, Silas. Just because our grandfathers found the Delta doesn't mean it's our responsibility."

Silas took a seat on the couch, and Rory joined him, sitting very close. She touched his knee, and he was instantly aware of the contact. "I'll hand them off to Waylen. Then it's someone else's job. I trust him, just not the people he's working for."

"There's probably a part of Commander Gunn that wished he would've done the same thing. He'd have lived his life without the constant burden of the token weighing on his mind," Rory told him.

"I believe that."

Silas glanced at the door, wondering when Cody would choose to return. It was locked, and Silas had the only key.

"This is our last night together," she said.

Silas swallowed and nodded in agreement. "Yeah." He was an analytical thinker, always measuring his actions before making important decisions, but he let that part of himself slip away. Rory was there, anticipating his kiss, and her chilled palm slid on his warm neck.

He closed his eyes, not wanting to see the trunk holding the spacesuit near the door, or the bag containing the tokens on the coffee table. If this was his last chance at happiness with Rory Swanson, he'd savor it.

5

Cody positioned himself by the fire, close enough to catch a sparking ember. He gazed around the party, remembering similar moments from his youth. Now, pushing forty, he felt out of place amongst the crowd. He guessed they were mostly strangers, brought together by sheer luck for the festival, yet they talked like old friends.

Cody knew he was odd by the majority's standards, and didn't really care. His hobbies had included space, anything related to aliens, and model shuttles as a child, while his peers shot hoops or worked on cars with their fathers.

His dad had been an engineer, with hopes of his own to join the ranks of NASA. Cody remembered being regaled with his dad's memories of the first Moon landing. Cody waited for another such development, but it never happened, and he couldn't understand why. Then his father left for work one day and never came home. He suffered a massive myocardial infarction while walking through his company's laboratory.

The funeral had been a somber affair, with his coworkers in attendance, and his bowling buddies, along with their extended family, whom Cody barely knew. He was eight years old. He overheard his mother's sister, griping that she shouldn't have married an older man. Cody bottled up his resentment against the world and focused on the stars.

When he looked at the Moon, he saw his father's face. The glimmer in his eye, the crooked smile that meant everything was going to be all right. Cody peered at it now, beyond a haze of smoke, wishing he could speak to him just one more time. To tell him that traveling to the Moon was indeed possible.

"Hey, want a beer?" a guy asked.

Cody nodded. "Thanks." He reached into the cooler, the ice biting a cut on his knuckle. He still ached from the assault in New York. "Quite the party."

"This? I guess so."

"Where are you from?"

"Salt Lake City." He lifted his beer. "But you'd never know it."

"Pretty town," Cody told him.

"You?"

"San Diego."

"Even nicer." They clinked beer cans, and he wandered off, stopping to chat with a woman who looked uninterested. The man didn't seem to notice as he continued pestering her. Cody knew the body language too well. He'd never been much of a dater, though not by choice. After a few years of casually trying, he'd basically given up.

The band playing through the speakers was one of his favorites, and he searched for the person controlling the music. Since half of them were on their phones, the task wasn't so simple. He spied a woman near the back, bobbing her chin to the drum beat, and deduced it was her. Cody navigated the various clusters of people, stopping beside her. "Good song."

She didn't look up. "Yeah, love them."

"I'm Cody."

"Rachael."

"Nice to meet you."

She finally glanced at him, then slid her phone into her jeans' rear pocket. Rachael grabbed her beer from the picnic table and gestured at the bonfire. "I don't like the smoke."

"Me neither." Cody had no particular aversion to it, but the comment came out, regardless. The lights to their cabin were off, and he wondered if Silas and Rory had gone to bed.

Rachael sat on top of the table.

"Mind if I...?"

"It's a free country," she said, sliding a large bag of unopened potato chips away.

"You here with friends?"

"Sure. Those girls." She pointed to the far edge of the grounds, where three women circled a tall man wearing a basketball jersey. He clutched two beers and talked loudly. "I'm realizing I don't like people."

"Same here." Cody smiled, and she returned it.

A truck approached the parking lot, the high beams on, blinding him. They finally flicked off, and someone climbed from the driver's side. Cody recognized the guy. "Shit."

"What is it?"

He rubbed his hands and recalled the face of the man who'd shoved him in the trunk of his rental car. "I have to go."

Rachael shrugged and took a drink while Cody set his beer down. He circled the group, heading to the cabin.

The door was locked, and Cody realized he didn't have a key. "Let me in!" He knocked, frantically searching for the goon, who was nowhere in sight.

He tried the handle, but it didn't work. After another ten seconds of feverish rapping, Silas unlatched it, and appeared without a shirt.

"Get in." Silas slammed the door behind Cody. "What's wrong?"

Cody reached for the trunk. "We need to leave."

"What's the problem?" Rory had a long t-shirt on, and nothing else. Cody took a second, looking from one to the other, and understood why they'd wanted to stay at the cabin.

"He's here."

"Who?"

"The guy from Tompkins Square Park." Cody peered through the blinds and pressed the switch off. The fire crackled in the hearth, giving them enough light to see by.

"Damn it," Silas muttered. "You're sure?"

"I think so. He's in a truck."

"We don't even have a car." Rory already had pants on, and pulled a hoodie over her shirt. Silas put on jeans and slid the trunk closer to the exit.

"Leave it," he said.

"No."

"How are we going to get out of here with this?"

Cody smirked. "We take his truck."

"You're serious?" Rory asked.

"Why not?"

"He might be carrying the keys. Vehicles don't have turnkey ignition any longer," Silas blurted.

"It's worth a shot." Cody started for the door while Silas gathered their packs.

Shadows of the Earth

"This isn't some elaborate scam for you to snake the Delta, is it?" Rory asked.

"No, I promise." Cody peeked past the glass and saw the guy stalking around the patrons. "He's on the far side. It's now or never."

"We can't bring the whole thing." Silas swung the trunk open. "Everyone, grab a piece." He took the primary suit, while Rory snatched the helmet. Cody hauled the tanks out, causing his muscles to strain with effort.

"Let's go." Rory opened the door, and they hurried behind the cabins, bypassing the units to the parking lot. "You check it."

Cody set the tanks aside and tested the handle, finding it unlocked. That was a good sign. The keys were in the cup holder, sitting behind a pistol. That wasn't so great.

Silas tossed the suit into the box and sped to the driver's seat. Rory jumped in the back, still holding the helmet, and Cody shut his door quietly.

The sound of the engine roared through the lot, and the bright headlights shone over the party. Silas tried to dim them, but eventually just backed up and sped from the scene. Cody watched the mirror, seeing the guy chasing after them as dust flew into the night sky.

Waylen had arrived at the jazz place thirty minutes early, and sat at the bar while waiting for Charlotte. She usually got off at six, unless there was an emergency; then she'd stay until all hours. He hoped she'd text him if something arose, but since he'd received no such message, he assumed she'd be joining him.

A band was setting up on the lounge's stage, and a man with a fedora practiced the trumpet without blowing air. A woman removed a large wooden bass from its case, and strummed a few deep chords.

"Drink?" the bartender asked.

He ordered a pint and turned to watch the entrance. Time ticked by, as it only did when you were waiting for someone in a public location. Excruciatingly slowly. He still had half a beer when the clock struck seven.

Charlotte was nowhere in view.

Waylen had spent the day at the FBI headquarters meeting with Ben, discussing the possibilities of his new team at Operation Delta. Their leaders obviously had a vested interest in the results of the Delta, but it was equally clear that only a few understood the magnitude of the situation. Ben had assured Waylen he'd be there if needed, but he'd also been instructed to let Waylen Brooks vanish from his memory.

At two in the afternoon, Ben had received a cryptic phone call, and he'd changed his demeanor, apologizing for cutting their meeting short. They shook, and Waylen walked away from the J. Edgar Hoover Building, stopping to look at the iconic yet nondescript structure. He technically no longer worked for them.

The jazz band played, snapping his attention to the present. It was ten after. Charlotte wasn't coming.

He started to leave when he heard her voice. "Waylen Brooks, you actually showed up."

There she was, dressed in a nice suit, with a glint in her eye. They shared a friendly hug, and Waylen grabbed his drink, waving down a server. They got a table across the room, far enough from the band to not have to shout their conversation, but close enough to enjoy the ambiance.

"You doubted me?"

"Let's be real. You don't have the best track record." Charlotte removed her suit jacket, and he noticed the necklace she wore. He'd given it to her for her birthday while they were dating. She must have seen his gaze shift, and she touched it. "I wear it all the time."

Waylen didn't know what to say, so he just smiled. "This place is as good as I remember it."

"They have an ear for bringing in talent." Charlotte nodded toward the band. "It's a great atmosphere."

The server brought a glass of wine for Waylen's date, and they settled into their chairs, both seemingly nervous. Waylen had spent a decent stretch with her, but that was in another era. Things had changed. Everything was flipped upside down since encountering the Delta.

"Why are we doing this?" Charlotte asked.

"Because I miss you."

"Really?" She raised a suspect eyebrow. "We haven't spoken in three years."

"I was giving you space."

"I have to admit, something happened when I saw you the other day. Memories flooded my mind."

Waylen grinned, thinking the same thing.

"Don't get too excited. I recalled the countless arguments, lonely nights, and canceled plans. Waylen, I'm thirty-eight and single. Time's not on our side."

"I can be solid."

"Can you?"

He thought about it, took a long inhale, then let it out. "Probably not."

"You have grown," she said. "The old you would have

lied to yourself."

Waylen watched her, thinking about how beautiful she looked. *Elegant* was the best word to describe the woman across from him. He didn't deserve her, but that didn't stop him from wondering how their lives might fit together. "I'm being reassigned."

"Really? What department?"

"Something new."

"New in the FBI?"

"Almost."

Charlotte frowned, then took a sip. "What aren't you telling me?"

"I'll be in New York for a while. We have something, Charlotte, but I can't do this to you again."

She broke her gaze, watching the band instead. "I see."

"If there was any way to—"

"That's your problem, Waylen. You pretend you aren't in control of your life, but you could change careers or ask for a desk job at the FBI headquarters. You know they'd accept."

"Later. When this is over."

"What is it that has you so committed?"

"I can't say."

"Fine." Charlotte stood. "When you figure it out, don't call me."

"Charlotte..." Waylen reached for her, but she was already halfway out the door. He slumped into his seat while his phone rang.

He didn't recognize the number, but the area code suggested it was from the region Operation Delta was housed. "Hello."

"*Mr. Brooks, have you procured the tokens?*" It was the

unmistakable voice of Theodore Belleville.

"I told you I'd get them this weekend."

"I've been informed that Leo Monroe's hired help may still be on the prowl. I'm working on picking up the last of them. We encountered one at a campground near the Mississippi River yesterday, a couple of hours from Chicago. Police had a call about an armed assailant stalking a party, and they found him breaking into cabins."

Waylen hadn't heard from Silas or the others since yesterday afternoon, but that was directly on their planned route. "How are you going to find the rest?"

"The perp cracked when we mentioned a clandestine military prison," Belleville said.

"Is that a real thing?"

"Keep up, Brooks, of course it is. He's given us the complete network, and admitted he was instructed to continue his search of the Delta until they had it, regardless of their boss' possible incarceration."

"How many?"

"Eight more. We've already used tracking on five, and two are in custody. We'll have them all before dawn, which is why I require the tokens' location now. I'll send an escort."

Waylen checked the time, and then the exit, wishing Charlotte would show up again. "I'm on it. I'll be in touch."

"See that you are. We're almost there, Waylen. Secure the Delta so we can begin our process." The call ended, and Waylen lowered his phone, going to Silas' number. He dialed it.

6

"You sure you don't want to visit the city with us?" Silas asked while driving into Woodstock, Vermont.

Viewing her town from this new vantage point was unsettling. So much had happened since she'd escaped Boston to head home, more than she could ever have imagined. Part of her struggled to believe she was going to leave the adventure all behind. Silas had been the one pleasant side effect of the last couple of weeks, but even his charming smile wasn't enough to drag her farther into the mess.

"I can't." She didn't expand on it, because it was the simple truth. Rory was done after their close call the previous night.

"What if those guys come for you again?" Cody asked.

"They wouldn't have bothered if you'd left the original tokens with Waylen," she countered.

"Then you wouldn't have gone to the Moon."

"I don't care…" But she did. Rory had stepped on the actual Moon, and now all she sensed when she closed her eyes was the Shadow. *The blessing might not outweigh the curse.* Rory liked the line, and hoped she'd remember it for her book. "I have to write, find a place, and move on with my

Shadows of the Earth

life. I suggest you two do the same."

Rory gave directions to Silas, who kept driving the stolen truck. Waylen had told them about the man being arrested thanks to their frantic phone call at the cabins. According to his new director, they were tracking down the remnants of the network tonight and capturing them, which would put Rory in the clear. Finally.

"This is your house?" Cody asked when they pulled up the driveway.

"Yes."

Cody stuck his head between the front seats, gaping at the estate. "It's incredible."

"Thanks. My parents like appearances." Rory glanced at Cody when Silas parked. "Can you give us a minute?"

Cody shuffled from the truck, and Silas killed the engine. The cabin grew silent.

"Listen…"

"Rory, I…"

They smiled at one another, and she took his hand. "Leave them with Waylen's boss and ditch this stolen truck, then go home to the city, your parents, wherever, and figure it out. Don't remain tied up in this, Silas. Promise me."

"I… I want to say I'll stop worrying about the Delta, but how can we?"

"Easy," she said. "Just let it go."

Silas gripped the steering wheel. "Is that why you have no reluctance about letting *me* go?"

"We can stay in touch."

Her mom and dad stepped out onto the porch, both waving at Rory. Cody went to greet them, but she couldn't listen to their conversation with the windows up.

"I'll catch you later, Rory Valentine. Good luck with

the new book."

"Thanks, Silas." She brushed a palm on his cheek, and kissed him for real.

Silas didn't speak while she gathered her bag and climbed out of the truck. She didn't look, knowing if she did, she'd call him back.

When her path crossed with Cody, she offered him a quick embrace. "Make sure you go home, Cody. There's nothing for you on the Moon. I promise."

Cody hung his head, and she reached her parents.

"Rory, you made the right decision." Oscar's arm circled her shoulders protectively, and she had to agree.

The truck turned around, heading to Vermont's only military facility, a training base an hour and a half north. The plans had changed, with the tokens being delivered to Waylen's new boss, rather than to the city. She assumed he'd arrive in a helicopter, take the Delta, and order them to never think about the tokens again. That was what Rory proposed to do.

It was night in Woodstock, but the birds still sang from her parents' tall treetops. Nostalgia washed over her, an awareness that hadn't struck Rory the first time she'd pulled up to her home. The trauma was too fresh then, but her experiences since had hardened her. Rory would no longer shed tears for the past; instead, she'd let it fuel her book.

"We're about to have dinner," Kathy said, holding the door.

They always ate earlier than this. "You waited for me?"

"Of course we did." Her father noticeably bolted the lock.

Her bag fell to the entrance floor, and a sense of pur-

Shadows of the Earth

pose flooded through her veins. "I'll be right there. I need to freshen up."

A couple of days in a van and a stolen truck had left her grimy, and she showered quickly, leaving her hair to air-dry as she put on matching grey sweats.

Before exiting the room, she powered on her computer. Since getting a new phone, she hadn't linked the email to it, and dozens of messages appeared. Rory sighed when she saw multiple emails from her agent, with URGENT spelled out in the subject line. TIME SENSITIVE was plastered on the latest, and Rory opened it.

Rory,

I've tried calling, but your number seems to be out of service. Have you read the other mail on your delivery date for the new manuscript? This is about something else. Boston University contacted me when they couldn't reach you. They have a position available this fall, and offered you to teach the English Lit class. I know it would be a distraction from writing, but it might be kismet. Call me.

Perri

Rory read it twice and blinked. A teacher? Could she do that?

She powered the computer down and returned to the kitchen, where her parents waited with the utmost patience. It was time to stop living under someone's thumb and begin her own life.

Kathy removed the foil from the glassware and dished out the food. Rory almost drooled at the sight of the home-cooked meal, after days of fast food and diners.

"Is it over?" her father finally asked, sipping a Scotch.

Rory nodded. "Yeah."

"Good." Kathy poured her a glass of wine and smiled at her daughter.

"I've been offered a job at Boston University."

"Is that so?" Oscar asked. "It's a great school."

"What kind of job?" Her mom probably assumed it was an administrative role.

"They want me to work in the English lit department. I don't have the details, but I wanted to touch base with you guys first," she said, to make them feel included. Truthfully, she'd already accepted in her mind. It was just the change she needed.

---

*T*he training site wasn't much to look at. Silas pulled up to the fenced gate and assumed there was somebody in the guardhouse. He honked, but no one came out. A few buildings lingered down the gravel driveway, only one with any lights on. It appeared to be out of commission.

"You sure this is the place?" Cody peered up, as if expecting a helicopter to land on the hood.

"That's what he said." Silas was about to turn the truck off when he spotted the headlights arriving. A man wearing army fatigues manually swung the gate, and motioned them in before locking it again.

"Follow me," he ordered, then returned to his Jeep. When they parked behind the primary structure, Silas checked his pocket, confirming the tokens were still intact. He couldn't wait to relinquish them to Waylen's superiors.

"Now what?" he asked the soldier.

He pointed up, and Silas watched the stars. The sky was perfectly clear, the air warm and comfortable. His gaze inevitably shifted to the Moon, and a minute later, a copter's shape blotted out the middle of the view, before lowering within the fence line of the base.

His hair blew to the side while the rotors loudly whooshed above. It landed fifty feet away, and the top continued spinning while a man in a suit hopped out. He jogged with two armed soldiers in black, moving as one directly ahead of him.

"Silas and Cody?" he asked.

"That's us."

"Do you have the package?" His hair was slicked and didn't seem affected by the unnatural wind. He reached toward Silas, who noticed the large gold ring on his wedding finger.

Silas hesitated. "Who are you?"

"That's none of your business, Silas. Give me the Delta."

He peered at Cody, who shrugged in response. "Waylen told us to come."

The soldier on the left raised his semi-automatic, and Silas' heart raced. He took the satchel carrying the three tokens from his pocket and gripped them. "Here they are."

The man snatched the bag from Silas and smiled widely. "Very good."

"Now what?" Silas asked over the noise.

The man started walking, but the soldiers didn't follow him.

Silas had a sinking feeling in his stomach.

"I don't like the looks of this," Cody muttered.

The first soldier grabbed Cody, while the second lunged for Silas. He fought the man's grip, but couldn't break free. The original guy, who'd let them into the base, removed a needle from his pocket. "Sorry. Just following orders."

Silas struggled harder while he jabbed Cody in the upper arm. "What are you doing? What is that?"

He kicked at the soldier holding him, but didn't connect. He watched as a second needle poked through his shirtsleeve, and liquid extruded from the tip. In a matter of seconds, his knees became wobbly, and his vision blurred at the edges. For a moment, Silas thought the Shadow was enveloping him, and the world grew dark.

When he woke, he was in a small room without windows. The door sat ten feet away, large and metal, with no lever on the interior. His teeth ached, his mouth pasty and dry. Silas saw a bottle of water, and he popped the cap off, drinking greedily until it was nearly empty. He forced himself to stop, in case he was trapped here for the long haul.

Silas assessed himself, checking the bullet wound where the round had passed right through his upper arm. The area was pink, the stitches fallen out or dissolved. His sight was better, but slightly fuzzy. He closed his eyes, then reopened them, finding it brighter. Silas cleared his throat. "Hello?" He gazed at the corner of the room when he heard a gentle whirring noise. The camera was barely perceivable, but more obvious now that he knew it was there. He stood, craning his head toward the lens. "Let me out of here. We haven't done anything!"

When no one responded, Silas sat on the cot again, resting his forehead on propped up arms. He was grateful they'd dropped Rory off at home, but not thrilled at his own circumstances. "Cody?" he hissed, and thought he might have caught a faint reply. He rose, moving from one end of his cage to the other, calling for his friend, but it remained quiet.

Silas eventually dropped to his back, resting his head

on the mattress, since there was no pillow. He didn't know how long he'd waited when the door finally swung inward. His temples throbbed when he slid to a seat, staring at the same man that had arrived in the helicopter.

"I apologize for the treatment, Silas Gunn," he said. "I'm Theodore, and I have a few questions for you." He stepped aside, as if expecting Silas to cordially join him for a casual meeting.

"Go to hell," Silas spat.

Theodore grinned at this. "Spirit. I appreciate that."

The moment Silas strode into the hall, the same two soldiers flanked him. After dropping him off in a private bathroom, Theodore led him to another room, this one larger, with fancy office chairs, and the Planetae logo on a massive projector screen on the wall. That suggested they were in the facility in New York, where Waylen had been with Leo Monroe just a couple days earlier.

"Is Waylen here?"

Theodore looked genuinely surprised by the question. "No."

Silas crossed his arms, glaring at the man. "Release me. We brought you the tokens. What else do you want from us?"

"Corporal Tucker, please have the food and coffee sent in."

The soldier turned and exited, leaving his counterpart while the door closed.

"Mr. Gunn, we have something to discuss. It's easier if you comply."

Silas frowned, but took the chair opposite Theodore. "Sure, Theo, why don't we do that?"

"Actually, I prefer Theodore."

"What can I do for you, *Theo*?" It was petty, but Silas

had little leverage here.

He didn't bother to correct Silas. "Who else is aware of the tokens?"

Silas ran through the short list. "How should I know?"

"You encountered other people over the last few weeks. Should I ask your parents? Maybe Clare and the kids?" Theodore's smug expression made Silas glower.

"Fine. My father knew about the one from Peter. Leigh touched the token from his safe, but they killed her for it. Rory and Cody have been with us for a while, and then there's the FBI agent."

"Waylen."

"No, the other one. Martina Sanchez."

"Right." Theodore made a note on his tablet.

"Why am I here?"

"How do you know Leo Monroe?"

"I don't," Silas said.

"You weren't hired by him to bring the token in?" Theodore's finger lingered over his screen.

"No! What the hell is wrong with you? Leigh is dead. They killed my grandpa, and I was shot!" He gestured to himself. "I never heard of Monroe or Planetae until a few days ago."

"And who is Cody Sanderson to you?"

"A stranger."

"That you met at a baseball game," Theodore said.

They must have already interrogated Cody, so there was no point in lying. "That's correct."

"When did Cody start working for Leo?"

"Hold on. What are you suggesting?"

Theodore stayed silent, forcing Silas to ponder the question. The guys in Colin Swanson's house had mentioned "Sanderson," who was obviously Cody. He'd directed them to the fake in Fred Trell's storage unit, showing he'd been in contact with the organization.

"I don't think he ever intended on giving them up to Leo," Silas offered.

"Where is Rory Swanson?"

Silas tapped his foot nervously below the table. "She has nothing to do with this anymore. Rory wants to be left alone."

The soldier entered after a brief knock, setting a plate of breakfast pastries and two coffee cups on the table. Theodore poured both beverages and slid one to Silas, who reached out, hoping the caffeine would help his headache. He drank it black, not bothering to try the open cream on the table, since Theodore hadn't used it. Who knew if it was laced with something?

"Silas, is there anyone else?"

"No," he swore. The coffee was hot and bitter, but he downed it, instantly growing more alert. "Can I go home now?"

"You quit your job, didn't you?"

How did he know so much? "Yes."

"Why?"

"Because I'm tired of running over spreadsheets about furniture importing," he said.

"Your grades were good."

"Is this a job interview?"

"Maybe."

Silas finished his coffee. "Theo, I have to admit, you've got guts, but I'd rather dig holes in cement with a dull shovel than work for you."

Theodore glanced at the soldier, then focused on Silas. "I'm afraid you don't have a choice."

7

*W*aylen squinted and put on his sunglasses as he drove to the fence. This was his future. Planetae and Operation Delta.

The guard stationed there moved to his window, and he rolled it down. "ID."

Waylen flipped his FBI credentials, and the guy nodded, opening the gate. "What's your name?"

The soldier smiled. "Corporal Tucker."

"Glad to meet you. I have a feeling we'll be seeing a lot of each other."

"Looks that way." Tucker nodded as he passed through, raising the window. He rounded the primary building and parked near the second largest structure. Belleville had called him an hour ago, letting him know the residences were primed for the team to take over. Leo Monroe had built it with enough space to house fifty on-site lab techs and staff for when they possessed the Delta. He'd planned on expanding it as needed, and Waylen saw the outline of wooden stakes in the earth a hundred yards to the north, where it would have been completed.

This residence was curved along the outer walls, the exterior dull grey. The parking lot had room for twenty cars, but a van with a Planetae logo stretched across four of them horizontally. Waylen took the one closest to the building and got out, picturing this as his temporary home.

He'd hoped for a connection with Charlotte in DC last night, but knew in the long run there was no way they could have sustained a relationship. Waylen wasn't in a position to be thinking about love while he was in charge of the Delta. They were going to test the apparatus in order to seek the threat level surrounding it. While he understood the defensive reasoning behind the secret operation, he suspected the US government selfishly wanted control of the possible mining or resource gathering rights.

Waylen didn't doubt that Theodore and his superiors were considering colonization, but there was no proof that the Delta linked to anywhere but the Moon. He'd heard about the secondary location from Cody, though the strange man from San Diego was the only one to have touched that token to investigate. That was about to change.

He grabbed the shopping bags from the backseat, looping his arms through the holes, and hauled them to the entrance. He checked his phone, confirming the code, and entered the five digits on the numerical lock before it granted him access. The space was empty, his footsteps echoing as he moved indoors. It smelled like new construction, and he noticed a couple of sticky notes on the walls where the paint was scuffed. It looked as though the crew had been called out, and no one had ever returned to finish the final strokes.

The apartment lobby had commercially carpeted stairs, and an office to the side. He took the flight of steps, heading to the main living floor. As promised, the suites were all unlocked, and Waylen checked a couple before settling on the one he assumed was the largest. His quarters sat alone beside a communal living room with a pool table, a bar, and a big-screen TV. Using the same code, apparently exclusive to him, he entered the suite and dropped the clothing bags. He kicked off his shoes and did a walkthrough. The kitchen was small but tidy. Theodore ensured a food delivery was coming today, so the pantry was empty, as was the fridge.

The bathroom had a nice stand-up shower, and considering everything, it was larger than his outside of Atlanta. The bedroom was just as pleasant, and he tested the mattress by sitting on it, finding an acceptable firmness.

"Home sweet home," he whispered, and began removing the clothing from the bags. He methodically sorted the packages, clipping the price tags off, then hung up the two new suits. He'd been unable to bring anything from his house, so he'd stopped in the city to visit Macy's. There was no en-suite laundry, so he tossed the new underwear and socks into the shared washer in the hall and set off to see where Theodore was.

Before he got to the front entrance of Monroe's massive laboratory, Theodore Belleville appeared, offering him a badge. "Keep this on you at all times. It works with the doors. No codes. They'll just read the RFID on the tag and unlock." He spoke fast, like he'd shot a double espresso in the last five minutes.

"Thanks." Waylen slipped it over his neck, and it dangled beside his tie. "Is Darren here yet?"

"No. And I'd appreciate it if you ask me before you hire anyone from the outside," Theodore said.

"You said I could bring in a team. I'm doing that." They walked into the place, and it felt far different from the time he'd visited with Leo Monroe. The tension was gone from his shoulders, replaced with a level of excitement usually reserved for the end of a case.

"We have a lot to discuss."

Waylen stared at his superior. "Do you have them?"

Theodore paused and removed the satchel from his suit jacket pocket, showing them to Waylen, without offering the tokens. "Yes."

"I tried to check on Silas, but he won't return my calls. Did you take his phone?"

Theodore stayed quiet.

"What the hell did you do with them?" Waylen suddenly saw the operation in a new light. They were clandestine, outside the law, with the backing of the government. Rules didn't apply, and he suspected that included burying bodies without remorse or consequence.

Theodore's gaze flickered down the foyer, and Waylen hurried that way. "They're fine!" he shouted after Waylen.

It didn't take long to realize where they were being held. The stationed soldiers gave it away. Waylen halted at the nearest door and reached for the handle. A female soldier stood in his path, her AR-15 sitting across her chest. "If you don't move—"

"Let him through," Theodore ordered.

Cody Sanderson was inside, his eyes dark. He sat on the cot, with messy hair and stubble on his cheeks and chin. "Look who decided to show. You could have asked us to come in, Waylen."

"Get up," he said.

Waylen rushed to the second room, where he found Silas. The Gunn grandson grimaced when he saw Waylen. "I wasn't behind this," he promised.

"Theo told us as much." Silas walked out, and it was

instantly obvious these men needed showers.

"I had to know they were on our team," Theodore proclaimed.

Cody rubbed his shoulder. "He drugged me."

"Is that true?" Waylen asked.

"I've also offered them jobs. Mr. Sanderson can assist with the computer system, and Mr. Gunn will be helpful on our projections."

"Projections?"

"You'll see. We'll reconvene over dinner this evening. Since you've decided to go rogue, I expect you'll have them together by then?" Theodore asked.

Waylen hadn't pondered what roles had to be filled, or how they'd go about these tests, but he nodded regardless. "Sure. What about Monroe's hired guns? Are they dealt with?"

"It's being handled," he said. "See you tonight." Theodore wandered in the other direction, heading deeper into the lab's halls.

He recognized the anger in Silas' eyes and the resentment in Cody's. "You guys okay?"

"We're fine," Cody said. "Now, let's get something to eat."

Silas wasn't so quick to shake off his night. "This is who you're working for?"

"I don't know him well enough yet," Waylen said. "But he's on thin ice."

The soldiers were no longer there, having trailed after Theodore. "You're seriously going to stay with the project?" Cody asked.

Silas shrugged. "I guess so. His arguments were compelling, not to mention the thinly-veiled threats to my family."

Shadows of the Earth

"He told me my job has already been notified of my resignation," Cody said. "I could leave and see if they'd take me back, but honestly, I hated the endless IT slips. I've always wanted to use the Delta, so what choice do I have?"

"Let's get you set up." Waylen returned with them to the residence building and gave them the brief tour. Silas was far less impressed, still fuming from his night spent in solitude, and Waylen couldn't blame him.

They each took a room, and were surprised to find fresh garments waiting when they got out of the showers. Waylen let in the soldiers carrying the delivery of food and clothing, sifting through the goods while they stocked the pantries of five units. "Is Theo staying here?" Waylen asked Tucker, who was off guardhouse duty.

"Mr. Belleville will not be remaining on site," Corporal Tucker said.

That suited Waylen fine. By the time he escorted the army members from the foyer, Silas and Cody were both in the communal living room, sitting at the bar. Cody had found a bag of potato chips from somewhere, and was washing them down with a soda. Silas had a cup of single-serve coffee, and Waylen headed over, making himself one.

"So, Rory…" Waylen let the comment linger in the air.

"She's at home," Silas said. "I kind of wish I'd done the same."

"Come on, guys." Cody guzzled from the bottle. "We're going to see the Moon. How epic is this?"

"They won't let us near it," Silas argued. "This is too important. They'll have trained astronauts or military personnel."

Both men watched Waylen, searching for answers he didn't have. "I know as much as you. I have the feeling we're flying well under the radar on this operation. The Secretary of Defense wants this kept under wraps, so it might just be us for now."

"We're also expendable," Cody said. "None of us are married. I assume the FBI would make excuses for Waylen, should it go wrong, and… the government can do anything they want. No one is going to be surprised in my family if they're told I died from a gas leak in an IT office or something equally unimpressive."

He thought about Darren Jones' ex-wife and kids, and almost regretted inviting him to the team. Waylen advised the pair about the addition to the crew, and Cody seemed intrigued.

"I've listened to his podcast for years. His theories always seem plausible, not like those TV guys suggesting aliens are behind everything from chem trails to the Aztec pyramids. He likes to imagine alternative options of what alien life may look like. It's a fresh take."

Waylen sipped the coffee, viewing the fenced entrance from the picture window near the bar. A car approached, and he received a text a minute later, telling him the guard wasn't letting Darren in.

"I don't even have a radio." Waylen sighed and got up. "Stay here. I'll be back with Darren."

He left Silas and Cody, striving not to think about Leo Monroe's one remaining agent on the loose.

8

Rory was finally free.

She wandered down the block and stopped to pick a rose from the pastor's yard. She was careful not to prick her finger on the thorns. How could something so lovely be so dangerous all at once? When the pastor's wife waved at her from the front porch, she tucked the stolen flower behind her and smiled.

Rory was at peace with her decision to leave for Boston in the morning. The start of the fall term was a few weeks away, but the board wanted to meet with her as a formality; then she'd need to work on the syllabus. Rory found she could speak in front of public forums with only a slight amount of apprehension, but having her own class seemed daunting.

Her phone beeped, and she checked it, hoping for a message from Silas. Instead, it was from Waylen's superior at the FBI, claiming the Monroe hires were behind bars, and that she shouldn't worry. Rory wanted to respond, but after a quick afternoon session with her therapist Justine, she thought it best to keep her distance from the triggers of the trauma she'd experienced.

Justine had also cautioned her from returning to the place where she'd spent a decade living under Kevin's rule, but there had been so many good things about Boston too. She loved the architecture, the college atmosphere, the bookstores, bodegas, and coffee shops. While she enjoyed the simplicity of Woodstock, Rory already longed for the city life again. She reminded Justine that Boston was a large metropolis, but the therapist countered it would shrink if her abusive ex learned of her arrival.

Rory would never let Kevin hurt her again. Or anyone, for that matter. She was done being the good girl. She'd gone to the Moon, for God's sake.

With a gaze to the sky, she found it too bright to see the stars yet. It was just as well.

Her parents were at the club, reluctantly going to dinner after Rory assured them she'd be fine on her own. She used her key to unlock the house, and spun the bolt once in. Another promise she'd made them before they agreed to leave.

Rory placed the solo flower into a narrow vase, doused the base with water, and carried it up to her room, setting it on the desk before flipping her laptop open.

The cursor blinked, and she typed, filling in line after line, making progress on her new book. She'd started early in the morning, unable to stop until her mother convinced her to take a shower and spend an hour eating lunch with them.

It was a good story, one that her agent would be very proud of. The publishers could get off her case about the looming deadline, Rory could teach in Boston, and things would be on the right track.

Rory glanced at the rose, admiring the orange bloom, then returned to the screen. What she saw sent shivers down her spine. She rolled from the desk, pushing off in

Shadows of the Earth

the chair, and stood. A series of dashes was centered on the monitor, forming an intricate design in the shape of an angled circle. It looked like the Shadow, complete with grayed-out markings rising from the edges. Had she typed that?

Rory rubbed her eyes, wondering if this was a dream, but the image remained. The cursor sat below it, flashing as ever.

She went to delete it, but took a screenshot first. Then she highlighted the entire pixelated creation and hit backspace on the keyboard. It vanished, and she shut the laptop after saving.

Rory lay on her bed. It was her imagination; she was certain of it. There was no cause for concern. The threat was over, and she was safe at home. Rory exhaled and settled in, feeling the exhaustion she'd been ignoring all day seeping into her bones.

Sometime later, she awoke to a strange sensation, like she was being watched. Her arms grew numb, the fingertips tingling as though she'd lingered outside for too long without gloves in the winter. Rory tried to reach for her phone, but it stretched from her vision. The Shadow encompassed the light fixture, spreading across the tray ceiling, until the room became ice cold.

"Mom…" she croaked, knowing her parents were out for dinner. A tear fell, sliding along her temple, but she couldn't move to wipe it. "Dad…" Her lungs ached, and she struggled for air. Rory's gaze jumped to the window, but instead of seeing the Moon on the horizon, she spied Earth, a resplendent beauty glowing with the light of the Sun.

She tried to scream, but only empty air escaped her lips. Rory was trapped.

Somewhere she heard glass shattering.

Her door flung open, and a man hurried in, his expression filled with concern. "Rory? What's the matter? You were screaming for help."

Rory blinked away tears and stared at the ceiling. There was no Shadow. She could move her arms, and she slid off the bed, rushing to the computer. It woke from sleep mode, and she opened the file.

"Rory, talk to me!" Doctor Greg shouted.

"I have to see something." Her file remained as it was, with no hint of the crude Shadow made from dashes. The screenshot she'd taken was gone too, suggesting it was all a nightmare. She laughed at her own reaction and returned to the bed, sitting on the edge. "I had a bad dream." Rory realized he held his left hand, where blood leaked past his other fingers. "What happened to you?"

"I ran into your parents at the club, and they said you were at home. I came to say hi, and you were shrieking, so I broke in."

"Let me look." Rory ushered him to the bathroom, no longer concerned about her own well-being. It was a dream, nothing more. She ran the water, and once it was rinsed, the cut didn't appear as terrible as she'd expected. After a bit of antiseptic, which he took well, she bandaged it, and they headed downstairs.

"You could have been a nurse. You did a great job, Rory," he said.

"Thanks, but no thanks."

"Are you sure you're okay?" Greg asked.

"Totally. Sorry about scaring you." They went through the kitchen, then to the rear mud room, and she seized the broom, sweeping up the shards of glass. Rory swore she saw mist rising from the broken pieces, but when she inspected them, it was only the reflection of her mother's dark fur jacket hanging in the closet.

"And for the mess." He gestured at the door. "I'll pay to have it repaired. One of my patients is in construction, and he'll be able to fix it up in no time."

"How about a coffee?"

"Sounds good." Greg flexed his bandaged hand and sat at the island while she ground some Colombian beans. "How was the funeral? Oscar said you and Kathy got mugged."

"I haven't had the best luck lately," she admitted. "But it'll change soon."

Greg narrowed his gaze. "You seem different."

Rory *was* different, but she couldn't tell him about it, could she? She'd already convinced herself not to talk to Justine about the Moon, because that would push her one step closer to being committed. Maybe Greg would accept her baffling story, because she felt the urge to confide in someone that wasn't part of it, to gauge their reaction.

"Do you have anywhere to be?" Rory busied herself by gathering two large mugs and added a touch of cream, bringing out two small stirring spoons. She grabbed the sugar, which neither of them used, and took a seat next to Greg. There were a couple of muffins on the counter, and she picked at the top of one.

"Nowhere in particular."

"I have to say something, and it's going to sound… impossible, but please, hear me out."

He pressed a palm to his chest, sitting up straighter. "Scout's honor."

"Remember at my book signing, when you asked if I'd go to the Moon?" she asked.

"Yes. And you promptly said no."

"That wasn't entirely true."

"So you would go."

"Not again."

"Again?"

Rory exhaled and faced him. "I have been on the Moon."

Greg paused midway through a drink and set the cup down. "What are you talking about?"

"The Moon." She pointed up. "I walked the surface three nights ago."

Greg watched her inquisitively. "Rory, I know I'm a different kind of doctor, but I can refer you to—"

"I'm not hysterical." Rory needed someone to know, and Greg was about as trustworthy as anyone, even if he was basically a stranger.

"I didn't say you were."

"You promised to hear me out."

"Then proceed."

Rory did, sharing all her experiences. He'd already known about the kidnapping and the FBI's involvement, which might have helped her case in convincing him there were factual elements to the story. After she described them abandoning a van along the Mississippi, and stealing the guy's truck while taking an old NASA spacesuit with them, his eyes began to glaze over.

"Well…?"

"I'm thinking," he said.

"I saw the Shadow again. That's why you heard me from outside."

Greg's gaze lifted toward the second floor. "Seriously?"

She described how she'd been writing, then the constructed image of the hole on the computer.

"Can I see the laptop?" he asked.

"It was a dream."

"Still…"

They returned to her bedroom, and Greg sat while she used the mouse to bring up her file. "It's gone."

"Yeah, strange." Greg motioned to the rose. "This is ready for the compost heap."

The rose she'd taken from the pastor's garden wasn't only wilted; it was severely decayed. The petals were strewn across the desk, the thorns brittle and black. "I put that in the vase this evening."

"You brought a dead rose into your office?"

"I didn't. It was beautiful an hour ago."

Greg touched it, and the last petal floated to the floor. "What would have caused that?"

Rory knew exactly what had done it, but couldn't find the words.

"Pumpkin, are you home?" Her father's voice boomed from the main floor.

Greg stood. "It's like I'm in high school again and getting caught in my girlfriend's bedroom."

"I'm not your…"

"Of course not, I just mean…"

"In here!" She crouched, picking up pieces of dead flower. She disposed of the remains into her garbage can and dumped the vase water down the sink.

Kathy and Oscar arrived, both smelling like booze. Her mother's expression was blank, her father's filled with concern. "Oh, Greg, you did come over."

"I was going to walk him home," Rory said.

"I drove," he whispered.

"Then you'll have to get your car in the morning."

Rory heard her parents chatting behind their backs as they descended the stairs. By the time they were outside, it was almost chilly enough to need a sweater. Rory grabbed one of her dad's old plaid jackets from inside, and they left, walking past his Mercedes on the street.

"You believe me?" she asked.

"Absolutely. Where's the Delta now?"

"Somewhere safe."

9

Silas enjoyed Darren's company. From the description, he'd pictured a nerdy middle-aged man obsessing over little green men, but Darren was anything but typical. Cody hung on his every word at dinner, nodding along to his comments, and interjecting with less frequency than normal.

Theodore Belleville had opted out of the meal, claiming he had important business to attend to, but the caterers came regardless, bringing far too much food for their intimate group of four. They were to meet in the primary laboratory at ten AM Sunday morning, meaning they had thirteen hours before their first actual meeting as members of Operation Delta.

Cody picked at his second dessert while a staff member cleaned up. Silas wondered what kind of NDA was required to work at a secret government facility like the one they'd taken over from Planetae, and suspected it wasn't an easy position to fill. The pair of women didn't speak as they cleared the table, even when Silas thanked them.

"You really don't believe we can access the other worlds without something else?" Cody asked Darren after much deliberation.

"That's my instinct, but I haven't seen the Delta in action, so take it with a grain of salt. You had this… Shadow in your living room, so you might have better insight. Were there any controls that you noticed? Or was it just a cloud of … blackness, as you've described?" Darren inquired.

"I was busy worrying about Rory. Cody, did you see anything?"

Cody shook his head. "Which leads me to the same conclusion as our friend Darren here."

Silas grinned at Cody's comment. Already sucking up to the resident alien expert.

"When can I see the computer system?" Cody asked Waylen.

"Theodore told me to keep everyone away from the lab tonight. He wants us to talk and be prepared for tomorrow."

Darren took a drink from his beer bottle. "What are we doing, then?"

"Your guess is as good as mine."

"I thought you were in charge?" Silas laughed.

"It's obvious that's not the case," Waylen admitted.

"What about his lab techs? Are they still here?" Silas asked.

"One of them is. She was there when I met with Leo, and helped him into the spacesuit. You'll meet her in the morning too." Waylen polished off his first beer.

It was nine, and Silas had the urge to go for a walk after the heavy meal. Unfortunately, they weren't near anything, and he didn't feel like being followed around by an armed soldier. "Anyone for a game of pool?"

"Sure." Darren rolled his neck and brought his drink. "Are they making you stay?"

Silas racked the balls, removing the triangle. He held it up, staring at Darren through the center, thinking about the Delta. "Yeah, probably."

Cody sauntered over with a beer and sat on a bar stool near them. "We're free to come and go, right, Waylen?"

The FBI agent shrugged at this. "I'll get us clarification."

Silas chalked his cue and let Darren break. The white ball cracked into the others, sending them scattering. "Come on, guys. We were drugged, confined, then grilled about the Delta. They're only giving us a 'position' because we know too much, and Theo wants to monitor us."

Darren sank a stripe, then missed a tougher shot. "What happens if I see the Delta and change my mind?"

Waylen was clearly growing frustrated, because he wouldn't stop frowning. Silas didn't know him that well, but his expressions usually gave him away. "No one's a prisoner," he said.

"What about you?" Cody asked him.

"Me?"

"You have more connections out there. Too many loose ends. They're isolating us, Waylen," he told the federal agent.

"Rory's not here," Silas said, sinking the three ball.

Waylen took his cell out. "Speaking of, I haven't heard from her."

Silas did the same after bouncing the five from the corner pocket. He grabbed his own phone and dialed Rory's number. There was no ring, no anything. "It's not working."

It beeped, and he found a message from Cody. *You*

suck at pool. "Funny."

"We can text one another. They must have us blocked from contacting the outside world," Cody said matter-of-factly.

Darren set his cue stick aside. "They can't do that."

"Sure, the secret government, watching over a weapons manufacturing facility, wouldn't do something illegal," Cody muttered. "They can and will do whatever they choose. We're lucky to be alive."

"Why did I think these tokens would be better off in the government's hands than Leo's?" Waylen glanced around the room and came in closer. He covered his mouth from any hidden cameras. "They're probably watching our every move. Let's try to act normal and see what Theodore has in store for us tomorrow. If I smell a setup, I'll find a way out."

Waylen believed he could escape, should it come to that, but Silas wasn't so confident. He walked to the window, studying the armed soldiers in the yard. He desperately wanted to contact Rory, but that was impossible.

"Once I have access to the computer, I'll send her a message," Cody assured him.

Silas nodded, glad someone was on their team.

"You gonna finish the game?" Darren called.

Silas had no desire to, but went through the motions, wondering if he'd ever get out of here alive.

Waylen had made three attempts to contact the director since he'd eaten breakfast, and all texts went unanswered, so they were heading into the meeting blind.

Shadows of the Earth

Cody wore a t-shirt with a video game logo, while Waylen had opted for a suit, as per usual. Silas and Darren were more casual, but each had a sweater and dark jeans provided by the military's provision delivery.

He stood at the entrance to the lab, recalling the moment he'd first seen it with Leo Monroe. He'd been so eager to explore the Delta, he hadn't even considered they might come for him. Waylen had imagined the guy was locked up deep underground somewhere no one could reach him, but now he wasn't so certain.

Corporal Tucker greeted them with a nod, and entered a code before stepping aside. Belleville was already present, standing by the hexagonal platform with a woman, the same one he'd seen helping Monroe on Wednesday.

The boss actually looked happy, and he softly clapped his palms together when they approached. "Waylen, thank you for coming." He glanced at the others, but didn't address them. "This is Doctor Rita Singh."

"Nice to meet you." Waylen smiled. "I'm Waylen. This is Darren, Cody, and Silas."

"Thanks for keeping me on board," she said directly to Waylen, as if he'd fought for her job security.

"You're the most qualified we have," he said in response.

Theodore gestured at the lockers with the suits. "Let's see what the fuss is about."

"Just like that?" Cody blurted.

"You'd prefer to wait? Leo was positive the Delta could bring him to the Moon, and now we have the means to do so," Theodore said.

"Rory…"

Silas nudged him in the ribs, and Cody stopped short.

They'd agreed not to share her experience on the Moon with Belleville.

"What about her?" Theo frowned and waited.

"She asked us to be careful."

"Well, Rory Swanson isn't here, and we are." Theodore moved to the locker. "We will be the first people to explore the Sea of Serenity since"—he glanced at Silas—"Commander Gunn."

Waylen had countless objections, but truthfully, he was as curious as any would be to view the Delta in action.

"Where's my spacesuit?" Cody blurted.

"The relic we found in your stolen truck?" Theodore asked.

"It's fully functional."

"You won't be needing that any longer."

Cody shrugged and touched a new version. "Impressive."

Waylen took one from the locker, and was shocked by how light it was. The Planetae logo was on the shoulder pad, the American flag on the other.

"Shouldn't we see if the Delta works before we go to the trouble?" Darren interjected.

"Yeah, and aren't these custom built for the wearers?" Cody lifted the suit.

"There will be alterations, yes, but these models should fit in general. If you'll notice, you each have a labeled locker," Rita said.

Waylen glanced at the doors, finding *W. Brooks* on the farthest. Darren and Silas swapped theirs after reading the labels, and Cody smiled, since he had already read the names.

Waylen was going to walk on the Moon. He'd spent

Shadows of the Earth

years of his childhood pretending to be an astronaut. He'd wander through the forest behind his home with friends, as if they were on a mission to a planet's surface. The local squirrels were alien threats they needed to evade.

Rita showed them how to dress, and helped Cody when the seals failed. Silas had his on, and held the helmet under an arm, before setting it down to assist Darren.

"What's this?" Darren touched a port.

"That's where the umbilical connects to the packs. These are a rehabilitated version of the models used in recent shuttle runs, but we've altered them to withstand spacewalks and, more importantly, Moonwalks." Rita removed a pack from the bottom of Waylen's locker, and Darren helped her lift it, clipping the unit onto Waylen's back. "It weighs eighty-seven pounds, which is a vast improvement from the older models. We did our best to disperse the bulk, but remember, everything on the Moon is much easier to manage."

Waylen had to adjust his stance as they mounted the pack, but it wasn't as bad as he'd expected.

"Where's the HUD and all that fun stuff?" Cody asked.

"In the movies," Rita said. "These are meant for communication. Each helmet helps control the pressure and distribute the air, and they have cameras mounted. One above the visor, one on the rear, by the occipital bone, so we can record what's behind you. The shoulders have built-in lights."

"What about weapons?" Cody added.

Theodore cleared his throat. "If we're done with the questions, I'd like to proceed."

It was obvious the guy had been directed to expedite this process. Waylen thought they were going about this wrong, but he'd follow Theodore's lead today, as long as no one was in immediate danger, and decide his next steps afterwards.

"This is the Hex." Rita walked to the containment field around the raised dais. "It's twenty feet wide, and we've built the walls to withstand heat, cold, and radiation. It's a proprietary polymer that I'm not able to reveal—"

Theodore smirked at the comment. "We'll be exploring that in detail later."

She stepped up after opening the door, and Waylen detected the clear seal around the frame. They all entered, each now wearing their helmets, and Rita closed it behind them. She settled at a desk with five monitors. They connected and flashed on, splitting in two, displaying their cameras from both ends. "We are recording all communication and video feeds for the initial contact mission. I suggest someone stays in the Hex and, as we've discussed, do not, I repeat, do not, bring the Delta into the portal."

"Shadow," Silas said. "That's what we call it."

"Okay, leave the Delta here. Any volunteers to stay?" Waylen asked.

They all quietly stared at one another, and Silas lifted his hand after a moment. "I'll hang back."

Waylen hadn't grasped the situation until he peered around the Hex, seeing the clear walls, the sealed door, and the central stand in the middle of the platform. His breaths were loud in his ears, the recycled air coming in and out faster than it should. When he spoke, the words echoed while they transmitted to the others through speakers. "Maybe we take this slower…"

Shadows of the Earth

"Waylen, everything's prepared. We're going to make history," Theodore said. "Of course, we can never tell a soul, but that changes nothing."

Waylen spied the satchel in his grip, and the director dumped the contents onto the stand.

"The Delta is ours, and now we'll discover what secrets it holds," Theodore said, and the edges folded over when he touched two of them together. Waylen held his breath as the third completed the triangle. The device glowed blue, and the Shadow drifted from the center, vapors pouring out, forming a misty hole like he'd seen in his early echo. It grew wider until the sides of it brushed the outer walls.

Theodore stood near it, setting the Delta on the stand. "Silas, ensure this isn't disconnected. It's our only path home. Rita, start a timer for ten minutes the moment we're gone. We must check if the comms work, so Silas can try to talk through the speakers when we're off Earth."

"I will," Silas promised.

Waylen wanted to give his people a pep talk, but the words caught in his throat as the enormity of what they were about to do took hold. "Good luck," was the best he could manage.

Theodore crept to the edge of the Shadow and stepped into it, vanishing. Darren glanced at Waylen, while Cody almost ran for his turn. Then the extraterrestrial expert disappeared, and it was only Waylen.

"Be careful," Silas told him.

Waylen strode into the mist.

10

"Thanks for everything," Rory said. Her few possessions were packed into a suitcase, and she realized how little she owned. Coming to her parents, she'd discarded all of her and Kevin's things into a dumpster, but now she had nothing left.

"Take this." Her father's hand folded around hers, and she opened it to find a credit card. "To set your new place up. When you're ready, we'll talk about the condo."

Rory appreciated his generosity, but she knew deep down that she had to do this on her own, eventually. This safety net would threaten to suffocate her if she wasn't cautious.

Rory kissed and hugged each of her parents, lugged the suitcase outside, and brought it to the car. Her old hatchback. At least that was hers, earned with her own money in college. It probably needed some maintenance, but she could take care of that in Boston.

The idea of returning to the town she'd just escaped from was daunting. But after being attacked, kidnapped, mugged, and chased, not to mention walking on the actual Moon, Rory was empowered. Nothing could stop her. Not a man, not anything.

Greg's car was already gone, meaning he'd come ei-

Shadows of the Earth

ther last night or early this morning to retrieve it. She liked him, but she'd made it clear they were strictly platonic, and he seemed to accept that fact. Besides, Silas had been a surprising connection, and she was moving to Boston. Thinking about Peter Gunn's grandson reminded her to text him, but the message failed again. That had been happening with all of them, and her anxiety resurfaced as a result. Cody's and Waylen's were doing the same. She'd try again once she got to the city.

And as quickly as she'd left Boston, filled with anger, tears, and resentment, Rory Swanson was heading back. This time, she had a sense of optimism and possibilities.

Passing through Woodstock was a pleasure, and she slowed, doing a detour past the town square. Being Sunday morning, it seemed quiet, with the diner packed and the bookstore doors propped wide. Rory waved at Mrs. Habbishire, who was watering flowers in a hanging basket.

Minutes later, she exited town, taking the 89, and hit the gas on the clear roads. She'd rushed out on a Sunday because traffic would be a third as hectic as waiting for another day. Soon she spotted a sign indicating she was in New Hampshire, and it made her think about Waylen Brooks' hobby of snapping photos of the state signs. She pulled to the shoulder, grabbed her phone, and climbed out carefully. A couple of cars sped by while she focused on the billboard. The slogan on the bottom stuck out. *Live Free or Die.* The motto was worth adopting.

Before returning to the driver's side, her cell rang. "Hello."

"*Is this Rory Swanson?*"

"Yes."

The other end crackled.

"Hello?" She slid into the car and closed the door, linking it to her Bluetooth.

"...*Swanson*..."

Rory took a deep breath, feeling a familiar unease creeping into her veins. "Listen, I don't know who this is, but..."

"*Sorry about that, Rory. It's Marg Chambers, the Associate Professor Department Chair for the English department.*"

Rory flushed with embarrassment and stayed parked. "Hey, Marg, it's great to hear from you."

"*We're scheduled for a meeting tomorrow, but something's come up. Are you in town?*"

"I will be in two hours," she said.

"*Splendid, what about dinner at six? There's an Italian restaurant right off campus.*"

"I know the place," Rory said.

"*Okay, then it's settled. I look forward to discussing your appointment. See you soon.*"

Rory heard the distinctive static, and her music began playing. She turned it down. "Not everyone is out to get you," she told herself.

She busied her mind by thinking about her novel. Rory hated to admit that her mother had possibly swayed her into the literary fiction route.

Rory signaled and sped onto the interstate, south on the I-89, hoping her story didn't mirror her new character, like it had ended up doing with Madeline in *View from the Heavens*. Rory loved writing the presently unnamed book and was eager to continue it. With the premise set, and a fluid outline, the typing came easily.

Rory smiled, feeling lighter after leaving Woodstock.

It was time to start fresh.

Nothing would stop her.

Shadows of the Earth

---

*W*aylen had seen heaven.

With no light pollution, and only a wisp of atmosphere, bright stars filled his entire field of vision. He'd never been a God-fearing man, but this might be enough to change his mind.

The four of them wandered across the sand and rocks. Theodore was muttering to himself, making verbal notes, Waylen surmised.

Cody ventured to the planted American flag, rubbing the material between his gloved fingers. Darren just made a slow circle while taking in the view.

Waylen was blank, an empty husk, not sure of anything in his life. He'd reached the Moon. They all had. What should have been impossible was anything but. He crouched and touched the ground, running his palm over the small bits of rock.

"Silas, come in," he said, remembering he was supposed to attempt contact with Earth.

No response came.

"Theodore," Waylen said, and the boss stopped near the lander module, glancing back. His face was unrecognizable in the mask's dark reflection, but his voice passed clearly.

"Brooks, get moving. We have to record as much as we can in ten minutes."

Waylen nodded and started forward, struggling to adjust for the low gravity. It was disconcerting, but he stayed upright and bounded closer to Darren and Cody.

"We did it," Cody told him. *"Come on, let's check out*

the...." He pointed to his boot, and Waylen got the gist. They weren't sure whether or not to tell Theodore about the alien print, if that was what it truly was.

He followed Cody to the site where Rory had been, and was grateful Theodore hadn't noticed the extra set of prints. The boots weren't custom for Rory, so it would be difficult to determine whether they belonged to Swanson, Gunn, or a third party.

Cody slowed, and Waylen almost bumped into him, but halted in time. There it was, just like he'd seen in the video. Theodore was fifty feet away, making quiet comments to himself, and Cody brushed the imprint with his boot, trying to look casual. Waylen wanted to reprimand him, but knew every interaction was being recorded for further analysis.

"*This is where they found the Delta,*" Cody said, covering his actions with a commentary. Waylen imagined finding the alien device while gathering samples from the surface. The pair of astronauts had trained for years in various fields before being sent to the Moon, and discovering the triangle-shaped artifact must have been awe-inspiring.

"Two hours," Waylen said.

"*Yeah, they were gone for that long.*" Cody's voice cracked through the speakers.

Waylen gazed at the landscape, wondering where the Shadow had appeared for them, and where it took the duo. Did they actually leave the Moon and visit another world? It gave him an idea, but he'd wait until they'd returned to the lab to broach the subject with Theodore.

"*Three minutes and twenty seconds,*" Theodore warned, arriving beside Waylen. "*This is incredible.*"

The Shadow remained in place, their only path home, and Waylen prayed nothing would break their contact with the Hex back in New York State. Darren stuck close to the mist, but his gaze was on Earth. Waylen couldn't blame him. The view was spectacular.

"I'd say this was a successful venture. Since we've confirmed nothing nefarious is awaiting us, we move to part two of the plan," Theodore said.

Cody glanced at Waylen, as if he might have the answers, but the agent just shrugged.

"Okay, you heard the man. Time to go home," Waylen told them, and lingered at the Shadow while Darren hurried through. Cody went next, and Waylen grabbed Theodore by the arm before he left as well. "What's your agenda? Why put me in charge of an operation, if you don't even talk to me?"

"Waylen, I had to see this for myself first. We'll talk."

"When?"

"Today," he verified.

Waylen released his grip and nodded. "Good."

Theodore strode into the black fog, vanishing from the Moon. For a moment, Waylen was alone up there, the only living being on the giant hunk of rock. He shivered and entered the hole, the ringlets of mist clinging to his appendages, darting across his mask.

Then he was within the Hex.

"Would you do the honors?" Theodore motioned to the Delta.

Waylen reached for it, and while there were no visible seams in the surface, the tokens separated with a little force. The blue light faded, the dark fog diminishing from the center, and they were once again just three pieces of flat metal.

Cody removed his helmet and set it aside. "That was riveting. When can we do it again?"

Theodore was already outside of the Hex, with Dr. Singh helping him off with the suit. "I have other tasks for you and Silas, as we've previously discussed. Mr. Sanderson, there are files locked in the server. I want access to them."

Cody glanced at Rita. "You don't have the passwords?"

"Leo trusted me, but not at that level," she admitted.

"I'm not a hacker," Cody reminded Theodore. "Just an IT guy."

"Can you do it?"

"I'll try." Cody's smile suggested he was underselling his abilities.

"And me?" Silas asked.

"Mr. Gunn, I'd like you to review the financials of Planetae. Search for anything out of place," Theodore said.

"And we have entry to those?"

"Somewhat. Whatever Cody discovers will shed more light on the situation. We've been able to review Planetae's tax information with the IRS, but we believe there is far more hidden from the US government."

"Makes sense. I doubt Leo wanted anyone to know he was selling invisible missiles to North Korea," Darren said. "And me? What are you hoping to get from my expertise?"

Theodore gestured to the tokens. "Those are the key. We've traveled to the Moon, but there are other worlds connected to them, I know it."

"It's true. The one from Trell is different… you don't see the echo of the Moon," Cody said.

"Use the tokens and acclimate to the echoes, then mark everything down. You and Waylen can start soon.

Silas, there's an office for you, and Cody, yours is next door." Theodore motioned to Waylen. "Get out of that suit and come with me. We have to talk."

Ten minutes later, Waylen was in a fancy office, which he could only presume had belonged to Leo Monroe. The wood finishings were exquisite, the entire room drenched in mahogany. Ancient books and strange artifacts sat behind glass cases, but Theodore didn't so much as look in their direction.

He took a seat at the large desk, and Waylen sat opposite him. "What are you supposed to find?"

Theodore leaned forward, resting his elbows on the desk. "I need to learn how far the Delta reaches."

"What do you plan to achieve?"

"Infinite opportunities."

11

Silas found comfort in reviewing financial statements. He'd started running the books for their family operation while in college. The outsourced accountant would compile the monthly data, and Silas confirmed the results while offering advice. His father instantly saw value in his opinions, and before he'd graduated, Silas was already the CFO.

He'd never chosen what to do with his life, not entirely. He'd taken to business because that was the direction in which his parents had guided him, but in retrospect, Silas wasn't certain he had any inclination toward the field. Silas understood that the world was a business, whether it was corporate, private, or government-funded. Even not-for-profit organizations had a bottom line to keep tidy.

The Planetae files were clean. Too clean. Whoever had done them was obviously well-trained, but Silas had smelled the stench of deceit the moment he'd begun perusing them. Hundreds of millions of dollars in government contracts were constantly being paid out, some in advances for new technology, others trickling in for product delivery. The USA appeared to give him nearly a hundred million a year for research and development. While that wasn't a lot compared to the country's yearly military budget, it was a hefty sum for any company, especially one with only two hundred listed employees.

Silas dug deeper, learning that Planetae owned seven commercial buildings in the United States, and had another three listed. One outside of Shenzhen, China; the second near Jakarta, Indonesia; and the last, a remote village in Germany. None of those locations had staff directly employed by Planetae, which raised a few flags, but they could be explained by outsourcing local manual labor. Still, they'd require management from head office at some point.

Silas checked the time, and realized he'd been at the desk for over three hours already. He rose, blinked, and shifted his gaze off the bright screens. In his usual day-to-day, Silas would often take an hourly break for five minutes to stretch his legs and rest his eyes.

He gazed around the room and moved to the window, flipping the blinds open. From the top floor, he could see a few blocks in the distance, past the chain-link fence. A convoy of military vehicles was approaching, and the sight gave Silas a tremor of fear. What were they tied up in? Could he leave of his own free will? His cell phone still couldn't breach the facility. According to Theodore, they had to protect the Delta's whereabouts.

He wasn't built for this type of job. Silas needed to see people, to go for dinner, to check out the odd concert. He also wanted to stay in touch with his family… and Rory. Silas sat, spinning slowly in the chair, and pictured her smiling face. Rory Swanson was the one shining star in the blackness surrounding the Delta, and now he couldn't even talk to her.

Silas reopened the files, and noticed a folder labeled

Balloons. He clicked it and noticed the usual. More spreadsheets, some documents of scanned PDFs from several organizations. He'd already searched through countless invoices for various components Planetae used to manufacture goods, including some extremely volatile compounds that were illegal for most of the world to purchase. With their authorizations, it was simple for Planetae to order anything, including plutonium and uranium.

He almost closed the folder, but his finger lingered on the mouse when he spotted a Notepad file. Silas sighed and checked the contents.

Helium—Somboon Suwan

That was it. Silas opened a web browser, typing the three words in. When the outcome showed nothing conclusive, he deleted the first word and found countless results for the name.

Silas hit the X and stared at the screen, then went to another section and began sorting through the endless information.

Cody Sanderson may not have been at the top of his graduating class, but he was certainly the brightest. Computers came easy to him, ever since he'd used the 386 as a preteen. He recalled his older brother getting a boot disk, so they had enough processing power to play a first-person shooter everyone was going nuts for. Cody had learned how it worked and modified the program, offering even faster gameplay. He was only ten, and his interest had grown from there.

These people thought he was an IT nerd, but he was

much more. Theodore Belleville must have had an inkling; otherwise, they would have brought in a team rather than offer a stranger access to a government-supported weapons manufacturer's database.

The network had a tracker built in, but Cody deactivated it before even sitting down. He understood that someone was always watching, but normally, it was just algorithms mining for useless statistics. This was different. Cody wouldn't permit Theo or anyone else to find out how efficient he could be.

After three hours in the chair, Cody knew everything about the facility, the staff, the contractors who'd built it, and the passcodes to every chamber, desk drawer, and camera system. He marked a few, giving Theodore something useful, but kept the rest for himself. Cody couldn't very well use the Delta if they were observing him.

He shut his eyes for a second, and gasped when he felt the sensation of low gravity. Cody snapped them open and sighed in relief to find he was still seated. Mist floated in the corners of his periphery, but when he turned his head, it was gone.

"You're fine. It's just an after-effect of the Delta," he assured himself. Had this happened to the astronauts? Fred Trell would have shared those details with Cody, or perhaps not. Cody actually had no evidence that the trio had used the Delta after returning to Earth. Fred claimed they made an agreement to separate the Tokens upon landing, but did they stick to it for their entire lives?

When the cobwebs faded, the room was once again a place of comfort. He no longer felt like he might float away, and the hints of the Shadow were gone. Cody closed his current application, switching to the security program. Two dozen camera angles appeared on screen, and he selected one, watching Dr. Rita walking with a tablet in her hand, reading as she moved.

He skipped by the rest until he found Waylen and Darren back in the laboratory. Cody clicked the unmute button, and heard their voices in the speakers.

"…won't harm us?"

Waylen stared at the three tokens. *"Sure, it's not fun, but Cody said it gets easier. I may have thrown up the first time, but we'll be prepared."*

"Why did I let you rope me into this again?" Darren Jones asked.

"Because I promised you a chance at the truth," Waylen said.

Cody muted their conversation and switched to the outer cameras. Six Humvees had arrived, and the soldiers stood in practiced rows.

Finally, he checked Leo Monroe's office feed, locating Theodore Belleville. Cody tapped the mouse, and heard one side of a conversation while Theo spoke into his cell phone.

"Yes, sir, I understand. There were no signs of hostiles on the surface," Theo said. *"I get that, but we're taking precautions. Currently, we can only connect to the Moon. Yes, sir."* He glanced at the phone, as if confirming the other person had hung up, then set it on the desk. Theodore rose and stared out the window.

A knock startled Cody, and he closed the program, switching to a coding screen. Silas was in the hall. "Want to grab dinner? I can't look at another spreadsheet."

Cody grinned and patted Silas on the shoulder. "Sure. I think I made some headway. Give me a second." He returned to the computer and shut it down, ensuring they couldn't trace his activity.

Shadows of the Earth

Rory strode on the sidewalk, noting how quiet it was on Sunday afternoon. It was exactly as she'd remembered it. The Italian restaurant was busy, despite the rest of the area being completely inactive. With no school on the weekends, traffic was almost nonexistent. Rory took a bus instead of driving, regardless, and went the last two blocks on foot.

A familiar tune played from speakers near the hostess station, and the woman greeted her.

"I'm here to meet Marg Chambers?" Rory said it like a question, and the young girl ran a finger over her tablet.

"Right this way."

Rory felt underdressed as she weaved through the dining room. Everyone wore skirts and ties in the vicinity. She flinched when a server popped the cork from a bottle of champagne, but thankfully, no one seemed to notice. Rory hadn't realized how much the recent violence had affected her. She'd shot a man and killed him.

Marg rose from her seat, extending her arm. "Rory Swanson?"

Rory recognized her from the quick study of the website's faculty photos, though she looked older in person. Wrinkles creased her eyes, and a hint of grays speckled her roots. "It's a pleasure to meet you, Marg."

They both sat while the hostess wandered off. A bottle of red wine already waited on the table, Marg with an untouched serving. "I took the liberty of ordering ahead. I hope you don't mind."

Rory smiled at her. "Not at all."

"Did you make it to Boston okay?"

"Traffic was light. I got to the hotel early," she said.

"So you haven't secured a place yet?" Marg waved the server down, and the man came, introducing himself. He poured a glass from the bottle for Rory and promised to give them a few minutes with the menu.

"Nothing concrete." Rory had a hotel booked for three days, but beyond that, didn't have a plan. It was extremely unlike her, but she appreciated not knowing what her next week would look like. It gave her a sense of freedom she'd lacked for some time.

"The faculty can offer you a room for the first year. The university has a lovely building for professors and guest lecturers, such as yourself, coming from out of town."

Rory was shocked, but tried not to let it show. "That would be great. Marg, why did you search me out?"

Marg smiled at this and took a sip. "I loved your book."

"Thanks."

"And when I saw the news of what happened at Peter Gunn's funeral, I had to contact you."

Rory paused and watched her. "Why?"

"You were caught up in something, weren't you?" Marg asked.

Rory's mind set off alarm bells. "Maybe this…"

Marg shook her head. "My sister was kidnapped when I was younger. From campus in Florida."

"Oh my God, is she okay?"

"Yes, but it took some time to recover." Marg glanced at her own hands while she spoke. "I heard you were living with your parents, and that you'd been through an ordeal…"

Rory bit her lip, knowing her agent, Perri, must have

Shadows of the Earth

let the cat out of the bag. "I'm fine."

"Either way, we have a role to fill this fall, and I thought you might like the stability. Perri told me you were working on your second novel, and I hoped you'd be willing to teach while you finished it. I figured you'd enjoy the change of pace. The students are great. I'd be giving you second-level courses, not 101, so you'll have a class filled with serious learners."

Rory listened, and by the time their entrees arrived, she was sold. "I'll do it."

"Excellent. We're thrilled to have you on board, Rory." Marg swirled her linguine with a fork.

Rory ate while they discussed the details, and before the check came, she'd already agreed to come by in the morning for a tour.

Her life was moving ahead, and on her way to the hotel in her taxi, she longed to call Silas to share the good news. Rory texted him, but it failed.

12

Infinite opportunities.

The two words replayed in Waylen's head while he walked with Darren Jones to the laboratory. Their footsteps echoed as they entered the space, with the Hex looming directly ahead. What had he gotten himself into? He glanced at Darren, assuming he was thinking the same.

He'd spent the last few hours trying to piece together their situation since meeting with Theodore, and it was wearing on him. Why was it only the four of them, Theodore, and Doctor Rita Singh? He had no contact with anyone beyond the base, which the boss claimed was for the Delta's protection. It gave him a bit of a reprieve, knowing that Assistant Director Ben and Martina knew his whereabouts. Waylen recalled Martina's deception and sighed.

"You okay?" Darren asked.

"You didn't tell a soul where you were going, did you?"

"No. I was asked not to. Remember?"

"Sure."

"Does that worry you?"

"Kind of." Waylen glanced at the walls, then at the Hex, which had cameras mounted at the outer edges. He pretended there was a piece of lint on Darren's shirt and leaned in, plucking it off. "We'll talk later."

Darren gave a slight nod, peering at the cameras as well. "What's it like to touch the tokens?"

"Your mind is transported to the site, seeing the echo from another point of view, or your own… I can't really recall. I was too mesmerized by the scene, and the shadowy hole lingering above the surface of the Moon." Waylen moved to the safe, hidden within the locker bay, and typed the code Theodore had discreetly provided. The three tokens were inside, each separated by a clear plastic sheath. Waylen pulled a pair of blue vinyl gloves out of his pocket and passed them to Darren before slapping a set on his own hands.

"We're really doing this?" Darren asked.

"Exposure to the tokens is essential. It'll lessen their effects."

"The echoes," Darren said.

"That's right."

"If these capture an echo, will they eventually replay our own movements?" Darren asked.

"That's an interesting question." Waylen didn't have the answer. "Maybe we'll learn that as we go."

Darren carried two chairs into the Hex's opening and faced them within the containment field. Waylen entered, closing the clear door behind him, and handed Darren a tablet he'd been issued. "We're supposed to mark down every sensation." Waylen took a piece of yellow tape, labeling the first token. He put a red sample on the second, then blue on the third. "They're each marked differently, so let's use the colors to indicate which token we're exploring. I suggest we alternate, with the other watching over to ensure we don't linger too long in the echo. At least for now."

"Good plan." Darren stared at the tokens in Waylen's gloved hands with trepidation, and Waylen understood why. Their recent addition was well-versed on the subject matter, and it was obvious he felt some apprehension at the prospect of exploring alien worlds.

Most of the laboratory lights were off, giving the Hex a brighter glow than its surroundings. Waylen grew hot, sensing he was being watched in the cameras with a spotlight. It made him uncomfortable, but he'd been given a job, and he'd see it through.

Waylen set the three tokens on the crate they'd placed between the chairs, like he'd dealt a hand of poker, then stripped the glove from his left hand. "I'll touch the token, instead of holding it. If I don't release after thirty seconds, pry my finger off."

Darren licked his lips. "Got it."

Waylen recalled the sensation he'd experienced in Loon Lake, and didn't know which of the three tokens he'd linked to, since they were all identical in appearance. Instead of choosing at random, he selected the one closest, which sat near his left knee. Waylen took a last glance at the cameras and pressed his digit onto the cool metal.

His lungs burned.

The Shadow fluttered above the Moon's regolith, misty tendrils spilling from the central mass. This was the same token as before. He now understood the movements he felt weren't his own, but someone else's. A person was in his peripheral vision, and he couldn't turn his head. Waylen guessed he was seeing from the eyes of Peter Gunn, and Colin Swanson was the figure next to him.

"*I need to find out.*" The words pressed into Waylen's mind, rather than hearing them.

Shadows of the Earth

His arm lifted, covered in a spacesuit, and the other man, now obviously Swanson, fell into the Shadow, vanishing from sight.

Waylen gasped for air when he broke contact with the token.

Darren knelt beside him. "You okay?"

He patted his own chest and searched for the bottle of water. Waylen spun the cap off and guzzled the contents before speaking. "I saw Swanson leave. These might tell us an authentic story."

Waylen's hand was shaky, but he didn't experience the level of nausea he'd felt the first time.

"I'll try the next," Darren said.

Waylen wanted to interject and go again, but he was the one who'd created the rules. "Thirty seconds."

"Gotcha." Darren had removed the gloves from both hands, and his index finger hovered over the metal artifact. "Here goes nothing."

Waylen watched as his eyes rolled into his head, his legs shooting straight out. Darren didn't fall off the chair, though he looked like he might, and his finger stuck to the token. Waylen checked the timer as the seconds quickly counted down. Darren coughed, and spit flew from his lips, landing on the crate.

Five.

Four.

Darren inhaled, and Waylen pried his hand from the alien device.

For a second, he thought Darren wasn't breathing, but he opened his eyes, wiped his mouth, and croaked.

"What did you find?" Waylen asked.

"I saw it… the other world."

Darren passed out.

Nathan Hystad

Location: Unknown
December 8ᵗʰ, 1972

Commander Peter Gunn was a man of few words. He preferred to listen to the people around him, assess the situation before commenting, but now he had nothing to say at all.

Colin Swanson lay in a heap on the ground, only noticeable by the odd grunt emerging into Gunn's helmet.

Peter rose from his seat, checking the connections on Colin's air, before confirming his own were working properly. He finally found his voice. "Helios, come in."

Static.

"Helios, this is Commander Gunn."

Static.

"Colin, are you coherent?" He crouched by his crewmate, and the man lifted his head.

"*I'm fine. I tripped.*" Colin glanced behind them. "*Coming through... that.*" The inky black hole remained, appearing just as the one on the Moon had.

Peter realized, for the first time, that they weren't in the Sea of Serenity or anywhere close to their previous destination. The star shining in the distance wasn't the same color as the Sun. It had a piercing yellow glow, which meant an actual atmosphere. The sky was tinged with red, dark clouds looming on the horizon.

He helped Colin to his feet, and they both stood with labored breaths. "Gravity is strong. Almost as much as Earth," Peter said, feeling better by making calculated observations. He estimated the weight of his suit and the various attached components were at least eighty percent as heavy as back home during training. Maybe ninety.

"*Where are we?*" Colin took a stride and nearly toppled forward. Peter snatched him by the pack and kept him upright.

"Careful," he suggested. "And I have no idea. We shouldn't have gotten so close to the… hole."

"*Peter, we found something very important. This is a portal. On the Moon!*" Swanson's eyes were wide, and somehow his mouth formed a smile, despite the incredulous situation.

"You know what this means…"

Swanson took a step. "*Yeah. We're going to be heroes.*"

"We have to go back."

"*We can't leave. Don't you understand how long it'll take for anyone to come again? NASA doesn't have another mission planned. It'll be years… and they won't send us. It'll be someone younger, maybe military, given the situation.*"

Peter mulled over his comments and agreed with every word. He could only think of his family, and ensuring he made it home to them. "I don't care."

"*You can go,*" Colin said, walking away from the hole they'd traveled through. "*I have to see more.*"

Peter Gunn was the commander of the mission, and he couldn't very well abandon Swanson on an alien planet. "We're not prepared for this."

"*We have air, Peter. Let's gather some information. We're the first people to set foot out here. Don't you understand the significance?*" Colin's enthusiasm was almost infectious.

"An hour. Then we return." Peter watched the hole, praying it would remain intact.

The pair of astronauts began to trek across the black,

rocky surface of the red-skied planet.

Peter eyed the shadowy portal before catching up to his counterpart.

PART TWO
REVELATIONS

1

The endless stream of files made Silas wish he'd never accepted the role—not that he'd taken it with open arms. After being drugged by Theodore Belleville, then hearing threats against his relatives, he had no choice. Silas disliked the man with a passion.

He closed the current spreadsheet and gaped at the blank desktop. The neatly organized folders sat in a clean row, in order of urgency. Silas had gone through the first three of five, and all the contents within. Give him one more day, and he'd be finished. Then what would Theo have him doing?

Silas initiated a web browser and checked the news. The dates were from last week. He used another source, finding nothing beyond last Thursday, when Theodore took control of the facility.

Silas switched to his web account, operated by the largest service provider in the world. He attempted to log in, but his email and stored cloud files didn't show up. The screen flashed dark and returned to the search field a steady three-count later. He repeated the command, with the same result. He needed email to contact his family. And Rory.

He'd been planning on working until lunch, but decided to break early and enter the hall. With a glance to the far end, it was obvious a soldier guarded the foyer beyond. The guy didn't even flinch in his direction when Silas exited his office, but his movements were likely tracked in some capacity. None of this current predicament sat well with Silas, yet he had to trust Waylen to figure it out. They'd only been on site for two nights, and the FBI agent swore things would improve and become clearer.

Silas knocked on Cody's door, and the IT specialist peered in both directions before waving Silas in.

"This is messed up," Cody whispered.

"Which part?"

Cody gestured at the monitor. "I've tried to break past the… firewall, but there's no way to access the internet. And email, forget it. Whoever designed this was smart."

"Smarter than you?" Silas asked.

Cody grimaced. "Apparently. I've blocked them from viewing my activity, and they don't know I have permission to the feed and audio from every camera in the place. But the rest is a mystery. It's like Leo Monroe built an invisible dome around the fenced yard. Our cells operate within the bubble, but can't reach elsewhere. Email and network data from before Thursday aren't available. We're stuck."

"Damn," Silas murmured. He'd hoped Cody would have uncovered a solution by now. "Can you pierce the bubble?"

"I'll try, but I believe it's a hardware issue."

"As in…" Silas waited for Cody to explain.

"Leo must have built an external device. It's not connected to the servers that I can tell."

"They made it impossible to reach the outside world," Silas said. "Why would they do that?"

"I have a theory," Cody said.

"Go ahead." Silas leaned on the office wall, since there wasn't a second chair.

"Leo Monroe was cocky. He had multi-million-dollar contracts with the US government."

"Actually, upwards of billions in the long run," Silas corrected.

"There you go, even more reason to feel above the law."

"But was he really arrested?" Silas asked.

"Maybe not," Cody said. "Monroe was so confident he was immune to intervention from any government agencies that he was hiring killers to hunt the tokens down. He even bribed Waylen's partner."

"And you," Silas said.

Cody bristled, but recovered quickly. "That's not what happened."

"Then t*ell* me."

"We should really discuss this with everyone," Cody said.

"Even Theo?" Silas grinned.

"No, not Theo."

Silas used his phone, contacting Waylen since they could still text within the dome.

Be right there.

"Let's meet at the residences instead," Silas said as he typed.

Sure. Ten minutes.

"Can you block the cameras in the common space?" Silas asked Cody.

"I could, but that would raise some flags, don't you think? How about the audio?"

"Give it a try."

Cody's fingers flew over the keyboard, and he closed an application.

"It's that simple?"

"For me it is," Cody casually said, then switched his computer to sleep mode.

The pair walked by the soldier, Silas trying not to be bothered by the fact he held a large black semi-automatic weapon. He'd counted last night, and estimated they'd brought in somewhere around thirty soldiers—mostly Marines, from what Silas could tell. He wasn't sure if they were to protect the team from the outside world, or to protect the Delta from their own group.

Silas went past Corporal Tucker, offering a nod before pushing through the exit. They were greeted with rain, the clouds dark and threatening overhead. Cody jogged the short distance to the apartment building while Silas let the drops soak into his clothing, remembering the time he'd been caught with Rory in the storm at Loon Lake. He needed to contact her. Or did he? Maybe leaving Rory out of it was for the best. She'd be able to move on with her life, like Silas had intended.

He was briefly angry at Cody for ever taking the tokens, and swapping the fakes for the real ones in New York. But another part of him thrived in the chaos. Silas would go down in history, should they encounter an alien race. He'd be able to visit the red-skied planet after locating a device that might direct the Shadow.

Waylen and Darren were already settled in the common space, the former agent making a pot of coffee. He had four cups out, and the machine beeped as the trickling slowly faded. "Coffee?"

"Always." Cody took a seat at the table and accepted the drink black.

Silas walked up to Waylen and checked the cameras. "Cody cut the sound in here."

"He can do that?" Darren asked.

"So he says."

"I'm guessing one of the soldiers is watching the feeds, so they'll realize the issue eventually," Cody said.

"But for the time being, let's speak candidly," Silas added. "We believe there's an advanced piece of technology secluding us from accessing the internet."

"That's obvious," Darren said.

"What do we do about it?" Silas inquired.

"Nothing," Waylen said.

Silas watched him closely, wondering if he'd taken to the other side, or if there were sides any longer.

"Listen, guys. Darren and I have been using the tokens."

Darren sat and looked slightly paler than before.

"What have you discovered?" Cody asked.

"The one Fred Trell had possessed leads to a different echo," Waylen said. "That's our priority, not friends and family. If there's a way for someone to operate the Delta from another planet, it'll bring them here. To our facility."

"It's why Leo Monroe created the disruption tech. He wanted to keep the information contained within his base," Cody implied.

"We're assuming whoever might possibly come through would attempt to use our network. We have to stop thinking of alien life as a mirror to our own." Darren's hands wrapped around the cup, as if comforted by the heat. "For all we know, we've already let something in." His eyes darted to the ceiling, then to the windows."

"That's highly unlikely," Waylen told him. "We were on the Moon a few minutes, and there were no signs of aliens…"

Cody sipped his drink. "The footprint."

"Which, I'll remind you, there was only one of." Waylen finally sat next to Silas. "And you wiped it clean."

Cody smiled at his deception. "I guess the camera feeds didn't catch it."

"Waylen, you're certain we can trust Theodore?" Silas asked.

"For now, I'll keep using the tokens. I've tried four times, and already feel less susceptible to its effects. I bet a few more days will really make a difference."

"And we keep searching files?" Silas still didn't see the value in that.

"Until you either find something useful, or we pivot with the Delta," Waylen said.

"There's another thing," Darren interjected. "Leo Monroe is obviously a smart man. He must have realized the Delta couldn't jump to any destination without a mechanism to control it. Monroe might have a lead on it, meaning we should talk to him."

Everyone gazed at Waylen.

"I'll chat with Theodore and see what he says."

"And in the meantime, we …" Cody glanced at the hall, where a pair of Marines in combat utility uniforms entered. They stopped and gestured at the two cameras in the room. One mumbled into his radio.

"Is there an issue?" Waylen asked.

"Comms are down," the closest man said.

Shadows of the Earth

"We were just finishing up. Go ahead and check them out. We wouldn't want our coffee shop talk to fall on deaf ears."

"You coming?" Cody asked Silas, but he shook his head.

"I'll be there in a few."

The others left, each going to their assigned tasks, while Silas entered his suite. He sighed and went to the bathroom, splashing water on his face before dabbing it dry. Alien worlds. Armed soldiers watching their every move. He wasn't supposed to be here.

Silas strolled to his room and reached under the mattress. According to Cody, they didn't have cameras in the suites. Silas sat on the edge of the bed, opening Peter Gunn's journal.

The date was smudged, but legible.

February 19th, 1973
Patty doesn't understand.

Silas touched the dried ink, imagining his grandfather writing this by hand fifty years earlier. He tried to picture his grandmother as she once was. She'd been kind, and styled her white hair in the same slicked bun each day. The woman Peter spoke of in this journal wasn't the same person. She was youthful and vibrant. Wife to a renowned astronaut, mother to Silas' father and aunt. He wondered how he'd feel about growing old, then read on.

Colin's begging we meet up, but I've declined every offer. Fred is slightly more agnostic about the entire thing, but he wasn't there. He didn't see what we did. A part of me believes Fred thinks we made it all up. I can only view the alternate destination when I close my eyes. It leaks into my dreams. Two hours. That's what it was, and I fear I'll never be the same because of it.

Patty, my dear, sweet Patty, maybe one day you'll know the truth, but I cannot burden you and the children with that. We must ignore it. Bury any trace of our experience deep within.

The journal entry ended with a large dot after the last word, suggesting he had pressed the tip of his pen to the paper, desiring to say more, but eventually decided against it.

Silas wanted to keep reading, to get a better insight into Peter's state of mind, but he had obligations. He returned the journal to its hiding place and ventured from the residence, through the rain, and back to the cramped office.

He opened another file and began highlighting anything suspicious. Silas hoped Waylen was right, because he felt trapped within these walls.

2

*T*he university looked remarkable. Rory had visited the campus twice, meeting colleagues in her early author days at the local coffee shop. Her most influential professor had challenged her creative writing students to find a group of like-minded individuals at the same stage of their fledgling careers to collaborate with. She'd done just that, joining various social media groups, and found three other women, girls really, which was what she'd been, from the Boston area.

One instance was in her final year at the university, and once a month, they'd meet to discuss their current project and share their writing progress. The group also spent two meetings reading each other's prose and critiquing it, which didn't turn out as well as they'd hoped. Some writers were precious about their words. Rory hadn't guessed she was particularly defensive until her first round of edits with her agent, and only then did she understand the author's reaction to being criticized.

After thousands of ratings and reviews on *View from the Heavens*, Rory's skin had thickened.

She gazed at the Charles River from one of the campus' only green spaces. Despite classes not beginning for a couple of weeks, there were already people lingering at the dorms on benches, talking over breakfast in brown bags.

Being here made Rory long for those days, in a time before Kevin or a publishing contract, when the world had seemed so large, yet somehow so simple. That was the thing about life. You had to move forward, no matter how much you wished for the past. Rory smiled and grabbed her phone, marking that line down for her new book. She scrolled through the spattering of similar notations in the file, and closed the app, checking her texts.

All messages to Silas, Waylen, and Cody had gone unanswered.

Her cell rang, an unfamiliar number on the screen. The area code wasn't quickly identifiable, meaning it wasn't Marg or someone else from the school, so she ignored it and stowed her phone into her bag. Rory adjusted her cross-body strap and ventured toward the people on the bench.

"Good morning," she said.

"Hey." The young woman covered her mouth when she spoke, lowering her half-eaten breakfast sandwich.

"Do you guys know where the Arts building is? I thought it was nearby, but seem to have gotten turned around."

"It's not open until September," the guy told her.

"I have a tour today and am already late."

"A tour?" the girl asked, and her eyes widened. "No way. You're Rory Valentine, right?"

Rory smiled and nodded. "Swanson. Rory Swanson."

"I was on the fence about taking the new creative writing class, but now I can't wait," she exclaimed.

"You heard? I only agreed last night."

"Word travels fast"—she peered at the guy beside

Shadows of the Earth

her—"seeing how this is Mrs. Chambers' son, Paul."

"And you are?" Rory asked.

The girl set the food aside and hopped to her feet. "Carmen Fend." She shook Rory's hand and kept grinning.

Rory gestured to the dorms. "Do you stay here for the summer?"

"Dating Paul comes with some perks. We both work at the campus bookstore. I want to be a writer."

"And you?" Rory asked Paul.

"I want to graduate." He laughed.

Rory absently lifted her arm, finding her watch-devoid wrist. "The Arts building?"

"Come on, Paul, let's escort Miss Valentine to your mom's office," Carmen said.

"Fine." Paul finished his sandwich, crumpled up the bag, and tossed it into the can from ten feet.

They walked in comfortable silence before Carmen began asking about Rory's second book. She fended off the barrage of inquiries with one of her own. "What kind of writing do you do?"

Carmen's steps slowed as she pondered the simple question. "It's kind of hard to describe. Somewhat transcendental mystery, with complex subplots…"

"It's witch romance," Paul answered for her, and Carmen turned red.

"It's more than—"

"This way." Paul cut through an alley, and they entered a courtyard. The building itself, like most in Boston, was beautiful. The beige stonework blended with the dark window frames. Rory loved the red brick sidewalk and the black wrought-iron stair railing leading to the entrance. Trees jostled in the breeze, filling the courtyard with their calming sound. Rory bet this place was never so peaceful during the school year, and she took a moment to appreciate it.

"It was nice to meet you," she told the duo. "Carmen, I'll see you in class."

She had a student. Someone wanted to occupy a seat in her classroom. They trundled off, Carmen's arm linked in Paul's.

Rory took a deep breath, depressed the handle, and entered her new workplace.

The clock struck noon as the door closed, and a few bells rang from the ornate timepiece. Nobody greeted her, and she didn't encounter a secretary or administrative assistant. Rory assumed they had interns during the semester, but in the off season, the building seemed as empty as the campus.

"Hello?" Rory called, then added volume to her voice when no one responded. She was about to text Marg when the woman's heels clicked on the hardwood from down the hall.

"Rory, you made it. I hope you didn't have any trouble finding the place," Marg said. She was dressed smartly, with a skirt and blouse accentuated with a half-gold, half-pearl necklace.

"Sorry I'm late. I ran into your son and his girlfriend. They showed me to the building."

"Paul... I told him to get a second job, but he's too busy playing video games and smoking weed." Marg composed herself and smiled. "But enough about my lazy kid. How did you sleep? Still interested in the position?"

"Yes, very much." The room smelled like education. There was a scent that could only be found in an institution such as this. It was a blend of old wood, musty pages, and layers of paint. She almost reached for her phone to mark down the description, but stopped herself when Marg cleared her throat.

"You know, you remind me of myself," Marg said.

"How so?"

"I wrote a couple of novels."

Rory had read her bio on the website, but didn't recall any publications. She should have done more research. "That's great."

Marg shrugged. "It was in the Nineties, and neither of them did very well. I couldn't even be called midlist, and in those days, you were only as good as your latest work. I got into teaching shortly after and never looked back."

"You stopped writing?" Rory asked.

"Not right away, but eventually," she admitted. "Don't worry, Rory Swanson. You can do both. I wasn't cut out for the game. Now, let's show you around. Did you bring your belongings?"

"In the car," she said.

"Excellent. Would you like a quick tour before lunch?"

"Sounds great." Rory was forging a fresh path without her parents' assistance, or Kevin's high-pressure tactics.

She saw the faculty's offices and the modest space she'd call her own during the first year. It wasn't much, but it would be hers. Someone's nameplate had been removed, leaving a pale spot on the wall, along with two barren screw holes.

"We'll have your name put up soon." Marg stepped aside while Rory entered the office. It was only large enough for a desk and a sole bookshelf.

"Is it okay for me to write ... after hours?"

"If you're done for the day, you can sleep at the desk for all I care," Marg told her. "We want you to enjoy the process, and I know the others in the department are eager to meet you."

"When do they arrive?"

"Next week." Marg started away. "I'll show you the classrooms."

Rory trailed through the office, out a back door, and past a building in the middle of a facelift. The brickwork was being patched, though none of the crew was currently present. She guessed they were on a lunch break. Her stomach growled, thinking about food. She'd been too nervous that morning to eat anything at the hotel, but after a few pleasant encounters, her anxiety had eased to a manageable level.

"You'll teach from a few different rooms, depending on the class, but mostly you'll be in Building D." Rory waited as Marg unlocked the main entrance. "Oh, before I forget, here's the list of courses we're asking you to teach. Don't worry, for the first semester, we're only asking that you carry three." She passed Rory a folder from her oversized bag.

Rory flipped it wide, finding a creative writing course, a class on diverse literature, and one on American literature. "These look perfect."

Marg smiled and opened the door, two down on the right. She didn't go in, just lingered while Rory stepped into the space and turned the lights on. She stared at the whiteboard, the rows of tables with chairs tucked beneath. While Rory hadn't anticipated she'd be talking in large amphitheaters, she also didn't expect such a small venue.

Shadows of the Earth

"We prefer intimate rooms for creative writing. Fifteen students are more than enough, given that it's your first foray into the teaching world. I imagine your other courses will be busier, since they're required for nearly every graduate program designation."

Rory went to the front of the room, standing to face the tables, and tried to picture being on this side.

Her phone rang.

"Go ahead. I'll be in the hall." Marg walked off, leaving her with some privacy.

Rory took the cell out and saw the same number. The caller hadn't left a voicemail earlier, but clearly, they wanted something. "Hello." She heard breathing on the other end. "Who is this?"

The call ended. Rory immediately tried dialing it, but no one answered. Instead of an outgoing message, it was just dead silence and a beep.

Frustrated, she turned the ringer off and joined Marg.

"Okay, we can get you set up in the faculty residence. Follow me."

Rory ignored the creeping sensation from the call. Leo Monroe had been brought into custody, and his people were under arrest. She was safe. Rory had to repeat that to herself a few times before her parasympathetic nervous system believed her.

Instead of worrying, she took in the view. The structure was gorgeous, with green vines catching the brick façade. Birds chirped from a high branch near the stairs, and the sun hit the windows, reflecting a warm glow over the area. It was meant to be. "How many staff members live in the dorms?"

"This semester will be around eight. There are a dozen units." Marg unlocked the front. "I lived here once.

Twenty years ago."

"Really?"

"You'll be staying in the same room. That might be lucky. You could take over my chair someday."

Rory couldn't dream of being in one position for two decades. Wasn't that how most people existed? They got a degree, a job, a family. Sometimes they'd change careers, but twenty years at a job wasn't so uncommon. The prospect caused Rory to freeze in place.

"Are you coming?" Marg held the door, and Rory forced her legs to move. There wasn't anything wrong with teaching for a semester or two. It would push her boundaries and make her a better writer.

Rory instantly fell in love with the place. They walked into the main level, and she rushed inside her unit, finding the same heavenly sunlight basking through the living room. The wooden floors creaked under her weight, and the ornate wall-mounted lanterns flickered when she turned them on. It was every author's dream: a warm, private area to work, close to her job, and more importantly, to coffee shops and takeout restaurants. "It's incredible."

The kitchen was cramped, but fully stocked. The appliances contradicted the age of the interior, and she was grateful to have new technology. It lacked a dishwasher, but Rory's two hands would do the trick. Her bedroom had a double bed and a single nightstand, as well as a decent-sized closet, which was a surprise. Everything was furnished, so she didn't need to worry about buying anything, and while it wasn't quite her aesthetic, she was content to use it while on campus.

Marg loitered in the hall. "What do you think?"

"I can't wait to get unpacked," she admitted.

"How about we do lunch, iron out the last details,

then you can grab your things afterwards? Do you like Japanese?"

"Love it."

Rory gazed at the layout, and closed the door behind her, knowing she was in the right place.

Her purse vibrated, but she ignored it while they chatted on the short walk to the sushi restaurant.

3

*W*aylen reached for the token he'd marked with a small piece of blue tape. He'd suffered the echo a few times already, and each was as frustrating as the previous. While he appreciated the sensation of walking on the Moon with Peter Gunn and Colin Swanson's viewpoints, he couldn't get enough of the moments on Planet Delta. That was what they'd decided to call it. Or Planet D. Cody often just shortened it to the letter D for expedience.

"When are we planning on returning through the Delta?" Darren asked, drawing his gaze from the tokens.

"Huh?"

"Why have we been sitting here all week, and not using it to explore the surface of the Moon?"

"Good point." Waylen wasn't certain he wanted to walk into the Shadow again. His visions of the mist were only starting to subside as he slept, but his contact with the tokens might have been holding them at bay.

Darren opened his file on the tablet and flipped it to show Waylen. "I've held the tokens fourteen times. So far, nothing's changed."

"Belleville asked us to stay longer," Waylen said. His meeting with Theodore Belleville had been short and sweet on Thursday afternoon, with the director ignoring his attempts at reaching out to Leo Monroe.

"How long?"

"Five," Waylen answered. To this point, the most time they'd allowed contact with the token was two minutes, but he was confident they could beat their own records unscathed. But Waylen had been thinking of raising the time to three minutes, not five.

"That's quite the jump," Darren said.

"Any issue with it?"

"I wasn't saying there was, it's just…"

"What?" Waylen asked.

"Does Theodore believe we can actually learn what they did on Planet D?"

"Seems that way."

Darren stared at the token with blue tape. "Should I try first?"

"I'll do it. Make sure I don't go over. And if you notice anything strange, stop me." Waylen took a drink of water and set the bottle aside.

"Strange as in what?" Darren asked. "Bleeding from the eyes?"

"Sure, that's a good marker." They'd been there for nearly a week, and Waylen didn't feel any closer to knowing what Theodore's intentions were, besides his early comment about making first contact. He'd been closed off, shut into his office when he was on site. Waylen inquired where he went, but never got a firm answer. Waylen had accepted the role with a certain expectation of transparency, but Theodore was no more informative than Assistant Director Ben had been for most of his career. Only in the last couple of years had his former boss begun to share anything significant.

Silas and Cody were growing weary of their tasks, and

both wanted something to change. Silas had found some irregular data in the files, and Waylen still had to double-check his findings. He was a smart man, and would have done well on one of Waylen's teams in his previous life at the Bureau. Maybe when all this Delta business was finished, he'd return to the Financial Crimes Division.

"Ready?" Darren watched him, and Waylen realized he'd been absorbed in his thoughts for an entire minute.

"Sure." Waylen attempted to psych himself up for traveling to the echo before contacting the token. He reached for it, not bothering with the dramatics of gloves. Darren started the timer, and Waylen's sight wavered, the scene around him dripping past his eyelashes, morphing into something new.

And he was on Planet D, seeing it through Peter Gunn's lenses.

Waylen held on to his convictions, the experience less threatening than in previous instances. His lungs didn't ache, his hands steady as he sat in the chair, aware that he was in two time periods at once. The echo he viewed was from fifty years ago, endured by a man that was buried in Campbelltown's cemetery. He dug deeper, trying to link to Peter, and sensed emotions below the surface. Waylen clawed in, noticing a shifting of his own mood. He suddenly had new memories, flashes of moments that weren't his to share. A wedding day. The birth of his children. The day he'd graduated. His first mission with the Air Force. His acceptance into the NASA space program. They belonged to Peter Gunn and, because of the token, to Waylen Brooks.

Waylen took in minor details, memorizing them. The rock was dense, almost slippery, though there wasn't liquid on it. No frost, water, ice… just stone. Peter's gaze floated over the landscape, and Waylen spied a few plants pressing past narrow cracks. They looked green through the NASA helmet's visor, and he assumed that was a good thing. If Theodore expected humanity to visit Planet D, surely proof of life would go a long way in convincing the government it was feasible.

He tried to control Peter's arm, to snatch a sample, but as usual, Commander Gunn's echo didn't obey.

Colin was ahead, advancing to the giant sun in the distance. This was new. Waylen realized he was entering unfamiliar territory, passing his previous two minutes within the echo, and his fingertips tingled because of it. There wasn't much to see from this angle. The ground, an ever-pressing blanket of dark rock stretching as far as Peter's gaze, rose and fell in dips and valleys, some sharp jutting sections stretching high, around a hundred feet into the air. The clouds intrigued Waylen. He hadn't noticed them in his earlier trips into the echo.

They moved along at a clip, the ground gray. The Sun—no, the local star, he corrected—was dazzling, and hard to ignore since it dominated the view. Peter didn't gaze directly at it, and Waylen attempted to avoid it as well, watching the scene unfold through Peter's memory. With a glance past the clouds, he saw the moon. Not Earth's Moon, but another, and tucked behind it was a second planetary object, this one a sliver of a crescent, all tinged with red.

"They'll never believe it," Swanson said.

Waylen hadn't heard them talking before, and flinched in his seat all the way back in the State of New York.

"That's because we aren't telling them," Peter replied.

"You can't be serious." Colin crouched, picking up a chunk of rock. *"They'll run tests and see it wasn't from the*

Moon or Earth. It's going to be…"

Waylen's vision faltered, and he returned to the Hex within the Planetae laboratory. He wavered in his chair, clutching the arms, and a surge of nausea rose in his chest.

"Five minutes is up," Darren said. "Anything to report?"

"Colin took a sample," he told Darren. "Peter said they wouldn't tell a soul about it."

"You heard them?" His counterpart appeared excited by the prospect.

"Only fragments. We have to stay for more time." Waylen tried to stand, but his legs didn't respond instantly, and he fell to the platform.

"Not a good idea." Darren helped him into the seat. "But you made progress."

"There was nothing resembling a control mechanism."

Darren rubbed his chin. "I can't wait to learn what they encountered on Planet D."

The doors to the lab opened, and in strode Theodore, with Dr. Rita Singh, Corporal Tucker, and two other soldiers Waylen hadn't formally met. Next to Tucker was a short man with a moustache and stubble on his chin; the other, a tall woman with a brown ponytail. Her frown seemed liked a permanent fixture.

Waylen rose, unsure why Theodore was interrupting them.

"Please exit the Hex," the director said.

He shot Darren a look, and they both walked out, leaving the tokens in place. "What can I do for you?"

"We're going to the Moon." Theodore said it nonchalantly, as if they were just heading to the corner store.

Shadows of the Earth

"Is that so," Waylen muttered. "I'll get my suit."

Theo gestured to the soldiers. "Just us."

Waylen noticed the extra crate by the lockers, which he hadn't seen on the way in. "Can I have a minute?"

Theodore seemed irritated, but relented. Waylen heard the door again, and Dr. Rita Singh arrived. "What is it, Waylen?"

"Why are you using the Delta?"

"I already told you. To travel to the Moon."

"But why? I thought we were trying to explore the tokens first, learn everything we can."

"Since you've found nothing of note, I'm implementing phase two."

Waylen tensed and tried to keep his composure. "I'd appreciate more transparency. Aren't we working together?"

"We are."

"When it matches your needs," Waylen added.

Theodore smiled and set a hand on Waylen's shoulder, which he quickly shrugged off. "Let's make one thing clear. I'm the director of Operation Delta."

"And we're on site because we're aware of the tokens. It was either kill us, lock us up, or put us on the team. Am I right?" The way Theo's eyes flickered down and left told Waylen everything he needed to know. "We're done."

"You can't go," Theodore hissed.

"Darren, pack your things. I'll grab Silas and Cody. We're not staying another minute."

Tucker aimed a gun between Darren and Waylen. He seemed conflicted, but kept the barrel up.

"That's how it's going to be?" Waylen poked Theo in the chest. "Who are you answering to? Is it Jacob Plemmons? I want to talk with Assistant Director Ben.

Why can't I access the world beyond this fence?"

The director kept calm through the tirade, which angered Waylen even more. "Waylen, we're on the verge of something remarkable." He motioned to the Hex, where the tokens remained. "Are you sure you want to abandon your post?"

"Yes."

"Darren? If I admitted we were close to locating the control, would you want to stay?" Theodore walked past Waylen, addressing the resident alien expert.

"Uhm, I guess so."

Waylen's anger faded, but only slightly. "How will you find it?"

He ignored the comment. "The reason I haven't been forthcoming is because your doubt is palpable. Mr. Sanderson is using his computer to mute microphones, and you look at me with contempt. I don't care if you like me, Waylen. I've never worried much about others' perceptions. I've been given a job, and I'm here to see it through. If you're not on board, I'll replace you. It's as simple as that."

"Why can't I leave and speak with Leo Monroe?"

"Do you believe your interrogation skills are better than those of a Marine who's been trained to grill insurgents? This isn't white-collar crime, Mr. Brooks. We're talking about federal espionage, extraterrestrial contact, and the defense of not only the United States, but the entire planet."

Waylen was at a loss, so he kept his composure, letting the severity of their situation wash over him. They were trapped on site, that was obvious, with no means to contact the outside world. But wasn't that a small price to pay for discretion?

Shadows of the Earth

"There has to be a clue on the Moon," Darren said.

"Come again?" Theo asked.

"I'm assuming you've expanded your search for something akin to the tokens." Darren's finger pointed to the high ceiling. "If they abandoned the Delta up there, leaving the Shadow running continuously, that tells me there's more than one Delta. Who knows how many planets or moons have portals? That's the first phase. Finding a race capable of space travel to discover the device would be the trigger, but it still needs a key."

"A key," Theodore said. "I like the name."

"Where is it? The Moon? Mars? Venus?" Waylen asked.

"I think it's here, on Earth. Each on its own won't do much. With the Delta, we can travel to the Moon, but nowhere else. It shows us that the Delta links to the other world from the Moon, but if you bring the device into the Shadow, we lose the connection to our Hex. You'd be stuck up there," Darren said.

"Or on the planet Peter and Colin visited during their two-hour window," Waylen finished.

Theodore rubbed his palms together. "I've been instructed to begin our plans for the mining operation Leo intended to start. That's what we're doing today. The soldiers will catalogue everything the astronauts left behind, then clear it out. The lunar module's ascent stages and anything else of note will return through the Shadow. And leave the flag."

Waylen stood aside while the three soldiers donned their suits, with Theodore once again joining the mission.

"You wanted to be part of the team?" Theo asked. "Get dressed."

Darren smiled, and Waylen could see he was sold.

Something was off about the entire scenario, but maybe he was just being paranoid.

Waylen began to climb into the spacesuit, while Dr. Rita assisted him.

4

"Anything exciting up there?" Cody peered over from the couch, where he played a violent video game. Currently, he was stuck in a jungle carrying an impossibly enormous gun, firing at massive aliens. It was a little too on the nose for Silas, so he'd opted out when invited to join an hour ago.

"More dust," Darren said. "Those soldiers make good astronauts, though. They didn't waste any time dismantling the ascent stages for the lunar module, not to mention all the junk Peter and Colin left behind."

Silas had spent all afternoon rechecking Planetae files, and for some reason, he'd returned to the section marked *Balloons*, specifically the sub-folder *Helium*. There was nothing in their entire network of processing plants or manufacturing facilities that required helium, but there it was, referenced on many occasions. He ran a cross on Balloons for the entire database, finding little of note. "Waylen, would you check something with me tomorrow?"

"Find an anomaly?"

"Possibly."

"Not a problem." Waylen drank some decaf, slumping in his chair. "I'm exhausted."

He'd told the group about his experience with the token, spending five minutes within the echo on Planet D. Cody nodded along with the story, saying he'd gone even longer at one point, but maxed out around seven minutes. The next time he'd touched the token, he'd grown violently ill, and hadn't tried to beat his record again.

Silas glanced at the pool table, but didn't have the energy for a game. The TV played a rerun of a classic sitcom. When he'd searched for the news earlier, the channels were blocked. "Did Theodore actually admit we could leave?"

"Not in so many words," Darren admitted.

"Then…"

"When I threatened to bail, he convinced us it was a mistake," Waylen said.

"Is it?"

"What?"

"A mistake?" Silas asked.

"Time will tell."

"I have nowhere else to be," Cody said. "Free food and lodging. I'm assuming we'll get a paycheck, right, Waylen?"

From the look on Waylen's face, he wasn't sure, but he nodded once. "Yeah, of course."

Silas observed the Moon through the windows. "I'm going for a walk."

"A walk?" Cody perked up. "Where?"

"Outside. I feel like a penned-up animal in here every night. I need to see the sky."

"Be careful," Waylen said.

"How much trouble can I get into? We're sequestered by a fenced yard, with twenty armed soldiers wandering around. I think we're in the safest place possible."

Shadows of the Earth

"It's them I'm afraid of," the FBI agent said.

Silas didn't take the bait, and grabbed a sweatshirt from his room before exiting the residence. No one stopped him, and he was relieved not to find a sentry posted outside. The area was quiet. No engines rumbling. No trains rolling across tracks in the distance. Nothing.

The guardhouse had lights on at the fenced gate, and a truck sat parked beside it. A lone figure could be seen in the small structure, reading what looked to be a paperback. Thinking about novels, his mind instantly pictured Rory Swanson, and he grabbed his cell phone, flipping to her contact information.

He tapped the text icon and scrolled, discovering his messages all with the FAILED notification beside them. "I'm trapped in a black hole."

Silas waved at a soldier idly marching the perimeter of the fence. They all knew who the crew members were, and no one bothered him while he strode slowly, gazing at the night sky. They were far enough from the city to be clear of most light pollution, and while there were fewer visible constellations than at Loon Lake, Silas still picked out a couple of familiar ones.

The fenced lot was large, and Silas judged it was a solid mile or so to circle the entire property. He started by reaching the barrier, then turned left, in the opposite direction of the patrol. They'd been there for a week, with little to show for their efforts. Waylen was skeptical about their progress, and the reasoning for the government's involvement in the project. Why wasn't a NASA representative present? Or a big team of scientists? The sole doctor on site was an astrophysicist hired by Leo Monroe. Shouldn't they have brought in an outside expert?

Silas considered their objectives while he walked, and

didn't expect to find anything significant hidden in the financial files. Monroe was too smart to leave something important exposed. He'd been caught, but that was because of his arrogance.

Eventually, he passed the soldier and kept going, his gaze still on the incredible stars high above. His phone chimed, and the sound of it almost seemed alien after a week devoid of notifications. He took it from his pocket and saw a text arrive from Rory. He couldn't tell which message she'd been replying to, but assumed it had been sent some time ago.

I'm worried about you. Please text me when you get this.

Silas peered around him, ensuring no one was watching. He faced the fence, avoiding the cameras, and lifted the phone.

Rory, it's me. There's no service here, but we're fine. I found a spot that might be outside their range. Are you okay? He hit send, and held his breath, waiting for it to display that it was SENT. When it beeped successfully, he exhaled again.

Three dots appeared, and he did his best to remain calm.

Where are you? New York? Why? What's happening?

Silas composed himself. *Still here. I think we're stuck. Not prisoners, but close.*

He checked over his shoulder, but no one seemed to pay him any mind.

Do you need help? Should I call someone?

Silas thought about it. *Don't bother. Theodore works for the government, which means I guess we do too. Waylen is keeping tabs on things. What about you?*

He waited, but the message failed. "Damn it." Silas moved as close to the fence as he could, and tried a second time, with the same result. Nothing came through from Rory, and he stared at the last one she'd sent.

Should I call someone?

If he didn't respond, would she try to help? Who was even available?

"Problem?"

Silas had been so caught up in his own business, he hadn't heard the silent footsteps of the soldier approaching. He fumbled with the phone, almost dropping it. "No, just going over some notes." Silas slipped it into his pocket.

"I think you'd better go inside," the woman said. He thought her name was Vera.

"I'm…"

"For your own safety, sir," Vera added, her thumb brushing her gripped weapon.

"Thanks, I will." Silas grimaced, and marked the location off for future reference. Beyond the fence was a section of spruce trees, next to the neighboring lot's commercial garbage cans. The area was deserted, probably bought by Planetae to ensure their interactions were discreet.

He returned to the common space, ready to tell them about the area clear of the cell blockage, but they'd already gone to bed. The TV was on, showing subtitles instead of sound, and Silas took a seat, rereading the brief conversation with Rory. He had a means to reach beyond the fence. All he could do was try again tomorrow.

Silas checked the phone, finding countless old messages from Rory and began reading through them.

———

*T*he screen was bright in his dark suite, but Cody didn't mind. His eyes were used to hours of working late at night. It was when he usually did his best coding. Cody had always wanted to be his own boss, ever since getting into the field, but with modern technology, a good IT person was a dime a dozen, and monetizing it on a large scale wasn't a simple task. So he'd done things for his own benefit, making websites for friends' businesses, creating silly online games with tracking software embedded into them.

Tonight, he utilized a backdoor program into Planetae's primary database. These local drives had lots of information, but mostly stuff pertinent to the Hex and the mission to use the Delta. There was very little about Leo Monroe's organization on the whole.

After an entire week of obsessing over it while he should have been sleeping, Cody finally made headway. The screen flashed black, and for a second, he thought he'd lost the connection. Then the program opened.

"This is it," Cody whispered. While this wasn't exactly what he'd hoped to reach, it was as good as expected with the current limitations. Instead of finding access to their entire network, Cody had what one might call a 'read only' version. Unless he had to change something, which he didn't, the mirror files would do just fine.

The countless files were cataloged and sorted professionally. Leo had an advanced computer software program dealing with the recording minutiae, which was smart, because it could always locate things on demand. Knowing that made Cody's life easier. The search function was more intuitive than some, and his access remained unrestricted.

Shadows of the Earth

Cody first scoured the mirror network for data on Leo's joint ventures with the US government, and had hundreds of hits within seconds. He drilled down the parameters, homing in on any land and development deals.

From what Cody could tell, Leo and the Department of Defense had teamed up on three construction projects in the past eight years. One in remote southern California. Another in northern Arizona. Cody smiled when he read the last. The facility was ten miles from the small town of Hermon, in upstate New York.

Cody hadn't wanted to bother Darren until he had proof, and this was all the evidence he needed. He stretched, saw that it was two in the morning, and decided he shouldn't delay until tomorrow. Or technically, later today.

He knocked on Darren's door, waiting patiently before trying again.

"What?" Darren finally answered, his dark hair disheveled. He hadn't opened it all the way.

"I have something to show you."

"Can we discuss this in the AM?" Darren tried to shut the door, but Cody stopped it with his foot.

"No, we can't."

Waylen showed up, holding a gun. "Is there a problem?"

Cody glanced at the drawn weapon. "Nothing that requires a bullet."

Waylen tapped the safety on and lowered it. "Sorry."

Silas must have overheard them too, because he also plodded into the hallway in bare feet. "What's the fuss about?"

"Cody made a discovery that's more important than sleep." Darren's comment was laced with sarcasm, and he yawned.

"Now that we're all up, how about some coffee at my place?" Cody lifted his eyebrows, and they seemed to catch his drift.

"Fine. I'll get my pants." Darren vanished and returned in a moment. Silas came out with a bathrobe on, and Waylen already had pajama bottoms and a tank top.

Cody glanced down the hall when they all entered, and locked the doors. "I'm pretty sure we're not being bugged."

"I didn't see any cameras," Silas said, brewing coffee in the mini kitchen.

"Same here. And when I was in the surveillance files, they were only observing the common space," Cody informed them.

"What is it?" Waylen asked.

"Darren, I remembered one of your podcasts. Everyone's always looked at Area 51 as this Mecca of UFO activity, but you didn't believe it for a second. You claimed it was a distraction, giving the public something to watch while they operated under cover elsewhere."

"Sure, I recall the episode."

"And you had theories on where the facilities may reside."

Darren took a seat on the couch. "California coast, for access to the water. Possibly New Mexico, since there are endless miles of emptiness."

"Close." Cody directed their attention to a map on his screen. He had the three Planetae buildings marked with green dots.

Darren stumbled over, leaning on the desk for a better look. "What are these?"

"The UFO facilities that Planetae made with the Department of Defense. I've been trying to penetrate their primary network, and I'm embarrassed it took this long, but I managed tonight," Cody said.

"Whoa." Silas crowded them, with Waylen at his side. "We don't know for certain these have anything to do with UFOs. They might be weapons storage."

Waylen shifted and set the gun on the table behind them. "Theodore mentioned teaming up with Monroe for classified projects, and I assumed they were related to space, or initiating first contact. It seems to be a recurring theme with the director and his boss."

"What does this mean?" Silas asked.

Cody shrugged. "I don't know, but here we are, trying to figure out how to operate the Shadow, and the US government already had evidence of extraterrestrials."

"Are you suggesting one of these facilities might hold the Key to the Delta?" Darren asked.

"If that's the case, why doesn't Theodore have it?"

Cody spun in his chair, facing the other three men. "Because our friend Theo isn't actually working for the government. He's been lying to us this whole time."

5

Rory adored her new accommodations. With one week to go before students began filing into campus, ready for orientation, the university finally had some life to it.

In the days since arriving, she'd written another twelve thousand words, putting her past the halfway mark of her first draft. She couldn't have been happier, until last night's message from Silas threw her back to reality.

She'd made contact, which meant Silas was okay, unless it was someone pretending to be him. Rory didn't believe that to be true. She'd tossed and turned, trying to figure out who she should call, but decided not to interfere. Waylen was with Silas and Cody, which gave her hope for their group.

He'd said they were stuck. It made her extremely grateful not to have joined them on the trek to deliver the tokens. They were supposed to hand them off unscathed, but things had obviously changed.

Rory finished a glass of water and washed it, leaving it upside down on a tea towel before heading to the window. The sun rose higher, casting a warm shine over the green space across from the faculty dorms. Birds chirped and pigeons cooed, bobbing for anything edible on the sidewalk.

Shadows of the Earth

Her phone rang, and Rory sighed, answering it. "Hello."

Silence.

"Listen, you freak, I'm tiring of these crank calls. Why don't you grow a pair and tell me your name?"

"*It's Kevin.*"

Her veins turned to ice.

"Kevin... this is an out-of-state number."

"*I heard you finally came back to your senses. Boston missed you.*" He didn't respond to her comment.

"Who told you? Why are you harassing me?"

"*We belong together, whether you think so or not.*" He was oddly calm, his words methodical. Careful.

Rory lowered the phone, ready to hang up, but thought better. "If you so much as glance in my direction, I'll have a restraining order drawn up so fast, it'll make your head spin."

"*I like this new Rory.*"

She ended the call and dialed another number.

Justine answered on the third ring. "*Rory?*"

"I know it's only been a week, and I should be stronger, but he called."

"*I understand,*" Justine didn't ask which *he* she referred to. "*Did he threaten you?*"

"Not really. I mean, with him, it all seems like a threat."

"*Visit the police if you feel unsafe,*" Justine said. "*And if the anxiety returns, work on the breathing exercises I gave you.*"

Rory nodded, then remembered Justine couldn't see her. "I'll do that."

"*While I have an opening, do you want to talk?*"

Rory knew she was being charged, so she might as well get a few things off her chest. They chatted for thirty minutes, while Rory focused her nervous energy on tidying up her place. She straightened the couch cushions and gathered her laundry while telling Justine about Marg, and the job offer, and her pleasant accommodations.

"*It sounds as though you have a lot going for you,*" Justine said afterward.

"I guess I do. If I could just make sure Kevin wasn't a threat to me."

"*You're right about the restraining order. If he does anything to make you uncomfortable, go to the police,*" Justine demanded.

"I will."

"*Is there anything else, or should we pick this up next session? We can continue to do phone calls, or virtual if that's better.*"

"The phone's good."

"*I'm glad to hear from you, Rory. Congrats on the new position, and the success with your writing. You're in a great spot, and no one will take that away, okay?*"

"Okay."

Rory grabbed her full basket, traveling to the unit's shared laundry room, and started a wash cycle. Instead of lingering to wait, she walked outside, deciding to buy a beverage from the nearby coffee shop.

All week, her trips around campus had been filled with joy and a sense of adventure. After Kevin's call, she viewed everything with dread. She hated him for it, and so much more.

Orientation was on the coming Friday, with the students moving in on Thursday. It wasn't enough time to prepare for the semester, but Marg had assured her it would be easier than she thought. Marg had even offered to sit in on a test run with her on Tuesday, which she'd agreed to. It didn't seem possible on such short notice, but sometimes it was better to dive right in. Rory would

Shadows of the Earth

be fine. She knew this, but with the ominous idea of Kevin looming in the back of her mind, everything became heavier, as though the Earth's gravity had shifted.

"You know he lives in Boston," she told herself. "Nothing has changed." The personal pep talk did little to ease her worry.

Rory closed her eyes, taking a deep breath, and opened them to find the grass gone. The cobblestones were replaced with gray rock, a fine dust covering all. The buildings had vanished, the Sun now behind her, the Earth a small marble in the distance, its blue oceans majestic and daunting all at once.

She glanced down, finding dozens of footprints, none of them human. The pieces of the lander module were missing, and the flag planted by her grandfather wasn't there. Directly in front of Rory was the Shadow. The hole beckoned her. Misty segments frayed and spread into the air, swirling before disappearing. More strings of fog broke off, almost like a finger, beckoning her toward it.

Rory did just that. Her flats kicked up a plume of dust with each step, and she reached for the portal, eager to find what lay beyond. All she had to do was walk, enter the darkness, and see for herself.

"Rory?" The voice sounded alien. "Rory, are you okay?"

She peered at the source, spying a figure shrouded in the same inky darkness as the portal. "Who are you?"

"Rory, it's Carmen. We met the other day."

She blinked, and regolith morphed into grass. The cobblestones returned. Earth became the Sun, the Shadow evaporating with each jerky inhale.

"What are you doing?" Carmen asked.

Rory stood at the edge of the courtyard, with a ten-foot drop from a retaining wall directly below her. She was inches from falling, her arms outstretched. "I…" She climbed down, dusting her hands off. "I thought I dropped something, but I didn't." Rory held up her cell phone.

Carmen looked dubious, but was gracious enough to change the subject. "What are you up to?"

"Coffee… clearly I could use some."

"Mind if I join? I need a pick-me-up. The bookstore opens Monday, and we're doing final inventory before the new batch of kids comes to pillage it." Carmen was maybe eight years younger than her, but at that moment, she felt decades older than the youthful spirit.

"You didn't see anything back there, did you?" Rory asked as they exited the courtyard, navigating a narrow alley.

"What do you mean?"

"Nothing." She didn't need any strange rumors circulating after the girl had found her standing on a ledge, staring into the abyss. Not the best way to start her fledgling career.

The sound of her phone's ringer made her grimace, but it was her mom. "Carmen, I'll be right in."

The girl smiled and entered the coffee shop, moving to the counter.

"Hey, Mom." They hadn't spoken in two days, and apparently, that was too long for Kathy. Rory struggled to believe it was the same woman that often went three months without so much as a text. That wasn't fair, though, since Rory rarely contacted her parents either.

"Rory, how's everything going?"

"That's a blanket question. Everything. Can you get more specific?" Rory smiled when she pictured her mom's frown.

"*This isn't the time for jokes.*"

"I'm fine."

"*Are you taking taxis or driving? We don't want another incident like in New York,*" Kathy warned.

"Yes, I'm being careful."

"*Good.*"

Rory sensed a purpose for the call, besides a quick check-in.

"*Greg asked about you,*" Kathy said.

And there it was. "He has my number. He can text me."

"*But you told him not to.*"

"Mom, I'm busy prepping for next week."

"*Are you sleeping? You know how those dorms can be…*"

"It's a dorm for professors, Mom, not a frat house. And there are only three of us in the entire building so far. Plus, the walls are brick or something. It's quiet, so yes, I'm sleeping well."

"*That's great.*"

"Mom, what aren't you saying?"

"*Someone's been watching the house,*" Kathy said, and Rory instantly peered over her shoulder.

"The house? Are you sure?"

"*Not specifically. Your father has the cameras running, and we alarm it. He hasn't noticed anything out of place, but I think I was followed to the club last night, and I've seen the car around town.*" Her mom's voice had lost its confident edge and was on the verge of paranoia.

"I was told they caught all of Monroe's men. There's no one tracking you, Mom."

"*Maybe it's Kevin,*" she said. "*I should have your dad call his friends at the sheriff's office.*"

"Kevin knows I'm in Boston, and he's already contacted me."

"*Then you have to go to the police!*"

"I will if he sets foot on campus, believe me."

"*Talk to security, and warn them you have a stalker.*"

That wasn't a half-bad idea, and Rory told her so.

"I should go. My friend's waiting." *Friend* was a stretch, since Carmen was actually going to be her student, but she'd had enough of this conversation.

"*A friend already. How wonderful! Okay, dear. Keep in touch, all right?*"

"I will."

"*I love you, Rory.*"

"Love you too."

Rory put her phone away, and caught sight of a silver sedan in the window's reflection. It drove by at a crawl, the glare of the sun obstructing her view of the driver. She slowly turned, and the car sped up, signaling at the end of the block. She shook it off, knowing it was only her mom's frantic voice worrying her.

Rory strode in, finding a dozen people at various tables. A young man sat with large headphones by himself, clacking at a laptop's keyboard, while a woman, clearly a real estate agent, handed brochures to a couple.

"I wasn't sure what you wanted," Carmen said. "I'm a cappuccino girl. Keeps me moving all day long."

"That sounds good." Rory motioned to the barista. "I'll take one as well."

A small TV was on behind the coffee bar, the news playing, and Rory almost looked elsewhere until the headline caught her attention.

FBI Assistant Director Trevor Ben proclaimed dead at the scene of a freeway pile-up in Arlington.

Shadows of the Earth

Rory froze and tugged her phone out. "No…" She searched the name and found similar stories trending. She had always assumed "Ben" was his first name. There were precious few details about how it happened. He'd been on the way home, where he left behind a wife and two children. Four vehicles were in the crash, but he was the sole casualty.

It made Rory think about the manner in which Leo Monroe had captured Waylen. He'd cut the brakes of Waylen's car and forced a crash to obtain the tokens, evacuating Waylen from their planned meeting in DC to New York. Had Assistant Director Ben been sabotaged as well?

She longed to speak with Waylen, but he was off the grid.

Carmen tapped her arm. "Rory?"

"It's… I knew him."

"Who?"

The news had already moved on to another story. "I have to go."

Rory hurried from the coffee shop empty-handed, and sent a text to Silas, praying he received it.

6

*W*aylen viewed the steady stream of soldiers emerging from the Shadow, returning to the Hex platform from their sojourn on the Moon. They pushed metal carts in, with samples loaded on each. The laboratory had filled up with rows of racking, and they were already teeming with a multitude of rocks and dirt samples.

Dr. Rita guided the carts down the makeshift ramp covering the steps, and told the soldiers where to put the supplies once they'd removed their helmets, then spacesuits. Two other women rifled through the suits, testing them by plugging the umbilical into a computer. They had spare oxygen tanks on site, and a large reservoir used to refill them.

This was the team's fifth trip with the Shadow, and Theodore showed no signs of slowing.

"Good, you're here." The director of their operation passed his helmet to Corporal Tucker and wandered over. His head seemed tiny protruding from the bulky suit, and his hair, usually slicked, was askew.

"I heard you wanted a word."

"Any luck with the tokens?"

"You know I can't use them while they're connected, right?" Waylen pointed to the Hex, where the Shadow was linked to the glowing Delta.

"We're finished for the day. Call Darren in and continue with the project. Let's try for ten minutes," he said.

"Ten… Cody's done seven, and it wasn't pretty."

"Then I suggest you work harder and get acclimated sooner. We have a lot to accomplish."

"How long are you in the lab for?"

"An hour or so. Once we have the gear stowed, the Hex is all yours." Theodore turned and shouted an order at someone when they spilled a tray of rocks onto the white floor.

Waylen left, careful to ensure no one was watching him, and entered the hallway. He sent Cody a message: *Now.*

The IT specialist sent a thumbs-up icon back.

Waylen would only have one shot at this, so he moved as fast as possible without raising attention. Most of the soldiers were present in the laboratory with Belleville, making his passage deeper into the facility that much simpler. Waylen eyed the office at the end of the corridor, and found someone lingering by the doors. He'd met the woman once, but couldn't recall her name. The gun remained slung over her shoulder, and she stood straight, eyes ahead.

Waylen stayed in the shadows and clicked another message, this time, to Silas: *Copernicus*. It was their codeword for needing a distraction. The floor was circular, with two access points to Theodore's office, and a minute later, he heard Silas' voice coming from the opposite direction.

"Hey, Vera. Can you give me a hand? We're supposed to add a desk to the third room for Darren, but I can't seem to pivot the thing through the doorway myself. The other guys are slacking off."

Vera glanced around and shrugged. "Sure, Silas."

They wandered away, and Waylen crept behind, staying far enough back that they couldn't see him. *Here.* The message went to Cody.

He received another thumbs-up. Waylen usually despised that response to texts, but they were proceeding with caution, should their network be under surveillance.

Waylen touched the handle and was relieved when the lever depressed. He pushed into the room and closed it behind him, locking it. He'd been in the office before, but without Theodore at the desk, it seemed dark and dank. Leo Monroe had once occupied the space, and evidence of his expensive tastes was everywhere. Waylen ignored all of it and opened drawers. He found the second phone in the top one, shocked there was no passcode. He checked the call history, and it was only a single number in or out.

Waylen remembered Cody's warning the other night. *Our friend Theo isn't actually working for the government. He's been lying to us this whole time.*

This might prove or disprove the theory.

Waylen hovered over the dial button and finally tapped it, raising the phone to his ear.

"*Were we scheduled for a call?*"

Waylen instantly recognized the voice. "No."

"*Then why are you bothering me, Theodore? Did you find the Key yet?*"

"We're close," Waylen lied. "Are you coming?" He tried to imitate Theodore's intonations, but wasn't sure he'd managed it.

"*When it's ready, I'll be there.*"

Waylen wanted to keep asking questions, but the

longer he conversed, the more likely he'd be caught. "I'm needed elsewhere. Talk soon." He hung up and returned the phone to its previous spot, before his vibrated.

She's back.

Waylen read the text and cursed under his breath. That meant Silas hadn't kept Vera from her post for very long. *I'm still…*

The handle jiggled, and Waylen blanched.

Hide.

The second message came through while Waylen searched for somewhere capable of sheltering his body. The shelves ran floor to ceiling, small lights illuminating the ancient collection of books. Beside the glass case was a matching storage compartment with wooden doors. Waylen tried it, hoping the doors weren't locked, and it opened. The shelves were empty, and Waylen detached the first, setting it on the bottom. He crawled into the newly hollowed-out cabinet and wrenched the door closed from the inside, almost catching his finger.

It was a tight squeeze, and his back brushed the shelf above. The position hurt his neck, but he couldn't move or he'd make a noise.

He guessed it was Theodore, and tried to breathe evenly, slowing his elevated heart rate. Waylen pressed out slightly, peeking toward the desk. Theo stood behind it, pouring a drink from the bar. He swirled the brown liquor in a crystal glass, conducting sparkling lights on the wall beyond before downing the contents.

An extremely uncomfortable minute passed; then came a knock.

"Yes?"

"Sir, Darren was hoping to have a word with you."

"Send him in."

"He's asked that you join him in the Hex."

Even if they got Theo out of the office, that still left Vera guarding the exit.

"Fine. Tell him I'll be there in a few." Theo took a seat and opened the drawer, checking his phone. Waylen watched from his hiding spot while the director typed hastily. He stared at the home screen for a solid thirty seconds before putting it back. He got to his feet and walked out, muttering something to Vera. The office sealed up, and Waylen sighed a wavering breath.

I hope you have a plan— Waylen hit send and waited.

Within the minute, a fire alarm sounded.

Vera's on the move, Cody said.

Waylen jogged to the exit, waited another ten seconds while the alarms continued to blare throughout the complex, and hurried into the hall, which was empty. He circled the rounded corridor and emerged outside, finding five soldiers running to the residence. Cody was on the front steps, waving his arms. "It's fine. I've put the fire out. I never was much of a cook. Burned the fish sticks."

Cody smiled at Waylen, and the soldiers marched off, leaving them alone. The alarm finally ceased, and Waylen peered at the camera mounted on the structure's exterior.

"Well…?" Cody whispered.

"You were right."

He lost his smile. "I'd hoped I wasn't."

"Meeting tonight. My suite. Tell Silas."

"Where are you off to?" Cody called.

"Darren and I have been ordered to go ten minutes in the Planet D echo. Wish me luck."

Shadows of the Earth

*F*ive hours later, Waylen plopped onto his couch, his hair damp after a cleansing shower. He'd never felt so wrung out. Even being on the job, working seven-day weeks, sleeping in nondescript motels around the country wasn't as harmful to his well-being as dealing with the tokens.

They'd made it eight minutes each before they'd respectively extracted the other from the token. Waylen pressed his eyelids shut and saw the Shadow lingering. He viewed the red skies, the dark rocky terrain, and the lumbering steps of Colin Swanson as he lunged to some unseen destination.

The pair had been out of contact with Fred Trell and NASA at Houston for an entire two-hour period, and they'd only witnessed eight minutes of the echo. What had they found that scared them so much? Waylen wished one of the astronauts was alive and well enough to be interviewed. Both Colin's and Peter's wives were gone too, and Fred hadn't married. He'd been close to the lawyer, Daniel, and Cody, but he hadn't divulged what transpired on that fateful day to either of them.

Waylen lay on the couch, resting his head on the square pillow, and fell asleep.

He had a dream.

He walked into the laboratory, and a man stood near the entrance to the Hex. When he turned around, he became a cloud of mist and vanished. Waylen walked onto the platform without a spacesuit and strode to the podium, where the individual tokens were. Without preamble, he clicked them together, forming a triangle, and against the laws of nature, the metal bent and stayed that way.

The Shadow spread from the center, crowding the

Hex until it filled his entire view. The fog saturated his lungs like smoke, and he coughed, struggling to inhale.

Waylen woke and sat up, feeling the effects in his chest. He hacked twice and drank a full glass of water in the kitchen before the unpleasant sensation eased.

Voices carried from the hall, and he opened the door, where Cody, Silas, and Darren were deep in discussion. They stopped, stared at Waylen, and quickly entered.

"You look terrible," Silas told him.

"Thanks." Waylen ran a hand through his hair, finding it had dried. How long had he been sleeping? It was seven, so he'd been on the couch for two hours, which didn't seem possible. "It's been quite the day."

"You're not kidding," Silas said. "Vera thought I was nuts requesting an office for Darren. Good thing no one questioned it, because we didn't get approval from Theodore."

"What happened? What did you get?" Cody asked Waylen. They were confident they weren't being overheard within the suites, so he came out and said it.

"Cody was one hundred percent right," Waylen said. "He's in touch with Leo Monroe, not Plemmons, like we'd assumed."

"We're screwed," Silas grumbled.

"Not necessarily. We can figure this out." Waylen gestured to the window. "There's a breach in their barrier. We'll contact Assistant Director Ben and demand he send help. I'll try tonight."

"Let's wait until tomorrow. I saw Theodore earlier, and he seems on edge," Darren told them.

"Fine." Waylen preferred that, given his current state. "Darren, are you okay?"

Darren took a seat at the table, cracking his neck from

side to side. "I've been better. Those damned tokens sure do a number on the mind."

"Eight minutes," Waylen said.

"Eight?" Cody looked impressed. "Might be dangerous."

"Theo wanted ten."

"He should do it himself." Cody took a beer from the fridge and offered Waylen's stockpile to the others.

Waylen wasn't in the mood, but accepted anyway. It might ease his constant memory of the lingering Shadow.

"Okay, what do we know for certain?" Darren asked.

Silas began counting the facts out on his fingers. "We were drugged. Theodore is working for Leo, which tells us he's not in prison. On the other hand, we're captives. Theo is going to kill Waylen and Darren by pushing them too far with the tokens, and it's only a matter of time before they do the same to Cody and me. Did I miss anything?"

Cody lifted his bottle. "They only stocked light beer."

Darren smiled. "Add it to the list."

"How can you be so chill?" Silas asked.

"We're on the verge of a breakthrough. I've dedicated my life to this sort of thing," Darren said. "Theodore can't kill us. We have people that are expecting to hear from us. I think he's just trying to get as much done in a short amount of time, and then he'll let us go."

"If he's working for Leo, nothing's off the table." Waylen drummed his fingers. "We don't even know if they actually caught the guys he'd had spread across the states, like Theodore advised."

Silas clenched his teeth. "Rory…"

"They have no need for her, not with the tokens here," Cody reminded them.

"But we still require the Key," Darren added.

"True. Rory doesn't know anything about that." Silas took a drink and stared at his phone. "I hate this."

"Everyone has to stay calm. I'll contact Ben tomorrow. He'll investigate and they'll show up for a routine visit. He'll get the White House's approval, if that's what it takes." Waylen sipped his beer, then idly peeled at the label.

Silas finally relaxed. "If you say so."

They stayed for an hour, changing the subject after going over Cody and Silas' updates. Their conversation eventually slipped to baseball, but Waylen couldn't shake the memory of the phone call.

Leo Monroe wasn't in custody, and he'd be coming back to his property. Waylen would do his best to prepare.

7

"And that's how I persuade the reader to turn the page." Rory added an exclamation point on the whiteboard for emphasis.

"Very impressive, Miss Swanson." Marg Chambers sat in the front row, making notes in a journal, rather than on a laptop.

Rory had gone through her entire lesson plan in thirty minutes, which meant she'd need to stretch the concepts out for the real thing, but for a test run, it went over better than expected. Rory assessed Marg, hoping for more than a simple comment. "Anything to work on?"

"Eye contact. You turn your back to the class quite frequently, but you'll get used to that. I like how you gave examples of your own experiences with *View*, but don't lean on it too often, or they'll grow bored. Creative writing doesn't have to follow such strict guidelines, because we're trying to inspire the writers, not stifle them, so good job on that front. I think you'll do wonderfully."

Rory beamed at the praise and made mental notes about the slight critiques. "Thank you, Marg."

"Don't thank me until you've done it in front of students. They can be relentless." Marg laughed.

She checked her phone when Marg left, but there

were no responses from Silas. Rory had seven unanswered texts to him alone, and more to Waylen and Cody.

She glanced out the window, finding dozens of students milling about. Today was Thursday, when they all came from out of town, filling their shared dorm rooms with hotplates, gaming systems, and brand-new comforter sets bought by ambivalent parents.

A few moving vans were parked on the street beyond the dorms, and she already noticed a keg being rolled into the building beside hers. Rory smiled, recalling her first keg party a decade ago. It was the age without worry, where the future wasn't set in stone, and the world seemed to be wide open, ready for the taking.

Rory gathered her things and slung her leather bag over a shoulder. The weather was beautiful, the kind of later summer afternoon that spoke to you. Birds flitted from tree to tree, annoyed at the commotion from the students. The Sun felt especially present, no longer hiding in the distance. She could still see the faint outline of the Moon, a semicircle of barely perceivable reflected light.

Rory pushed aside the sensation threatening to encompass her, and miraculously, it vanished. The echoes continued to bother her during the week, but none nearly as badly as the experience on Saturday. Did the others have the same reaction to the tokens, or was it because she'd used the Shadow? Had they all gone to the Moon? Rory couldn't ask them since it was impossible to reach anyone.

She'd figured Silas could risk sending another message, but so far, it was crickets. Were they dead? Had Leo Monroe hired more help from behind bars?

Rory grabbed a bagel and coffee. She saw her name scrawled on the side of the paper cup without giving it, indicating the barista remembered her. That gave a sense of reassurance, but the gnawing feeling that Silas needed help was almost overwhelming. She'd abandoned them.

No. It wasn't her fault she'd ever encountered a token. That fell on her grandfather, though he never would have wished Rory harm. He was a sweet man, too sweet for his own good. He shouldn't have allowed Peter Gunn to bully him into keeping the tokens and Delta secret.

She peered at the faculty dorms, and considered returning home to work on her novel. It was flowing better than *View* ever had, even at her peak. Rory couldn't handle the distraction Silas' absence was providing. He was fine. She repeated this like a mantra and headed to the building, using her key fob to unlock the main entrance.

The sound of music rolled into the foyer, and she saw a door propped open. A man bobbed his body as she walked by, filling a bookshelf with old volumes while the record spun, playing jazz from another era. She nearly interrupted, since she hadn't met this professor yet, but continued home instead.

Once the handle latched, the music quieted, and she was grateful for it. Rory sloughed the bag off, setting it on the table, and walked to the desk, flipping her laptop up. She set her coffee down, unwrapped the bagel, and read her last scene while eating. It was good, both the breakfast and her writing.

She glanced at her phone when it buzzed.

We have to talk

It came from an unknown number. She'd already blocked Kevin's, so it couldn't be him, unless it was yet another burner. Rory wished everyone would just leave her alone. She didn't respond, and continued typing.

Rory, it's Special Agent Martina Sanchez

That got her attention. Rory's heart fluttered nervously as she picked up the cell. *What's up?*

The phone rang, and Rory considered blocking her too. In the end, she accepted it after five startling chimes. "What?"

"*I know I'm not your favorite person. I'm not mine either.*"

"Is this about Waylen?"

"*In a sense.*" She paused momentarily. "*I can't reach them.*"

"Same here. I heard from Silas once, but that was it."

"*You did?*"

"He said there was no service, and they were stuck there," she said.

"*That's peculiar. I've visited the site, but the soldiers won't allow me to enter. They don't care that I'm FBI. Something bad is going on.*"

"Bad?"

"*I took the money from Monroe, but I was also trying to get Waylen out of the mess with the tokens. We're talking about big government, weapons manufacturing, and possible international wars over this thing. Monroe is a ghost. I can't find any record of him being held captive. The White House is claiming ignorance. I was given a case across the country when I started being too vocal. And Assistant Director Ben is dead.*"

"Car crash," Rory said.

"*Sure, and you believe that? He was targeted because he asked too many questions. I'll be next.*"

Martina did sound distressed, but she hid it better than Rory might have. "What do you want me to do?"

"*They're looking for something. That list Theodore Belleville gave Ben was a bust. Monroe didn't hire those guys. They were just lowlifes, protecting drug dealers. You might be in danger.*"

Rory stared past her laptop, through the window to

the street. The car she'd noticed a few times lingered near a garbage can. "I'm think I'm being watched." She sounded paranoid, like her mother. It was probably a student or teacher at the university. Of course she'd keep seeing the same vehicles around campus. She looked away, processing Martina's comment.

"*I'll come to Boston,*" Waylen's old partner said.

"Why?"

"*I don't know exactly why, but I believe you're the missing piece. I'll explain more when I'm there. Monroe might have your friends captive.*"

"You're telling me they're being held by the Planetae CEO? He was arrested!"

"*Weren't you listening? No one's sure where he is. Ben pushed buttons, and he's dead. We're going to end up the same if we don't work together,*" she said.

"I can't!" Rory shouted. "I'm starting a new job and writing a book. I want to be left out of it all!" She hung up before Martina could respond, and blocked the number without thinking twice.

The car she'd been watching turned on, and a young man opened the back door, tossing an empty food delivery bag inside. There it was. Proof she was losing her mind. The vehicle kept showing up because it was a delivery driver for one of those apps.

Martina thought Ben was killed… murdered for investigating the Planetae base. Between the recent phone call and the threats from Kevin, Rory was seriously second-guessing her return to the city. Her course outlines sat in binders on the table, and she grabbed them.

Instructor: Rory Swanson

She brushed a hand over the name and sighed. Martina could come to Boston for all she cared, but Rory had to forget the Delta. It was difficult, considering the damned echoes lingering in the stillness, but she guessed the mark wouldn't stick forever.

Rory jumped when someone knocked, and she suddenly wished she had a gun. Silas seemed to have no issue walking around carrying them, but the laws in Massachusetts were much different from Wyoming.

"Who is it?" she asked through the door.

"Garnet Barry... I live across the hall!" he answered.

She opened it and saw the guy who'd been playing a jazz record. "Hey." Then she extended her arm, remembering social form. "Rory Swanson."

Garnet shook and moved his other hand from behind his back. "I'm a big fan. Would you sign it?"

He passed her a worn copy of *View from the Heavens*. "You liked it?"

"It was brilliant. I was never much for science fiction, but I dated a woman who kept raving about it, so she lent it to me. We broke up, but I kept the copy." He smiled, so it clearly didn't bother him.

He followed her in without an invitation. Rory found a pen and opened the cover, locating the blank part below the title page. *To Garnet, find your view. Rory Valentine.* She added the heart over her last name, as she usually did, and he read the quote when she gave it back.

"I'm writing a book too," he said. "I'm also in the literature department. Teaching kids studying law or sciences how to analyze a classic piece. Doesn't get much more fun than that."

"I can imagine." Rory liked Garnet already. He wasn't imposing, and the tweed jacket really sold his role at the university. She bet the students loved his classes.

"We're having a mixer for the faculty after orientation

tomorrow. Drinks at McLaren's at five. Come by, and meet the gang," he said.

"I'll be there." She steered him to the exit, and he seemed to get her drift. "You have excellent taste, by the way. Smooth jazz."

He looked embarrassed. "Sorry about that. The room was stuffy, so I let the air flow. I'll keep it down."

"There's nothing to apologize for. See you tomorrow," she said, and waited until he was in his own suite to close her door.

Martina's warning crept into her thoughts, but she ignored the pressing worry as she found her manuscript file and began typing, determined to forget the Delta.

8

"We're onto something." Waylen stretched, then rubbed his eyes.

Silas felt the same way, strung out after another week at the facility with no answers. Theodore Belleville had become a ghost, vanishing for days at a time. He'd banned them from using the laboratory since Wednesday, though they'd witnessed others entering the space.

They'd been pushed out.

Since Waylen and Darren were no longer the token's guinea pigs, Silas had asked the special investigator to stretch his financial crimes skills to examine what Planetae was up to. Cody could access their primary network to view files, and they'd found the name Somboon Suwan occasionally, inferring this man was a key player in the mystery before them.

"Somboon worked at a plant run by Planetae out of the Philippines, but he's also linked to the UFO facility in upstate New York. It's all connected to this Balloon program, whatever that is," Waylen said.

"We have to break out of here," Silas whispered.

Waylen nodded and opened another file. "I'm working on it."

They'd been unable to venture outside to send any

more messages. The moment Waylen left to shoot Assistant Director Ben a text, he'd been informed that the yard was off limits because of the threat of exposure to potential enemies.

Since then, Theodore had become a ghost.

Silas hated this more than he'd thought possible. The days dragged on, with them pretending not to be captives. Cody was cracking, his calm edge smoothing to panic in the last while. Darren Jones started keeping to himself, refusing to leave the residences. He was sure they were going to be shot and buried in the forest visible to the north. Silas didn't disagree.

Silas stood, taking his phone. "Enough of this."

"Where are you going?"

"Outside!" Silas stormed into the hallway, with Waylen on his heels. The second they pushed through the main exit, Corporal Tucker followed. "You don't need to escort us."

"It's for your own safety," he said.

"Tucker, where are you from?" Waylen asked as they walked to the residence building.

"Me, sir?"

"Yes."

"All over. Lastly stationed out of Pendleton."

"California?"

"Yes, sir."

Silas wasn't sure where Waylen was going with this.

Waylen stopped before climbing the steps. "Who sent you here?"

"Sir?"

"Why are you at this facility?"

"I was…"

"Do you know who Leo Monroe is?"

"Yes, sir."

"You're not an active-duty Marine, are you?"

Corporal Tucker averted his gaze, and his arms fell to his sides, but he didn't answer.

"I work for the FBI, Tucker. My job is to protect this country and her inhabitants. Whatever Monroe's doing, it's bad. I won't let him hurt people. I can tell that you're a smart man. When you got the call to wear fatigues and pretend to be enlisted, you jumped at the chance for the cash, didn't you? Escort a few civilians around, watch a gate. Nothing too strenuous. Do you have a family?" Waylen pointed to his chest pocket. "I'm guessing you're carrying a photo of them."

Tucker slipped a Polaroid from his BDUs and passed it to Waylen. "Wife and two girls, sir."

Waylen offered it back. "It's about to get ugly. My advice, stay clear. Starting right now. I'm going for a walk around the perimeter with my friend, and I can't be interrupted. Do you understand?"

"I won't get in trouble?" Tucker asked.

"No, I promise."

Tucker glanced at Silas, then removed his radio, speaking into it. "I ordered a shift change. You have ten minutes."

"Thanks." Waylen clapped him on the shoulder and they started across the concrete to the grass field, then toward the fence.

The Sun was behind the treeline, and lengthy shadows mingled with the chain-link, casting strange patterns on the ground. Silas stepped on them and hurried to the location where he'd found service days earlier. "This is it." His phone showed no bars, but Waylen's smile suggested he didn't have the same issue.

"Got it." Waylen dialed someone, and Silas heard it quietly ringing through the speaker. "Ben, it's…"

A woman's voice replied, and Waylen looked confused. "A car accident? Is he…" A second later, "I'm so sorry, Olivia. I can't believe it. The service is this weekend? I'm out of town on assignment, but I offer you and the kids my deepest condolences." Waylen said goodbye and hung up. His eyes were red, his frown creasing his brow. "Ben died in a car crash. Monroe did this."

Silas didn't know what to say, so he dialed Rory.

"*Silas!*"

"Thank God. It's good to hear your voice," he said. Waylen was on the phone again too, leaving a voicemail for someone.

"*Where are you?*"

"The same place. Leo Monroe is still controlling the operation. They won't even let us see the Delta. He's sending soldiers to set something up on the Moon, and we haven't found a device to control the Shadow. I think we need help."

"*Martina Sanchez called me today. What's the address there?*"

Silas wasn't quite sure. "Where are we?" he asked Waylen, who seemed frustrated as he redialed.

"Let me talk to her," he said, taking Silas' phone. He described it to Rory and gave it over.

"You get that?" Silas asked.

"*What am I supposed to do? I'm in Boston.*"

Waylen nodded down the fence line. "I guess our ten minutes is up."

Silas grimaced and clutched the cell so tight, he thought it might break. "Tell Martina what we discussed. She has to bring this up the chain of command, and let them know our national security is being threatened. Hell, get her to contact a general or something. Say there's a group of ex-Marines waving AKs around."

"*I... I blocked her number, but I'll call her back.*"

The soldier noticed them and jogged closer, her gun hefted across her chest.

"I have to run," he said. "I might not have another chance to reach you."

"*Be careful. Help is coming.*"

They each slid their respective phones away when Vera arrived. The barrel wagged between them. "Hand the cells over."

"What..."

"Don't be stupid. Give me the phones."

"Where's Tucker?"

A quick burst of gunfire sounded in the yard, followed by silence. Vera didn't break her stare. "He's going home early."

Silas felt sick to his stomach. Had they just shot one of their own?

The fenced gate opened, and bright headlights shone over the parking lot. A long black car rolled toward the laboratory, and Silas cursed while offering his phone to the armed soldier. Whether or not she was presently an enlisted Marine, she had the upper hand.

Waylen did the same.

"Turn around," Vera said, and when neither did, she repeated herself with more force. "Turn around and grab the fence!"

Silas saw a man exit the car, and instantly recognized Leo Monroe. His minion, Theodore Belleville, was right on his heels, talking nonstop. They were too far away for Silas to hear the conversation, but Leo paused and stared. He pointed; then the woman's radio beeped.

Silas noticed how Theodore held one too, and his voice carried through the nearby speaker. "*Bring them to the lab.*"

She shoved Waylen with her left hand and kept her aim. "You're on borrowed time."

Silas wondered what had Vera so angry, but decided it was best not to ask. They made quick work of the couple hundred yards, and Leo Monroe stood near the entrance, patiently waiting.

"Good evening, Mr. Brooks. I told you it was foolish to go against me, didn't I?" Leo grinned widely, and Silas wanted to wipe the expression off his face.

Waylen came across as neutral, almost amused by the revelation. "I should have known better."

"Theodore tells me you're causing trouble. Why am I not surprised? I figured the four of you might actually be useful, but I was obviously mistaken."

Two more big soldiers arrived. Cody and Darren were in front of them, Darren with a swollen cheek.

"If you're not helping Operation Delta, then there's no point in keeping you around," Leo said casually.

"So we can leave?" Waylen asked.

Leo opened his mouth, but didn't comment right away. He straightened his tie and glanced at Belleville. "I'm afraid there's too much risk. We're proceeding with phase three."

"Which is?" Silas asked.

"Mining the Moon. I have state-of-the-art equipment being brought in as we speak. By next week, this facility will begin to process the very first batch from our own celestial body. It no longer belongs to humanity, but to Planetae." Leo reached for the door. "Kill them."

"Wait!" Waylen rushed to block Silas and the other

two. "You need the Key."

Leo leaned toward Theodore, spoke softly, then nodded. "What about it?"

"You want more than just Moon rocks, don't you? I know your real purpose for spending all this effort to retrieve the Delta. You want to walk on other planets. *We* can ensure that happens."

"There's no evidence that proves any of the worlds are inhabited by intelligent life," Belleville interjected. "Or that they'll prove useful in any fashion."

"That's not quite true." Waylen stepped closer, even with three high-powered weapons aimed at his chest. "I've spent twenty minutes with the echo from Planet D."

"So what?" Theodore barked. "Those astronauts found nothing, and neither did you."

But Silas knew that wasn't true, because Waylen had told them all about his latest experience with the token.

"We did, but since your accomplice wasn't here, I didn't inform him," Waylen said.

"What… what did you find?" Leo's voice grew tighter.

"A monument. Peter and Colin encountered proof of an alien civilization."

Silas' skin filled with goosebumps at the mention of aliens. He observed Leo, recognizing the moment he'd changed his mind.

"And the Key?"

"It's in the facility near Hermon," Silas said.

This seemed to shock Leo Monroe. "The base I helped construct for the government?"

"They got to your Project Balloon contact, Somboon Suwan." Silas hoped they were right about this theory, because it was their only shot at survival.

"How did—" Leo recoiled and entered the building. "I have no jurisdiction there. Plemmons thinks I'm incarcerated, and my lookalike won't deceive them forever. Waylen Brooks, it's up to you to secure me this Key."

"We'll leave now," Waylen said, motioning to the other three.

"Do you think I'm a fool? Take the UFO expert, but Sanderson and Gunn stay put. Call it collateral."

Silas didn't like being left behind.

"Fine, but I get the Key for you, and we all walk out of here alive," Waylen told him.

"I'm a man of my word, Brooks. Bring the Key, and you can go," he said.

"A minute ago, I was already dead," Waylen reminded him.

"Then count your blessings. You've been granted a new lease on life. Take a truck. I want the Key by Monday."

"How will I get into the base?" Waylen asked.

"That's your problem." Leo held the door for Belleville, who stepped through. "Monday, or I shoot this duo myself."

They were left alone. The guards made themselves scarce after returning the two cell phones.

"What the hell? They were going to kill us!" Cody paced, his legs moving so fast, Silas thought he might trip over his own feet. "I should never have touched those stupid things. What was I thinking? My life wasn't so bad, was it? I had a job, a decent condo. I wish I hadn't met Fred Trell."

"If you're done freaking out, we have to talk," Waylen said. "Silas, even if I travel to this base, they could ignore me. Do I walk up to Somboon and demand the secondary piece of the Delta?"

"My suggestion? Grab a couple of spare sets of BDUs and pretend you fit in."

"Impersonate soldiers?" Waylen asked.

"However you do it, keep it brief. I don't think he's bluffing about the deadline."

"That's only four days," Darren said.

"Then we'd better stop talking about it and leave." Waylen shook hands with Silas, then Cody. "I won't fail you."

9

*H*er sleep was restless, with the conversation replaying on a loop. Silas was in danger, and Rory couldn't do anything to help. She'd unblocked Sanchez's number, and instantly dialed her, explaining what had happened. Martina claimed to have a similar voicemail from Waylen Brooks, and because of that fact, she took the warning seriously.

With no way to physically help Silas, Rory attended the orientation sessions, and currently sat in the front row of the smaller amphitheater. A few hundred anxious students filled the room, ready to begin their journey into the Arts program this coming semester.

All the mixed-department faculty members were introduced. A handful of people hooted when her own name was mentioned. Rory stood, giving them a wave, but found it difficult to be in the moment after the worrisome call from Silas the night before.

She was grateful to not have to stand on stage and give the new students a rousing speech. Instead, she listened as a man and woman wearing plastic badges around their necks described how events would transpire over the duration of next week and beyond.

"What a bore." Garnet leaned from the chair behind

her. He smelled like cigarettes and whiskey. She checked the time, seeing it was already four in the afternoon.

"Shhh," Rory said in return, making him smile.

"Still coming to McLaren's?"

"Sure." She had her cell phone, and would place the ringer on high after leaving the amphitheater. Rory didn't feel like mingling with the other professors, but she needed to start off on a good foot. Martina would help Waylen and Silas. She worked for the FBI, and Rory was just an author. After repeating this to herself the last few hours, she was beginning to believe it.

"With that, we welcome you to the Arts program, and hope you'll be as inspired as we are." The woman began clapping, and the crowd followed, some getting to their feet.

Rory joined Garnet by the exit. "Poor suckers. They don't know what they're in for."

"Which is?" Rory asked.

"Four impossibly tough years, which they'll later realize were the best times of their lives as they struggle to find any viable employment in this field. It's either work copy for a website or do graphic design, and both of those are quickly becoming antiquated, aren't they?"

"Then they can teach," Rory added.

"Touché." Garnet held the door, and she beat the rush into the hall.

"I'll meet you at the bar," she said, heading outside.

Garnet didn't respond as he caught up with another counterpart.

Rory hurried to her apartment and closed the door. Without thinking, she dialed Martina, but there was no answer. She tried Silas, and as expected, nothing.

The entire fiasco had to end. It wasn't her fault that

Shadows of the Earth

Grandpa Swanson had flown to the Moon and walked through a damned Shadow to another world. While she missed Silas, she also wanted to start fresh. Rory stared in her bathroom mirror, finding lines around her eyes that weren't there before coming home to Woodstock.

Her hands always seemed shaky, her breathing less even. Rory had to get it together, and quickly. She tried to remind herself what she was grateful for.

This position at the university.

Her freedom from Kevin.

The book contract and the fact that the manuscript felt organic.

This fantastically old, furnished apartment.

Her parents, for all the support they'd given her in the recent months.

Rory forced herself to smile. She'd heard it could trick the mind into thinking you were happy. It released a dopamine response. Whatever it was supposed to do didn't happen, and the knot in her stomach remained.

She smoothed out her hair and straightened her blouse, which was something her mom might have chosen, and wiped a smudge off her shoes. They weren't quite basic flats, but had little-to-no height. She recalled her mother calling them kitten heels. Rory wasn't about to be caught in an alley without the ability to run. She disliked that mentality, but after being mugged, shot at, and kidnapped, the statistics didn't lie.

Before leaving, she walked to the kitchen and tucked a sharp knife into her purse.

The complex was silent as she wound her way through the halls, into the foyer, then outside. Everyone staying on site would be gathering at the mixer. Rory felt nervous, and not because of the tokens or the Delta. She had to befriend an entire faculty, and wasn't in the headspace to make a good first impression.

The moment she entered McLaren's, seven blocks off campus, she flushed with anxiety. Before approaching the obvious cluster of professors, she circled around them, hit the bar, and ordered a shot of tequila and a martini with an olive. It was her mother's drink, and she wanted to seem elegant and refined. With her back to the teachers, she downed the tequila and winced. The bartender grinned, and she slid a twenty to him before grabbing the martini and putting a mask of resolution on. She wore it well. A smile that suggested she was having fun. A glimmer in her eyes conveying interest in any subject her colleagues brought up.

All the while, she wondered if someone was going to call her with an update out of New York.

"Rory, glad you came." Garnet slid an arm around her shoulder, and she did her best not to briskly shrug it off. He must have sensed her annoyance, and dropped the act. He introduced her to a few people, and she amiably chatted with them.

Two hours and three martinis later, she was spent, choosing a seat near the dart boards. A young couple laughed while they threw darts, the man repeatedly missing the board.

"Mind if I sit?" It was Marg Chambers, and she looked completely sober.

Rory gestured to the empty stool. "Sure."

"How are you doing? It can be a lot, starting a job like this. There are so many people to meet, trying to remember faces and names."

Rory clutched her glass. "I'm okay."

"We're happy to have you, and I do think you'll fit

right in."

"Thanks, so do I."

Rory's head ached, and her mouth felt too dry. She squinted her eyes closed, and her lungs tightened, like she couldn't get enough air. When she looked again, Marg was covered in mist. Thick black fog engulfed her superior.

"You have the weekend to prepare, and then it's classes on Monday," Marg said through the cloud of darkness.

The Shadow spread down the high-top table, creeping along the wall to the dartboard. Tendrils stretched to the ceiling, pieces plunging into people's drinks. Garnet was ten feet away, animatedly talking to a young woman, and the Shadow wrapped around his leg, climbing until it enveloped Garnet's entire body.

Rory rose, her glass falling and shattering on the floor.

"Rory? What's the matter?"

She heard Marg's voice, but all she saw was the incessant void.

Rory caught sight of the red exit lights and pivoted in that direction, staggering from McLaren's. She shut the door, glad to be free of the Shadow. What was happening to her?

She took a seat on a bench, facing the river, and watched the last rays of the day vanish in the horizon while struggling to catch her breath. Were the others experiencing similar effects? How could Rory put it in her past when the damned Shadow clung to her brain like a disease?

Rory glanced behind her, making sure the mist hadn't followed, but the vision was gone.

Her gaze lingered on the street, particularly the car with tinted windows by the garbage can. She thought it might be the food delivery guy, but realized his vehicle, though a similar model, didn't have the tint.

Rory got to her feet and started in the opposite direction. When she checked, the car had turned around, and drove leisurely before parking with its headlights on her. She sped up, glad for her choice in shoes, and cut into an alley a block down. Her heart was pounding. A couple of large, dirty trucks sat parked behind various businesses, and she wrinkled her nose when she passed a Chinese restaurant's grease trap.

So far, no one had approached the alley. She skirted the next narrow street, veering toward campus. For a Friday night, it was eerily quiet at almost eight o'clock. Then she remembered the kegs being hauled into the dorms, and guessed that most of the students were currently drinking warm beer from red plastic cups.

When she was four blocks from her apartment, Rory slowed, assuming that no one had been following her. Here she was again with the overactive imagination. She wanted to shower, pour a lemon tea, watch some mindless television until she fell asleep, and forget the incident at the bar had ever happened.

Rory saw a man standing along her direct route, facing the opposite direction. "You have to get over your shit," she muttered to herself, and entered the slender alley between the Arts buildings, rather than walk past the stranger. Rory's purse swung with the change of trajectory, and slipped off her shoulder. She checked, and the figure was gone.

She was almost at the end when someone stepped under a streetlight and held his arms up. "Rory, I just want to talk."

Rory's heart seized behind her chest. "Kevin…"

Shadows of the Earth

Headlights blasted them, throwing her shadow long as the light bounced across the brick exteriors. Kevin lifted a hand to block the glare, and Rory heard his heavy footsteps approaching. She had nowhere to go.

10

Silas paced from one side of Cody's suite to the other. "We're trapped."

"They'll kill us." Cody had said this exact line about a dozen times in the last twenty-four hours since Waylen had left. "He abandoned us, Silas."

The soldiers had scoured their units, taking anything that might be deemed a weapon. Waylen's spare pistol had been claimed by Vera.

They hadn't stolen Cody's laptop, but he wasn't in the helping mood. All he did was mope in his sweatsuit, griping that Waylen wouldn't succeed, and that they were dead in another three days.

"For the love of God, Cody, focus." Silas wanted to slap the other man, but doubted violence would help shake him from the funk.

"I had cancer," he said.

Silas stopped pacing, and fell into the chair across from Cody. "Seriously?"

"Yeah, when I was seventeen."

"That sucks."

"You're telling me. Leukemia. It was terrible, but they caught it early, and the treatment worked."

"I'm glad you're okay," Silas said.

Shadows of the Earth

"When they diagnosed me, I was so certain I would die. My mom and step-dad did their best to assure me otherwise, but I've always been a pessimist. I read a lot, watched sci-fi movies, and worked on my computer. I'd lock myself in my room for days, weeks, only leaving for appointments at the hospital. Then one day, they told me it was gone, I'd beaten it. I didn't trust them, but they were right. Every year after, the results were negative. I was in remission, and it never returned. But in the back of my mind, I expected it to show up again. It's a looming dread, a gloom over my life that I don't think I'll ever shake."

Silas listened with compassion, and couldn't imagine what that must have been like. "I'm sorry it happened to you."

"Don't be. Because I'm about to die, and I won't have to worry about cancer anymore."

"Enough," Silas said.

"What?"

"Waylen won't fail. Use the computer, and do something to help us!"

"They've tightened security."

"Then bypass it," Silas ordered, and lifted the laptop, opening it. He placed it by Cody.

Cody began typing. "Grab me a beer."

"How about a coffee instead?"

"Whatever." Cody's fingers clicked quickly on the keyboard. He had an unlabeled baseball cap on, flipped backwards like he always seemed to do when deep in work.

Silas brewed two single-serve cups, and brought them to the couch, setting them onto coasters by habit. Cody drank a hot sip, grimaced, and without looking, put the cup directly on the coffee table. Silas didn't adjust it.

"Anything?" Silas asked after five minutes.

Cody smiled for the first time that day. "Actually, yeah."

Silas sidled closer and saw the camera feeds on the monitor. "You got it to work?"

"I didn't even think it was possible. Planetae must be outsourcing their IT and security to some third-party college students." Cody navigated the various camera angles, and stopped when they came upon the Hex. Leo Monroe and Theodore Belleville stood fully suited up. Vera lingered nearby, a gun slung over her shoulder.

"A lot of good that'll do," Silas said.

"Guns will fire on the Moon," Cody responded. "Not that there's anyone to shoot."

"Yet."

Cody gave him a doubtful look. "Let's see if I can get audio."

They watched as a couple of other soldiers climbed into spacesuits, and eventually, Cody tapped a key in triumph.

"… last session before we dismantle the Delta. If there's a monument on Planet D, I want it verified," Monroe said.

"Twenty minutes? Who's going to do it? You have to be well practiced to survive so long," Theodore told him. *"Sanderson is the only person on base with that kind of experience."*

Silas noticed how Cody sank into the couch, becoming smaller.

"Not him. He'll make anything up to save his own hide. I was thinking… you."

The camera was mounted twenty feet from the middle of the Hex, and displayed most details of Theodore's face. He was terrified. *"I can't! There's too much to do."*

Shadows of the Earth

"*I'm here now. You'll begin after we transport the next round of supplies. Understood?*"

"*Ask one of the soldiers. They'll do it. Just offer them a bonus.*"

Vera stood next to Monroe, and her gun shifted enough for the hint to be obvious.

"*You'll use the echo of Planet D, and confirm there's an alien monument.*"

After a solid minute of silence, Theo spoke. "*Yes, sir. It will take time to acclimatize…*"

"*I want results by tonight.*" Leo turned his back, reviewing something on a tablet Dr. Rita passed him.

They continued to observe it for a while. Eventually, Cody cut the audio and set the computer on the table, where they could view the various feeds.

"It'll probably kill him," Cody said.

"Good."

"Yeah, good."

"What's the point of this?" Silas asked.

"What do you mean?"

"The Delta. So a mysterious race left it open on the Moon, and we discovered it. What then?"

Cody had regained some of his previous composure, and he crossed his legs, sitting more upright. "There's a theory Darren and I have debated."

"And that is…?"

"We weren't supposed to dismantle the Delta."

"Interesting." Silas finished his coffee and slowly rotated the cup in his palm.

"It was intended to be used by whoever found it."

"My grandfather screwed it up."

"I think so."

"What did they really find? Waylen saw a monument,"

Silas said.

"To be fair, they noticed a shape in the distance, but it wasn't close enough to make out any details. He exaggerated with Monroe to give themselves leverage," Cody retorted.

"Let's keep the ideas flowing." Silas watched Cody. "Let's say they wanted visitors. Why didn't they encounter anyone on Planet D?"

"They might have already moved on, or they're dead. Or they put it up there so long ago, they'd forgotten about it in the generations since. We don't know what the hell people did thousands of years ago on Earth. It's not like we kept some elaborate KMS for all of humanity."

"KMS," Silas said quietly.

"Knowledge Management System. In business, it's a software program intended to store all pertinent business functions. It allows for staff to be replaced without as many headaches, but it's rarely that successful."

"I know, I went to college, remember?"

"Right."

"What's on Planet D?" Silas wished they could investigate it like early explorers.

"First contact."

"Then there's the footprint Rory recorded."

"Yeah, I've been thinking about that. It had to be placed before they took the Delta, not after."

"Why?"

"Because their portal was gone, meaning the aliens couldn't access the Moon. We saw no evidence of a starship landing, or a length of footprints leading to the Shadow's location."

Silas nodded his agreement. "My grandfather missed the footprint."

"Likely, and can you blame him? They were literally on the damned Moon, and came across a misty blob. It would be hard to see anything but the Shadow at that point," Cody said.

"Do you actually believe there's a Key?"

Cody shook his head. "Probably not. I bet we need to bring the actual Delta back to the Moon."

"Either through itself, or by shuttle."

"Yeah. If Monroe carries it into the Shadow, whoever makes the trip is stuck."

"Or on Planet D," Silas said.

"Yes. If they use a shuttle, which I highly doubt they can, they'd have the means to escape after with a lunar module."

"That would mean Planetae teams up with NASA or one of the billionaires' pilot projects, whom I don't believe are at that stage yet."

"China might be," Cody suggested.

Silas absorbed the comment. "Monroe probably isn't beyond partnering with another country. That's what he's doing here: proving to a potential buyer that he has a remarkable asset."

"There's nothing we can do."

"Without a Key, Waylen can't save us." The realization sank in. "Why did Monroe even let Waylen go, if he's partnering with America's enemies?"

"It's all speculation, Silas. But… if he can avoid bargaining with anyone, and find a Key to control the Delta from within his Hex, he'll risk freeing Waylen."

"Agreed."

"Either way, I don't think we'll be around to see the end of this," Cody whispered.

Silas exhaled, and couldn't argue with Cody's logic.

"How about that beer?"

"You read my mind."

Silas walked to the kitchen, bringing the empty cups, and cracked two bottles of beer. "Good luck, Waylen."

11

The facility sat motionless in the dark.

The area was filled with forests and farms but little else. The government base had a chain-link fence circling it, and a company logo was plastered on a large metal sign out front beside the entrance gate. The three letters were bold: CME. From what Waylen could tell, it was fabricated, with no website, phone number, or trace of commerce.

He assumed no one paid the place any mind, considering there were probably fifty people living in the surrounding hundred-mile radius. They were in the boonies, through and through.

"It's a bust," Darren said.

"It can't be."

"We need the Key," he added.

"We'll get it."

Darren glanced at him from the passenger seat. "Waylen, face the music. There's nothing here. It's empty."

"I can't let Silas and Cody take the fall."

"We can ask for help. Find the authorities."

Waylen remembered the chief in New Hampshire, and recalled that Assistant Director Ben was dead. "I don't know what good it would do. Even Plemmons thinks Monroe's incarcerated. They trust Theodore Belleville for some reason. I'm just a financial crimes special agent, and I technically don't even work for the FBI any longer. They stripped my credibility, and I accepted it without hesitation. It was a mistake. I'm sorry for dragging you into this disaster, Darren. Why don't you leave? Go back to Providence and see your kids."

"You'd really let me do that?"

"Of course. I'd suggest hiding out. Rent something for a couple of weeks, until Monroe is dealt with."

"I couldn't bail on you guys now."

"You sure as hell can," Waylen said.

Darren gazed at the dark building, but shook his head after a moment of quiet contemplation. "Nah. I've come this far."

Waylen reached into the glovebox, taking the handgun left behind by its previous occupants.

"What are you doing?"

Waylen exited the truck and softly closed the door. "I'm going in."

Darren joined him outside. "Like this?" He wore the same sweater and jeans combination from Operation Delta, and Waylen still donned the suit from yesterday. He'd freshened up at a rest stop a few hours earlier, and ditched the tie in the backseat.

"If it's empty, then what does it matter?" Waylen patted his pocket, ensuring his FBI credentials were present. Before walking to the gate, he tried Martina again, without any luck. Where was she?

The gate was on rolling wheels, the top covered in barbed wire. Darren typed a code on the keypad, but it buzzed and flashed red in response.

Waylen motioned for Darren to step aside, and re-

Shadows of the Earth

called the five-digit number Silas had found in the Balloon files. It seemed to be linked to the projects Planetae colluded on with the US government. Waylen methodically entered the numbers, repeating them out loud to ensure he did it in the proper order. Instead of buzzing, it beeped, and the gate's lock clicked.

"Nice guess," Darren said.

"Smile, you're on camera." Waylen gestured at the blinking light. He waved, hoping no one was in their proximity before they'd scoured the place.

Darren kept his chin low, and they jogged toward the entrance. The building itself was too nice for this rural setting, with curved exterior walls and dark, reflective windows. In the night, starlight bounced off the material, shining brightly against the concrete lot.

Waylen tapped the second code, this time a seven-digit sequence, and as he held his breath, it worked.

They'd penetrated the secret government base.

His gun hung low as he scanned the foyer. It was exactly what someone on the outside might expect. A large reception area, a spot labeled *Security*, and an open space with ten chairs. Waylen doubted they'd ever been used, since it seemed like no one had utilized this complex yet. He flipped a bank of light switches on, and the area basked in the LED fixtures' glow.

Darren went to the stout coffee table and picked up a magazine. "It's dated from seven years ago."

"When they built it," Waylen said.

"If it's empty, why did you and Silas flag it?"

"We realized it was one of the three facilities Planetae helped build. The files showed Somboon Suwan was given a position here, but obviously, that's not true." Waylen walked deeper, coming to the bottom of the wide staircase. "Up or down?"

"Down," Darren said. "If they're holding on to an alien craft, it's not in the attic."

Waylen took the lead now, lifting his gun as they descended into the ground. He didn't stop until there was no other option to go further, and set a palm on the lever, unsure what to expect. To his surprise, it opened without a lock or a code, and he entered the vast space. Waylen's footsteps echoed in the cavernous room, and he found the lights ten feet to his left on the wall. He flicked the first switch, and winced when he recognized the platform centering the space. "It's another Hex."

"Incredible," Darren gasped. "Leo Monroe stole the design."

"Or he built it for the government first."

"But why? The Department of Defense didn't know about the Delta."

"It's possible they didn't understand the purpose," Waylen said. They stepped up to the hexagonal platform. "What was their intention?"

Darren touched the podium positioned in the middle of the Hex. "They tried to recreate the Delta. This would allow them to move between buildings. From California, to Arizona, to upstate New York."

"Maybe we were wrong all along," Waylen said, "and the government did know about the tokens."

"Very good," someone said, his voice crisp and clear.

Waylen lifted the gun, searching for the source. He rushed to the platform's exit, not wanting to be trapped inside. "Who's there?"

More lights flashed on, and the sudden burst almost blinded him.

"Waylen Brooks, I presume?"

Shadows of the Earth

His eyes acclimated, and he saw a figure striding from the far side of the room. He didn't appear armed. He stopped ten feet away. "My name is Somboon."

"Do you have the Key?"

"What Key?" Somboon asked.

"You know what I'm talking about," Waylen said. "Did Monroe or Belleville tell you I was coming?"

"I don't work for Mr. Monroe any longer."

"Then who…"

Somboon glanced over his shoulder to a second person standing by the exit.

"I should have known it was you," Waylen told them.

"Rory, we need to talk," Kevin said again.

The headlights continued to shine down the alley, and Rory was stuck between the two opposing forces. Kevin didn't seem to notice the threatening car aimed in their direction.

"I have nothing to say to you," she hissed.

Kevin took a step closer. "Rory, it's fate. You came back to Boston. We have an unbreakable bond."

She saw the scar on his nose from where she'd decked him a while ago. Rory felt a small amount of satisfaction that it was slightly crooked. The car hadn't budged. It stayed running, the brights wrapping the fire escapes and trash cans with their ambiance.

"Leave me alone. Move!" Rory started forward, but he lunged to block her path.

He slapped her on the cheek, and her face burned. "You're a real piece of…"

A horn honked.

Kevin seemed to note the vehicle, and he waved a middle finger at the driver. "What the hell do you want?"

Rory took her chance and darted past Kevin, but didn't get far. His hand snaked out, gripping her.

"Stop making this harder than it has to be, Rory."

She fumbled in her purse for the knife, but couldn't hold on, and it dropped to the ground with a clatter. Kevin's gaze followed it, while the engine revved and the sedan's tires squealed as it tore off. She broke free from Kevin and dove between two buildings. Kevin was struck, and slammed into the hood with a sickening thump. He rolled off, and the car screamed to a stop. Rory froze in horror as the driver got out. He was tall and lean, a scowl on his face like they'd interrupted his evening cruise.

She didn't notice the gun until he pulled the trigger. A silencer made it sound like nothing more than a burst of wind, and two bullets fired into Kevin's writhing form. Blood pooled on the dark concrete beneath her ex-boyfriend. Rory couldn't find her voice, and she remained motionless, her limbs failing her.

"Get in," the gruff man said. His hair was gray, all cut to the same length, and his chin and cheeks were dotted with white stubble.

"No." Rory found her voice and backed up until she hit a brick wall.

He stalked toward her menacingly. "I'm not asking."

Rory peered at Kevin's corpse, then at the running car. Someone walked down the sidewalk, and they shouted drunkenly. "Help!" Rory called, and the man lunged, covering her mouth. She tried to bite him, but his leather gloves were thick and caused her to gag.

"I don't want to hurt you," he groaned, and dragged

her to the open door. "This is for your own good."

He threw her into the backseat and slammed it shut. She attempted to escape, but the child locks were activated. Rory bashed her elbow into the glass and cried out in pain when the nerves fired up. Her abductor grabbed the knife, wiped the handle clean, and tossed it into a nearby trash can.

They were already moving, and all Rory could do was gaze out the window at Kevin's dead body. "You killed him."

"He was in the way. I thought you wanted him gone," the man said.

"How would you know what I want?" she yelled.

"You told campus security about him, remember? Said that Kevin Heffernan was a threat to your well-being, and asked them to be on the lookout," he said, and dialed a number while driving slower. "Yeah, I need a cleanup. Sure. Here's the address." He outlined directions, then hung up.

"Who was that?" Rory tried to see where he was taking her, and noticed a large group of kids lingering outside the dorms, the keg party in full effect. For the second time in the last month, Rory was being kidnapped.

"Never mind."

"Who are you?"

"My name's Brett."

"What do you want with me? I don't have anything," she said.

"We've met before."

Rory stared at Brett's reflection in the rearview mirror, but didn't see a face she recognized. "When?"

"You were around seven, visiting your grandparents," he said.

Rory pondered his meaning. "You knew Colin?"

"Very well."

"How?"

"We worked together," Brett told her.

"I don't understand." Rory's cheek ached. They drove south, away from the river.

"Rory, Colin Swanson told someone what happened on the Moon," Brett said. "We've been trying to figure out how to use the Delta ever since."

"But you didn't have it."

He slowed, stopping at a red light. Rory peered at the SUV beside them, wondering if she could get their attention, but her curiosity overcame her dread.

"You're making a big assumption there, Rory."

"Why's that? Peter, Fred, Colin… they had their own tokens. What am I assuming that's so wrong?"

The light switched to green, and he pressed the gas pedal. A smile formed as he turned his head so she could see him. "That their tokens were the only ones."

12

Clark Fallow, the NASA administrator, looked even older in the laboratory. He clasped his bony hands together as if deep in prayer. "Waylen Brooks. Imagine my surprise at seeing you on the camera feeds."

"Clark," he said. "What's going on here?"

Somboon stood with the elderly NASA executive, his arms crossed. They both wore expensive suits, and seemed amused to have company.

"Let's talk somewhere more comfortable," Clark said. "I'm not a young man."

They followed the duo through a hidden doorway, down a winding corridor, and into an oval office five stories below ground.

"Does this place double as a fallout shelter?" Darren asked.

"Good eye. We have enough supplies here to last ten people two decades," Somboon said.

The office was comfy, but the notion of being so far below the surface made Waylen sweat. All those tons of stone and dirt above them…

"Who's your friend?" Clark sat at the head of the table, and Darren approached to shake his hand.

"Darren Jones."

"Yes, the podcaster," Clark said. "We're fans."

Darren sat without comment.

"Okay, we're having a civilized conversation. Why is the administrator of NASA in remote upstate New York with a man on Leo Monroe's payroll?" Waylen asked.

"Somboon has always been part of our team," Clark advised them.

"What team?"

"Would it surprise you to learn there's an organization right here in the United States, determined to prevent alien invasions?"

"Not really," Darren said. "I've heard rumors of these groups for decades. The UAF, ALN, BER."

"Mostly created by ourselves." Clark laughed, and it sounded slightly wet, like he had an infection in his lungs. He used a handkerchief from his breast pocket and dabbed his lips. "Every now and then, we'd perpetuate a rumor with people in your field to keep eyes off of us."

Waylen thought about the three letters on the fence and the building. "The CME?"

"Another bogus company. We're the D.O.O.S. Department of Outer Space."

"Is it connected to NASA in any way?" Darren asked.

"No. The President chooses who he puts in charge of that administration, and he's aware I've been running the branch for years."

"How long?" Waylen watched him. He'd read Clark's file before interviewing him at Peter Gunn's funeral, and knew Clark was in his late seventies.

"Since the first Moon landing," he said.

Darren whistled low. "That's a long time. You weren't that old."

"Twenty-seven." Clark glanced at Somboon, and the

man rose, returning a minute later with four glasses and a whiskey decanter. He poured four servings and doled them out. Waylen didn't touch his, while Darren downed the contents without looking at it. Clark continued his story. "My biggest regret was that Kennedy never got to witness his dream come to fruition. He was such an advocate of the program."

"You met Kennedy?"

"You could say he was a mentor to me," Clark said. "The moment we entered the space race, certain people were confident we'd trigger a reaction from an outside race. Some thought that just exiting our atmosphere might notify a cosmic being. Others, in the church, said we would touch God. More pragmatic men, like Kennedy, believed in the science, and without proof of aliens, he didn't suspect we'd reach them on the Moon. I guess he was wrong."

"But we haven't encountered anyone, have we?" Waylen asked.

Clark and Somboon shared a glance that suggested otherwise. "Mr. Brooks, where are you coming from? How did you find us here?"

"That's a long story."

"We have time," Clark said, and coughed again. "Though some less than others."

Waylen took a sip of the liquor and spoke candidly. He filled them in on the events since he'd last seen Clark on Park Avenue: from the incident at the home rental with Martina, to being taken via helicopter to Monroe's facility, before they stormed the gates to arrest him. When he mentioned Monroe being free of his cell, and that he was holding Silas and Cody hostage, Clark's hand clutching his glass trembled.

Nathan Hystad

"I told Plemmons he was a bigger risk than he gave Monroe credit for," Somboon said.

Waylen recalled the matching Hex in this facility. "Why did you work with Monroe in the first place?"

"He built the best tech, and Planetae operated with the utmost discretion," Clark said. "Now we believe he's eager to sell his operation to the highest bidder."

"That's what this is all about?" Darren blurted. He poured himself a second drink and took it slower. "Money?"

"Whether we're dealing with aliens or war, it's always about money," Clark told him.

"So what is this place?" Waylen inquired.

"We've spent years preparing for something to happen, to no avail. Peter Gunn and Colin Swanson visited an alien world in 1972, but no one has come to Earth, as far as we're aware. Or the Moon. Whoever created the Delta is long gone." Clark smiled briefly, but it fell off. "We found the second Delta on the far side in 1984."

Darren choked on his drink and set the glass down. "What? You went to the dark side?"

"It was obvious something happened during those two hours. Peter and Colin were fairly composed about the entire endeavor, their story never wavering, but Fred Trell broke under scrutiny. While he never admitted to the tokens, he explained they'd found something, but didn't divulge the details. Colin told me the truth twelve years later."

"You weren't working for NASA," Waylen said. "How did you get a secretly manned mission to the Moon?"

"It went under the guise of a test for the *Challenger* shuttle launch."

"Who did you send?" Darren asked.

Shadows of the Earth

"Colin Swanson came with me," Clark said. "I spent ten years in the Air Force, while still with the D.O.O.S., and a man named Brett Davis was our pilot."

Waylen couldn't believe his ears. "You're saying you flew to the Moon on a classified mission, and found a second set of tokens?"

"That's precisely what I'm saying." Clark had a slightly smug expression, and rightfully so. That they'd pulled off such an arduous task was impressive.

"How do we get Silas and Cody? Monroe isn't kidding. He'll kill them. I have"—Waylen looked at the time, seeing they'd passed into the next day—"two days to bring him the Key, which I'm supposedly taking from here."

"There is no Key," Somboon said. "Not a physical one, anyway."

Darren finished his second drink. "What does that mean?"

"Only a person can guide the Delta to its destination. Colin may have had the ability. We've tried everything since, but it always fails."

"Colin Swanson was the Key?" Waylen didn't understand. "Is that why he got sick?"

"We believe so. At first, he couldn't stop seeing the echoes, and his vision filled with memories of the Shadow. By the end, he'd managed to control it, but his brain betrayed him," Clark said.

"And you haven't had a Key since he died, years ago?"

"That's correct."

"So where does it lead?" Darren asked.

Waylen leaned forward in anticipation. "It's not the Moon?"

"No, the second Delta doesn't go there."

"Planet D?"

"Is that what Monroe's lap dog, Belleville, calls it? How uninspired," Clark said.

"You knew Theodore was working for Leo?"

"We had our assumptions. Unfortunately, the Secretary of Defense didn't agree with us. Now we can act and throw them both into confinement. With both Deltas in our possession, we should be able to locate the third."

"The third?" Waylen asked.

Somboon made a triangle by touching his index and thumbs together. "A triangle has three sides. The Delta you've seen is one of three."

"What the hell…"

Silas woke with the sound of Cody's voice. He groggily opened his eyes, remembering they'd been talking late into the night, drinking. He tried to cop out, but couldn't once Cody suggested they might be their last beers ever.

Cody's laptop screen glowed against his pale skin. "Silas, over here."

"What'd you find?" Silas yawned and moved to the couch. He glanced at the corner of the monitor and saw it was two thirty in the morning. "You're still watching the cameras?"

"They didn't kill Corporal Tucker," he said.

"What?" Silas squinted as the footage played.

Cody paused the feed. "This was from earlier tonight." On the screen, Vera shoved a man, and he staggered. She spoke to him, but the words were too muffled to decipher. He was escorted into a room, and she locked the door from the outside. Vera talked in her radio, then strode away.

"Tucker's not dead. How does this help us?"

"We can free him. He's a soldier, and now a disgruntled one. Tucker will help get us out of here," Cody said.

Silas glanced at the empty six-pack, and wished they hadn't sat around moping over their impending deaths. He was a little tipsy, and extremely tired. "How are we supposed to do that?"

"Vera has the keys."

"So?" Silas went to the kitchen and poured some water, drinking it in three long gulps. He refilled the glass and returned to the living room.

"She's sleeping." Cody showed a feed of her going to the bunks. Vera must have been promoted when Monroe came back, because while the other soldiers slept on cots in an open room, she had her own space.

"You want to go knock on her door?" Silas asked.

"It can't be that difficult."

"You're acting like we have experience with this kind of thing. Waylen, maybe, but you and me? Not to mention, we can't even get into the main building. It'll be secured."

Cody grinned and retrieved something from his pants pocket. He held a keycard with the Planetae logo on it. "It won't be an issue."

"Where did you find that?"

"While the rest of you were busy trusting Theodore Belleville, I was preparing. Actually, I'd planned to steal the Delta and flee, but this'll have to do."

"What is it with you and stealing the Delta?" Silas asked.

"It doesn't belong in Monroe's hands," he said.

"But it's safe with *you*?"

"Better than being traded to another country's government, right?"

Silas watched Cody and shrugged. "Maybe."

"Let's go."

"Now?"

"It's the middle of the night." Cody switched the camera view, and Monroe was in his office, sleeping in a pull-down Murphy bed.

"What about Belleville?"

It switched to the Hex, where Leo sat on a chair, holding a token. A string of drool clung to his lower lip.

"That doesn't look good."

"No, it does not." Cody put the keycard into his sweatpants' pocket. He reached under the couch cushion and brandished a shiny chrome pistol.

"You never cease to amaze me, Cody."

"Glad I can keep you on your toes." Cody offered it to Silas. "You should take this."

Silas fought the urge to leave the gun and lock the suite doors, but Cody was right. If there wasn't a real Key, Waylen would fail, and he knew Monroe would kill them both and bury their bodies without a second thought. He dropped the magazine, confirmed it was full, and racked one into the chamber.

He doubted there was a better time than three in the morning, with the entire facility devoid of activity.

Silas used the bathroom, relieving himself, then washed his hands and face. He hurried to the next-door suite, changing into dark jeans and a black hoodie. It was the best option for staying invisible. Cody did the same, wearing a navy-blue sweatsuit. In the dim lighting, it appeared as close to black as it could.

Shadows of the Earth

Cody checked the cameras one more time, ensuring there had been no changes, and opened another program. "This will loop them for twenty minutes." He used his digital watch, tapping a button. "I've started a countdown."

Silas kept the gun in his grip, and they moved through the residence, past the communal space with the pool table, then into the foyer, before heading outside. It was almost September, and fall had come early. The wind blew in a cold front from over the ocean, chilling the grounds as they jogged to the exterior of the laboratory's building. Instead of trying the main entrance, Cody led Silas around to the side and stopped at a nondescript brown metal door. The keycard touched the box, and it unlocked. Cody hesitated, then grabbed the handle, tugging it open. Silas went in, suddenly worried they'd come face to face with Vera and the rest of her hired soldiers, but the hall was empty.

Only the emergency lights remained on, but they were strong enough to see by. Silas was grateful for the shroud of darkness on the edge of the corridor, and he clung there, with Cody following two paces behind. They passed by the offices they'd previously occupied, and he tried the first, finding his previous workstation had been dismantled. A few loose cords remained, and a single bolt from the desk's partition. Cody's was the same, but slightly messier. His chair sat in the middle of the empty office, the hydraulic lift lowered all the way.

They shared a dubious glance before continuing.

Silas wished they'd thought this through, because even if they accessed Vera's room, how could they steal the keys without waking her? He wasn't in the mood for getting into a gunfight with a trained opponent.

The hall curved, and Silas slowed around the bend, stopping completely to listen for sounds of anyone's approach. When there were no apparent noises, Silas walked again, and slowed as they neared the soldier's quarters. Behind the double doors, the space was filled with bunks and a large, shared washroom. He bypassed that and chose the smaller door, where Vera had entered over two hours earlier, according to the camera's time stamp.

He hoped Vera was the type to go to sleep at this hour. Silas was surprised they didn't have a patrol wandering the building. Instead, Belleville kept a guard at the gate, and another walking the perimeter. They clearly weren't worried about a coup, and Silas and Cody weren't a tangible threat with Waylen on another mission.

Cody slid the keycard into the slot, and it clicked. Silas grimaced at the sudden noise and tugged the handle. It was pitch-black inside, so Silas did his best to keep it that way. Cody motioned for him to stay, and he slipped into the quarters, blending into the darkness.

Vera was on the bed, a slight lump beneath her covers. The white pillow almost glowed with the minor amount of light leaking past the crack in the exit. Silas held his breath while Cody fumbled through the clothing folded on the chair.

Vera made a gurgling sound, smacked her lips, and turned to face Silas with her eyes closed. She scratched her nose and mumbled. Cody froze, her pants in his hands.

After they were sure Vera wasn't going to spring awake, Cody eventually located the keys. He clutched them tightly, the metal grinding on the ring. He moved slowly and deliberately until they'd left Vera's quarters.

"Can I help you?"

The voice startled Silas, and he swung the pistol to aim at Dr. Rita Singh.

"I'll shoot if I have to," he said.

"Put that thing away. We have work to do." Rita waved for them to follow, and Silas looked at Cody, who shrugged and chased after the doctor.

Silas, not sure he had any other choice, did the same.

13

The Moon was high, a beacon that wouldn't stop drawing Rory's gaze through the car's sunroof. They'd gone west as soon as they exited Boston, and Brett wasn't forthcoming about their final destination. They entered New York State a couple of hours after leaving, and now she thought they were heading south, but she couldn't be certain. Rory glanced at the dash, and the letter S near the odometer confirmed her suspicion.

"Where are we going?" she asked again, sensing he might have changed his mind.

"It'll be safe," he said.

"You killed my ex."

"He seemed like a lowlife."

"He was, but you ran him over, then shot him."

"I hate loose ends. Not to mention, he hit you and didn't look ready to stop until you... did whatever he came for."

Rory wanted to forget the expression on Kevin's face as he'd barreled into the hood. She recalled the streak of his blood. Were there cameras in the alley? Would someone watch the footage and come after them? She doubted it. By now, Kevin's body would have been found, and he was probably already at the morgue. Police might have the area cordoned off, detectives trying to figure out what had occurred.

"What were you saying about the tokens earlier?"

He'd warned her to keep quiet at the beginning of their road trip, but the hard edge around his eyes had eased with time in the miles between them and Boston. "I mentioned earlier that I knew your grandpa."

Rory tried to determine how old Brett was. He looked gruff, but in great shape. He was maybe early sixties, but could probably give men half his age a run for their money at a physical challenge. "How?"

"We had the same friends."

"Is that where we're going now? To see your friends?"

"Maybe."

"I loved him."

"Colin?"

She nodded. "He was so kind and caring."

"You wrote a book, didn't you?"

Rory watched Brett from the corner of her eye while staring at the empty road ahead. "Yes."

"He would have been thrilled with that." The tension was erased from his voice.

"I think so too."

"Are you seeing things?"

Rory stiffened.

"He did. Echoes… right? The rest of us tried, but we never saw much when we weren't in contact with the tokens. But Colin… he could picture the different worlds. He'd describe them to us, even before visiting them. He lived with the effects for most of his life, but it slowed after he abandoned the program."

"The program?" Rory asked.

"What the hell does it matter? You'll find out soon

enough. We were in the Department of Outer Space together." He laughed, and the skin around his eyes crinkled. "Sounds cheesy, but it's real."

"My grandpa was in this group?" Rory struggled to understand what Brett was revealing. "Did anyone know?"

"Probably his wife. She was an exceptional woman," Brett said. "I never married, but they always made me feel like part of the family. So did Clark."

"Clark?"

"Fallow."

"The NASA administrator?"

"Before that, he was our boss. Technically, he still is."

"What did you do in the Department of Outer Space?"

"Our aim was to protect the country from outside forces."

"UFOs?"

"Unfortunately, we never did encounter any. Lots of drones, weather balloons, and Russian fighter jets, but nothing resembling an actual alien craft," he admitted.

"You sound disappointed," she said.

"When you're working on something for forty years, you kind of want to know it's for a good reason."

Rory had been so caught up in the moment, she'd almost forgotten about her job. "I can't be here."

"In the car?"

"In New York, with you… I have a job starting Monday."

"We're just passing through this state."

"Like I said, I have to get to work."

"Teaching gig, right?"

"How long were you following me?"

Shadows of the Earth

"Not that long."

"Meaning?"

He laughed again. "Since you left Boston for Woodstock."

"Then why didn't you stop Jack?"

"I couldn't be there all the time. I kept tabs on you because I owed it to your grandpa."

Rory sighed. "You asked if I see things."

"Do you?" He lifted both eyebrows and glanced at her while staying in his lane. The headlights reflected off the yellow lines.

"Yes."

"When did it start?"

"Only since I went to the Moon. Actually, before that… after I held it at my grandparents' house."

"You don't remember," he said.

"Remember what?"

"You were seven."

Rory stared at him, shifting in her seat for a better view. "What are you talking about?"

"I came to the hospital."

Rory blinked her dry eyes and rubbed them. "I've never been to a hospital. Not as a patient."

"Yes, you have. Colin had already started becoming forgetful. You found it in his study, and they came across you unconscious with the token in your hand."

Rory imagined herself on the floor, like she'd been when Jack tore through the house searching for it. This time, she was small, wearing a yellow polka-dot dress, her hair done in the two braids Grandma always did when she visited. Grandpa Swanson's arms circled under her when the metal object fell to the area rug. The phone call to the ambulance. Her lungs aching, her fingertips feeling like they might fall off.

"I remember," she whispered. "Why has no one ever mentioned it again?"

"They labeled it an anaphylactic response to something you ate, and your lungs were monitored for two weeks. I brought you a stuffed tiger." Brett signaled and pulled into a gas station in the middle of nowhere. A couple of long-haul trucks sat parked near the diner, which had an *Open* sign lit up.

"I had that tiger for years."

He smiled at the news. "They were so scared for you, Rory. Clark hated that Peter refused to give up the tokens. He closed off all communication with NASA and the others, Colin included. We tried to work with Fred Trell at some point, but he stuck to his agreement, even if he never spoke to Peter. It didn't matter, because no one knew about the Delta we possessed, and we were content keeping it under wraps."

"What changed?"

"Monroe… he learned of the original tokens' existence."

"How?"

"It was Trell's loose lips. He told his lawyer, then Sanderson. Once Leo got a whiff of their existence, it was too late. He'd already helped us build three facilities, and of course, he duplicated the technology in his own secret base."

"That's where my friends are being held," she said.

"We'll get them out," Brett promised.

She thought about Kevin, and touched her cheek where he'd hit her.

He broke the lull of silence. "I'm sorry."

"For what?"

Shadows of the Earth

"Your ex."

She didn't respond.

"I'm not sorry he's dead, just that you were there to witness it."

"Let's leave it at that." Rory hugged herself, and Brett turned up the heat when he noticed.

"Take a load off. We have quite a drive ahead of us," he said.

Rory closed her eyes, the mist creeping into her peripheral. *Are you seeing things?*

Yes. Yes, I am.

"In here." Rita gestured to the second door on the right. A soldier lazily protected the makeshift cell holding Corporal Tucker. "Wait for me." She held a palm to Cody. "The key."

Cody looked trepidatious, but gave her the metal ring with a single key on it.

Dr. Rita strode off, and her entire posture changed. She clutched a clipboard and put her glasses to the bridge of her nose. She dangled the keychain in front of her. "I require the prisoner."

The soldier stood at attention and coughed once. "I've been given no such orders."

"Get out of my way. Monroe wants Tucker as a lab rat. Unless you'd like to volunteer?"

The soldier's gun rested on the wall, the barrel pointed to the ceiling. He still had a radio on him. Silas inched closer, staying on the dark side of the rounded corridor.

"No, ma'am." He moved, giving her access to the

room. Silas breathed a sigh of relief, then padded along, being as quiet as possible.

"Tucker, with me," she ordered. Silas couldn't see them until Rita escorted Tucker out the exit. He had a black eye, and his lip was swollen.

He met Silas' gaze from ten feet away, his mind processing what was happening.

Silas ran, shoving the soldier into the open door. His heart hammered in his chest as he whipped the gun up, aiming for the man's chest. He was on the ground, scooting to the cot. "Don't shoot."

"Give me the radio."

The soldier glanced at the device and slid it across the floor. Silas caught it with his shoe, then tossed it to Cody. "Don't make a sound, or we're coming back to finish the job." He closed the door, and twisted the key in the lock before pocketing it.

"Tucker, are you with us? We need to grab the Delta and leave," Silas said.

He winced and nodded. "Anything to make these bastards pay."

Cody handed him the soldier's assault rifle. "Take this."

They rushed into the laboratory, and Silas stopped Cody. "How much time for the cameras?"

He lifted his watch. "Four minutes."

"That's tight." Silas gestured to the Hex. "Find the Delta."

They arrived, and Rita entered the Hex first. Theodore Belleville was slumped on the platform, his chest no longer rising and falling. A notepad with scrawled-out times and descriptions was next to him. Rita checked his pulse and shook her head, and Silas carefully removed the

Shadows of the Earth

token from Theo's dead hand. Once all three were secure, it was time to go.

Tucker led the way, and Silas knew they'd have a gunfight to escape. He mentally prepared himself as they hurried into the late-night air. They were a hundred yards from the gate when Cody glanced at him. "Cameras are on."

Silas peered at the exterior of the building, then at the fence. A large four-wheeler was parked nearby, and Cody was already inside, moving through the cab. The engine started a moment later, and Tucker stayed where he was while the rest filed into the vehicle.

"Why are you leaving?" Silas asked Rita.

"It wasn't supposed to be like this. Leo was a visionary, not a monster. He's lost his mind."

"We have company," Cody said from the driver's seat. His headlights blared at the facility's entrance, and Vera rushed out in a tank top and shorts. It would have been funny if she wasn't carrying the biggest gun Silas had ever seen in person. More soldiers joined her, and she halted, facing the vehicle.

"Get out!" she shouted.

Cody didn't flinch, and neither did Silas. The trio of tokens were each wrapped, tucked into his pocket.

Time stood still while they decided on their course of action. Drive and be shot. Stay and… be shot.

Leo Monroe emerged, his dress shirt unbuttoned, his tie missing. He looked angry, but almost amused, at their attempted escape.

Silas had been fueled by adrenaline, but it started to dwindle. "We're not getting out of here."

Cody's hand landed on the gearshift. "I can make a run for it."

"Turn it off," Silas said. The moment he drove, they'd shoot the tires.

Cody did. "This is how it ends."

"I guess so," Silas muttered.

They climbed out, and Tucker came to stand with them, his posture defensive.

"I expected better from you." Monroe nodded, and Vera swung the gun up faster than anyone could react. Silas froze, sensing he was next. "Doctor, you are on thin ice." Vera didn't fire. Monroe stretched his hand toward Silas. "Give it to me."

He thought about Rory. Their limbs entangled on his bed in Loon Lake. The scent of the ocean when he was a kid in Cape Cod. The breeze in his hair at graduation day.

Silas reached for the bags, and a bright light enveloped him. The heavens opened, prepared to bring another lost soul into His comforting arms.

The whooshing of rotors drew his gaze. Soldiers dropped from ropes. Gunfire erupted while Silas dove behind the large vehicle, tackling Cody in the process. He stayed down, face pressed into the ground, hands shielding his head.

The helicopter landed, and Silas took in the scene. Half of Monroe's hired help were dead. The other half had dropped their weapons, arms raised in surrender. Vera's corpse lay sprawled out beside Monroe's shiny shoes.

"Leo Monroe, you're under arrest." Waylen had a pair of handcuffs. "Again."

Ridgewood, New Jersey

Shadows of the Earth
December 24th, 1972

Peter Gunn stared at the Christmas tree and listened to his children discussing Santa Claus.

"If Dad can fly to the Moon, Santa can deliver all the toys around the world," Arthur said with confidence.

Bunny stuck her tongue out at her brother. "You were bad, so you're getting coal."

Peter's gaze drifted to his wife, who worked tirelessly in the kitchen. The scent of fresh cookies wafted to his chair, and he rose, heading to the source. Patty was the most beautiful sight in the world.

"You seem tired," she said, pausing her cookie icing.

How could he tell her he'd not only been on the Moon, but that they'd traveled to another planet? Seen things he couldn't unsee? Peter hugged his wife, feeling her warmth. He was real. She was too. This wasn't a dream.

He closed his eyes and saw the field under the red skies.

Shadows. Hundreds of them. Misty black pits, each holding a mysterious destination. What had they come across?

"I love you, Patty." He kissed her on the forehead, then, making sure the kids were occupied, on the lips. She seemed shocked by the moment of passion, and melted into him, dropping the icing bag. It spilled on the cupboard, but she didn't clean it up right away.

"I love you too, Peter," she said breathlessly.

"Dad, tell Bunny that Santa's bringing me presents!" Arthur shouted from the other room.

"Bunny, stop picking on your brother. Or maybe Santa won't come at all!" Peter winked at Patty, and she gripped her icing, returning to her task.

He poured a drink and watched the Moon through the window. The lights of the tree reflected in the glass, and he didn't know what to focus on.

His family or his secret.

PART THREE
THE DEPARTMENT

1

The Planetae compound seemed far different in the daylight, under the protection of the military. They'd disposed of the bodies from the firefight, but the bloodstains soaked into the concrete near the building's entrance. Waylen was shocked that Leo Monroe had evaded prison and returned in the first place.

During the cleanup, they found Theodore Belleville's corpse in the Hex, and Clark Fallow ordered him to be brought elsewhere for testing. It reminded Waylen of his own mortality. He could have just as easily died from contact with the tokens, since they didn't fully understand the relics.

Waylen searched Leo's former office, where he'd once hidden within the bookshelf, and found nothing of use, but the Department's team would take a closer inspection.

Waylen sat on the swivel chair, rotating slowly. They almost killed Silas and Cody. "But they didn't," he assured himself, and straightened when a knock came to the door.

"Come in," he said, as if it was his office.

Jacob B. Plemmons, the Secretary of Defense, entered. His demeanor was somber, and Waylen assumed he was about to be reprimanded. Instead, the big man offered his hand. Waylen met him halfway in a shake. "Special Agent Brooks, I have to apologize for my lack of foresight."

Waylen had enough experience with situations like this to stay silent.

Plemmons paused for a heartbeat, but when Waylen didn't interject, he kept talking. "I met Leo Monroe when he was twenty-seven. I hadn't encountered a more brilliant man. He'd gone to the finest schools, and came from a reputable family. He was a fourth-generation entrepreneur, each generation growing wealthier than its predecessor. Leo was cocky, but his engineering skills were obvious. It's why I wasn't overly eager to throw him into prison."

They entered the hallway. "How did he get out?"

"Monroe has a lot of contacts. He was only in holding for a day before they swapped him for a duplicate. The doppelgänger acted violently ill, and he was quarantined on doctors' orders. No one wants an epidemic in the prison system." Plemmons' sigh deflated his chest. "Theodore was a government figure you always saw around but never questioned. I'd usually encounter him while visiting the White House. Hell, he was in the President's foursome at our annual charity golf tournament. I've been too trusting."

"What'll happen to Monroe now?" Waylen asked as they toured the length of the hall to the laboratory.

"He'll rot in a cell."

"Good."

"We're going to figure out what his plan was," Plemmons said.

Shadows of the Earth

"Can I be there?" Waylen asked.

Plemmons opened the door to the lab, and they watched as a group of Marines donned their spacesuits. "Let me think about it."

Waylen was a mess after the last month, and found himself conflicted about his future. Part of him wanted to return to the FBI and continue his career in Financial Crimes. Another part was too curious to end his business with the Delta. Then there was the mysterious Department of Outer Space. Perhaps that was his next great adventure.

"I'd like to witness this for myself," he told Dr. Rita Singh, who remained on-site despite her connection to Monroe. They'd kept her around after Silas and Cody's retelling of the previous night's events.

"Sir, I don't think we should—" a large man interjected, clutching his space helmet to his chest.

"Thank you, Lieutenant Colonel Banner, but if your team acts as escorts, there shouldn't be any issues, correct?"

Banner glanced at Waylen, then at his superior. "No, sir." He turned to the other three Marines and began barking orders.

"What do you say? Aren't you the least bit curious what Monroe was doing on the surface?" Plemmons asked.

Waylen thought about Martina, then Rory. Neither had answered their phone, and he was worried about their well-being. Monroe had ordered Assistant Director Ben killed, and that angered him more than anything else from the last few weeks.

He fought the urge to leave, and stared at the Hex, where Theodore's body had been found only hours earlier. Rita had a suit near her, and she motioned to it, inviting him to wear the space gear. Waylen knew something important existed on Planet D, but how could they travel to the other world?

He didn't answer Plemmons as he approached Rita and began dressing in the suit he'd worn previously.

Ten minutes later, they were in the Hex, their heavy boots clinking on the white polymer floor. Plemmons had the tokens, and he offered the set to Waylen. "Do the honors."

Waylen gaped at the flat, smooth pieces, and removed the trio from their vessels. With the gloves on, the echoes were unable to link to him directly, and seeing Theodore's corpse had been a lesson in caution.

He connected the first token to the second, and the metal wrapped as it formed part of the triangle. The third section combined with the others, and the Shadow poured from the center, filling the platform. Banner and his men looked poised, despite the situation, and Plemmons only exhibited the briefest of panic. When it finished, Waylen placed the Delta on the podium, not wanting to strand them on the Moon.

"*Are you ready?*" Banner's voice carried through Waylen's helmet's speakers.

"We're a go." Waylen proceeded after Banner's three soldiers and beheld the surface of the Moon.

Plemmons came next, his steps wary as he moved in low gravity. Banner's composure finally snapped when he emerged from the portal. The mist hovered in the hole, fragments vanishing as they extended beyond the portal. The foggy substance was constantly replaced by the black middle of the Shadow.

Waylen was so distracted by the Shadow itself, he'd

Shadows of the Earth

ignored the set up around him. Banner clung close to the Secretary of Defense, but his soldiers bounded through the makeshift mine, assessing any imminent threats. They searched crates, determining that the only explosive materials in the area were intended for mining operations. Waylen suppressed a grimace when he thought about Monroe transporting explosives to the surface.

"*Run an inventory,*" Plemmons said.

"You're not taking it back to the laboratory?" Waylen asked.

"*Progress above anything is the goal. Can you imagine the value to our GDP if we mined even a tenth of Monroe's projections?*"

Waylen bristled within his spacesuit. "So this is about money?"

"*Not only that, but the world runs on currency, Waylen. Having this resource means a change to our entire spacefaring futures. Picture a processing plant up here, building shuttles and rockets in orbit. Generation ships for exploration of neighboring star systems. It's within our grasp.*"

"Why do I get the sense it'll be used to make more war machines instead?" Waylen asked.

"*You don't have to like it, but the President has ordered us to take stock before we decide whether dismantling what they'd started is the best course of action,*" Plemmons said. Not much seemed to have been completed, past stacking hundreds of crates of gear on the Moon.

Waylen left him to it, walking off for some solitude. He eyed the area from the echoes. He'd lived in Peter Gunn's mind for a week, continuously replaying the memories lodged into the tokens. As he lumbered to the region, he felt Colin Swanson with him. When he peered over his right shoulder, no one was there.

Once he was a hundred feet from the soldiers, Waylen

gazed into the distance. The Earth was behind him, the Sun a brilliant white light millions of miles away. The landscape rose and fell with subtle hills, and he checked on Plemmons, then continued. He listened to chatter in his helmet, but none of the conversation seemed to be directed at him. There were no footprints, nothing to show that anybody, human or otherwise, had ever inhabited this part of the Moon.

This was being an explorer, venturing through unmapped territory, eager to discover something extraordinary for humanity? Waylen glanced at the group again, finding them much smaller as he put distance between himself and the soldiers.

He crested a smooth mound of gray rock and examined a small crater. Waylen descended the meager slope and lost sight of the camp near the Shadow. For a moment, he was the only person on the Moon. He stood at the edge of the universe, gazing at the bright clusters of stars with nothing to impede his view.

How could he return to Earth after this?

The weight of his own past threatened to drown him. A childhood he'd mostly chosen to forget. The brief relationships he'd allowed to creep past his defenses.

"*Brooks, where are you?*" Plemmons' voice was deep.

"I'm giving you space."

"*Well, don't. We're going back. Unless you intend to stay.*"

Waylen sighed and tore his gaze from the most beautiful sight he'd ever witnessed. His footsteps were lighter, and not just from the meager gravity.

The others came into view as he rounded the incline, and Waylen hurried, leaping as he jogged.

"*Everyone ready?*" Banner watched his troops, and they each gave the affirmative.

Shadows of the Earth

Before Waylen entered the Shadow, Plemmons took hold of his arm, keeping him planted on the Moon. "*Would you stay to investigate the Shadow with us?*"

Waylen was close enough to hear the words echo through his spacesuit and into the speaker. "No. I can't." He broke free from the Secretary's grip and strode into the Shadow, returning to the Hex in the Planetae laboratory. He removed his helmet, exited the platform, and ditched the suit while the soldiers discussed their mission amongst one another.

"*Waylen, we're not finished with this conversation!*" Plemmons called, but Waylen was done with these people. They were too reckless, allowing innocent victims to be killed. All for what? Profit? It made him sick.

He ignored Plemmons' beckoning and walked through the front doors. Cody and Silas were outside, duffel bags at their feet. "You waited," Waylen said.

"We figured you'd come around." Silas patted him on the back. "Thought you could use a ride."

Waylen lifted a finger. "There's just one thing I have to do."

Silas tossed the bags in the truck's box and jumped into the driver's seat, while Cody trudged behind him, leaving the passenger side free.

Waylen dialed a number on his cell phone, aware of the slim chance she'd be in the office on a Saturday morning.

"*Hello?*"

"It's me."

There was a slight pause. "*I was wondering when you'd call.*"

"Charlotte, I want to give this a shot."

223

2

Rory saw the signs for Louisville exits on the side of the road. "Can you tell me where we're going yet?"

"We have offices all over. One of them is in Louisville."

Rory checked her phone, finding the service was still out. "Why doesn't this work?" She lifted the cell. It reminded her of the technology Silas must have been surrounded by in New York.

"Look, we're the good guys, but you're important, Rory. You can't share your location. Haven't you learned this by now?"

Rory wondered if she'd made yet another poor decision. Whoever Brett was, he might not be an ally like she'd originally thought. He sure seemed to have the right answers; plus there was his story about her and the token when she was a kid, then the tiger stuffed animal... He'd been present. She was certain of it.

Rory wished she could talk to her grandpa, to ask him whether she should trust the man that claimed to be a friend, but didn't have the luxury. He was dead, and there was no changing that.

"I'm hungry."

Brett nodded and signaled, switching lanes. "We'll

pick up food on the way. My favorite pizza joint is only a few blocks from the site. Unless you have another preference."

"Pizza's fine," she said.

They bypassed most of the city and wound to the southwest corner. It was a blend of neighborhoods and industrial parks, complete with a shopping center and the aforementioned pizza place.

"I have to use the bathroom," she said.

He stretched his hand out. "Phone."

Rory considered darting from the car, but guessed that Brett would easily catch her, even if he was two decades older. She conceded, curious what this Department of Outer Space was doing with an office in Louisville, Kentucky. They entered together, and a young teenage couple glanced at them, quickly resuming their conversation. The girl sipped cola from a straw, and the boy shoved another piece of pepperoni pizza into his mouth.

She used the bathroom and assured herself this was going to be fine. They'd talk, and she'd reject whatever kind of offer the organization expressed, then return to Boston to teach her first lesson as a guest lecturer on Monday.

Before leaving, she checked the windows, finding them too small to squeeze out of. The edges were covered in old, cracked paint, and the entire room had a mildewy odor. With a plan in place, she relaxed and washed up, finding Brett at the order counter when she emerged.

Rory asked for vegetarian after seeing how deep the slices were, and Brett scoffed, choosing something layered with meat. They waited around, talking idly about Colin's youth, until it was ready. He passed the warm boxes to her in the car.

"You have a lot of stories about Grandpa," she said.

"He was a character."

"Do you miss him?"

"We all do. Clark, especially," Brett said. "You'll meet him soon."

The roads were clear, lacking traffic on a Saturday afternoon.

"Clark's the NASA administrator, right?"

"That's him. And yes, we've been on the same team for decades."

That eased Rory's worry even more. He was an old man, around the age Colin had been when he died.

The region was covered in green fields and large swaying trees. The sky was crystal blue, without a cloud in sight, and she felt the heat through the window, not just from the pizza boxes on her lap. Rory noticed a traffic camera on a set of lights, and they continued for a minute, turned right, and went down a secondary road, eventually drawing into a warehouse parking lot. The letters *CME* were the only indicator of who owned the building. "What does it mean?"

"Nothing. It's a shell corp, something we funnel government funding with. You can't have numerous structures throughout the country without labels, or people ask questions."

"Did Leo Monroe build this?" she asked.

"Nope. Leo helped manufacture three D.O.O.S. bases, but that's as far as our trust went. Some things need to be kept confidential," he said.

Brett pushed a button on what looked to be a garage opener clipped to the visor, and the bay door slid high. He pulled into the building and closed up behind them. For a second, the space remained dark, only illuminated

Shadows of the Earth

by the sedan's daylights. Brett used his phone, and the warehouse filled with a comfortable glow.

"Welcome to the Department of Outer Space," Brett said.

Rory glanced at her cell sitting in the car, and left it, assuming she'd have the same issues here.

"How about we eat, then I can show you the project," he said.

"Project?" Rory followed him across the smooth sealed concrete floor and into a lunchroom. It was about as basic as it could be. The appliances were white, the microwave clean, the counters laminate. Nothing looked new, nor well worn.

Brett flipped his pizza box lid and inhaled deeply. "You'll see what I mean in a few minutes." He checked a cupboard, finding a couple of plates. "Be honest about the food. I swear it's half the reason Clark chose this location in Kentucky."

Rory shoved aside her frustrations and anxiety, knowing she needed energy more than anything, and she ate. The first bite sent her to heaven. "This is delicious." She wasn't one to speak with her mouth full, but it was that good.

Brett chewed and didn't comment.

Rory finished the piece and hastened to a second. They each had three before slowing. She'd only pecked on some appetizers at the bar the night before, and the need for personal grooming was becoming apparent. "Is there a shower here? Toiletries?"

"Of course," he said. "We had a lot of late nights back in the day."

"Did Colin ever visit here?" Rory asked, receiving a nod.

"Many times. Until he said he had to stop using the Delta," Brett told her.

"Why?"

Brett set the crust down and tapped his temple. "It took a toll."

"I get that." Rory hadn't seen the Shadow or any effects of the echoes since the bar, and she was grateful. "Will that happen to me?"

"Colin spent weeks with the Shadow," he admitted. "We'll take better precautions."

Rory understood what Brett wanted, at least on a surface level, but wouldn't deny him until she learned more about the project. She almost ate one last piece, but decided against it in favor of cleaning up.

Brett walked her to a set of stairs that led to a partition on the building's top floor, which was four stories high. "There's a bathroom at the end of the hall, and sweats in the laundry room. Nothing fancy, just old stuff with the lettering *CME* on the chest. You can toss them in the dryer before you shower." Brett left her without another word. The door closer hissed shut, latching the push handle, and Rory leaned on the wall, wondering if there was a landline or something to contact Silas with.

What had happened to them in New York? Was he safe?

Rory found the piles of matching sweatsuits, and set a medium against herself, judging it a suitable fit. She tossed it into one of two dryers in the bathroom, and threw in a crisp laundry sheet before throwing it on a tumble setting.

There weren't any locks, but she didn't think Brett was a concern on that front. She still stripped with a musty towel wrapped around her, and only took it off when she

Shadows of the Earth

was in the stall. Cold water splashed her toes, and it was a solid three minutes before steam began rising from the flow. Rory stepped under the nozzle, washing off a long night and a day of travel.

She hurriedly put on the sweatsuit so she could have a few extra minutes to look around without suspicion. Rory checked the first room, which had two sets of bunk beds. The bare mattresses sat on plain metal bed frames. No phones.

Once she scoured the entire floor and was confident there was no means to contact Silas, she returned to the stairwell. Rory stopped near the top step, hearing a voice. Her gaze lingered on a duct vent, and she walked closer, pressing an ear to the dusty surface.

"...*Delta... Yes. I'll show her now. Clark, she's a good sport, and I believe... Okay, will do. Goodbye.*"

The door at the bottom of the stairs opened, and Rory jumped at the noise. She wore over-sized slides she'd found over old socks, and made enough sound that Brett wouldn't think she'd been skulking around.

"Better?" Brett asked when she arrived.

"Much." Her hair was still wet, and she shivered. "Can we check this out?"

"Sure." Brett led her past an office and into the warehouse where they'd originally parked. He settled onto a forklift and powered it on. The backup bells sounded as he moved the unit, and he turned it off with the twist of a key that stayed in the ignition. He crouched, sliding an empty wooden pallet to the side, revealing a gray hatch. He opened the edge of a lock and touched the surface with his thumb. It scanned the print, and unlocked.

"That's high tech," she said.

"Can't be too cautious." The muscles under Brett's t-shirt bulged as he hefted the weight, letting it fall with a bang. Rory doubted she could have lifted it if she tried, judging by the effort he'd exuded.

"After you," he said, gesturing to the metal rungs.

Rory gazed into the dark hole, having second thoughts. "I should…"

Brett nodded in understanding and entered first, making quick work of the ten steps. A moment later, a bank of lights turned on below, transforming the space under them to something far less frightening. It looked decades newer, with shiny black tiles and computer screens in the walls. Rory hurried down, careful her feet didn't slip, and landed with grace at the bottom.

"What is this?"

"Welcome to the D.O.O.S., Rory Swanson. This is your destiny," he told her, grinning. "He'd have been proud to see you here."

Rory glanced around as the cramped foyer expanded into a much larger space. The room continued farther, with another set of stairs heading to the middle. More lights activated with their movement, and Rory spied a strange contraption along the far edge. "What's that?"

"It's what we were working on before Colin could no longer assist us," he said. "Come, I'll show you."

Rory was in an almost dreamlike state as they descended into the Department's underground lab. She tried to picture her grandfather with Brett, both of them younger, like they had been when she was a little girl.

Rory squinted and saw Colin ahead. He turned to a misty Brett, talking as the shadowy figures walked toward the end of the room. Fog swirled around them, and eventually, they disappeared.

"Did you see that?" Rory croaked.

Shadows of the Earth

Brett strode through the apparition and shook his head. "See what?"

"Nothing." Rory hugged herself, wondering what it was about this place that gave her a vision so soon after entering. Would she lose her mind like Colin? What did they need from her?

The apparatus was ten feet high, with a cylinder on either side. It was dark gray, with no visible windows. The middle was flat, and Rory didn't recognize the door frame until they were standing directly in front of it. Brett pushed on a corner, and it clicked, the thin slab swinging wide to reveal the contents. To her surprise, there was nothing but a single chair facing a black wall within.

"What's this?" Rory touched the back of the chair.

"This is how we find the third Delta."

Rory's knees grew weak. "Third?"

Brett walked to the corner, on the interior of the left cylinder, and scanned his thumbprint again. A hatch opened, and he removed three sheets. Brett didn't even wear gloves as he held a token. The only inkling he'd touched the alien device was a slight wince in his eyes. "We have the second Delta, and I'm told they've recovered the first set in New York."

"Silas is all right?"

Brett nodded, and the tension literally lifted from her chest. She sat in the chair, her legs lacking the energy to stand. Rory rested her face in her hands and ran them down her cheeks. "Thank God."

He took the second token, letting it wrap around the first.

"Why are you able to touch them?"

"Because I've handled them thousands of times," he said.

Nathan Hystad

She reached for the third, which hadn't connected to the others. "May I?"

"It's a bit of a shock. Not like the ones you've already explored."

"I can manage," she said, hopeful that was the truth.

Brett hesitated, then offered it. "I'll take it away when it becomes too much. Just remember, you're not really there."

Rory inhaled and accepted the token, noticing the color was slightly lighter than the other version they'd had in Loon Lake. The moment her skin made contact, her life changed forever.

Rory wasn't on the Moon, or the red-skied planet. No. She was somewhere else.

She saw a Shadow, and to the right of it, a domed projection. A holographic representation of a solar system. Rory struggled to breathe, and reminded herself this was only an echo, not reality.

The image zoomed, the detailed dome focusing on a planet. A single moon orbited the world, and Rory recognized Africa, then the Middle East.

It was Earth.

Rory gasped when Brett plucked the token from her grip, and panted while regaining a rhythm in her lungs.

"You saw it?"

"Who are they?" she asked.

"I don't know, but we were close before Colin abandoned the program."

"What am I supposed to do?"

"Finish what he started, Rory. Find the third Delta so we can seal them shut forever."

3

*H*e drove the rental over the speed limit, not caring if he was given a ticket. With nowhere else to go besides home, Cody had agreed to join Silas on a road trip to check on Rory. She'd been unresponsive, and that worried Silas tremendously. Waylen had returned to D.C., and Silas wondered if their time with the special agent was at an end.

"Why can it never be easy? I should be able to pick up the phone and text Rory. *Hey, how's the book coming?* And she'd respond, *Kinda slow.* Then I'd say... *Good, better than being chased by murderers and running from aliens*, and we'd laugh."

Cody grunted from the passenger seat, mowing down a bag of chips. He spilled crumbs continuously, and Silas was glad it wasn't his car; otherwise, he'd have tossed the chips and his friend onto the street by now. "She's probably hanging with her parents or something."

"Without her cell?"

"You know how these author types are. Plus, Rory didn't come across as someone caught up with social media," Cody said.

"Perhaps you're right," Silas conceded. Since they were already a few hours out of Manhattan, the GPS displayed another thirty minutes until they'd reach the university. "Try her again."

Cody dusted his fingers off on his jeans before using his phone. He held it up, and ended the call when Rory's voicemail was triggered. "No dice."

Silas was still in shock that they'd survived the night. Leo Monroe had been apprehended, Theodore was dead, and the two of them were alive. Waylen refused to accept any position with this clandestine government agency, and Silas couldn't blame him. Let the military take over. If aliens came through a portal, leave it to someone like Plemmons to greet them, not Silas.

Cody fidgeted in the seat, rolling his window down slightly. The cabin was filled by an unsettling pressure until Silas tapped the rear glass open to balance it out. "You heard what Waylen said earlier?"

"Sure." Silas didn't know which part Cody meant, but assumed that if he didn't engage, the other guy would keep talking.

"Another Delta? That's insane. They returned to the Moon and couldn't tell a soul. How is that possible?"

"Makes you wonder what else the government is hiding, doesn't it?" Silas asked, intending to goad Cody on for amusement.

"Don't get me started," Cody said, rolling his eyes. "I spent the last ten years trying to secure the Delta after Fred blabbed about the blasted thing, and now I wish I'd never touched it."

"What are you going to do?"

"Head home, I suppose. To be honest, I kind of miss the ocean."

"We're not that far," Silas pointed to the east.

"The Pacific…" Cody smiled. "It's a much more hospitable beast."

It was nearly four in the afternoon, and Silas wondered if Waylen had made it to D.C. yet. He'd taken another Planetae truck with him, saying he'd ditch it at the FBI headquarters. Silas almost told Cody to check, but didn't want to interrupt Waylen.

He slowed in traffic and wound toward the school. "Where is she living?" Cody asked.

"I don't know." Silas stared at the grounds, which brought him back to his own days in college. Classes wouldn't have started yet, not until Monday, but he noticed a lot of students in the area. Many would stay off campus with their parents, or in rented apartments, but there were a lot of dorms in schools like this.

He searched for a faculty office, and when he didn't find one, he stopped at the sidewalk. After rolling his window down, he asked a couple of guys carrying a six-pack and fast food. They directed him, and Silas turned around, parking a short distance away. He used a credit card to pay for parking, and Cody groaned. "These prices are extortion. No wonder the debt load is so—"

"Can you keep your opinions to yourself?"

Cody locked the car when they'd both exited and found the office. He heard a man's voice and saw him talking on the phone. Silas knocked, and the guy lifted a finger, ended the call, and walked to the door.

"Yes?" he asked through the glass. The OPEN sign was dark, the lights off.

"We're looking for Rory Swanson!" Silas spoke loudly.

The guy smiled and undid the latch. "Sure, I know Rory." He offered his hand. "I'm Garnet."

"Like the jewel?"

"My mom was into that stuff. It was the Seventies."

He shrugged.

"Rory…?"

"She's living in the faculty dorms. I saw her last night, but I think she had too much to drink. Poor thing spilled a cocktail and left. She's probably sleeping off a nasty one."

"Can you point us in the right direction?"

"I'll do better. Allow me to show you." Garnet grabbed a scarf from a coat hanger and draped it behind his head, even though it was sixty degrees out. He twisted a key, closing up shop, and jogged ahead, his loafers quiet on the cobblestone sidewalk. Cody hung back, moving slower as he gazed around.

Silas made small talk out of habit. "You teach here?"

"Yes. I should upgrade to a professor by next year, if they approve it. Then I can stop living in these cramped quarters and buy a real condo. Though I enjoy the price"—Garnet put a hand beside his mouth, leaning closer—"which is free. And I love the proximity to my classes, especially for those mornings after downing a few too many glasses of wine while grading mediocre English lit papers. Then I'll get my own aide to torment and let do the heavy lifting. Finally… tenure… life is coming together." They approached a brick building, which wasn't uncommon, since almost all of them were covered in a similar red brick, and he gestured to the entrance. "How do you know Rory?"

"We're old friends."

Garnet led them in and pointed at a room down the hall while his phone rang. "She's in number eleven." He answered it, heading into his own suite. "I'm glad you called, Sharon." The door closed, and Silas waited for Cody to catch up before rushing to Rory's unit. He knocked, and it swung slightly inward. "Rory?" The entrance wasn't latched, so he pushed it with a finger. The hinges squeaked in protest, and Silas stood face to face with the barrel of a handgun.

"You're really back?" Charlotte seemed shocked by the revelation.

"I am." Waylen sat on her couch, glad Charlotte had accepted his call, and that she'd gone as far as inviting him over. "I should book a hotel before they're all sold out."

"Nonsense. You're already here, and it'll be dark soon," she said.

Waylen didn't remind her that wouldn't happen for two hours or so. "I appreciate it." His tie was under his jacket, draped on a kitchen chair, and Charlotte eyed it. Saying nothing, he walked to the closet and grabbed a hanger to stow it away. "Sorry, I'm used to living alone. Jackets are everywhere. And the ties, forget about it."

She laughed and melted into the oversized seat across from him. "I wasn't expecting to hear from you."

"But …"

"Waylen, you broke my heart. What are you really doing in D.C.?"

"Come Monday, I'm calling my real estate agent and putting my home in Atlanta on the market. I have a meeting at Hoover tomorrow with Ben's replacement, and I'm going to ask for a position in town. No more road trips, unless absolutely necessary."

Charlotte followed, absently playing with the hem of

her shirt. "And what... about us?"

Waylen needed sleep. A week's worth, but being in proximity to his ex did something to him. He felt rejuvenated again. "That's up to you. I'm here for the duration, if you're willing to try."

She had a pair of black tights on, and her hair was clipped up lightly. Judging by the lawnmower in the front yard, and the garden hose still loose on the hanger, she'd been doing Saturday afternoon chores. As he sat there, watching Charlotte, he thought that might be the life he'd been missing. She appraised him with wide eyes. "What about the case?"

"It's done," he said.

"For real?"

Waylen knew he paused too long, but couldn't help it. "Yes." After everything, Waylen wouldn't be involved with the scandalous 'Department', not with a clean conscience. He'd been manipulated by various government agents, and was finished with it. He was meant to work at the FBI, not with secret alien devices. They were Jacob B. Plemmons' problem now.

His phone beeped, and Waylen looked down.

"You can check it," Charlotte said, peering at the screen.

He saw Darren's name and shook his head. "Nope. It's behind me." Darren Jones had elected to stay and accept a role with the organization. Good for him. Waylen thought Darren was better suited to the project than himself.

Charlotte rose and walked to him, taking his hand. "I have to jump in the shower."

"I can wait."

She wrinkled her nose. "You could probably use one

Shadows of the Earth

too."

Waylen made eye contact, gauging her meaning. "You want me to…" He got up, and when she wandered down the hall, he took the hint.

A while later, they were in her primary bedroom, staring at the ceiling with the comforter tossed onto the floor. Charlotte's palm rested on his chest, and Waylen couldn't decide if he'd ever been so content.

"We can stay in tonight and order from that Vietnamese place you love," she suggested.

"That would be perfect." Waylen didn't have a meeting with the Bureau until the morning, and for one night, he'd forget everything.

The laboratory was silent as Darren Jones entered. The only sound came from the heavy door latching behind him, then his dress shoes as he traversed the distance toward the Hex. Waylen had left him there at Darren's request. While the FBI agent didn't seem eager to hang around and learn more about the Delta, Darren had the urge to stay as close to the tokens as possible.

He'd spent as many hours with the alien artifacts as he'd been permitted under Theodore Belleville's command, more than Waylen had been aware of. Darren wasn't certain why he'd originally asked Theo to let him into the Hex with the tokens late at night, but he'd allowed it.

He stepped onto the platform and sealed the Hex. Darren unfolded a chair and stared at the trio of tokens. Waylen's tape remained on them, distinguishing the ech-

Nathan Hystad

oes from one another. Darren could now stay in contact for thirty minutes, no longer feeling the sickening sensations. The last time, he'd almost reached the end of Swanson and Gunn's journey.

The trio of flat metal pieces reflected the dim lights dully, and Darren inspected the closest to him. This would show him the Moon. Instead, he opted for the last, wishing to see Planet D again. He'd detected a way to skip past the early stages of the echo, and that had proven invaluable.

Darren slipped the token from its clear cover and took a seat, resting the object on his thigh. No one had granted him permission to be in the Hex, but they hadn't warned him away either. He touched it, and his vision swayed as he became Peter Gunn. After a moment of vertigo, Darren recalled the last scene he'd witnessed, and the echo sped up, dragging him through the hike on the alien world at a speed four times as fast.

Around ten minutes into the experience, Darren didn't recognize the scene surrounding him. He'd caught up to his previous visions.

His brain ached, and his sight grew heavy, laden with a red tinge. Darren moved his chin to the side and realized he was in control. He lifted his arm, and it was his that appeared, not Peter Gunn's spacesuit. "Hello?" He heard his own voice in the echo, which he knew to be impossible.

Ahead, he noticed a field of Shadows. Darren stepped closer and walked through the misty forms of Gunn and Swanson. Their silhouettes wavered with the progress, but didn't return to solid.

Once he began to hike, he couldn't stop himself. The Shadows grew nearer, and he struggled to count how

Shadows of the Earth

many filled the region. Hundreds. Maybe thousands.

Darren froze when something emerged from the center of one, about two hundred yards away. They both stopped and faced each other.

A voice pressed into his mind, and the being beckoned him.

Darren Jones had no choice but to accommodate the alien's wishes.

4

"You..." Silas stayed where he was, blocking Cody from the gun's line of sight.

"Get in," Special Agent Martina Sanchez blurted, grabbing Silas by the collar. "And close the door."

He entered; then Cody hastily obeyed.

"What are you doing in Rory's room?" Cody demanded. "Where is she?"

"I was hoping you'd know," she said. "I got here earlier today, but no one's seen her. Rory's cell phone is dark, no trace at all."

"When?"

"Around eleven last night." Martina looked exhausted. She had bags under her eyes, and her lids hung heavy.

Silas did the math. "She's been missing for eighteen hours."

Cody loitered at the fridge, peering at the precious few items Rory had inside.

"Do you mind?"

"There could be a clue," he muttered.

"What are you doing here?" Silas asked Martina.

"I checked everywhere today and decided to wait for her. She joined a faculty members mixer, so at first, I assumed she hooked up with some middle-aged professor

Shadows of the Earth

and turned her phone off. But then I spoke to a few people at the event, and they claimed she seemed distracted. Maybe drunk, but no one admitted she over-drank."

Silas thought about the fact that an FBI agent was skulking through campus, asking after her two days before her teaching debut. "You're not making this easy on her. Now they're all going to think Rory's tied up in a big FBI case."

"I told them I'm her cousin from out of town, trying to surprise her."

"You don't look related," Cody said.

Martina shot him a glare and holstered her gun.

"Lugging that piece around probably didn't help," Cody added.

She motioned to Cody. "Would you get him to mind his business?"

"You think I control him?" Silas laughed. "Good luck."

"Hey, I'm right here." Cody closed the fridge, holding a pudding cup.

"What did you find?" Silas asked.

"Nothing. She vanished." Martina went to the window, sliding the thick red drape wide. "Rory Swanson isn't on campus."

"Is the bar close?"

"Not too far."

"I have to see it. Let's retrace her steps."

"I already tried that."

He moved to the exit. "I don't care. Show us."

Cody gestured at her gun. "You might want to practice some discretion."

They left her room and, without the key, kept it unlocked. The three of them walked past the neighbor's door, and Silas was glad Garnet didn't show his face.

The sun was beginning its descent into the west, and would eventually be swallowed by the horizon. They headed in the opposite direction, the waning rays only visible through its reflection off the endless windows from the student dorm complex.

A security guard patrolled the sidewalks and stopped them in their tracks. "Are you students?"

"Is it a crime to exist?" Cody asked.

He was an older man, probably a retired police officer, and snapping at him wouldn't get them anywhere.

"Sorry about him. He's just hangry." Silas smiled. "We're visiting one of the new guest lecturers, Rory Swanson."

"Rory… I like her. She came to see me this week. Something about her ex harassing her. You three know him?"

"Kevin," Silas murmured.

"That's the one. I'm on the lookout for him, so tell Rory she's in good hands. Have a pleasant night." He continued on his previous route.

"Damn it," Martina said. "I assumed it was related to the Delta, and it may have been her abusive ex-boyfriend." She grabbed her phone and wandered off.

A few minutes later, they stared at the bar. McLaren's was packed, and a group of students, seemingly too young for drinks, entered.

"Rory acted out of character when she was here. Maybe she had another vision of the Shadow," Silas said, assessing her potential path.

"Or Kevin showed up," Cody told him.

They spent the next ten minutes scouring alleys between the bar and Rory's place, probing for a clue. It grew

Shadows of the Earth

more difficult as the light lessened, and dusk cast its hazy glow over campus. Streetlights popped on, and the pathways grew darker. Cody gestured past Silas, toward a lidless garbage can, and he noticed an object inside. It was a knife. He picked it up. "This is a cheap piece, not something the nearby Chinese restaurant would use."

Martina's phone rang. "I see. Winchester and… yep, got it. Thanks, Hal. I owe you."

"Anything?" Silas asked.

"Kevin's cell led him here. At the exact time we think Rory vanished."

"Here?" Silas pointed at the alley.

"Yes." She crouched beside the knife. "If I didn't know any better, this was a crime scene. And someone tried to cover it up."

Silas spun in a slow circle, searching for a camera. A balcony overlooked the entire back street, and a red light flashed every few seconds. It was directly above the restaurant. "Come on."

Bells chimed as they entered the establishment, and Cody snatched a menu. "We may as well grab a bite."

Silas couldn't decline, and they ordered while waiting for the server to get the owner. A woman emerged from the back, wiping her palms on a worn apron. "Yes?"

The place was fairly quiet, with only two tables occupied. "Can we talk somewhere private?" Martina asked.

"Sure." She waved them into the kitchen, where steam rose from frying veggies on a hot grill. "What is this about?"

"Do you live upstairs?" Martina asked.

"Yes." The proprietor nodded.

"And there's a camera?"

"We had a break-in, and the insurance didn't cover it.

I won't be taken advantage of."

"I need to see the footage."

She crossed her arms defensively. "Why? Who are you?"

Martina retrieved the credentials and flipped the small book open, showing her picture and title. "FBI, ma'am, and I believe a crime happened last night near your premises."

They were ushered upstairs. The walls had been lined with cases of sauces, and they went into the living room, where a cluttered desk held an old tower computer. The owner booted the monitor on, entered a password, and brought up a program. The fan whirred angrily behind the boxy tower, but it worked. "What time?"

"Can we start at ten thirty?" Martina sat, taking control of the mouse.

Silas held his breath and viewed the footage, playing it at 10X while waiting for someone to appear. A minute later, Rory surfaced. "That's her!"

Martina shot him a glance, and he kept quiet.

The scene illuminated, like a floodlight was shining on Rory, and she turned when a man entered the camera's scope.

"Kevin," Silas hissed. He'd seen photos of the bastard on Rory's old social media.

They were in conversation, but the recording had no audio. He wished he could hear what was being said. Silas flinched when Kevin struck her, and he had an awful feeling in the pit of his stomach. He clutched her arm, and Rory broke free as the scene brightened. Kevin stood there while a car pummeled into him. Silas froze, watching the injured man slide to the concrete. A guy exited the vehicle, peering around as he pulled a gun from his breast.

Shadows of the Earth

He shot Kevin twice and ordered Rory into the car. She seemed terrified, but she got in. They drove off.

"That happened last night?" the woman asked.

"Yes."

"Where were the police?"

Martina fast-forwarded again, until a pair arrived thirty minutes later in a white van. They wrapped Kevin in a black blanket and hauled him into the rear doors, then applied something from a commercial sprayer onto the area his corpse had settled. The van left as fast as it had arrived.

"What the hell was that?" Cody breathed finally.

"We're going to find out." Martina had the original film on screen and zoomed to the best shot they had of the fleeing car. Most of the license plate was visible, which, given the angle of the camera, was a miracle. "I'll send this to the office and have it cleaned up." She looked at the owner of the apartment while she removed a small thumb drive from her pocket. "Is it okay if I take this footage?"

"Yes. I'm not in any trouble, am I?" she asked timidly.

"Not at all. You've done us a great service." Martina led them downstairs, where their meals were placed at a table near the door.

"We should eat," Cody told them.

"He's right." Silas sat. "We don't have any leads until your contact…"

Martina's cell beeped, and she smiled. "Got him. I'm putting out a tracer. If this guy is still driving that car, we'll find out where they went." She took a seat, removing her chopsticks from the paper, and rubbed them together before picking up a piece of beef.

"Why are you so adamant about finding Rory?"

Nathan Hystad

"I haven't been completely honest about my motives," she said.

Silas didn't know much about Waylen's partner, only that she'd betrayed them while trying to gather the tokens.

"You think I screwed Waylen over for Leo, but the truth is…" Martina set the ends of the chopsticks on her plate. "I work for an organization called the Department of Outer Space, and they might believe Rory's some Key. They'll stop at nothing to use her until they break her mind. Now that the Shadows have been activated, they'll want to find the third Delta. Since Colin died, and the tokens were in hiding, they stayed buried. They're getting older now, and with Monroe and Gunn out of the way, Fallow will finally fight to possess the Deltas."

Silas couldn't even process the words, and his food sat untouched. Cody shoveled his meal while listening. "Wait, the Department of what?"

Martina took a long drink from her glass of water and dabbed her lips with a napkin. "Let me tell you a story."

Silas rested his elbows on the table, eager to hear the tale from the woman sitting across from him.

"You two have spent the last few weeks believing there's only one Delta. They found it on the Moon in 1972. My boss, Clark Fallow, Brett Davis, and Colin Swanson went to the Moon in 1984 and attained the second Delta."

Silas' cheek twitched. "What?"

Even Cody stopped eating.

"Colin had this ability to read the tokens. He became obsessed, constantly struggling to figure out what information they held. There were echoes already in the three pieces, but not their own experiences, like you've witnessed within the alien device. Colin determined the location of another Delta, and they were trusting enough in his story to fly a manned excursion to the Moon, without telling a soul."

"How is that possible?" Cody asked.

"It was a different time. Things were much easier to hide in the Eighties than they would be now. An era before cell phones and private security cameras."

"What happened?" Silas tapped the table, wanting answers.

"They found a second set of tokens, complete with an active Delta."

"Did they… go in?"

Martina glowered, her gaze falling to her dish. "They never told me."

"How did you get mixed up with the Department?"

"My father worked for them until 1999, when he died," Martina said.

"On the job?"

"No, a heart attack at home. I grew up around the guys, including Colin Swanson. I heard stories about the Moon my entire life, and when I graduated from college, they recruited me into the fold, and I learned there was more to it. I've seen the second Delta in action, but I've never been allowed to enter the Shadow."

"How does Waylen fall into this?"

"That was completely random. With things at the Department on pause, they kept most of us on retainer, but we were told to live in the real world until the proper time came. I got the call the night of our big bust on the West Coast. It was after I learned of Peter Gunn's murder, and Waylen and I…" Martina dropped her utensils. "He must hate me."

"We can explain…"

"It won't matter. Once he learns about the Department…"

"He already knows," Silas said.

"He does?"

He described what had happened at the Planetae facility in New York, and how Waylen returned with Fallow to arrest Monroe. She seemed pleased to hear Theodore Belleville was dead, like she had a personal vendetta against the man.

"Wait, if you work for the Department, what's the issue?" Cody finished his meal, then poked at Silas' dish with his fork.

"They'll do anything to obtain this third Delta, even if that means killing Rory," she said.

"Why? What's so important?"

"They pretend they want it to close the Shadows, and seal off Earth from any invasion."

"But," Silas prompted.

"But they really believe it will give them access to countless worlds. They have no intention of closing anything."

Silas no longer had an appetite. "We have to help her."

5

*D*arkness.

The scent of freshly cut grass.

A foreign sound, similar to a bird, but different from anything Rory had ever heard.

She shifted in the chair, glad the bottom was cushioned. Rory wasn't certain how many hours she'd spent within the contraption, but it had to be at least four. Her eyes saw nothing, even after they should have acclimated. Rory sensed the Shadow's fog surrounding her body, but couldn't feel any of the mysterious substance.

She told herself to concentrate. People were depending on her to finish Colin's work.

Where is it? Rory wasn't certain whether she'd said that in her own head or out loud, and the question echoed in her mind, each iteration a different person's voice. Had this been done before? How many subjects had sat in this very chair, hoping the third and final Delta's location would be revealed to them? It reminded her of a vision quest she'd read about in an anthropology class years earlier. Rory was alone with her thoughts, but how could she transform into an altered state of mind with no aid?

She stopped concentrating and exhaled slowly. Instead of staying focused, Rory let it all go. Flashes from her childhood came to the forefront. Rory was in her bedroom, playing with a doll, brushing its coarse hair while her dad listened to a classical album on the main floor. Her standing on stage during a Christmas recital, forgetting the words in their school play.

The mental footage melted, replaced by another. Rory glanced at her own feet, finding them barefoot. She was at her grandparents' house in Rye, New Hampshire. She could tell by the hideous pattern on the carpet. Grandpa Swanson's desk was a big, clunky thing, blocking her path to the window. It was cranked open, and Rory heard children laughing through the screen. She meandered around the desk, climbed on the swivel chair, and rolled to the window.

Two boys played on the street, and one glanced up at her. Rory was seven and lifted a hand, waving. The skinnier kid returned the gesture, and got whacked in the face with the football they were tossing back and forth. Rory giggled, and the kid ran to retrieve the ball.

She gazed at the top of Grandpa's desk. Rory wasn't allowed in here, but she was so bored. Her parents were gone with Grandma, and her grandpa was on the phone again. She was about to leave the office when she spied the purple bag. What was in it?

Rory undid the tie strap and dropped the contents onto the desk when the doorbell rang.

"Brett, to what do I owe the pleasure?" Grandpa Swanson asked, his voice carrying upstairs.

Rory stared at the flat piece of metal, and pushed her tongue through the gap in her teeth while reaching for it.

She snapped to the present with a gasp. The vision was so vivid.

"Let me out!" she called, and the door opened a moment later.

Brett stood in the entrance, and his silhouette glowed with backlighting after being in darkness for so long. "Did you find it?"

"What…" Rory almost forgot what she'd been doing in confinement. "No, I haven't located the other Delta."

"That's okay. It takes a while to acclimate," he said.

"Have you used it?" Rory asked.

"Me?" Brett pointed at himself. "Nah. I don't have the aptitude, it would appear. Otherwise, I'd have finished this ages ago."

"Why me?"

"Maybe it's your connection to Colin? Or perhaps the tokens prefer to link to certain people. Everyone within the Department has attempted this venture at one time or another."

"Even Clark Fallow?"

"Especially Clark," he said. "He's tried frequently, but nothing happens for him either."

"Is it late?"

Brett answered without looking at his watch. "Nine thirty."

Rory stepped from the chair and nearly fell over. Brett lunged to catch her. "It takes a lot out of you."

She realized the Shadow remained activated, and hurried from its range while Brett disconnected the three tokens, one by one, returning them into their allotted cases.

"Did you see anything?"

"No. Mostly memories from my youth."

"Colin always liked those," Brett said.

"But I did smell something."

Brett acted intrigued, and he lifted a bent notepad from his back pocket, then clicked the end of a ballpoint.

He tested it with a scribble, and when it just scratched the page, he licked the tip of the pen.

"Fresh cut grass."

"That's what you smelled?"

"Yes."

"Was it from one of your own echoes?"

"I don't know. It was there before the visuals."

"Any sounds?"

"Birds… or maybe not. I couldn't see them, but it was a distant cawing, almost like seagulls at the coastline."

He made notes.

"Is that good?" Rory asked.

"Very. Most people fail on their first try, so you're way ahead of the curve," he said. "But you're probably used to hearing that, aren't you?"

"Not as often as you'd think." Rory fought to stifle a yawn, but failed.

"How about we fix something to eat? I had a grocery order delivered while you were inside. I make a mean veal parm…"

Rory smiled and gave him a nod. "I'm famished." She couldn't believe how hungry she was suddenly.

"And I put a laptop in your guest room. Figured you might want to do some writing while we're here," he said.

"I really should go back to Boston," she told him, testing to see if she could leave willingly or not.

"You will," Brett assured her. "From what you've already done, I believe you'll figure this out tomorrow, and I'll personally escort you home once we have the Delta's location."

Nothing about his posture, cadence, or demeanor seemed contrived, but Rory couldn't trust everything out of his mouth. "Thanks. I assume my new computer won't let me email?"

"The Department hasn't survived this long by us lacking caution. I'm sorry, but these are the rules," he said. "Come on, let's get some food."

They left the warehouse and climbed up to the kitchen, where two brown paper bags stuffed with groceries sat on the table. Brett motioned for her to have a seat, but she headed to the bathroom first. She hadn't gone in hours, and took a minute to relieve herself before washing her hands. Rory stared in the mirror, trying to picture that young girl she'd felt the echoes of earlier. It felt impossible that her seven-year-old version, so filled with joy and vigor, could end up this sad and traumatized by thirty. It wasn't fair.

All Rory had to do was figure out where the damned third Delta was, and then she could return to her new life. Kevin Heffernan would never bother her again. The thought was cold, but she didn't care. He'd harassed her for the last time.

Captivating scents of frying vegetables filled the kitchen air. Onions were in the pan, being sautéed with oil. Brett had two glasses of wine poured into plastic cups, and he drank from one, then slid the second to her.

"What happens when the Department gets the last Delta?" she asked.

"Colin saw a vision of the three, and he believed we could close them all."

"All?"

"You don't know?"

Rory sipped the wine, finding it acceptable, and shook her head. "Know what?"

"What they found across the Shadow in 1972?"

"Obviously not."

"They walked for an hour, Peter trailing behind your grandfather. The pair passed a monument early on, something stone, with odd lettering on it. The edges were weatherbeaten, suggesting it was ancient. Eventually, they reached the lower half of a valley, and there was the field."

"Field?"

"Of Shadows. Hundreds of portals to countless worlds. It was why Peter Gunn demanded they keep the tokens confidential. He was smart enough to realize what that implied. Peter swore them to secrecy, and he appeared to be the only one of the three to adhere to their promise. Trell told his lawyer and Cody Sanderson. Your grandfather came into the Department's fold and helped us secure the Delta you were using just a short while ago."

"And you want to close everything off?" Rory asked.

"Yes. There's more, but…" He stopped.

Rory noticed a flicker of his gaze, and he went quiet before turning to his onions, which had browned. He cursed and flipped them, adding the meat to the pan. It sizzled and spat, and they ended their conversation about that subject.

Instead, he asked her about writing, and her new plot. Rory told him about the story, and he seemed genuinely interested in what she had to say. They drank another glass of wine, ate what she figured might be the best home-cooked meal she'd had in years, and chatted until the clock hit eleven. Then the food settled, the wine took hold, and Rory could barely keep her eyes open.

"I'll clean up. Catch you in the morning," he said, rising from the table. "If you want to be back at a reasonable hour, I suggest we start early. How about six AM?"

Rory couldn't imagine sitting in that dark box again,

but nodded in agreement. She just wanted to leave, and if that would get her to Boston, then so be it.

She brushed, avoiding the mirror, and crawled into bed. Rory felt the mist surrounding her, but wouldn't dare check as she easily drifted into slumber.

6

*W*aylen loved how light traffic was at eight in the morning in downtown D.C. Tourist buses were already out, but the area seemed peaceful, especially now that school was starting up again. Families had burned through summer vacation days and were focused on settling in for the fall.

He parked underground, still driving the Planetae-branded truck, and hopped into the elevator, rising to the FBI head office's main foyer. He showed his credentials, dropped his gun and keys into the tray, and walked through the detector, collecting his belongings on the other side. Waylen knew his way around and traveled to the third story, where Ben's temporary replacement had suggested they meet.

It was Sunday, a lazy day for a lot of Americans, but the FBI offices were busy. People sat in cubicles when he emerged from the elevator, talking on phones, and clacking the keys as they entered data from reports around the country.

"Over here, Brooks," someone said, and he saw Adam Elling in a doorway.

"Adam." Waylen shook his hand. They'd worked on a case early in his stint with the Bureau, and while they'd never butted heads, they hadn't always seen eye to eye.

Shadows of the Earth

That was years earlier, and they'd spoken at numerous functions, catching up on each occasion. He didn't consider them friends, but they were relatively friendly.

"Waylen Brooks, as I live and die. Come in." Adam glanced down the hall, then stepped aside, letting Waylen pass. He shut the door and stood with his hands on his hips. "Now what in the hell has been going on around here?"

"Sir?"

The office was plain, something clearly pieced together at the last minute. The furniture didn't match, as if they'd borrowed items from various floors and jammed it in to make Elling feel content. "Sit."

Adam took the chair behind the desk, leaving Waylen the plastic one facing him. He did as was instructed.

"I was working a case in Billings. Ever been there?"

"No."

"Beautiful landscape. Ranchers. They're far more dangerous than you'd ever guess. We're talking embezzlement, bribing judges, and murder. Over land, cattle, and horses."

"Sounds like a big case," Waylen said.

"It is. It's also obvious the local PD is on the take, so I'm tiptoeing around with Blair… You remember Blair Perron, my partner?"

"Sure."

"She's confident we're about to break this damned thing wide open, if we can convince the newest recruit to spill, and I get a phone call from the Director. The Director himself! I assumed he would grind our gears, like the President was personally interested in the outcome of some rancher feud in rural Montana. You wanna guess what he told me?"

Nathan Hystad

"That Trevor Ben was murdered," Waylen said.

"Murdered? He died in a car accident, Waylen." Adam's expression became grim. "They demanded I replace him, then sent a couple of newbies to help Blair finish her investigation. I was ordered to fly home and make myself comfortable until they decided on a permanent alternative. I never asked for this, and imagine my surprise when I heard your voice on the phone. You were always Ben's poster boy. Waylen Brooks, the best in the Bureau, even up to last month when you nailed those scammers."

"Thank you, sir." It was weird calling him that, but Waylen shifted into his role quickly to save time.

"Then I had your files pulled, and guess what?"

"What?"

"You were listed as 'temporarily relieved'. It's rare enough that I checked into it. Full salary. There was also a lump sum transferred from our accounting division to your bank account." Adam rubbed his bare chin. "Tell me what you're mixed up in, and do it now."

Waylen glanced through the office window at the bright D.C. skies, and decided to come clean. He didn't know who was on what side any longer, but it was obvious Adam Elling wasn't with Planetae or the Department of Outer Space. "You'd never believe it."

"Try me."

"I need my job back," he said.

"With Financial?"

"Yes. Not in the field. I want to stay posted in D.C."

"I see," Adam said.

"Do we have an agreement?"

"Talk, and we'll figure that end out."

Waylen started with the moment he'd been drawn into the conspiracy at the storage units in Oregon. He told

Shadows of the Earth

Adam about Fred Trell, the dead astronaut, then the timing of Peter Gunn's murder. Adam had read about the break-in at the Air and Space Museum, so he glossed over the details.

Adam listened to the tale of Waylen's trip to Loon Lake, and the attack on Gunn's neighbor. When he got to the tokens, Adam interjected, "You're saying that contact with this metal … thing makes you hallucinate. Is it radioactive? Are we dealing with some new WMD?"

"No, this isn't a manmade weapon of mass destruction, Adam. It's …" Waylen pointed up. "From another world."

Adam slammed a palm on the table and started laughing. "Jeez, Waylen, you got me. Who put you up to this? Are you my big test to see if I can handle the role?"

Waylen gritted his teeth and lowered his voice. "Adam, this is real."

He continued, describing the two men Leo hired, and how they'd killed Silas' new friend Leigh by burning her family grocery store down. Before he told Adam about their trek into the hurricane, the acting assistant director ordered someone to bring in coffees and donuts, and Waylen paused when the refreshments arrived.

Then came the part with Rory's grandparents' house, and the capturing of Jack, after another person was killed.

"You've woven quite the story, Waylen." Adam bit into a jelly donut, and sticky red jam clung to his lip.

"That's only the beginning."

Next, he described the interaction with Leo Monroe, and his abduction before the FBI SWAT helped clear the facility, arresting Monroe. Adam paled when he learned that Operation Delta wasn't approved by the administration, and that Monroe seemed to have connections to every major department within the government.

Waylen almost left out the Department of Outer Space, but decided against it. He needed Adam to see the entire picture, and every detail counted.

The coffee carafe was empty, and Adam had packed down three donuts by the time an hour expired. Waylen finished his discussion and waited for the new assistant director to speak.

"What have I gotten myself into?" He kicked back and clasped his hands behind his head, leaning at a forty-five-degree angle to stare at the discolored ceiling tiles.

"I'm not sure, sir."

"And you abandoned the project?"

"Should I have stayed? The Secretary of Defense seemed to have it under control," Waylen said.

"You've rubbed elbows with some bad people, Brooks. Why disclose everything?"

"You have to understand what we're dealing with. They killed your predecessor."

"Will that happen to me?" Adam landed his elbows on the desk.

"With Monroe locked up, maybe not. Unfortunately, no one will admit where he's been taken," Waylen said.

"What do you want from him?"

"There's more to the story than I'm aware of, and I believe Monroe has the missing information." Waylen was done with the Delta. Rory was in Boston, starting a new chapter, and Silas had left with Cody. They weren't mixed up in the chaos, and Waylen didn't choose to be either.

"Okay."

"Yeah?"

"I'll get the details from the Director," Adam promised.

Shadows of the Earth

"Today," Waylen added.

"Seriously? You're asking me to call the Director on a Sunday? He's probably at church with his family."

"I have to finish what I started," he said.

"Fine. Give me a few." Adam offered his hand again. They shook, and Adam had regained some of his color. "It's all true?"

"Every bit," he confirmed.

"I didn't sign up for this, Waylen." Adam puffed his cheeks out and closed his door.

Waylen heard him through the glass, apologizing to the Director. Instead of eavesdropping, he wandered down the hall and found another coffee. He was already jittery from the stuff, but didn't know what else to do with himself in the meantime.

Waylen impatiently gazed at Adam's office and sipped the thick black concoction. It seemed like everyone in the Bureau preferred it that way.

"This is a surprise," someone said, and Waylen glanced at the newcomer.

"Gary Charles." They skipped the compulsory handshake, and he grabbed a cup. "Why are you here on a Sunday?"

"That's how it goes. Crime doesn't sleep. And neither do I these days," Special Agent Charles said.

"Why's that?"

"I've always had a fear of"—Charles' gaze drifted to the window—"*them* coming to Earth. With everything you've encountered, it seems inevitable."

"Not necessarily," Waylen said.

"No?"

Waylen made sure they were alone, and leaned on the kitchen's cabinets, facing Gary Charles. "These portals have been in place for ages, thousands of years. It seems doubtful that they'd choose now as the moment to spring a surprise visit on us."

Charles tilted his cup and grimaced at the taste. "This is brutal." He sipped it again. "That eases my mind a bit. What are you doing here?"

"I need to verify Monroe's whereabouts," he told Gary.

"What a disaster. And Assistant Director Ben... such a shame."

"What's your take on the new guy?"

"Adam? He's okay."

As if he'd been listening, Adam Elling exited his office and took long, heavy strides to the coffeemaker. "Slacking off at the water cooler, hey, gentlemen?"

"We were just..." Gary started.

"Forget it. I was busting your balls. Good news, Waylen. I found your guy." Adam pointed at Gary. "Since you're already here, go with Waylen. We do things by the book from now on, *capiche*?"

"Understood, sir." Waylen nodded at the other agent, who seemed perturbed to be included in his assignment. "Where's he at?"

"Sing Sing."

"That's only a short drive from the Planetae laboratory," Waylen noted. "I need an audience with Monroe." It was an infamously rough prison, and Monroe belonged there after all the chaos he'd caused.

"Then you'd better leave. They're expecting you at three this afternoon," Adam said. "Don't forget this when I send you on a mundane case involving a sketchy pension fund next week."

"Nothing would please me more after what I've gone

Shadows of the Earth

through." Waylen stopped before pressing the elevator button. "You wouldn't have a spare helicopter waiting nearby, would you?"

"Incredible," Adam muttered. "Check in with me tomorrow. Those pensioners are making a lot of noise, and the governor isn't pleased."

"Guess we're driving," Waylen said.

Gary met him in the underground parking, and shook his head when Waylen walked up to the Planetae truck. "Really?"

"You have something better?"

Charles gestured to a ten-year-old oversized sedan with tinted windows.

"Can you be any more cliché?" Waylen asked.

"She guzzles gas, but the ride's as smooth as they come." Special Agent Gary Charles hopped into the driver's seat and fired the engine on.

Waylen joined him. "Okay, let's lean on Monroe."

"What makes you think he'll comply?"

"Because he's a narcissist. Monroe can't go five minutes without hearing his own voice. He'll talk because we're listening, and that'll be enough."

Waylen texted Charlotte that he was leaving for a while, but hoped to be back before midnight. She gave a cursory neutral response. Her trust was something he'd have to build up before she'd let him in, and Waylen understood why.

It wasn't long before they were coasting down the Interstate, heading for Baltimore.

"You're right," Waylen said. "It is a smooth ride."

Gary smiled and turned the radio on.

7

Silas woke when Martina honked at a truck driver. He blasted his horn in return, and she swerved to avoid being cut off. "I hate men!" she shouted.

Silas figured there was more to the statement than the guy ahead of them. Cody stayed sleeping in the back seat.

"How does he do it?" Martina asked, breaking the silence.

"Cody? I have no idea, but he can sleep through anything." They were a few hours from reaching Louisville, and his anxiety increased with every mile.

They'd tracked the car's plates, and Martina's network at the Bureau had located the vehicle in Louisville. They were narrowing the trace within the city limits, but so far, nothing had popped up. There were always federal and regional jurisdiction issues when it came to private cameras, or even municipally-funded street feeds, but Martina was confident they'd get another hit before their arrival.

"They could be gone," he said. "That was from an entire day ago."

"I bet they're staying."

"What's in Louisville?"

"I'm not positive," she answered.

"What if Rory wasn't even in the car?" Silas asked.

Shadows of the Earth

"The feed was inconclusive."

"They usually are." Martina drifted into the passing lane and jammed on the gas, speeding ahead of the truck. She waved her middle finger at him and received a lengthy honk. Soon they were in front, and cruising at seventy.

"Why are you so keen on helping her?"

"I owe it to Waylen. And you guys."

"She's been through the wringer." Silas made a fist, remembering she'd been taken from the guest house in Woodstock, then killed one of Jack's men in Rye. Add in Kevin, and Rory had enough material for a hundred best-selling novels, and a hell of an autobiography.

"I promise we'll bring her home," Martina assured him.

"Thanks." Silas wondered if this would ever stop. Monroe was in prison, yet Rory had still been taken from campus against her will. There had to be a way to end everything, and if that was really what the Department of Outer Space wanted, then Silas was on board. From what he saw, humanity wasn't ready for first contact. The entire world seemed to be holding on by threads, and one false move might throw them into pandemonium.

"I wonder what they look like," he said.

"Who?"

"The aliens."

"It might be better not to know."

"We saw their footprint," Silas said.

Martina slowly glanced at him, then swerved into her lane when she almost drove off the road. "What did you say?"

"We recorded it when Rory traveled to the Moon in Cody's old spacesuit."

"Why didn't you mention that before?"

"It didn't come up."

"Tell me about this footprint," Martina ordered.

"Two toes, thicker than ours, and the print was longer than Gunn's and Swanson's boots. There was a third digit where the heel should have been."

Martina let loose a string of words in Spanish, and performed the sign of the cross. "Who else knows?"

"No one. Waylen and Darren Jones."

"Where was it?"

"By the Shadow, near the spot where they found the Delta."

"Shit." Martina kept driving, but he saw how white her knuckles had turned. The news of the print had her worried.

"Cody figured it was old, probably from when they first dropped the Shadow on the Moon," Silas said. "Are you positive the guy in the video was from the Department?"

"Yes."

"And you're not aware of any facilities in Louisville?"

"That was above my paygrade. I was aware of the place in Hermon, and the ones in California and Arizona. Everything is sitting empty. Once Colin died, the program became a myth, and we moved on."

"Until Monroe found out about them and killed Gunn."

"Right."

"Why didn't the Department have the tokens?" Silas asked.

"They do, from the far side of the Moon."

"No, the original set."

Martina gazed at him. "I can't answer that. Clark Fallow second-guessed the program after Colin died. He was

Shadows of the Earth

given the job at NASA, and the D.O.O.S. was a thing of the past. For all of us."

"Clearly, not everyone felt the same way," Silas said. "Will Rory use the Delta to find the third device?"

"I doubt it. If Colin couldn't, why should his granddaughter?"

Silas considered the conundrum. "What if it's a puzzle?"

"Go on," she said.

"Aliens leave one set on the Moon. We happen to encounter it. Colin Swanson utilizes the echoes to secure the second Delta." The more Silas considered the problem, the more certain he was of the solution.

"And?"

"They thought in linear terms. Colin could have used both sets of the Delta to triangulate the location of the third," he said.

Martina took an exit and pulled into a gas station. The diner was packed, and she had to reverse into a parking spot next to the convenience store's entrance. She killed the engine and stared at him. "If you're right, they've been waiting for nothing all these years."

"Except, if the theory about Colin being a Key is correct, they had no one to test the hypothesis in the last decade," Silas said.

"Now they do."

"Rory," he whispered.

Her phone beeped, and Martina scrolled through the message. "Got him. The car was spotted heading into an industrial area. Twice. The latest time was today. Leaving, then coming back." Martina smiled and inserted the address into the car's GPS. It said they were two hours and seventeen minutes away.

"We're going to need the tokens from New York," Cody said from behind them.

"We'll be playing right into their hands," Silas said. "If we find the last Delta, the Department will have exactly what they want: access to an infinite number of worlds."

"I can help on that front." Martina dialed a number. "Waylen, it's me."

---

*L*ight.

An infinite of stars.

Rory squinted into the blaring glow, and the brilliance faded. It was the first time in hours that she'd seen anything but darkness, which made it even more powerful. The bird songs grew louder, the scent of grass prevalent in her nostrils.

She noticed a shape, an outline of a building. Rory reached out, feeling the surface of something against her palm, even though her arm was within the box in the Department's warehouse. It scratched her skin like stone. She ran a finger along the top, guessing it was the mortar between the building blocks. Rory closed her eyes and inhaled, picking up another smell. Flowers. Summer.

Then, like a house of cards, the vision came tumbling down, the blackness of the Shadow shielding the space and spilling over her face. The mist clung to her, and Rory choked as the substance floated into her mouth. She coughed and staggered to the exit. "Brett!"

The doors opened, and Brett stood with a steadying hand outstretched. "You okay?"

"It was closer." Her head ached, and she walked to

Shadows of the Earth

the couch he'd dragged from another room.

"What did you find?"

"A building. It's stone, and the weather is nice and sunny. I smelled flowers and grass this time."

"Good. Take five and—"

"Brett, we're missing something."

"No, you need to focus."

Rory downed half a bottle of water. "I disagree."

Brett gaped at her and clenched his jaw. He looked as tired as she felt. "You said it yourself, you're closer. If you want to get home…"

Rory had had enough of his behavior. "Is that a threat?"

"Not at all. We need to shut the portals down. Don't you understand?"

"Sure."

"You have classes tomorrow, remember?"

"How could I forget?"

Brett's expression loosened, and his smile almost passed as genuine. "Find the Delta, and we're done. It'll all go away. Forever."

The words were promising, but Rory didn't believe it. "How will you close them?"

"We'll figure it out." Brett took her empty bottle, and tossed her another. "Take a couple more and try again."

Rory wasn't sure she had a choice. She grabbed an acetaminophen capsule from a first aid kit and chugged the second bottle. After a quick trip to the bathroom, she decided to continue. The sooner she did what Brett asked, the faster she was on her way.

She glared at the darkness within the box and walked in, realizing there was no handle on the interior. Brett was required to let her out. She worried he might not open it if she failed to provide good news in one of these trials.

"Focus," she told herself as she sat facing the large black wall. The Delta remained inside, its Shadow filling the surrounding air.

Instead of her usual approach, she switched tactics. The definition of insanity was doing the same actions and expecting different results. Rory would change the game.

This time, she smelled nothing, saw no lights, touched no stonework. She pictured the house on Loon Lake, where she'd torn Silas' clothes off after being caught in a rainstorm. The living room in which she'd traveled through the Shadow, wearing a retro NASA spacesuit. If they thought Colin Swanson was a Key, Rory would be a stronger version.

She was glad there weren't cameras in the black box. She rose, aware of the Shadow's presence, but Rory couldn't see it. She sensed the mist, and saw the Delta at the center, composed of three separate tokens. Three. Delta. Triangle. The number stood for many things.

Birth. Life. Death.

Mind. Body. Soul.

Three.

Rory kept envisioning the log cabin, and stepped in.

She emerged on the other side, no longer in Louisville.

Rory took a tentative stride from the lingering black portal, hovering a foot off Peter Gunn's hardwood floors. She'd done it.

She ran to the phone and dialed her parents from memory.

"*You've reached the Swansons. We're probably at the club, so leave your name and number.*" Her father's cheerful voice filled her ear, and Rory hated that was the only number

Shadows of the Earth

she had memorized.

When it beeped, Rory recorded a message. "Mom, Dad, it's me. This is going to sound crazy, but I've been taken to Louisville, Kentucky. I don't have my phone, so please contact Special Agent Waylen Brooks. He left you his business card when he was in town." She did her best to describe the building, and was cut off when the voicemail carrier beeped, dropping the last few words.

She'd somehow used the Shadow to travel to another place without carrying the Delta. From what she'd heard, this had never been accomplished before. Perhaps she was the Key.

Before leaving, she walked to the fridge, grabbing the black marker stuck to the stainless steel with a magnet. She popped the cap and wrote a message on the small white board. '*Rory was here*'.

After gazing at the lake momentarily, she returned to the Shadow, suddenly not sure if she should go through or stay behind. She didn't have a car, and with no money, she wouldn't get far. Brett would eventually open the doors and find her missing. Then he'd most certainly follow. Rory was in no shape to be running from another agency, no matter if they touted themselves as the 'good guys' or not.

She walked into the fog and was once again shrouded by darkness.

With the test complete, Rory sat, determined to locate the third Delta before her time ran out.

8

Waylen hadn't visited Sing Sing prison before, and would have been glad to avoid it his entire life. It was extremely dated, with much of the facility original to the era of its construction.

"Six hundred fourteen people were executed here," Gary said. "That's a lot of ghosts."

"You believe in that?"

"There are aliens. Are ghosts out of the realm of possibility?" the other agent asked.

"I guess not." The recent call from Martina had rattled Waylen. She'd asked him to get the Delta from Plemmons, but he doubted it would be so simple.

Gary pulled into the parking lot, and they entered the prison.

A doughy man waited for them, his eyelids almost shut. He was overweight by a good hundred pounds, and his undersized suit clung to his form. "Is one of you Waylen Brooks?" he asked.

"I am."

"My name's Barney Feldstein, and I'm the warden." He didn't offer to shake. "They've instructed me to escort you to visit our newest inmate."

"Thank you," was all Waylen said.

Shadows of the Earth

"I've raised my concern over allowing a prisoner to be incarcerated without a trial. It's entirely unconstitutional," he blurted.

"I agree," Special Agent Charles added. "But he's guilty of many offenses, mark my words."

"I'll have to trust you on that." The warden unlocked a set of doors and stepped past two guards. "Come with me." They stopped at a desk with a uniformed clerk behind it. "You'll need to surrender your weapons."

Waylen undid his holster, and Gary did the same, although with slightly more hesitation. Barney must have noticed. "It's standard procedure."

"Nothing seems to operate as it should these days," Gary Charles told him.

"Sing Sing has strict protocols, and that's how you stay alive." Barney clutched a metal rung on the barricade separating the guards from the general prisoner area. "This way."

They spent the next ten minutes walking past various cell blocks. Most of the prisoners remained in cells, some cat-calling the duo. They must have assumed the pair of suits strolling through with the warden were high-powered attorneys, and Waylen heard multiple men declaring their innocence at the top of their lungs.

It grew quieter when they momentarily walked outside before entering another building. Despite his size, the warden made the trek without slowing.

"We've moved him to a private room. He'll be handcuffed to the table," Barney Feldstein said.

"Is that necessary?" Waylen asked.

"Since we had someone almost tear a reporter's head from their neck twenty years ago… I'd say, yes."

Waylen didn't interject, trying to block the image from

his mind. The on-duty guard unlocked the door and held it for the warden.

"You have an hour." Barney peered into the room, but stayed in the hall. "Good luck."

Leo Monroe sat upright, and as promised, he was chained to iron loops welded onto the table. He folded one palm on the other hand and stared at Waylen, then Gary. "Who's your friend?"

"Special Agent Gary Charles," he said.

"I was told you were investigating me in D.C."

"That's right." Gary sat.

Waylen took off his suit jacket, draped it on the door handle, and rolled up his sleeves. After losing the tie, he faced Leo. "I don't like you."

"Emotions are irrelevant," Leo said.

"Tell me about the Department of Outer Space," Waylen said.

The blank look on Leo's face suggested he either wasn't aware of the organization, or he was that good at hiding it.

Waylen finally sat and dragged the chair closer to the table, making a loud squeaking noise on the concrete floor. "The D.O.O.S."

"Is this a joke?"

"Stop messing with me."

"There's no such department," Leo said.

"You helped design three of their buildings. Now, does it ring a bell?"

"Those aren't related to any space organization," he said. "It was Plemmons. He hired me."

"Then why do they have your Hex technology?"

"The Hex was designed to test military-grade explosives within. You can detonate a low-yield nuclear device inside them and no one would be the wiser."

Special Agent Charles made notes, and Leo ignored him.

"You're saying the Hex wasn't created for the Delta?"

"Not even close. I only duplicated it in case something came through the Shadow while we were using it. Those three sites aren't alien UFO buildings. They're classified weapon testing facilities. It has nothing to do with the Delta."

Waylen had follow-up questions, but preferred to jump around during an interview. It kept the target on their toes. "What was the point?"

"Of what?"

"Killing people to get the Shadow."

"You don't understand the magnitude of such a venture, do you? There are people setting their sights on Mars, to set up impossible colonies that will never succeed. Others are banking on mining asteroids, which is almost as hopeless, though with improved robotics, that might come this century. Space Law will become the next big thing, with fierce and reckless competition. Precedents will be set, but for now, it's the Wild West." Leo made finger guns to enhance his reference.

"Why did you keep us on site? You could have killed us and brought the tokens to another country," Waylen said.

"I'm locked up, and don't expect to be let out anytime soon, so I must take ownership of what happened. But from me to you, I was doing it for the greater good."

"Of your business," Gary finished.

"I planned to pave the way for future generations, and with the Shadow, we'd be able to stop harvesting our own lands. Imagine if we could access a blank slate, a planet to refine oil, an alien continent to manufacture plastics. Without the need for landfills, the oceans would once again thrive. There would be no more threat to our ozone. Are you beginning to see the picture?"

"How altruistic of you," Waylen said. "You'd rather dump our trash on another world than deal with the issues."

"The Delta could lead us to thousands of options. How many will be husks, wastelands ripe for the picking? This is the future. Instead of a mass exodus on Earth when the ice caps melt and we're doomed, we can fix it."

Waylen peered at Gary, who nodded absently, still scrawling notes. "I have to admit, you're making sense. Did you pitch this to the government?"

"Yes."

"When?"

"Theodore did."

"They knew about the Delta," he said. Waylen considered what he'd learned so far. It didn't sound as though Monroe was aware of the other Delta. Instead, he'd hoped to mine the Moon, and given his few interactions with the Planetae CEO, it seemed feasible that was his primary objective.

Waylen narrowed his gaze, focusing on the prisoner. "Leo, I'm going to tell you something. There's a second Delta."

"Impossible."

"It's been in the government's possession since 1984, when Clark Fallow, Colin Swanson, and Brett Davis flew to the Moon and found it."

For the first time since meeting the man, Leo looked stunned. "How?"

"Colin used the original token, and determined where

another lay in waiting," Waylen said.

"Why? Why are there two?"

"There aren't."

"You just said…"

Waylen lifted three fingers. "It's a trio."

"And what… happens when all three are located?"

"We were hoping you could enlighten us, but apparently, you weren't part of the inner circle."

Leo Monroe's eyes closed, as if he was getting a migraine. "I was blinded by the Delta's potential. If the rumors about Planet D are substantiated, we might be in trouble."

"You'll never know." Waylen rose, guessing there was little left for Monroe to share.

"Don't leave," he pleaded.

"Goodbye, Leo." Waylen pulled the tie over his head and cinched the loop up before throwing his suit jacket on. Without another word, he banged on the door, and stepped out when the guard opened it. Gary followed, and Leo shouted at him to come back while he strode from that part of his life forever.

Once they got to the sedan, Waylen rested his hands on the roof and took a deep breath. "That was useless."

Gary smiled. "Not entirely. We understand Leo's motivation, and while it was mostly monetary, there was an element of philanthropy to it. He also admitted those buildings like the one in Hermon weren't designed for the Shadow. Those are military structures."

"Why did Fallow lie?"

"Because the Department of Outer Space isn't real. It isn't a sanctioned authority, it's just a group of fanatics working on their own behalf." Gary climbed in.

Waylen immediately rolled the window down, since

the heat made the car exceedingly stuffy. He found his old water bottle and twisted the cap, finishing the warm liquid. "They flew to the Moon, Gary. That's not something a weekend club does."

"Is there proof they did?" Gary asked. "Aren't we taught to follow the trails? To ensure evidence is legitimate before making arrests? We're taking a liar's word for it."

"They're all liars. I don't know who to trust anymore, and that includes Martina Sanchez."

"Was there something going on between you two?" Gary asked.

"I'd rather not say."

"Fine. Where to?"

"Martina guessed we might find the last Delta if we bring the two sets together, so what the hell? We have a full day to waste. Why not give it a shot?"

Gary nodded and sped away from Sing Sing. They arrived at the Planetae gates only thirty minutes later, and were greeted with silence.

Waylen got out and wrapped his fingers on the chain link. "Hello?" he called.

"Something's wrong," Gary said.

"You have any surveillance gear in here?"

"Trunk." Gary popped it, and Waylen grabbed a pair of binoculars from a black case.

He used them, scanning the exterior of the building, and halted on the cameras. They appeared to be running. If anyone was inside, he'd be seen on the monitors. A helicopter remained within the fenced yard, along with three light armored vehicles.

Waylen wiped a bead of sweat off his brow and lowered the binoculars. "Not a single sentry. When we were

Shadows of the Earth

stuck here, they had patrols on the fence. Plemmons wouldn't be this sloppy."

"They probably left," Gary said.

"Without those?" Waylen motioned at the military vehicles. "How are you at climbing over barbed wire?"

"I'm forty-eight with a bad back. How about we try this another way?" Gary hopped into the car and rolled the window down. "It's the Bureau's. They won't mind."

Waylen stepped aside while Special Agent Charles threw it in reverse, stopping a hundred feet away. He stepped on the gas, making the tires squeal, and barreled into the rolling metal gate. It broke loose, and Gary slammed on the brakes while the gate clattered to the ground.

"That's one hell of an entrance," Waylen said, peering at the building. No soldiers came rushing out to stop them.

"That answers that. Let's check who's home."

Waylen's stomach was in knots as they crossed the couple hundred-yard span, past the LAVs and copter, and reached the doors. His hand wavered by the keypad, hoping his code still worked.

He typed it in, and the latch unlocked.

9

"Did you know about this place?" Silas asked Martina.

"Nope."

"How long has it been since you were in touch with the other members of the Department?"

"A few years."

"When all this started, did you contact them? Or vice versa?"

"I didn't."

From what Silas was hearing, Martina might not have been a high-ranking member of the secret organization. They watched the series of warehouse bays, particularly the one with the sedan parked out front. The plates matched the car that had run down Rory's ex. He bet they could test the paint and find Kevin's blood on the hood. Not that Silas had any guilt on that front. Kevin Heffernan was a scumbag.

"What are we waiting for?" Cody reached for the handle, but Martina glared at him.

"Hold on to your pants, Sanderson," she said. "I want to know where they are."

"Only so many options. How about we start with the one his car is parked at?" Cody's voice was laced with sarcasm.

Shadows of the Earth

Martina opened her door. "You two should stay put."

"Not a chance." Silas was already out before he finished the sentence. "I thought these guys were on the same team as you, Martina. Are guns really necessary?"

Martina kept her piece holstered. "Time will tell."

They crossed the mostly empty lot and tried the front entrance. At first, Silas assumed the building was unmarked, until he noticed the letters *CME*. "What's that?"

"Something the Department uses on occasion," she said. "Which means this is the right place."

There were four glass doors separated by a series of bays for delivery trucks to back into. Martina chose the left option and tried the handle. Of course, it was also locked. "I don't have time for this," she muttered, and searched the sidewalk.

"What are you doing?" Cody asked.

"Looking for something to break this with."

"Won't that trigger alarms?"

Martina gazed at the parking lot. "I don't see any cameras, and if they're inside, the alarm will be off already."

Silas thought it was strange for a secret government organization to lack surveillance at one of their buildings. It was obvious Martina Sanchez was apprehensive, which didn't sit well with him either.

Silas found a brick around the corner, and judging by the cigarette butts on the ground, someone kept it to prop the side entrance open. "Will this work?"

Martina threw the brick at the center of the door, shattering it. Fragments clinked to the concrete, and a few followed the brick inside the foyer. She slipped her hand in and flipped the knob.

Silas waited for any sounds to emerge from down the

dark hall, but nothing happened. Martina took the lead, brandishing her gun, and Silas activated the flashlight feature on his phone to give them a better view.

They bypassed a couple of offices. "You said the Department wasn't active," Cody reminded her.

"We aren't."

"Then why are there fresh flowers in this one?" He gestured at the simple bouquet, with petals on the verge of wilting.

Martina paused and entered the office. She picked up a sheet of printer paper with a corporate letterhead on the top. "They might be subletting."

"Sure, makes sense." Cody snatched the page, crumpled it, and tossed it into a wastebasket.

"Where's Rory?" Silas asked.

"Let's try the warehouse." Martina hurried, and they walked into the large space. Instead of being empty like she'd predicted, the tall metal racking was filled with pallets. They looked to be selling commercial electrical supplies.

"Rory!" Silas shouted.

"She's not here." Martina spun in the middle of the warehouse. "Let's visit the next bay."

She was closer than ever to finding the answer. She walked through the villa, not in her own body, but in the echo of another's memory. Her boots were gigantic, maybe belonging to a male groundskeeper. He stopped near a stone bridge, where a narrow stream bubbled by. The air seemed thick with summer, the grass as green as any she'd ever witnessed.

Rory wanted to gain a better view of the building, hoping for a marker that would determine where the echo took place, but she didn't have control of the person's memory. They looked at their feet a lot, pausing at the gardens to check the flowers, dead-heading a few. They dropped the withered flowers into the dirt and continued to the shrubbery a short distance away.

Her eyes ached, and Rory knew she couldn't stay any longer. Someone called a name, but the words were indecipherable. The man's chin lifted, and a figure came into sight.

Is that…

The vision swirled, and she awoke on the floor beside the chair, the room completely black. She sensed the Shadow all around her and sat up, trying to piece together the latest echo. Was the other Delta truly in the building she kept seeing? And had that person been who she thought it was? It seemed not only improbable, but impossible. What did he have to do with the third Delta?

Rory stumbled to the exit and banged on the slab. "Let me out."

There was no response.

"Brett, for the love of God! I have to pee. I'm hungry, and my head is in a vise!"

She pressed her ear to the cool metal and heard footsteps.

"Did you find it?" Brett's voice was quiet.

Rory considered her options. "Yes! I'll tell you where the Delta is, just open—"

"You're lying."

She sighed, trying to temper the anger growing in her chest. "I can't do this forever! I have to leave for Boston.

You promised—"

"I said you could return when you gave me the location," Brett said. The barricade between them slightly muffled his words.

Rory felt the Shadow's edges tickle her face, and she waved the fog into the darkness. She could leave. Would it work again?

The door opened, and a dejected Brett filled her view. "Sorry, Rory. I'm under a lot of pressure to get this done. We're concerned that with the recent activity, someone's been notified."

Rory glanced at the writhing Shadow stuck in the box. "You think that by using the Delta, another race is aware we're here?"

"It's a good possibility," he said.

"Then why keep it running all day?"

"To find the third Delta, so we can shut them off."

"There's no data to suggest that's possible!" she exclaimed.

"Your grandfather believed it. He saw things…" Brett pointed to the chair. "In this very room."

Rory rushed in and grabbed the Delta. "We have to shut it—"

Brett blocked her and wrestled the alien triangle from Rory. "This is too important. Were you really close?"

Rory nodded, but didn't want to tell Brett who she'd seen in the latest vision. "I need a break."

It was six o'clock. How could she travel to Boston by tomorrow morning? She didn't have her cell phone, and had no way to warn Marg of her absence. Brett held the Delta, with the portal shimmering around him. If he wasn't careful, he'd travel through. Rory wondered what the destination was, since she'd already used it to get to

Shadows of the Earth

Loon Lake.

Brett's phone rang, and he answered the call after setting the Delta in its original place. He turned his back on Rory, and she almost dismantled it, until she heard Brett's side of the conversation.

"What do you mean no contact? Plemmons? Cameras are down? No, I haven't found... *We* haven't." He peered at Rory. "Are you sending a team?"

He hung up and looked ten years older.

"What's the matter?" she asked.

"Jacob B. Plemmons stayed in New York with Clark, and they were using the Delta," he said.

"Okay, and... ?"

"They're not responsive. The entire team. Fifty soldiers."

Rory's gaze flickered to the Shadow. "What does that mean?"

"I don't know, but it can't be good."

"You've had incidents before, haven't you?" She strode closer to Brett. "Tell me!"

"A few of our subjects... vanished."

"Vanished?"

"Through the Shadow."

"In there?" Rory gestured to the contraption she'd spent all day inside.

"Yes."

She punched him in the chest, then bashed the bottom of her fist on his arm. "How dare you! You said it was safe!"

"It's been so long. I..." Brett tapped his leg up and down.

Rory bit her tongue and stared at the box, then the exit across the warehouse floor. "I'm leaving." She walked and didn't hear him following.

Before she made it up the steps, voices carried from ahead, and she saw three figures arriving.

Brett shouted behind her, and Rory turned to see the Department of Outer Space member step into the box. A light shimmered from the room she'd sat in for hours, and when it lowered, Brett was gone.

"Rory?"

Her jaw dropped when she recognized the voice. She barreled into Silas, and his arms wrapped around her.

"What was that?" Martina Sanchez asked.

"That was Brett Davis."

"Where did he go?"

"I'm not about to find out." Rory released Silas, and undid the tokens.

10

*W*aylen found the first body ten feet inside the complex. The soldier was unrecognizable, their uniform melted with the rest of them. A weapon lay untouched beside the pile. He swallowed a lump in his throat and kept walking. He and Gary Charles were both holding their guns, trying to piece together what they were seeing.

"Where do we go?" Gary asked.

"This way." Waylen winced when they passed another mess on the floor. His phone buzzed, making him quickly check it. Rory's parents' home number was on the screen, and he declined.

"Was this a chemical attack?" Gary sniffed the air. "We should get out of here, Brooks."

"No." Waylen kept walking. "There's no scent. Whatever caused this is long gone."

"How can you be sure?"

Waylen couldn't, so he didn't comment. He was sick to death of the Planetae complex, and once again, he plodded through its halls, only this time, the occupants were smudges on the floor. They slowly entered the laboratory, watching the Hex. At least two dozen soldiers were dead, and he found countless bullet casings. There had been a battle, with the gunfire focused on the platform.

They'd left Darren Jones here, along with Corporal Tucker, Dr. Rita Singh, Clark Fallow, and Jacob Plemmons, the Secretary of Defense. From what Waylen could tell, none of them were present.

He stepped in something sticky and didn't look down to see what it was. If he did, he might never recover from the experience. Waylen used his training and compartmentalized the scene, shoving any fear into a dark recess of his mind.

Special Agent Charles muttered curses to himself, but kept his composure while they strode to the Hex. The Shadow lingered within the confines of the six-sided containment field. Waylen touched the exterior, finding tiny bumps over the surface. "They shot it. The soldiers were aiming at the Hex, and unleashed their fury."

"A lot of good it did them," Gary said. "They're all dead."

"But how?" Waylen spun on the steps to stare at the exit. Every single person in the room was dead, a pile of mush on the floor. "We've been so stupid."

"Yeah, why?"

He banged a hand on the clear barrier. "Because we were working on the assumption that no one was watching!"

"You're saying aliens did this?"

"Unless you can prove otherwise," Waylen said.

"What if another planet's atmosphere leaked through? Or the pressure changed, and they imploded."

"The structure seems fine."

Gary shrugged. "It only affected organic beings."

"That theory has a few holes."

"Like what?" Gary asked.

Shadows of the Earth

"The fact that twenty-something soldiers fired heavy artillery at the Hex in a last-ditch effort." Waylen observed the misty fog surrounding the void. Pieces lifted and dipped, breaking off to vanish after a few seconds, constantly being replaced with more soupy substance.

"How do we explain this? Who do we tell?" Gary asked. "The Secretary of Defense is dead. NASA's administrator, gone."

"We don't know they're dead," he said. Waylen gazed at the portal, then to the lockers where the spacesuits sat. A few were noticeably missing. He recognized pieces of one near the stairs, the edges smeared with what might have been part of a human.

"You're kidding me," Gary groaned.

"Stay here."

"Gladly."

Waylen expected Gary to protest, and was surprised when he accepted Waylen's orders.

He put on the suit, remembering the notes from Rita, and seven minutes later, he stood in the Hex, realizing he might be the dumbest man in the world. Before leaving, he sent a text to Charlotte, silenced it, and passed it to Gary. "Call… Martina."

Waylen attached the helmet and double-checked the settings, ensuring he'd done it properly. Before, he'd had a professional to fall back on.

"You don't have to do this. We can dismantle the Delta and—"

"And what? Wait for someone to show up? What do we tell them? Look around!"

Gary glanced at the remnants of the soldiers and lowered his chin. "Be careful."

Waylen entered the Hex and took a few breaths of recycled air. *You can do this.*

He had no clue what he'd discover across the portal. Would it still lead to the Moon?

The Shadow loomed, no longer an intriguing scientific marvel. Instead, Waylen regarded it with distrust and anger, mixed with a hearty dose of fear. He glanced at Gary, who watched from beyond the Hex's walls.

Mist parted as he stepped into the foggy hole and away from Earth.

"Where did that guy go?" Cody demanded.

Rory shivered, and Silas did his best to comfort her. "What happened here?"

She glanced at the tokens. "Brett found me in Boston. Kevin was there, and—"

"We saw video footage," Silas told her. "Are you okay?"

Her watery eyes met his gaze. "Yes. Brett said we had to secure a third set of tokens, and that my grandfather used this room to search for it. It was how they located the second set. Which is right there."

"This is bananas," Cody mumbled.

"Did you find it?" Martina asked.

"I was so close. Silas, Peter Gunn knew about it."

"Huh? How?"

"I saw an echo from a groundskeeper at this villa… I swear it was a younger Peter that came into view near the end of my vision," she said. "Did you hold on to that diary?"

"I left it in New York, under the mattress."

Shadows of the Earth

"We're going to need it," Rory said.

"Okay. And Brett? What was that all about?" Cody walked to the edge of the warehouse. "Something took him into the portal."

"Then it's a good thing I broke the connection." Rory noticed she was touching the tokens, with little effect. She dropped them to the floor. "I used the Shadow."

"Where did it take you?" Silas asked.

"I traveled to your house on the lake."

Silas lifted his eyebrows in surprise. "And it worked?"

"I think so."

Martina's phone vibrated, and Silas saw Waylen's name on the display before she answered it. "Waylen, finally. Did you get the tokens?" She put it on speaker for everyone to hear.

"*Martina, it's Gary Charles.*"

"Gary, where's Waylen?"

"*We went to see Monroe today, then drove to the Planetae facility… they're all dead.*"

"Dead? Who is?" Martina asked.

"*The entire regiment of soldiers that escorted Plemmons on site. They're… it's like something melted them. I don't know how to explain it. We can't find Plemmons or Fallow. There's no one here.*"

"Where is Waylen?" She spoke the words slowly.

"*He walked into the Shadow. Waylen thought the others might have hidden on the Moon.*"

Silas glanced at the box holding the Delta. "Could you do it again?"

Rory shrugged, but nodded. "I'll try."

"Gary, stay where you are. We're coming," Martina said.

"*You're in Louisville? It'll take… you won't be here until to-*

morrow."

"Hang tight. And, Gary, don't shoot." Martina ended the call. "Rory, why don't you try to control the destination?"

"I'd visited the house in Loon Lake," Rory said. "I haven't been to Monroe's lab in New York."

"Maybe it doesn't matter. What if the Shadow can go anywhere it's been activated?" Cody surmised. "Rory, you're the Key. We don't need another device; it's you."

Rory sealed her lips. "Let's see if this works."

"We're right here. Focus on the Delta, and bring us to it," Martina said.

The tokens adhered, establishing a perfect triangle, the gentle blue light spreading out, forming a black portal.

Rory stepped into the box, her heart racing. She took a meditative breath and relaxed a fraction. She'd done it before. Why not again? Silas' presence fueled her. Rory wasn't alone. They'd gone through this together, and Waylen needed their help.

She stayed upright, rather than using the chair, and faced the Shadow. When her eyes were closed, she pictured a different Delta, one far away. They were connected. Rory sensed its existence and smiled grimly as an echo played.

Rory had only seen Clark Fallow once, and didn't know Darren Jones well. She'd looked him up after learning he was working with Waylen and Silas. The man holding the Delta was tall and wore a stiff suit, an American flag pinned to his lapel. She assumed it was Jacob

Shadows of the Earth

Plemmons. He set it on the table within the Hex, and before the Shadow filled the space, the black mist flashed brightly.

The rest was pandemonium. Rory couldn't tell what had happened, but saw soldiers falling. Echoes of gunfire cascaded around, and Plemmons lay on the platform, his cheek pressed to the floor. The vision faded, and Rory found herself in the same position within the box. She rose and knew the destination was set. "I think it'll work." Rory barely spoke loud enough for her allies to overhear, but Silas approached the apparatus' entrance.

"Do we all go?" Cody asked.

"Unless you want to drive my car," Martina said, grabbing her keys from her pocket. She offered them, but Cody shook his head.

"Nah, we should stick together."

Rory picked the Delta up, and dozens of images flashed in her mind. Colin Swanson as a young man, arguing with Peter Gunn, Fred Trell in the backdrop drinking a beer. Brett Davis being torn from the very room they were in. Waylen… walking on the Moon. Silas held her up when her knees gave way.

"You okay?"

"Yeah. I'll bring the Delta through."

None of them knew what might happen if they used the Shadow while possessing the alien triangle, but it had to be done. Rory glanced from Cody to Martina, then stopped on Silas. "It's time."

Rory walked into the gaping hole, and her foot landed on the solid floor, eight hundred miles away.

11

*W*aylen was shocked by the present scene on the Moon. They'd developed buildings with large steel beams and overlapping riveted metal walls. Seeing manmade structures in such a foreign location was unsettling, and it took his brain a minute to comprehend everything.

He heard every breath, in a constant reminder of being utterly alone on the surface. The Shadow remained behind him, unchanged since he'd emerged through the portal. Waylen didn't know what he'd expected to find, but this wasn't it.

"Hello!" he called. Unless their suits were linked to his, no one could contact him. Waylen had next to zero experience with these advanced space walking suits, and tried not to feel dumb for forgetting the GPS trackers earlier.

Waylen guided the HUD through its few options. He tapped the icon of a helmet, and a radar grid filled the bottom right edge of his facemask. It took a second to focus, but when he did, Waylen noticed three green dots. They showed any linked suits. Waylen moved, trying to understand his map. One dot arose in the opposite direction from the other two, so that was obviously him. Waylen spun around, seeing Earth. He began his approach,

Shadows of the Earth

passing the largest structure. Two huge wheeled machines blocked his view of the first blinking target.

Waylen circumvented the nearest, and paused when he saw a body. The occupant's helmet's mask was cracked, and the face within had turned blue. His eyes were open, red and bloody. It was Clark Fallow, the head of NASA, and the Department of Outer Space.

That left one more person. Waylen prayed they weren't dead.

He judged by the distance on the radar that they were approximately five hundred yards straight ahead. The ground dipped, and Waylen slowed at the edge of the depression. He stared at a cluster of rocks. The green dot was directly across the crater. Waylen circled around it at a crawl.

The trip took longer than expected, and his air tank notification showed it had decreased another ten percent. Clearly, no one had refilled these since their last outing. It indicated he had twenty minutes remaining.

When he arrived at the rocks, he saw they were twice as tall as him, and the middle of the cluster doubled that size again. Waylen thought he caught movement in his periphery, and scanned the mining camp, but nothing was out of place.

He noticed the feet first, then the legs, as he rounded the peninsula of rock. Waylen hurried when he saw the person's finger twitch. "Help's here."

Waylen crouched, taking Dr. Rita's hand. Her eyes blinked open, and Waylen heard the subtle chime coming through her helmet. "I'm out of air."

"Obviously not." Waylen tapped her mask. "You're still alive."

"It's at one minute."

Waylen was down to twelve. "We have to go."

Rita didn't budge. He grunted and hefted her weight onto his shoulder. Considering the low gravity, it was a simple task. Waylen didn't hear any protests as he returned to camp, bounding as quickly as his legs would take him. He reached the first roving vehicle and tripped, sending Rita to float and land on the regolith beside the building.

Her mask glowed red, and she appeared to be unconscious. Waylen recalled what she'd told him about the umbilical cords, and removed his, knowing the valve would seal shut the moment it was released. He undid her plug and snapped his in. The red lights stopped, and Waylen held his breath, conserving air.

Rita's mouth opened, then closed, her nostrils shifting ever so slightly.

He waited a full minute, then reverted the cord back to his own suit. Waylen hauled her up and carried her like a child in his arms. The Shadow awaited, and he rushed for it, careful not to fall again. He almost dove into the portal, but something caught his eye. A figure watched him in the other direction. The solitary being was a hundred feet from his position, and it started walking toward Waylen and the Shadow.

Without another thought, Waylen stepped into the hole.

And landed within the Hex.

Waylen grabbed the Delta, tearing the tokens apart. The connection broke, and the snippets of mist burst apart like vapor. He let the tokens fall, clinging to the platform, and dropped to his knees, unclasping Rita's helmet. For a second, he thought he'd lost her, until her chest rose and fell.

Shadows of the Earth

"Waylen?" The Hex door was open, and Rory gawked at the pair. He looked past her, seeing another Shadow activated within the lab.

"Turn it off!" Waylen shoved in, almost knocking Rory to the ground, and broke the other alien device. The portal shuddered and vanished. Only then did Waylen find his seat. He lay back, staring at the ceiling through his mask while the air alert sounded in his suit. He undid the cord, removed the helmet, and laughed.

"Something funny?" Gary Charles asked.

"I saw them."

"Who?" Rory's arms crossed protectively across her chest, with Silas hovering beside her.

"Them. The aliens." He got to his feet, stripping out of the spacesuit. He was drenched in sweat. "Well, one alien."

"Whoa," Cody said.

"Where were you?"

He finally noticed that Martina Sanchez was in the room. "The Moon," he answered.

"What on God's green Earth went down here?" She gestured at the mess in the laboratory. Dozens of guns were on the floor, next to what used to be their operators.

Rory scooped up the dropped tokens, and Waylen noticed she didn't use gloves or any kind of barrier between the metal and her skin. Silas took the pieces of the Delta, placing them into small cloth bags found in the lockers.

"We broke the gate and walked into this," Gary said. "Waylen spied the missing suits and traveled into the Shadow to investigate, and apparently found a woman."

"That's Dr. Rita Singh. She worked for Leo Monroe," Waylen explained.

Martina touched her fingers to Rita's neck after removing the helmet. "She has a pulse, but she's unconscious. I think we'd better get her to a hospital."

"We have to call this in," Waylen said, but wasn't sure who to contact.

"Was anyone else up there? I count more missing spacesuits," Cody told him.

"I crossed paths with Clark Fallow." Waylen shook his head. "He didn't make it. The other two... nowhere to be seen. Let's do a walkthrough of the entire facility. Martina, can you call the local Bureau and have an ambulance brought in?"

"On it." She had her phone out, and walked off while it rang.

"Rory, Martina filled me in on your adventure. Did they hurt you?" Waylen had assured the woman she'd be all right. Then the moment he wasn't around, something terrible happened to her.

"I don't think Brett Davis meant any harm. He really wants to find the third Delta," Rory said.

Waylen couldn't even think about the damned alien tokens. "We've closed them. Nothing happened for years while the Shadows were off, and it can stay that way if we leave them disconnected. Silas, I'm understanding why your grandfather was so adamant they remained apart."

"So am I," Silas said.

Waylen had Gary stay with the civilians while he and Martina walked through the laboratory, past the offices, eventually checking the residences.

"Do you forgive me yet?" she asked when he entered the apartment block.

"Martina..."

She stopped and faced him. "Waylen, I lied to you. I'm part of the D.O.O.S. too."

Shadows of the Earth

"Of course you are."

Waylen thought about that night at the storage facility. If he remembered it correctly, she'd encouraged him to talk with the proprietor. Then she'd dismissed him, suggesting she could handle things while he investigated Loon Lake. "You knew…"

"I had an idea. The Department didn't stick together, and even Swanson wasn't sure where Trell or Gunn kept them. No one at the Department could have predicted that Gunn stored his token at his own home."

"What's the point? Can't we leave them all off? Won't we be safe?"

"Your guess is as good as mine," Martina said. She moved to the side, and they walked up the stairs. There was evidence of prior occupants, but the rooms were empty. The common space where they'd played pool only a week earlier was messy, but deserted.

Waylen plodded to the kitchen and grabbed a beer from the fridge. He offered one to Martina, but she declined. "The last time we did that, our unspoken rule flew out the window."

Her comment made him think about Charlotte. "I need this to be over."

"Give me the tokens. I'll handle it," she said.

"I think I'll hang on to them."

"You're seriously going to Boston? After all this?" Silas argued.

"I made an agreement with the university," she said. Rory peered at the building, glad to have left the gory laboratory. None of them had even speculated on what might have done such horrific damage to dozens of trained soldiers. Waylen had seen the alien, but only from a distance. The lab's camera system had malfunctioned. Dr. Rita was safely in a hospital bed, but the doctors were keeping her in a medically induced coma until her vitals strengthened.

There was nothing Rory could do here.

"I'll go with you," Silas said.

Rory saw the desperation on his face. He wanted to protect her, so why was she arguing with him? Every other man in her life had disappointed her in some way, but not Silas. "Okay."

He exhaled. "You won't regret this."

"What will you do all day?"

"I'll be the best damned roomie you've ever had."

Rory hadn't thought this through. Was she even allowed to bring a guest into the faculty dorms? Truthfully, she wasn't in the mood to sleep alone, not after yet another abduction. The Department's numbers had taken a loss, with Brett vanishing, and Clark Fallow's tragedy on the Moon.

They waited near the Planetae truck, and just past midnight, Waylen and Martina emerged without Special Agent Charles. Cody plodded behind the FBI agents, looking dejected.

"You're off?" Waylen asked.

"Yep," Silas answered. "What about you?"

"Cody's checking if we can access any of the camera feeds," Waylen told them.

Cody didn't seem excited by the prospect. "What's the matter?" Rory asked him.

"I dunno. You're leaving, and I have to stay…" Cody

glanced at the building. "People died today. We traveled from Kentucky to New York... through an alien portal." He shivered and stuck his hands into his jeans pockets. "This is probably goodbye."

Rory stepped closer. "What about after you're done?"

"I'll fly home to San Diego. I've been gone long enough."

Rory hugged him, and he accepted the quick embrace. He bumped knuckles with Silas, then started to the building. "Good luck with everything. It's been a slice."

They said farewell to Martina; then it was just Waylen escorting them to the truck. He leaned in and pursed his lips, as if choosing his words wisely. "There's still another Delta."

"I don't want to think about it," Rory said.

"That doesn't really matter. What we want is irrelevant. Aliens killed fifty soldiers today, and we don't know how or why."

"There could be another answer," Silas added.

"Do tell."

"Monroe's a weapons manufacturer. What if this was one of his at work? Those bodies could have undergone some version of chemical warfare."

"I've thought the same, but that doesn't justify the sheer number of shots fired toward the Hex. No, I believe something emerged from the Shadow."

Rory glanced around the complex. "They might not have returned through it."

Waylen's jaw tightened. "Another possibility."

Silas stood closer to Rory. "What about Darren and Plemmons? Where are they?"

"That's what I intend to find out. After I set Cody up, I'll go to the hospital and wait for Rita to regain consciousness. She'll have answers."

Rory hugged the agent, and Silas shook his hand.

"Take care of each other," Waylen said firmly.

"We will."

Waylen left without another word, and Silas tossed his pack into the backseat. "You have the journal, right?"

"It's there." Silas went to the driver's side and started the truck.

They drove past Gary's sedan, then the damaged gate, and onto the nearest freeway.

Rory wished to dive into the journal, to see if Peter Gunn made a comment about the alternative Delta, but her eyes fought her every step of the way. Each time she attempted, they felt more strained.

"Maybe we can stop for a coffee," she suggested after thirty minutes.

"No. Rory, if you plan on teaching in the morning, you need sleep. Do you have any idea how exhausted you are?"

"I have some idea," she said with a smile. Rory took a blue jacket with the Planetae logo from the back and folded it to make a pillow. She placed it between her head and the window, and closed her eyes. The truck bumped along, jostling her slightly, but she barely noticed. The hum of the tires at high speeds became a buzzing in her ears.

Rory saw the stone building, and smelled the grass and flowers. She felt the heat of the sun on her face.

"We're here," Silas said, startling her.

She sat up and dabbed her damp lips. It was daylight, and they were parked on campus by the faculty dorms in Boston. "How…"

"You were out. It took longer than I thought, and I

had to refuel an hour ago, but we made it." Silas offered her a cup of coffee. "Picked it up in a drive-through. Thought you might be hungry too."

Rory sniffed, identifying the breakfast sandwich, and glanced at the bag on the center console. "Thanks."

She couldn't believe she'd slept the entire trip, and that it was six thirty in the morning.

"Are you ready for your first day as a guest lecturer?" Silas asked.

"No," she said plainly.

Silas laughed and got out. "Too bad."

Rory stared at the dorm and mentally steeled herself for the coming semester.

12

*A*nother hospital.

Waylen paced the waiting room, trying not to interrupt the rest of the visitors. He noticed a couple, the red-cheeked woman holding her husband's hand. An older man with an actual newspaper slowly flipped the pages and grumbled under his breath. A young girl sat cross-legged on the floor, playing with a doll.

Cody had stayed at the lab with Martina and Gary, attempting to repair the computer system. He'd suspected the entire localized network was fried, but Cody thought he might have a work-around for it. Waylen checked his phone, but there were no messages.

Charlotte had texted him late last night, and it had been short but not curt. Waylen was already on eggshells with her, and wondered if he should have waited to contact her until the Deltas were in the past.

Visiting hours weren't for another hour, but those rules were different in the ICU. A doctor came out, and for a second, Waylen thought he was about to learn about Dr. Rita's condition. Then he turned and walked up to the couple. He spoke a few words, and their composure instantly crumbled.

Waylen needed fresh air. He walked to the main floor,

taking the stairs rather than the elevator. He hated being within confined spaces in a hospital. He could almost picture the superbugs clinging to the bright fluorescent fixtures, waiting for him to breathe something in.

He walked by a woman in a wheelchair, some apparatus beeping as he passed, and Waylen gave her a smile. She ignored him and continued to scowl at an invisible assailant.

The line for the cafeteria was short, and he went to the back of it, drumming his fingers on his hip while making sure his wallet was there. He knew they should notify Rita's family of her health crisis, but that would involve a lot of explaining. *I'm sorry, Mr. and Mrs. Singh. She ran out of air on the Moon.*

"Next!"

"Coffee. Black." Waylen pointed at a blueberry scone. "That too."

They poured the hot beverage, then packaged the pastry, and he paid, leaving a decent tip, mostly because he didn't want to accept change from a hospital. He wasn't normally a germaphobe, but any kind of health care facility had this effect on him.

Waylen took a seat at the farthest table, despite only four people residing in the cafeteria. He picked at the food and sipped the strong coffee while wishing for a doctor to tell him anything. He'd saved Rita's life, and now he needed to know what she'd seen. What happened at the laboratory? And where was the Secretary of Defense? Not to mention Darren Jones, whom he'd invited into this disastrous case. Darren had an ex-wife and children, and someone would seek him out.

Waylen got a second cup, then took his time relocating to the ICU waiting room. He checked in at the nurses' station before sitting.

A clock on the wall ticked. The girl dropped her doll and left it there, staring at the lifeless blonde plastic toy. The couple was gone, no doubt escorted to a grieving room.

Waylen tried to compartmentalize the last few weeks. He'd been moving a mile a minute, not settling down to think things through. While he had nothing but hours of solitude, he realized he should have been concentrating on the case's details. He drank the bitter brew and pulled his phone out to make notes. The Department of Outer Space may or may not have been a real organization. A few rogue people didn't make up an actual sanctioned government agency, even if they believed it to be. Brett Davis had taken Rory, killed Kevin Heffernan, and vanished into the Shadow in Kentucky.

Clark Fallow, the leader of the organization, was dead. Martina's dad was part of the crew, and he'd passed in 1999. Colin Swanson had joined them, leading to a secret mission to the Moon to retrieve the second Delta.

They were each currently dead or missing.

Waylen felt the weight of the six tokens in his jacket pocket. He wouldn't leave them with Martina and Cody, both of whom had acted suspect in the past. Gary Charles seemed trustworthy, but Waylen couldn't risk something as big as an invasion by letting anyone near the tokens.

He tried to recall what the being had looked like on the Moon, but his memory betrayed him. Had it been tall? From the distance, and the lacking reference points, he didn't know for certain. He couldn't remember any visible weapons on its person. Maybe it didn't need guns. Perhaps it was human... He shook his head and finished the second cup of coffee before tossing it into the garbage can. When he glanced up, another woman sat in the waiting room, nervously twisting a lock of hair on her finger.

Waylen hated hospitals.

"Special Agent Brooks," a nurse said.

He nodded and rose, clasping his palms together. "That's me."

"The patient is alive, but unresponsive. The doctor asked me to notify you. We're moving her into a room, and I'll come for you when she's awake and ready."

Waylen thanked her and exhaled with gratitude. All he could do now was wait.

"There are many paths to writing a book, as you're aware, but there's one constant. Can anyone take a guess what that is?" Rory asked.

A student in the front row raised her arm.

"Yes, go ahead." Rory didn't know any of their names, but was going to work on that.

"Outlining?"

"Not exactly," Rory said. "Some authors find outlining an affront to their craft, saying it stifles them."

"What about you?" the student asked. "Do you outline?"

"I have to. I've tried the other way, and it's not for me. My brain needs parameters." Rory could tell she'd lost some of them, and they were all making notes, mostly on laptops. "We'll expand on the basics later, but let's return to the original question."

A young man waved a hand. "The writing. You need to sit and type."

"Right. That's it…"

"Wallace."

"As with anything in life, if you want to be good at something, you must practice. Writing should be done every day, whether or not you feel like it. That's part of this class. In the course program on the online portal…" Rory stopped, and blinked, imagining the Shadow enveloping the classroom. She composed herself and continued. "In the portal, you'll find a shared spreadsheet of a word counter. Use it daily, filling in your counts. Seeing each other's progress will be excellent motivation."

"How much time are we talking? I have a full course load, and…" another man asked.

"Whatever you can. Two hundred words. Five hundred. A thousand. It depends on your experience and personal goals. This is not a competition, just a visualization tool that will help grow your confidence and make you realize that books, poems, or short stories can be written while working jobs or being a student."

They all seemed on board. The course was full, and Rory was hoping none of them dropped the class because of what might be perceived as daily homework. The bell rang, and she couldn't believe she'd survived her first teaching engagement unscathed.

"I'll see you all on Wednesday, when we'll discuss tropes and genres. Enjoy the rest of the day," she told them.

Rory stayed at the front of the class while they filed out, talking excitedly to one another. Rory remembered her time at school, being away from home, making new friends.

Shadows of the Earth

She gathered her things, and exited after she was alone. Marg Chambers lingered in the hall, waiting for her. "How did it go?"

"Well, I think."

"No one bolted, which is a positive sign," Marg said.

"Does that happen?"

"It did to me," Marg admitted. "Truth be told, I came off a little strong when I started. I don't think you have anything to worry about."

"Thanks," Rory said.

"What's your schedule like for the rest of the day?"

"I have my American Literature class this afternoon, so I'm heading home to review the syllabus again."

"Fantastic. See you soon, Rory."

Rory, delighted that it all seemed to go so well, went outside, finding the gloomy Monday morning refreshing. Wind tousled the treetops, and a few green leaves fell to the cobblestoned sidewalks. She watched the dark clouds moving quickly overhead, and walked with urgency, not wishing to be doused in her one decent professor-type outfit. She still had so many to-dos, shopping included. Maybe she could call her mom and dad to visit.

Rory hurried, then stopped by the alley Kevin had appeared in three days earlier. She pressed her eyes shut and continued, not thinking about the sickening sound he'd made hitting the hood of Brett's car. She'd done nothing wrong.

Silas was dressed and on the couch, reading *View from the Heavens*. "This is brilliant."

"Finally remembered you could read?" she teased.

Silas flipped it upside down and scratched his head. "Is this how it's done?"

"You don't have to read my book, Silas."

"I wanted to." Silas hopped up and kissed her. It was a strange feeling, having someone waiting at home for her, and being greeted with an intimate gesture. "How was class?"

"Actually... amazing." Rory described it, and Silas listened to her story, not interrupting like Kevin would have.

"I'm so proud of you," he said.

"Don't be. We have to wait to see if they learn anything. Should we grab lunch?"

"I already ordered from the sandwich shop, but I'll go pick it up. You have work to do, right?" he asked.

"Yeah, that would be perfect. Thanks, Silas." She lifted on her toes and kissed him this time.

"See you soon." He left the book open to his page, and Rory grabbed a bookmark to save his place. She held the copy and flipped to the inside flap, seeing her author photo.

"You've come a long way," Rory told herself, and set it on the coffee table.

She noticed Silas' bag on the floor near the bedroom, and she picked it up, removing the journal. Rory sat, going to the last few pages.

It's over. They've been dispersed. If anyone ever reads this, I believe it's best to leave geometry to the experts.

Rory read the line twice, realizing he was obviously meaning the triangle. She went back a few pages, stopping on a different entry.

I don't feel real. I have dreams of another life. Patricia notices it too.

"What the hell does that mean?" Rory said out loud. It sounded to her like Peter Gunn had found the third Delta, and judging by the other notation, he'd split the

Shadows of the Earth

tokens up. It really had been him she'd witnessed in the echo.

She heard footsteps approaching, and Rory closed the journal and slid it into the pack. She was done with that. Let the tokens stay in hiding.

Silas entered the suite, carrying a brown bag, and his smile lit up the room. He could be the source of light she needed to disperse her own shadows.

Cody stretched and took a bite of pizza. His laptop had greasy splotches on the keys, and he used a paper napkin to wipe them. He'd viewed surveillance footage from the day before, but it stopped at 3:47 P.M.

At that time, all the spacesuits were in place at the lockers. Only a few soldiers loitered in the laboratory, and Plemmons was in Monroe's old office with Clark Fallow. Then it stopped. The image froze, and Cody zoomed on every camera feed, hoping for a clue.

Nothing stood out.

"This is ridiculous." Cody ate the crust and leaned back in the chair, cracking his knuckles above his head. What had he learned about Planetae? He heard Martina on the phone in the hall, but did his best to ignore her.

They had backup systems in place, but everything on site was fried. Although… what if the satellites were operational? Cody smiled and clicked the mouse, switching gears. He used the same sneaky entrance he'd discovered in the early days at the laboratory, and accessed the satellite link. Clearly, their IT team hadn't anticipated someone trying this program. Cody could tell that if he'd been outside the Planetae building, he'd have been rejected. It was an intuitive system, but foolish on their part in hindsight.

Cody combed through millions of bytes of data, seeking a fraction of the network. It took him hours, but after a bathroom break, another soda, and two more pieces of cold pepperoni pizza, he had it.

The footage appeared on his screen, and he almost couldn't believe it. Someone had fried the network, but it continued to record, regardless. Cody considered watching it alone, then decided he should bring in Gary and Martina instead.

They both came instantly. "Did you get anything, or is this bad news?" Special Agent Charles asked.

"I have it." Cody played them the footage, starting from 3:47 P.M.

Martina grabbed a swivel chair from the neighboring room and slid it closer, while Gary hovered behind Cody, leaning in for a better view of the small laptop screen.

An alarm sounded in the feeds at 4:01. A voice called orders over a speaker, and the soldiers reached the laboratory soon after. The Shadow formed once Darren Jones clipped the tokens together. Plemmons and Fallow burst from the office, and Cody observed from five different camera angles as they jogged to the Hex. Fallow, being close to eighty, took longer, but they both arrived, as did Dr. Rita.

"What was the issue?" Martina asked.

Darren was the only person within the Hex, and they shouted at him. Cody couldn't hear the words, since the cameras were some distance away. He tried to retrieve proper feeds, but they were blank.

Darren stepped aside, and three figures emerged.

"Oh. My. God," Martina breathed.

Shadows of the Earth

Cody's heart pounded as they watched a trio of aliens enter the Hex through the portal. Darren acknowledged them.

Plemmons backed up, with Rita behind him, and rushed toward the lockers.

The door to the platform opened, and the first alien stepped to the stairs. He looked in both directions and lifted an arm. A red light pulsed, and Fallow shouted something. The soldiers took aim, and all fired at once. The sound was intense. Cody flinched with the noise of battle. The red pulse shot out, covering the room. The cameras went red, then black, and when it subsided, there wasn't a single soldier standing.

Fallow and Rita were behind the Hex, curled up small, as if avoiding detection. Plemmons had evaded his own death by hiding at the lockers.

The alien strode to the floor, followed by his two counterparts. Darren reached for the Delta, but stopped when the being shouted at him in a foreign tongue. Darren pointed at Plemmons, and the first alien grabbed him. Plemmons crumpled like a rag doll, and was carried away.

They walked slowly and methodically through the laboratory, and eventually outside. Darren got into one of the armored vehicles, opened the gate, and escorted the aliens from the premises, closing the barrier.

None of them spoke while they observed the lab again. Fallow and Rita donned their spacesuits, and for some reason, entered the Shadow, perhaps trying to figure out where the aliens had come from.

The clock counter on the bottom of the screens showed 4:11 P.M. Cody fast-forwarded, and forty minutes later, Waylen and Gary arrived.

"That was intense," Gary said. "We barely missed

them."

Cody rewound the scene and paused on the beings in the hallway after finding a decent angle. He zoomed in. "Aliens are real."

"Who do we tell?" Gary asked.

"I have no idea," Martina said.

Cape Canaveral, Florida
August 12th, 1988

"Smile for the camera!" The photographer took a dozen shots, and Peter did his best to keep the friendly expression. The three of them hadn't done a photo op together in a couple of years, and somehow it looked like they'd aged a decade.

Fred Trell was the first to wave the woman off. "I think we've had enough. Have a good day." He turned to Peter. "God, I need a stiff drink. What do you say we get the hell out of here?"

"Fine by me," Peter said. He'd left his wife at home, knowing Patty would be bored at such an event. He didn't want her to be around when he finally talked some sense into Colin.

They entered a car that was waiting for them, and as usual, Fred found the seediest establishment in town. Peter grimaced as he sat across from Colin, and waited until they had beverages in front of them before speaking. For good measure, he ordered a second round, asking for it to be delivered in five minutes. The server just nodded and walked off without a word.

Shadows of the Earth

"I'm glad we could all…" Colin said, and Peter cut him off.

"Stop it."

"What?"

"I know what you're doing. This D.O.O.S. bullcrap. We're done, Colin. Fred and I are not giving you our tokens, and I don't intend on hearing another word about it," he said.

"I can change your mind." Colin's smile was unsettling. He sipped the drink and slowly spun his tumbler, waiting for someone to speak.

Fred took the bait. "How?"

Colin checked over his shoulder while pulling something from his jacket. He slid the tokens out, and Peter clenched his fist under the table.

"What are those?" Peter asked.

"You know what they are," Colin said.

"No, you're lying. We hid them…"

"This is another set."

"I don't believe you."

Colin pushed one closer to Peter. "Then hold this."

"What do you want?" Fred asked.

"With the third, we'll control the portals, travel to other worlds, explore like real astronauts," Colin said.

Peter stared at the three pieces of alien metal. "Why can't we just forget it?"

"Because we're not meant to."

Peter sighed, and downed his whiskey. "To hell with it." He grabbed the token, and nothing would ever be the same.

PART FOUR
DECISIONS

1

"Son, the car's out front!" Arthur called.

Silas adjusted his tie and wiped a scuff off his shoe with his thumb. "I'm ready." They got into the black vehicle, and his usually somber father was beaming. "Why are you so excited?"

"You're joining me at the office," he said.

"Just for a visit."

"You're not really going to stay in Boston on campus while your... girlfriend teaches, are you?" Arthur was one of those men that thought about work from the moment he rose out of bed until the second his eyes closed at night. If you weren't the same, he held you at a lower esteem, which suited Silas fine.

"She's not my girlfriend," was all he could think to say.

"No?"

"Maybe. We haven't had time to discuss it." Silas watched as an older woman powerwalked by in a sweatsuit.

"If you want to return to work, there's a position

waiting," his dad said.

"You replaced me already. What would I do?"

"I'm sure we can find something. High level. I won't always be here to do this job."

"As if," Silas muttered. "You and retirement are like oil and water. They don't mix." It was nice to have a normal conversation, not one revolving around tokens, Deltas, and aliens.

"We'll see. One day, I'll hand over the reins and start woodworking in the garage or fly-fishing with Uncle Bob. Your mother's side sure loves their fishing."

"You could use the house at Loon Lake," Silas offered.

"I don't think so, son."

"Why?"

"That was your grandfather's, and he wasn't my biggest fan."

"Is this about the inheritance? Because if you want anything from it, I'm more than happy—"

"Stop right there, Silas. I'm glad he left it to you and Clare. I have more than enough," Arthur said.

"I heard from the locals that Loon Lake is spectacular for fishing if you rise before the sun. You do that now, so I doubt it would be much of a strain."

"It's the only time I can get a walk in and read my papers."

Silas was proud that his father had canceled his actual physical newspapers and graduated to perusing them on his tablet.

"Dad, what really happened with Grandpa?" Silas recalled what Rory had told them, regarding the echo from the second Delta. How was he involved with the disbursement of the last alien triangle?

"What do you mean?"

They inched across the busy bridge, heading into Manhattan.

"When did you stop talking to him?" Silas asked.

"It wasn't a quick process. He was distant. I don't know how my saint of a mother put up with him. He was always irritable over trivial things like the wind."

"But they visited you in New York?"

"Sure."

"When?"

"Clare was two. Remember the story about them coming for Christmas? You weren't born yet, so it was around 1995."

Silas thought the dates aligned with what Martina had suggested to Waylen about his traveling.

"Why do you ask?"

"It's nothing."

"Are you still in any danger?" Arthur asked.

Silas shook his head. "Nah. We closed the... We're out of the woods."

"Glad to hear it." His dad patted his knee and directed the driver to take an alternate route. They stopped a block from the office, where the road was barricaded because of construction.

Silas savored the sounds of the city as they exited the car. He'd avoided his own condo, choosing to stay with his parents. With Rory's folks in town for a visit, he wanted to make himself scarce.

Walking to their midtown office seemed normal. The sun reflected off high windows; the air held the subtle scent of garbage and sewers. His feet vibrated as a train car rumbled by in the subway below them, bearing south. It was like he'd traveled back two months, and it was just

Shadows of the Earth

another Monday.

They took the elevator to the twelfth floor, and he smiled at the front desk administrator. Thea waved as she tapped the earpiece, answering a call.

"You need a desk for today?" Arthur asked.

The moment the boss set foot in the building, the energy changed. Silas had never noticed it before, but their postures shifted. The sound of the place grew muted. Brian arrived, thrusting a tablet at Arthur. "Sir, Mark's running into a shipment issue. The containers are stuck in port, and now we're being told we have to pay for the storage and crane delays."

"Not on my watch." Arthur took the device and stormed down the hall.

Silas went in search of Beverly, Peter's old assistant when he ran a consulting firm in the nineties. Since then, she'd been a staple at the furniture company. Recently, Silas learned she'd funneled information about Clare and Silas to their grandparents.

She was near Arthur's office. Beverly looked older than he remembered, but maybe it was him that had changed. The entire place seemed different: stale, stuffy, and a little suffocating.

"Silas!" She rose and gave him a hug. "Are you here to stay?"

"Just visiting."

"Your dad is in there." She pointed at the door.

"That's okay. I came with him this morning. I actually wanted to talk to you."

"Me?"

"Can we grab a coffee?"

"I really…" She looked at the clock, which ticked to 8:37 A.M.

"It's fine. I already told my dad."

She smiled, then led him to the break room. It was empty at the early hour, with everyone at their desks. He poured them drinks, making her a tea, since she only drank one coffee a day, and that was at home before work.

"You remembered," she said, dipping the tea bag by the string into the steaming water.

"Beverly, it's been a month." He laughed.

"Feels much longer." She took a seat and folded her hands on her lap. "Now, what can I do for you?"

"It's about Grandpa."

She cleared her throat and examined the cup. "Yes?"

For a moment, Silas wondered if something had happened between them. His younger secretary... constantly away from home for meetings and conventions. Her expression sure held a guilty visage. "You worked for him in the Nineties, right?"

"I did."

"What can you tell me about a vacation he took?"

She seemed to be relieved at the question. "He traveled a lot, Silas."

"This was different. He might have kept it discreet."

She pursed her lips and dragged the tea bag around the inner rim of the cup. "I know which you're referring to."

"What happened?" Silas leaned conspiratorially close, and when he realized it, gave her space.

"I booked the flights and train rides. Peter instructed me to never speak of it again. I swear I had no clue what your grandfather was doing. I had to lie to Patty when she called me, and that broke my heart, but he was my boss, and I wasn't one to ask questions."

Shadows of the Earth

It noticeably pained her to relive the memory. "Do you remember the details?"

"No," she said, dashing his hopes. "But I have records at home, if you'd like me to find them."

"Really?"

"My house is too big, and because it's just me, I've filled the basement with thirty years of files. I keep meaning to sort and toss them, but haven't had the energy to do so," she said.

"Can I come over to check?"

Beverly sipped her drink and glanced at the clock. "Would Peter be angry at me for sharing this?"

"From the sounds of it, he was upset at everything, so probably."

The comment brought a smile to her face. "Oh, he wasn't so bad. More bark than bite. He changed around the time of that trip."

"How so?"

"I couldn't pinpoint it. Three weeks before he left, Patty called me, asking if I'd noticed a shift in his behavior. I said no, but that wasn't quite true. She begged him to see a doctor." Beverly tapped her temple. "This made him furious, but he did it."

"He did?"

"Peter would have done anything for his wife."

For all the harshness surrounding Silas' grandfather, Peter obviously had a soft spot for Patty.

"Can I…"

"Yes. After work, come to the house and I'll make you dinner."

Silas noticed Clare walking by, and nodded. "That's perfect. I'll be ready at four."

"I'd better get to it." Beverly placed her cup in the

sink and rushed off.

Clare entered a minute later, holding her *World's #1 Mom* mug, and filled it with coffee. "What are you doing here?"

"Hey, sis. Nice to see you too."

"Seriously? I thought you were at Loon Lake, or Boston, or wherever the hell you've been running around to." Clare squinted as she watched him. A layer of expensive perfume wafted from her like mist from the Shadow.

"I chose to visit my family. Is that a crime?"

"Sure. You decide to keep the house?"

"I haven't made up my mind."

"Well, decide, because the lawyer is withholding funds until we've signed off on it," she said.

Silas lifted an eyebrow. "You don't have enough?"

"The kids' prep school raised its fees this year, and I'm looking at a remodel…" She stopped and sat, sighing out a breath. "Sorry for coming at you like that. I have no reason to." Clare gazed at the doors, ensuring they were alone. "I'm frustrated because you quit."

"Why?"

"Because I was going to. Since you're gone, Dad will freak if I leave on top of that. He wanted this to be a legacy company, something to pass on to generations of Gunns."

"Now I feel bad," he murmured.

"You should." Clare sipped her coffee. "Blake mentioned moving to the country, and I thought…"

"Blake?"

"I've been dating someone. Shhhhh, Mom and Dad don't know. They're the worst with me and men, especially since the first marriage was a dumpster fire."

"You're not considering doing that again, are you?"

Shadows of the Earth

"Not yet, but I… We can't move on if I'm trapped running operations for a furniture company."

"Do you realize how ridiculous we must sound?"

Her nods were slow and long. "Absolutely."

"I'll talk to Dad."

"You will?"

"He's had offers from larger companies to buy him over the years," Silas said.

"Seriously?"

"Sure. I've been involved as the CFO."

"Are they decent offers?" Clare asked.

"With a little negotiation, they would be," Silas told her.

"That's the angle. Tell him neither of us wants to take it over, and play the sale tilt," she whispered. "And don't say a word about this, because the staff will freak."

"He mentioned retirement this morning," he added.

"Perfect." Clare cradled her cup. "Besides the usual, how are you doing?"

Silas couldn't tell her about being drugged and held hostage by a rogue organization aiming to mine the Moon. Or the subsequent gun fight, and definitely not about the mess of melted soldiers only an hour north of their current position. "I'm fine," he said instead.

"And Rory Valentine?"

"Swanson," he corrected. "She's… pretty great."

"I haven't seen that lopsided smirk since you kissed Amy Trundleman after my seventeenth birthday party."

Silas laughed, recalling the moment with vivid clarity. "It's too bad her boyfriend saw us." He rubbed his cheek where the brute had clocked him.

"They're married," Clare said.

"No kidding." Silas didn't keep in touch with many

people from the old neighborhood.

They stayed and chatted for a few minutes, temporarily distracting him from his real reason for coming to the city.

2

"Normally, I'd suggest removing anything you don't use every day from the countertops, but it looks like you've already prepared the kitchen," Logan, his realtor, said.

Charlotte ran a finger down the quartz. "It's dusty."

"The cleaners will show this afternoon," Waylen told her.

"Cleaners? Cancel them. Jeez, Waylen, we're two grown adults. Where do you keep the dusters?" Charlotte started opening cupboards.

"You think we can get a decent offer?"

"The market's hot, and the timing couldn't be better. New school year is in full effect, and people are regretting their districts. Since it's September, you'll have lighter competition, but also fewer buyers. In the end, I believe we'll score asking, maybe ten over."

Waylen did the math, knowing he'd paid a hundred thousand less, and only owed one twenty. "That'll work for me. Thanks for swinging by, Logan."

"No problem. Make sure the place is spotless, and I'll come by with the photographer to take photos later today. I'll bring the sign and load the specs online tonight. You'll be booking viewings within twenty-four hours. Is there somewhere you can go while people scour the property?"

"I won't be in town."

Charlotte stopped looking and frowned at him. "So soon?"

"I told you it was just a drop-in."

Logan said his goodbyes, and Waylen caught him before he drove off. "I forgot to give you this." Waylen passed him the spare key.

Charlotte linked her arm in his, and they stared at the house from the sidewalk. "It's a nice place."

"I think so."

"Will you miss it?"

"I never felt like it was home, since I barely slept here."

"Is that going to change?"

"Yes."

She leaned her head on his shoulder. "Don't bother renting that apartment in the city."

"No?"

"Stay with me."

Waylen closed his eyes, picturing the freeze-framed capture of the aliens walking off with Plemmons, Darren Jones at the lead.

"Okay." Charlotte couldn't know about them, not yet. "I'll be in and out of town while the new assistant director gets his bearings. He's got me on a pensioner's scam at the moment, but mentioned I might be sent away," he told her.

"Waylen, that's fine, but I need to see you're into the relationship this time," she said.

"I am." He took her hands, squaring off to face her. Waylen touched her chin and kissed Charlotte. "We can make this work."

Shadows of the Earth

"Good." Charlotte started up the walkway. "Now, where's that cleaning gear?"

He shrugged. "I only have the basics. The lady came once a week when I was around. We can hit the store."

Thirty minutes later, they were at one of those large supermarkets, and had a cart half-filled with supplies. "You realize we're leaving tomorrow, right?"

"Then stash it in the closet for the new homeowners," she said.

They wandered through the place, Waylen feeling like a stranger in such an establishment. How many times had he set foot in a supermarket of this magnitude? "Do you shop at this store?"

"Usually, I go to the market by me. It's a lot smaller. I prefer the creaking wooden floors and the butcher you know by sight, if not name."

"You have a way with words," he said. "Anyone ever tell you that?"

"Only all the time." She smiled.

"This is pretty nice," he admitted. Waylen tried to remember what the relationship used to be like, and struggled to.

"Waylen, you really have been focused on work. Shopping's a chore."

"Not when it's with you," he said.

"Okay, enough flattery. I already agreed to let you stay."

They stood in line at a busy checkout, and Waylen's gaze drifted to the stacks of magazines. He removed one from its spot and flipped to the article listed on the front cover. *Aliens. Are they among us?* The image was blurry, but it showed what slightly resembled a UFO in the sky above a barn. The location was listed as rural Kentucky. Another picture had an obviously photo-altered head inside a window. It was so comically bad that it made Waylen laugh. He shoved it back as the conveyor cleared up.

He paid, and they hauled the score into the parking lot. When the car's trunk was full, Waylen returned the cart and saw a car screech to a halt near their rental. His first reaction was to reach for his gun, but he wasn't carrying it.

Charlotte looked terrified, but Waylen relaxed when he spied Assistant Director Adam Elling exiting the passenger side. He recognized Special Agent Charles behind the steering wheel.

"Who are these men?" she asked him.

"Charlotte, meet my boss, Adam. That's Gary." Waylen gestured at the big man in the driver's seat.

"We have to talk." Adam bounced on his feet, like he'd recently downed a double espresso.

"Here?" Waylen glanced around the parking lot. Someone honked, eager for a spot to open up.

"It's important."

"You could have called," he told the new assistant director.

"There's been a sighting." Adam's words were impactful.

"I understand. Follow me." Waylen got into the car, and when Gary moved, he backed up, and the anxious driver swerved in to fill the vacant spot.

"What's this about?"

"You don't want to know," he said.

"Try me." Charlotte clicked her seatbelt.

Waylen checked his mirror and saw they were trailing him. "I haven't told you everything."

"Why isn't that a surprise? I thought this would be

different."

"It can be. It's ..."

"What?" she shouted.

"Once you hear it, you can't unhear it. Do you understand?"

"Waylen, you're making me nervous."

He weighed his options. "Aliens are real."

"Aliens?"

"I've been to the Moon," he said.

"The Moon? Waylen, what's the matter with you?"

"All this time, I... the astronauts found something on the last trip to the Moon," he drawled. "It was a portal, a hole in space that allowed them to visit another planet. The crew lied about the missing two hours, and no one was aware of these *things* until recently. Turns out, an organization called the Department of Outer Space was formed years earlier, and with the help of Colin Swanson, they located a second alien contraption. They flew on a clandestine mission to the Moon to retrieve it. Now, we're under the assumption there's a third and final Delta. That's what they're—"

"Waylen, you need help."

He glanced at her, seeing disbelief written all over her face. "There's more. Jacob Plemmons knows everything, and he was at the facility with me in New York a while ago. Clark Fallow too."

"The NASA administrator and our secretary of defense?" Charlotte paled at the mention of the high-level officials. "What do they have to do with this?"

"Clark's dead. They took Plemmons."

"Who? Where?"

"What's it been like at the White House?"

"Normal."

"The President?"

"He's not in town."

"This is real. You have to believe me."

"Then why are we in Atlanta selling your house?" she asked.

"I told them to leave me out of it," he admitted. "I wanted to return to the Bureau, and…"

"Return? You left it?"

"That's another long story." He braked and parked in his driveway, with Gary blocking him as they took a spot on the street.

"Waylen, none of this makes sense," she said.

"It will. Come on." He went outside, and Adam glared in Charlotte's direction.

"Can she give us some privacy?" Adam asked.

Waylen shook his head. "I'm sorry, but no. I've told her everything."

Adam looked ready to rip into him, but refrained. "Inside."

Waylen left the cleaning supplies in the trunk and unlocked his door, letting them in. "What's this about a sighting?"

Adam flipped his cell toward Waylen, showing a video feed. It was Darren Jones.

"He looks familiar," Charlotte said. Waylen saw a flash of surprise.

"I met him at your house."

"Who is he?" she asked.

"From what we gather, that man is working with the aliens," Adam said.

"And you brought him to my home?" she exclaimed.

"Assistant Director Ben recommended him…"

"Waylen, this video was taken in Rhode Island. I want

Shadows of the Earth

you to head to Providence, search his place, and find out anything you can. The Director has ordered me to do whatever I need to locate Plemmons, and to do it quietly. They haven't announced Clark's death, and this Doctor Rita's still not talking," Adam said.

"What are you doing?" Waylen asked Gary.

"I'm going with you. We believe those three beings from the Shadow are hiding out with Darren."

"Beings?" Charlotte cried.

Adam removed something from his pocket. "I can't keep these."

"Why?" Waylen wanted nothing to do with the tokens. He'd pawned them off on Adam before leaving D.C. yesterday, and had felt far lighter after getting rid of the burden.

"Take them!" Adam ordered.

Waylen hesitated, then snatched the separated tokens. Charlotte's gaze landed on them, and she stared without blinking.

"Good luck." Adam shook his hand.

"You too."

They left, and the room remained silent for a full minute.

"The Moon?" Charlotte sank to the couch. "I'm coming." Her gaze lingered on the tokens.

"What?"

"To Providence. And you're going to tell me every detail of this case," she said sternly.

"Can we do this while we clean?" Waylen gestured to the door. He checked his phone when it chimed. "The flight's not for another two hours." He noticed a seat for Charlotte as well.

"Fine, but you're scrubbing the toilets."

3

"Don't forget to finish your paper on themes from your current Steinbeck novel," Rory said while the students started closing laptops and packing up their bags.

The second the room was empty, her father entered, giving a slow applause. Kathy offered a faint smile as she tugged at her gold necklace. "My darling daughter, you've reached a pinnacle."

"It's nothing, Dad."

He gestured at the lectern, then to the seats. "This is... something."

"Did you guys stay busy?"

"There's a lot to see in Boston, and since we rarely visited when you were living here before, we kept ourselves occupied," Kathy said. Her comments were usually laced with cynicism, and this was no exception. "We won't be seeing Kevin anytime, will we?"

"If he shows his face, I'll make sure he gets the point." Oscar slapped a fist into his palm. Rory didn't think of her father as a fighter, but the glint of anger said otherwise.

"He's not going to bother us," Rory said. "Come on, let's go to my place. Then we can figure out where to have dinner."

"You haven't made a reservation?" Kathy asked. "It's

Shadows of the Earth

already…"

"Mom, it's three, and this isn't Woodstock. There are countless options on a Monday evening." Rory gathered her bag and slung the heavy satchel over a shoulder.

"May I take that for you?" her dad asked.

"Nah, I'm good." Rory exited the class and waved at Garnet as he spoke to one of the maintenance people near the bathrooms. "I have to drop by the office."

"Hear that, Kathy? Our Rory has an office," Oscar said.

They entered the building ten minutes later, and Rory instantly regretted bringing her parents. Marg Chambers hung up the phone when she noticed her, and rushed into the foyer. "Rory, you've brought guests."

"Marg, meet my parents, Kathy and Oscar."

They did the customary handshakes, and Rory zoned out as her dad regaled Marg with a story of Rory in middle school, writing her first book. She went to her office and removed the computer and heavy textbook from the bag.

Rory sat in her cramped space and wondered how Silas was doing in New York. He'd gone to visit his own family, but she knew him better than he thought. She was fully aware he'd chosen to leave while her parents visited, and she couldn't blame him. Rory wasn't going to tell them there was a man living with her on campus, no matter how much his reputation helped.

Her cell buzzed, and she found a message from Martina Sanchez.

The D.O.O.S. is dark. No one is talking.

Rory fought the urge to ignore the text, but eventually relented. *What about Somboon Suwan?*

Ghosted me. I can't find him.

He was the only member Rory knew of besides Martina still out there, but surely, they had others. Clark Fallow was dead. Brett had somehow vanished into the Delta in Louisville, and Rory was done with it.

Silas wasn't just in the city visiting Long Island, and she hated that he hadn't been fully transparent with her. Could they last if they lied or kept omitting their actual feelings and motivations? Justine would tell her no.

Waylen's on his way to Providence.

Rory stared at the words. It was too close to Boston for her liking. She didn't wish to be in the same vicinity as the Deltas, and they were only a quick trip down the 95.

She put the phone away when Marg appeared. "There she is," Marg said. "Y'all have a great night, and don't forget to try that fusion place I mentioned."

Marg wandered off, and Oscar's gaze floated around the small office. "It's… quaint."

"Dad, I'm here temporarily. They're not giving me a corner suite," she said.

"It's fine. For your first semester," Kathy added. "Let's get to your apartment so your father can take his pills."

"Kathy."

She waved a dismissive hand. "It's not like Rory doesn't know about your high blood pressure."

Students walked throughout campus, and the scene relaxed Rory. They were starting their lives, taking courses to enrich their minds, regardless of whether they saw it that way yet. Some of them would do great things, and others would fail. Rory hoped they'd hop back on their feet like she had.

Her mom seemed pleasantly surprised with her accommodations and didn't say one judgmental comment while she showed them around. Rory had gone all out on preparations, even though they were staying at a swanky hotel near the water.

"Are you going to change?" Kathy asked.

Rory glanced at her outfit and nodded. "Sure, I was just about to," she lied.

Oscar opened the fridge, probably checking to see if she had it stocked with the staples, and Rory headed to the bedroom, closing the door.

When she emerged in a simple black dress, her mother was talking with a uniformed police officer. "Rory is right there."

Rory's heart leapt, and she did her best to remain composed. "Can I help you?"

He walked in, his partner lingering in the hall, hand on the holstered gun. "We're responding to a missing persons report for one Kevin Heffernan. Do you know Mr. Heffernan?"

Rory nodded. "I used to date him."

"Date?"

"We lived together."

"When did you last see Mr. Heffernan?"

Rory had to think, because she couldn't rightly admit to witnessing his death a few blocks away. "A month or so."

"He came to Woodstock and harassed my daughter!" Oscar shouted.

The officer glanced at him, as if gauging his threat level. "Can you expand on that?"

Rory blew at a hair in her face and sighed. "I moved home after we broke it off, and he showed up unannounced."

"What happened?"

"He threatened me, and I punched him."

"You hit him?" the cop asked.

"On the nose."

"What did Kevin do?"

She didn't mention Jack, because that might lead them down a long, arduous path she wanted no part of. "He was angry."

"Has Kevin contacted you?"

Rory assumed they were aware he'd phoned her. "Yes."

"The campus security staff mentioned you warned them he'd been stalking you again," he said.

"He's called twice, I think."

"Have you seen him?"

"No," she said evenly.

The officer didn't break their locked gaze and made notes. "If you hear from Kevin again, drop us a line." He offered a business card and stepped into the hall. The second cop nodded solemnly as the duo departed, heavy-footed on the worn hardwood.

"He's missing?" Oscar asked.

"I guess so," she said, breathing lighter.

"About that reservation…" Kathy changed the subject so quickly, Rory almost laughed. "I'm not really interested in this big-city fusion Marg suggested. I prefer a chef that stays in their lane; otherwise, it's a waste of a good palate. Oscar, what about Spanish food? Rory, is there somewhere we can get fish? Your dad has been eating far too much red meat."

Rory, glad for the usual banter, set a palm on her mother's arm. "I have the perfect spot."

Her parents left, and Rory stood in the entryway, gazing into her apartment. Mist clung to her ceiling, her bookshelves, and the TV in the corner. She shut the door, aware it wouldn't do her any good. The Shadow always followed.

Silas almost forked another piece of roast, but decided against it. "That was delicious," he told Beverly.

Her home was quite decadent, with old wooden furniture so large that looked like it must have been built inside the house.

"I'm glad you enjoyed it, Silas. Imagine if Peter knew we were dining together all these years later," she said.

"I bet he'd be ecstatic."

"Yes, he would." Beverly rose to clear the table, and Silas hurried to help. They stacked the dishes in the galley kitchen, and she told him to start in the basement. "I'll bring you a coffee in a few minutes. The files are all labeled by year, so you shouldn't struggle to locate what you're after."

Silas thanked her and walked to the door, peering into the darkness below. For a second, he thought it was a Shadow, threatening to swallow him whole, until he flipped the avocado-colored light switch and banished the blackness with the power of a sixty-watt bulb.

The space was unfinished, with low ceilings and a musty odor he guessed would never leave, no matter how hard one might try. The floor remained dry, keeping the boxes from retaining any moisture. Beverly may have struggled to get rid of things, but she sure didn't leave them in disarray. Everything was organized beyond belief. Her Christmas decorations were closed, with each box labeled for the purpose. *Main floor tree. Veranda decorations.* Silas smiled and continued to the file storage boxes. She had fifty stacked four high, and most of the containers had crumpled at the lids from the weight.

Silas checked the dates, moving from the Eighties to the early Nineties, and stopped at 1997. He removed the top box and slid the one below it free, popping the lid off. He searched for anything labeled with Peter's consulting firm's logo, and discovered seven hefty folders.

"Here you go," Beverly said, surprising him. He hadn't noticed her footsteps. She handed him a coffee cup centered on a small plate.

"Thank you."

"Take your time. I'll be upstairs." She left him in the stuffy basement.

Silas investigated the dates on an itinerary and judged them accurate. He ran over the company financials for that fiscal year, and saw that despite a few months of travel, Peter added no new business in 1997. "What were you doing?"

He kept thinking about Rory's echo and seeing Peter Gunn in the vision. Silas took anything resembling train stubs and flight details, as well as hotel bills, and shoved them into one folder. He returned the files to their previous place, and headed upstairs with his empty cup.

"That's it?"

Silas held the folder up. "Can I take this?"

"I'd be happy if you cleared it all out."

"Are you serious?"

Beverly nodded. "It's time."

"Why don't I call the shredding company we use at the office? I'll book it for this weekend and pay them extra to take the boxes."

Shadows of the Earth

For a breath, he guessed she'd decline his offer, but she hugged him. "You've always been a good kid, Silas. Thank you. You have no idea how difficult it is to let go of the past."

"I have a bit of an idea," he murmured. "Thanks for dinner."

"Will you be coming back to the office?"

"I don't think so."

"That's too bad." She saw him out and held the door open while he wandered off.

He strolled slowly, enjoying the pleasant evening. Silas eventually hopped on a bus going east, and arrived a block from his parents' house thirty minutes later.

Arthur was in the living room, and his mom sat in her chair at the table, knitting a scarf. "How was dinner?" his father asked.

"Good."

"What's that?" Arthur looked at the files.

The baseball game was loud, and Silas grabbed the remote, turning it down. "Nothing."

"If you say so."

Silas took a seat and muted the game.

"I'm watching that, son."

"I need to talk to you."

"About?"

All they could hear for a second was the clicking of Silas' mom's knitting needles.

"You should sell the business."

"Sell?" Arthur reached for his beer and took a sip. "Why would I do that?"

"It's a good time. Your books are clean, you're having a great third quarter…"

"I know all this, Silas. But why sell?"

"Clare wants out," he said.

"Is that so?" Arthur's voice stayed steady. "And you?"

"Dad, I'm already gone."

"I guess I had hopes you'd come to your senses. I was actually going to mention we had another offer."

"That's great."

"I suppose it is. I started this business as a legacy for my children."

"We appreciate your efforts, Dad."

"Why couldn't Clare tell me?" Arthur asked.

"She cares too much and didn't want to hurt your feelings."

"Honey, it's time," Alice said. She set a hand on his shoulder from behind him. "You've always talked about traveling the world."

Arthur looked up at his wife. "You're probably right."

Silas left them to discuss the details and headed to the spare room. He spread the pages across the bedding and grabbed a blank journal to record his findings.

If what he believed was true, Peter Gunn had found the third Delta and dispersed the three tokens, intending on keeping them separated.

Until now.

4

*W*aylen had always enjoyed Providence, Rhode Island. It was an old city, nestled along the water, with a decent population, but it seemed more like a town.

He glanced beside him, almost stunned to see Charlotte there. "You sure you want to do this?"

"Yes."

Waylen was breaking all kinds of laws, but Darren Jones was a serious fugitive. He'd stood by while they murdered fifty soldiers and escorted threatening aliens from the Planetae facility. Waylen needed to learn where they'd gone, and quickly.

Special Agent Gary Charles flashed his lights ahead, showing it was a go. "Stay here and call me if you see anything alarming. We have the cameras recording."

Charlotte held the professional camera with the telescoping lens, and nodded at him. "Be careful, Waylen. I just got you back."

He leaned over the console and kissed her. "I'll be fine."

Darren lived in a pleasant building, an old brick brownstone only a block from the harbor. It seemed like a great area, within walking distance of coffee shops and trendy bars. At ten PM on a Tuesday, it was quiet. The streetlights gave off a consistent buzzing sound when he exited the car and met Gary on the sidewalk. "I'll take the rear. You hang out front, in case we get a runner."

"We really haven't thought this through, Waylen," Gary said. "What if… *they* are here?"

Waylen pictured the mess the alien device had left in the lab, and shuddered. "I doubt Darren came to his house with his guests. I'd bet all of Monroe's money they're off grid."

Gary unclipped his holster and removed his gun, remaining in the shadows. "Go."

Waylen did the same and circled the townhouses. They each had their own narrow yard, with a wooden fence. He tried the rear gate and found it unlocked. As he moved through the overgrown grass, he triggered a neighbor's motion sensor light fixture, and the glow filled the next-door yard. Somewhere in the vicinity, a dog barked, making its presence known.

Waylen reached the steps and jogged up, searching for cameras. He touched the handle and spun it, finding the door locked. He grabbed a bundle of burlap sitting near a potting station on the deck and took a landscaping brick from the garden. Weeds had overtaken the region, and Waylen saw a couple of pumpkins reflecting the moonlight between them.

He wrapped the brick and cautiously hit the glass with the covered weight. It shattered as quietly as one might hope, and Waylen turned the lock from the inside, letting himself in. He stepped across the shards and into Darren Jones' house.

What had happened? Waylen couldn't understand the steps that must have transpired for Darren to become an accomplice to an alien race. Was this the first move in an

Shadows of the Earth

invasion? He had so many unanswered questions, and he prayed he'd find evidence in Darren's home.

Before continuing, he listened for any signs of occupancy. A clock ticked loudly from somewhere in the house, and water dripped in the kitchen sink, but otherwise, it was dead silent.

Waylen kept the lights off, since the living room's drapes were wide enough to brighten the space. With a quick inspection, he opened the front door and let Gary in.

"Clear?" the special agent asked.

"Not yet." Waylen glanced at the stairs. "You go down, I'll go up."

"Deal."

He crept to the steps and climbed them slowly, hitting the second floor. The townhouse was lean and tall, with three stories. This level had two bedrooms and a bath. All were tidy and empty. He noticed kids' stuff in the rooms. This was where Darren's children slept when they visited on weekends.

How could a family man conspire with aliens?

Waylen got to the top and found the primary suite. It took up the entire floor, with a reading nook, a full bathroom, and a king-sized bed. He picked up a book on the nightstand, flipping to the cover. It talked about making first contact through the use of radio waves. It looked to be from the Eighties or earlier.

Gary arrived a minute later, shrugging. "The only stuff in the basement was podcast gear. He probably recorded there."

"This was a bust," Waylen said. He texted Assistant Director Elling and sat on the bed while waiting for a response. "We may as well…"

Nathan Hystad

Look for a key to his vacation property.

He showed Gary the phone. "Does everyone make more than us?" the other agent asked.

"Apparently." Waylen typed in the address and found it wasn't too far, just an hour south in Little Compton.

They scoured the bedroom, then returned to the kitchen, discovering a spare set of keys on a chain with a golf course logo on it. "This has to be the place," he said, dangling them on a finger.

"Do we go now?" Gary asked.

"Yeah, while it's dark." Waylen left the damaged door in the back, and they accessed the front, using the keys to flip the lock shut.

Charlotte looked petrified in the car, and he smiled in consolation. "Did you get anything?"

"A lead. Sorry, but I have to drop you off at the hotel," he said.

"No way." She lowered the camera. "I'm coming."

Waylen suddenly felt the weight of the tokens in his pocket. "Okay." Now he'd have to protect her *and* the alien pieces.

"It's that easy?" Charlotte asked as he started the car. Gary took his own ride, and they turned around, leaving Waylen to proceed first.

"You'd rather I argue? I know better."

Charlotte gave him a smile. "You're learning. Who ever said one can't teach old dogs new tricks?"

Waylen laughed, then stuck a palm to his chest, feigning pain. "Who are you calling old?"

"Where are we going?"

"An hour south, to Darren's place on the water."

"You believe he brought these… aliens to his vacation home?"

Shadows of the Earth

"Darren can't just wander around with three aliens. He's got to be close."

"Why not put a nationwide APB out on Jones?"

"They will if we fail, but we're talking about actual beings from another planet, Charlotte. This is a fire that needs to be extinguished quickly and quietly."

"You have the... Delta?" Charlotte gazed at the front of his jacket.

"Yes. Both of them."

"So they can't bring any more to Earth, right?"

"That's the expectation."

"But you mentioned a third?"

Waylen hit the steering wheel with the butt of his palm. "Damn it."

"What?"

"That's Darren's plan. He was using the tokens with me at Planetae. He's aiming to pinpoint the last three segments."

"Then?"

"They'll open a portal, I suppose."

"To where?"

Waylen let out a lungful of tense air. "I don't want to find out." The clock changed to 11:01 on the dash as they rolled onto a bridge. Gary's headlights bobbed in the mirror, and his signal followed Waylen's when he turned left.

"How did it feel?"

Waylen assumed she meant touching the tokens, so he didn't ask for clarification. "Strange. I became sick the first time, but the effect lessened with each test run."

"You could still only stay in contact for so long?"

"Yeah. Theodore Belleville is dead from living in the echo for too many minutes."

"I knew him," Charlotte admitted.

"From the White House?"

"He walked around like he owned the place. No one knew what his role was, but we didn't question his presence. Not even the President. Isn't that odd?"

"Not after the last month. I don't know who I can trust," he said.

"You can trust me, Waylen."

"I'm counting on it."

"Can ... I want to try the tokens," Charlotte said.

"Now?"

"We have an hour."

"It's a bad idea."

"Think of it from my vantage point, Waylen. Aliens, portals, and metal bookmarks? Sounds pretty ridiculous."

Waylen flipped the wipers on as a few drops splattered on the windshield. "Okay, but only for a second. I don't want you hurting yourself."

He carefully removed a plastic-covered token, keeping a hand on the steering wheel. He still had the piece of tape on the corner, denoting its echo. "This is from the Moon."

Charlotte stretched for it, but he held it out of reach. "One second."

"I promise." She took the offered token and exposed an inch, tightly gripping the bottom. Her finger shakily rose, and he noticed her French manicure. He should have paid closer attention to those kinds of details, but his mind was elsewhere. Charlotte touched it, gasped, and released it, dropping the token. "I saw it... the Shadow and the Moon." She rubbed her eyes as if they were dry. "You were serious."

"Why did you think I was breaking into someone's house in the middle of the night?" he asked.

Shadows of the Earth

"I had to see for myself."

They discussed lighter subjects for the duration of the drive, catching up on their lives from the past three years. Waylen offered precious few details, given the fact he only worked, and had next to no other hobbies. Charlotte, on the other hand, had taken up yoga, joined a book club, and was thinking about learning another language. He watched her talk about her dreams, and realized he never anticipated the future. Waylen had no expectations from himself, past solving each case he was assigned.

When she asked if he'd do any of those things, he nodded earnestly. She settled into her seat, despite having experienced the token only a short while earlier.

"How are your parents?" Waylen asked after a brief pause in conversation.

"They're fine. Dad's fishing a lot, and Mom's keeping herself busy around the house."

"Vermont, right?"

"I'm surprised you remembered," she said.

They'd never visited Vermont while they dated, with Charlotte claiming they'd make a fuss over Waylen if he showed up. It was obvious she wasn't ready for that kind of commitment, and truthfully, he hadn't been either.

He checked the GPS, ensuring they were on track, and the roads grew far darker as they exited from the rural city limits and took what passed for a freeway out there. Without streetlights, he had to rely on the headlights. The road was narrow, with no shoulder to speak of. He approached a flatbed truck going ten under the speed limit, and went around, with Gary twenty feet behind.

"It's a nice area." Charlotte stared at a sign for a bed-and-breakfast two minutes ahead.

"I wish we were coming here for a weekend getaway."

"Maybe when we're done," she breathed.

"I'd like that."

He entered Little Compton, and the dash screen said they'd arrive in three minutes. Waylen followed the trail on the GPS and slowed when he saw the house numbers. He guessed that some of these homes were permanent residences, and not all second properties.

Waylen parked across the street, turning the car off. Gary did the same, and Waylen dialed his counterpart, leaving it on speaker.

"Hey, let's hold up and see if we get any movement," he said.

"*Roger that, boss.*"

They stayed on the line while they watched the place. Waylen peered into windows, not seeing any lights on. There were no cars in the gravel driveway, which suggested it was vacant, but he noticed a garage on the side of the home after a second.

"Stay here," he told Charlotte, and this time, she didn't protest.

Waylen glanced at the sky, filled with endless stars.

"Nice view," Gary said, stalking over to him.

He was about to respond when he spied a light on in the house. He reached for his gun, while Gary started making for the front door.

When Waylen rechecked, the light had vanished.

5

Silas was on the road yet again. He contemplated what it would be like to drive a long-haul truck, and to have seen every corner of their great nation. Did they grow tired of the sights, and just wish to be home? He figured the sheen would wear off eventually, as with most occupations.

He'd examined the details a dozen times before deciding to venture off on his own. His sister had reluctantly loaned him her older SUV, which seemed brand new and only had twenty thousand miles on it. Putting miles on a car in the city took a while to do, especially when she had a company car at her disposal.

It was almost midnight, and absolutely nothing in the town of Harbinger, North Carolina, was open.

Silas drove down the aptly labeled Church Road, since one of the few structures along it was a white church with an empty parking lot. He continued, finding the destination he sought after a wrong turn. Even with the GPS on, it was difficult to recognize the proper exits.

Harbinger. The town's name made Silas wonder if that was what drew his grandfather to bring the token here. He thought that a harbinger was a bad thing, an indication of terrible things on the horizon. It also signaled the approach of another. Was it a clue to the fact there might be aliens across the Delta's Shadow?

Silas wished Peter Gunn had left more detailed information on the subject, rather than arbitrary notes in a journal, and a secreted token beneath his floorboards.

Rory had described the echo from her brief stint in Kentucky, and Silas let his foot off the gas when he neared the villa. It was out of place and stood out like a sore thumb. There was no gate, and the sign at the end of its driveway gave honor to the previous owner, a woman named Florence Bethany. The gardens were meant to leave something to remember the philanthropic efforts of Florence, who'd died in 1989.

The building itself was large and acted as a museum of local history. A sign out front announced a local artist display on the coming weekend.

"Why did you choose this location, Grandpa?" Silas whispered. His lights shone on the white brick, and he saw the vast gardens on either side of the cobblestone walkway. It was obvious that Peter had come to Harbinger on his trip in 1997, but finding the building from Rory's vision had been a challenge, particularly because she didn't approve of his venture. Silas hadn't told her he was leaving for North Carolina. She thought he was still in New York visiting his family, while Oscar and Kathy were in Boston. By using the online street view application, he'd located the sole place in the region that matched her description.

Silas turned the SUV off and scoped out the gardens. Rory had spoken about the fresh cut grass, and the overwhelming scent of flowers in the echo, so maybe Peter had left the token somewhere nearby.

He donned a windbreaker, attempting to keep warm.

Shadows of the Earth

The night air was chilly, and a breeze blew in from the Atlantic, making it even colder. Silas slid his hands into his pockets and strolled to the building.

The villa itself could probably house a dozen on the top floor. He peered into the windows, finding a gallery set up. Many of the easels lacked the paintings that would fill them on the coming weekend. They'd decorated the space in gold and black, with upside-down wine glasses lining a table, and a large commercial drip coffee maker on the opposite end.

"What do you want?" A low voice grated on his ears, and completely surprised him.

"I…"

The man came around the corner, and into the light of the Moon. He was big, wearing dirty boots and coveralls. He grimaced, and Silas noticed a missing front tooth. "You tryna steal something?"

"No, nothing like that."

He eyeballed Silas. "Then what? Car break down?" He gazed at the SUV.

"No. My name's Silas." He remembered Rory describing what she thought was a groundskeeper in the vision from the echo.

"I'm Nash."

"How long have you worked here?"

Nash blinked, probably surprised by the direction of the conversation. "Thirty-four years."

Silas doubted this could be the same guy. "Did you ever meet Peter Gunn?"

His expression changed, and he smiled widely. "The astronaut. I watched him on the Moon when I was a little boy." He held a hand to his knee.

"I'm his grandson."

"I see," Nash said. He lost some of the rigidity of his spine, and his chest heaved as he coughed. "You came for it."

Silas nodded slowly, wondering if he'd actually leave carrying a segment of the third Delta.

"Follow me." Nash started off without another word, and Silas jogged behind him.

"Do we…" Silas stopped when it was clear Nash wasn't in the mood to talk. They made it to a garage tucked between two meadows of trees. It looked like Nash lived there. The rocking chair on the front porch was well worn, and had an empty soda can beside it.

Nash walked past the building to a shed and extracted two shovels.

"What are those for?" Silas had a vision of himself being buried alive. There was no one to hear him scream. If Nash's intentions held malice, he didn't act on it. Instead, he passed Silas the shovel, and gestured at the garden.

"We dig."

Silas joined him at the edge of the flower garden. Some blooms remained wide, as if seeking sustenance from the stars. It was difficult to distinguish colors at night, but their fragrance was pure.

"What did he tell you?" Silas asked, after Nash broke ground near a patch of azaleas.

"That it's special. And I had to protect it."

"Who owns this place?"

"Peter Gunn," he said.

Silas smiled, since that meant he did. The owner of a villa in Harbinger. He doubted it held much value, but probably did to the locals, who could use it for events like the art gallery sale.

Shadows of the Earth

"I was sorry to hear of his passing," Nash said, showing a hint of remorse.

"Me too." Silas dug, throwing clumps of hearty earth into a pile Nash had started. "Do you live on site?"

"Yes."

"And you're being paid?"

"Will that stop since there's nothing left to guard?" Nash asked.

"Do you want to stay?"

"Yes. I have nowhere else to go," Nash said.

"Then you'll keep being paid." Silas really needed to examine the portfolios. He'd been too caught up in the Delta since reading the will at the lawyers' office in Campbelltown.

They spilled another ten spades filled with dirt, and Silas asked a question that had been burning in his chest. "He told you someone would come for it?"

"He said it might happen, and I was to judge whether or not to give it up," Nash said.

"Really?" Silas was surprised Peter had put so much responsibility on Nash's shoulders.

Nash pushed the end of the shovel into the ground and stared at Silas. "I haven't decided yet."

A shudder coursed through Silas, but he did his best to stay composed. "I'm a good guy, Nash. I can't let this get into the wrong hands."

"And you'll protect it?" Nash asked.

"Yes." He held a palm to his heart. "I swear on Peter's grave."

Nash narrowed his gaze. "Okay. I believe you." He walked another ten feet to the left and dug.

"It's not here?" Silas motioned at the soil they'd moved over the last five minutes.

"No, I was tricking you. Trying to see if I liked you or not." Nash shoveled quicker, and Silas jumped beside him, doing the same. Soon, they had a hole large enough to bury a body, and Nash hopped in.

"Are we almost there?" Silas asked.

"Think so. It's been a long time." Nash scratched his chin while gazing at the middle.

Silas spotted headlights on the country road and jabbed the tip of the shovel down, walking closer to the pathway. A vehicle was on the villa's driveway. "This is bad."

Nash frowned. "You keep digging. Let me see who it is."

Before Silas could object, Nash was stomping toward the incoming vehicle with his shovel in hand.

Silas moved as fast as possible, throwing dirt without caution. He glanced at the white utility van when it stopped, and heard a man's voice. They couldn't quite see him from their position, and Silas crouched, continuing to excavate the soil.

Nash spoke with the man, but Silas couldn't make out the words or tell who had come. He hurried when he saw part of a whiskey bag. Peter had used the original marker for the token, and that added to the reality of his situation.

"Get out of here!" Nash shouted.

Silas clutched the bag, shaking it free, and wiped some of the mud from the surface. He peered in, finding the token he'd been expecting.

He sprang from the hole, keeping his grip on the shovel after placing the Delta segment into his pocket. Silas rounded the villa, clinging to one side, and saw the face of the newcomer.

Shadows of the Earth

Darren Jones had his palms in front of his chest.

"Why so hostile? I'm passing through and heard great things about your gardens. I can pay you for your time," Darren said, using his best podcast voice.

Silas clenched his jaw, furious that Darren had so easily deceived them. How did that happen? He checked the van and had a sinking sensation. Darren had left the Planetae facility with three of the beings, and was now driving a windowless utility vehicle. Were they in it, and what had they done with Plemmons?

"Disappear, stranger," Nash grumbled.

Darren took a step closer to the big groundskeeper, but Nash didn't back down. "What'll it take? Money? I have a thousand dollars with your name on it. Just show me where Gunn hid the token."

Nash's gaze flickered to the garden.

"Don't do it," Silas whispered from his hiding spot. His own SUV was parked thirty feet from the van, and he wondered if Darren had even noticed someone else was there. Unless he assumed Nash owned the hundred-thousand-dollar ride.

"No deal."

"Fine. Ten grand. Bring it to me and I pay you," Darren said.

Nash seemed to contemplate taking the money and selling Silas out, but he spoke after a tense minute. "No. Leave."

The van shook, and the rear door popped open. Silas froze when an alien appeared, looming behind Darren. "I told you to accept the payment. Now you've made my friends upset."

The alien lifted an arm, and a red light shone from his wrist. Nash grasped his head, letting the shovel fall, and the noise carried to Silas, making him sick to his stomach. Silas averted his gaze, and when he checked again, Darren was marching past the smear left by Nash.

The alien went with him, and Silas wouldn't have believed it if he hadn't seen it up close. They'd watched footage before, but that was on a laptop screen. Observing the obviously non-human entity stalking through the villa shook him to the core.

It walked gracefully, like it didn't have a care in the world. Standing two feet taller than Darren, it was half again as wide at the shoulders. The arms were long, but given its stature, they didn't seem out of place. Silas figured it wore gloves, because he couldn't see much detail in the poorly lit courtyard. It was the feet that stood out, with a rear toe like they'd seen on the Moon after Rory's initial excursion from Peter's living room in Loon Lake. This was the same race.

Silas waited until they were out of sight, and ran, pumping his limbs with everything he had. When he got to the SUV, he dropped the keys and fumbled for them as they jangled under the vehicle. Silas dove to his belly, stretching for the fob. He paused when he spied two sets of legs emerging from the van a short distance away.

Silas grabbed the keys and hopped to his feet as the alien pair advanced in his direction.

He took a better look at them. Instead of having large, oval eyes usually depicted in science fiction, they were nearly imperceptible. Rather than a protruding nose, the bone was rounded, with three holes acting as nostrils. They flared on the right invader's face, and its mouth opened to reveal a plate of teeth similar to a whale's.

Silas realized he was gawking. The moment one raised its wrist, the light began to flash red, and he took it as a

Shadows of the Earth

sign to get the hell out of there. Otherwise, he'd end up like the soldiers in New York, or the groundskeeper, Nash. Silas rushed into the SUV, used the push button to start it, and considered running them down. That might put him in range of their peculiar weapons, so he reversed, speeding backwards. The nearest chased him, the powerful legs carrying it at a loping sprint. Silas stuck in reverse, almost at the road, and the being lowered, now using its arms like a cheetah darting through the Serengeti in search of prey.

When Silas hit the pavement, he spun the wheel, threw it into drive and took off.

The alien filled his rearview and stopped, standing at the street. "Take that, you…" The second was thirty yards ahead, arm lifted defensively. The device on his wrist pulsed red, and Silas felt nausea forming in his stomach. He had no choice. Silas pushed harder on the gas pedal and slammed into the bastard. The alien bashed into the windshield, cracking the glass, but not shattering it. Silas heard the body roll over the roof and saw it land, spinning after it struck the asphalt.

He didn't check to see if it survived.

Silas wiped his nose with a sleeve, finding blood.

He'd made it out alive, and had the first token.

# 6

*W*aylen waited for the person in Darren's Little Compton house to reveal themselves. After an hour, his impatience got the best of him. They made a plan, and for the second time in the last few hours, Waylen trespassed on Darren Jones' property. They didn't require the keys, after all, since someone else had already broken in.

Waylen put a finger to his lips and entered the house, gun drawn.

Rather than splitting up, he and Gary checked the main floor together, discovering it had been ransacked. Instead of sifting through the debris, they rushed upstairs.

Gary turned left at the top, and Waylen took a right, silently creeping through the home. The first bedroom was adorned with nautical memorabilia and appeared to be an office. The desk was beachy and light, the fixture on the surface covered in seashells. A wall had pictures of boats in the water and photos of Darren and his family. Waylen looked at one, and judging by Darren's age, he guessed it was taken five or six years earlier. The kids were small, wearing oversized lifejackets, and he had his hand on the girl's shoulder, all four of them smiling proudly.

Gary Charles met him in the hall, and they headed to

the last room together. It wasn't latched, and Waylen used the barrel of the gun to prop it open. The bed was occupied.

He gave Gary a nod, and mentally counted to three before barging in and flipping the lights on. "Hands where I can see them!"

The figure shifted beneath the comforter, and he noticed the gun resting on the nightstand, then saw who was reaching for it.

Martina Sanchez had it in her grip before Waylen nearly fired, and he lowered the weapon, urging Gary to as well.

"Why are you sleeping in Darren's bed?" he shouted.

Martina was fully dressed, and she slid out, holstering her gun. "I came for a lead. It didn't seem like anyone else cared that we're on the brink of an invasion, so I took it upon myself." She glanced at Gary. "Special Agent Charles."

"Sanchez," he muttered.

"Did you find anything?" Waylen asked.

Martina started to make the bed and stopped midway. "What am I doing?" She messed it up more, tossing his pillows to the floor. "God, I hate this guy. How could he work with them?"

Waylen had been wondering that same thing. "I was with Darren for a couple of weeks. We used the tokens together every day."

"You're forgetting that you worked with Sanchez for years, and she kept a lot from you. The mysterious Department of Outer Space, for example."

"Yeah, what's up with that?" Waylen asked.

"It wasn't like we had annual Christmas parties. They rarely told me what they were planning, which, evidently, wasn't much." Martina led them downstairs, then to a second door. She opened it, and Waylen squeezed his nostrils closed.

"What is that?" he asked.

"I think they were here. Darren brought his friends to this place for a day or two. I'm assuming he needed to procure some supplies before finding a more permanent solution. You can only stay so long with three aliens living in your basement," Martina said.

Waylen took each step slowly, the smell growing far stronger. The basement was finished with painted white wood paneling and white oak floors.

"I found the source of the smell." Gary checked the furnace room and gestured at a pile of bones.

Waylen waved a few flies from his face. "What are those from?"

"I didn't look close enough, but I'm guessing they're from a cow," Martina said.

"Where did he go?" Waylen pulled it shut, and his phone vibrated. He saw Silas' name and answered it.

"*… hit one of them.*"

"Slow down," Waylen said, sensing the panic in Silas' voice. He put it on speaker so the others could hear. "What did you do?"

"*I chased after the third Delta…*"

"Why didn't you tell me?"

"*I don't know. I figured you'd try to talk me out of it,*" Silas said. "*I have the locations, or at least this one for certain. The other two are more difficult.*"

"Silas," Waylen said while Gary and Martina stepped closer. "What did you hit?"

"*An alien!*"

Waylen glanced at the mechanical room. Somehow,

the scent didn't seem as bad the longer he lingered in the stench. The sound of the buzzing flies lowered as they were cordoned off.

"I drove to Harbinger, North Carolina. Rory's parents were visiting, and I took it as an excuse to head home for a few days. I talked with Beverly, Peter's former assistant, and she had all these files. It wasn't too difficult to discover where he'd gone on his trip around the country, not when you knew what to look for. Once I decided Harbinger was a solid lead, I searched for the building Rory described, and found it," Silas said.

They listened as he explained the experience with the gardener, then Darren's arrival, and Silas' anxious exit.

"Where are you now?" Martina asked.

"*Who's that?*" Silas demanded.

"It's Martina. I'm here with her and Special Agent Charles." Waylen thought Silas might comment on the fact it was after midnight, but he didn't.

"*I'm on the way north.*"

"Meet us in Boston," Waylen said.

"*Why?*"

"There are aliens on the loose, and they're after the same thing as you. Plus, we might need the Deltas I'm carrying to figure out where to locate the rest."

"*Rory's going to be pissed,*" Silas muttered.

"When do her parents leave?"

"*Tomorrow.*"

"Stay in touch and be careful. Where are the other two?"

"*I think one's in California. The last in Arizona,*" Silas said.

Gary and Waylen shared a knowing glance. "Gotcha. Silas, you did well. But next time, keep me in the loop?" The tokens in his jacket felt heavier, like an immeasurable weight he couldn't shoulder for much longer.

A sound came from upstairs. "Charlotte," Waylen said when the call ended.

"Who?" Martina asked with her gun drawn.

The basement door creaked open. "Waylen?" Charlotte called.

"Down here," he said.

She slowly descended, and her gaze shifted from Waylen to Gary, then settled on Martina. "Why is…"

"I asked you to stay in the car."

Charlotte's nostrils wiggled. "What's that smell?"

Martina didn't hesitate to shove the furnace door. "It's a pile of bones. We believe aliens ate whatever kind of animal it was."

"Who are you?" Charlotte asked, her gaze still on the pieces of skeletal remains.

"Martina Sanchez." She holstered her weapon and offered a hand. Waylen felt two different versions of his life collide.

"Charlotte Halstead."

Martina looked at Waylen. "The White House press chick?"

"I work with the press secretary, yes."

"We're all caught up." Waylen started for the stairs. "We have to beat Darren and his friends to the last tokens."

"Then what?" Gary asked.

"I wish I knew."

"*I* don't want to go home," Kathy said.

Shadows of the Earth

"Honey, I have that event tomorrow, and need to prepare for it." Oscar placed their luggage in the back of the car, and Rory anxiously observed her parents. While she'd had a delightful visit, she was ready to continue with her semester, rather than catering to them each evening after classes.

She hugged her mom, then dad, Oscar lingering longer before kissing her on the cheek. "You need anything at all. Call me."

"I will," she promised. The clouds were low and heavy, threatening to douse the campus at any moment. Rory noticed bits of mist floating through the air, but the sight barely registered. She was confident the sensations would wear off eventually, given enough time away from the Delta. Whatever she'd done in that box in Louisville had triggered a reaction, but she didn't expect it to stick forever.

Kathy stared at her once in the car and rolled the window down. "I love you, Rory Swanson. And we're both extremely proud of the woman you've grown into."

Rory's eyes filled with tears while she waved. "Thanks, Mom. I love you too." They drove off, leaving Rory standing outside her faculty dorm building as the first drop fell.

"That was heartwarming." Garnet appeared from the entrance, hands clasped to his chest.

"You were watching?"

"I thought about sneaking by, but didn't want to interrupt," he said. "I'm heading for a coffee. Care to join me?"

"I should work on my plan for tomorrow," she told him. "I'm way behind after the visit."

"Nonsense. The kids don't know any better. Just give

them a reading assignment and kick up your feet. That's what I do when I'm tired… or hungover." Garnet grinned at her and gestured in the coffee shop's direction.

"Fine." Rory patted her pockets, realizing her phone wasn't on her. "But an hour max."

That seemed to appease her colleague, and they began the short walk. "Your parents seem nice. Mine were awful."

"Were? Did you lose them?"

"No, I just refuse to speak to the lousy killjoys." Garnet opened an umbrella when the drops came faster, and held it out so they might share. "I left at seventeen and never looked back."

"You've done well enough for someone with no support system," she said.

"It could be better. I've had great feedback from a few of your students, Rory. You almost inspire me to try harder."

"Me?"

"Showing up early, keeping them interested with anecdotes, and all this real-life publishing contract business. It helps to hear it from an author currently writing a new bestseller, rather than a stuffy suit who'd won an award in the Seventies like their previous guest lecturer," Garnet said.

When they neared the coffee shop, the downpour grew in intensity. Water splashed her feet and the cuffs of her pants as it barraged the sidewalks. There were already pools of rain gathering at the welcome mat, and Rory stepped over them as Garnet held the door for her. It was quiet, given the fact most students were still in their last class for the day.

They ordered, and Garnet rested the damp umbrella

Shadows of the Earth

on the wall when they took a seat. Mist and darkness floated from the windows, and Rory did her best to ignore the creeping sensation that always followed.

"Rory, what did the guy you warned security about look like?" Garnet asked. He faced the windows, frowning, with her aimed at the coffee bar.

She spun around in the chair, seeing a man peering through the glass, hair plastered to his brow. Rory rushed to the exit. "Silas, what are you doing?"

"Rory." He hugged her, his clothing soaking wet. "You didn't answer your phone."

"It's at home," she said. "And I was in a class all day… then my parents…"

"We've been trying to reach you."

"We?"

Silas motioned to the street, where two cars waited. Waylen lifted a hand off the steering wheel. In the vehicle behind, Special Agent Gary Charles and Martina Sanchez observed their interaction. Rory realized the Shadow that had been following her seemed to have vanished.

"Why are you all here?" Rory demanded.

Silas touched her wrist. "It's not over."

Rory backed up. "Silas, I told you I'm done."

"I… I found the token."

Rory slapped his shoulder. "Silas! I said I was finished with this!"

"We need your help."

"No." Rory stalked off, splashing through puddles.

Silas chased her, keeping pace. "I met with Darren, and the aliens attacked me. Rory, they're after the Delta too. We can't let them have it."

Rory froze in her tracks. "How… You were in the city to see your family." His lack of response answered her question. "You lied to me."

"We can't just leave it. We're in this until it's finished. There's another Shadow on Earth, and we have to secure it before them. It's as simple as that!" Silas was drenched, and he halted in front of her, his eyes pleading.

Rory wanted to tell him to screw off, but she couldn't. She gazed at the car, seeing Waylen waiting patiently, and she let out a heavy sigh. "What can I do?"

7

Rory's apartment became much smaller once they were all crammed into it. She wouldn't look at him, and Silas couldn't really blame her. Rory wasn't wrong. He'd lied.

Waylen took charge of the preparations, with everyone ceding to his authority. Rory's table was covered in papers, pieces from Peter Gunn's itinerary during his trip in the Nineties. The two sets of tokens sat on the table, but within reach, while Silas kept the latest in his pocket.

Charlotte was in the conversation, and Silas was surprised Waylen had allowed her to join their adventure. Clearly, she hadn't given him a choice; otherwise, she'd be safe in DC, out of harm's way.

"If you're right, and the remaining two tokens are in California and Arizona, it'll take Darren and his acquaintances a while to get there," Martina said. "It's not as though he can buy them coach seats on a plane and no one will notice."

"You'd be surprised," Gary added. "You should have seen the guy next to me on my last flight."

The joke only received a light laugh from Charlotte. The rest were too distraught about the next few days.

"Martina, the Department of Outer Space built their bases in Arizona and northern California," Silas said. "It can't be a coincidence that those are the same locations as these last tokens, can it?"

"Your guess is as good as mine," she said.

"The token from Harbinger wasn't near the Hermon, New York base," Waylen offered.

"We could travel between the Hexes." Silas glanced at Rory, who hadn't commented on anything in some time. "That would save us a ton of hassle."

"We'd definitely beat Darren to the tokens if we do," Gary suggested.

Rory must have felt their gazes on her, because she finally looked up. "And you want me to use the Shadow to accomplish this, don't you?"

"We also have you to learn where the rest are hiding," Waylen added.

Rory fidgeted with her hands under the table. "You guys won't leave me alone until this is done, will you?"

"Rory, no one's making …" Silas said, but she cut him off.

"I don't have much of a choice." Rory pointed at the tokens. "Fine, snap them together. Let's go to California or Arizona."

"I think we should find where Peter put them first," Waylen said.

"Good idea. Do we leave and get to the facility in Hermon, or should we drive to Planetae's operation?"

"I'm not going back there," Waylen confirmed. The aliens had murdered fifty trained soldiers in the laboratory, so Silas wasn't in the mood to visit it either.

"We don't have to go anywhere." Rory rose and walked to the living room. "Set it up here."

"Now?"

She glared at their group. "Let's do this as quickly as

possible. Waylen, connect the Delta."

"Which one?" he asked.

"The one Brett used," she said.

"We could duplicate the box." Silas pointed at the bedroom. "In the dark."

That seemed to put the others at ease.

"Okay." Rory left, heading to the room with her bed.

"Give us a minute." Silas followed her and shut the door, turning a bedside lamp on. "Rory, please don't be angry with me. I don't want this any more than you do."

"Then why did you go chasing it?" she asked.

"There are aliens wandering around trying to find them."

She sat on the corner of the bed. "We know nothing about them."

"For the first time, all the Deltas will be exposed at once," Silas said. "We can't allow them to access the Shadows. You haven't witnessed what can happen. I have." He pictured Nash at the villas in Harbinger, then the mess left behind after the alien operated his strange weapon.

"I'm tired of being used," Rory said.

"I'll stay with you."

Rory sat up straighter. "You will?"

"Sure. We've both handled the Shadow and touched the tokens." Silas grabbed Waylen, and he entered slowly, peering at the bedroom.

"Where do you want it?" Waylen connected two pieces and held the third crisscrossing the segment.

"On the bed." Rory moved off the mattress.

"Silas, you going to leave?" Waylen asked.

"I'm staying."

"You sure?" Waylen put the last segment together,

Nathan Hystad

and the Shadow instantly formed from the glowing triangle.

"Yes." Silas observed with Rory as the portal grew over the bed. The dim misty fog rose to the ceiling, engulfing the light fixture.

"Shout if you need anything," Waylen said, and closed the door.

Silas noticed the second set of tokens on the nightstand, and he pocketed them. "Now what?"

Rory flipped the switch off, making the space dark. "We focus on your grandfather."

Silas pictured the old man as he'd been the last time they'd visited. He recalled the lines in his eyes with vivid clarity, the slight tremor to his fingers, the gruff voice. There was a hardness to his gaze that Silas had always found unnerving, and now he knew why. Peter Gunn had spent every day since landing on the Moon hoping to prevent aliens from coming to Earth. Why couldn't they have let sleeping dogs lie? Why did Monroe have to open up this can of worms, and force their hand?

Even the D.O.O.S. had seemed content to leave them alone, and the moment they were activated, their director was killed trying to stop them from being overtaken.

Silas felt Rory's grip on his hand, and he took her energy, hoping she could duplicate her success from Kentucky here in Boston.

"It's useless. I can't sense a thing," she said.

Silas barely heard her. His view filled with contradicting images, one from a desert landscape, one in what appeared to be the redwood forest with a flag flapping in the breeze nearby.

"Rory."

"Yeah?"

Shadows of the Earth

The gentle blue glow centering the Delta wasn't enough light to see by, and he gazed at the woman he was falling for. "I know where the tokens are."

"How?"

Silas understood an important fact the second he experienced the visions. "My grandfather was the Key, not Colin. And I am too."

Gary cut the deck of cards and continued to shuffle them, doling out six to Waylen. His pegs were almost past the double skunk line, and Waylen grimaced when he saw the poor hand he'd been dealt.

"How can you play cribbage at a time like this?" Martina asked.

"No kidding." Charlotte was in the kitchen, brewing a second cup of coffee.

"It keeps the mind off things." Gary slid two cards onto the pair Waylen had given over.

"Something's been bothering me," Waylen said.

"A lot is bothering me about this entire disaster." Martina helped Charlotte by refilling the cream.

"What happened to Somboon Suwan?"

"Who?" Charlotte asked.

Gary laid a card on the table. "Monroe's guy?"

"Silas found details on Somboon in the Planetae files, and that's how we linked him to the Hermon facility. Everyone but him has been accounted for. Dr. Rita's still in the hospital. The aliens took Plemmons. Darren is working with them. But Somboon wasn't on any of the footage," Waylen said.

"Have you asked anyone?"

"Who would you suggest I ask?" Waylen pegged with a fifteen-two. "Clark Fallow's dead. Brett Davis vanished in Kentucky through the Shadow. The Department has crumbled, right, Martina?"

She coughed once. "There's one person who would know."

"Who?"

"The President."

Charlotte sat with a steaming cup of coffee. "President Grant is aware of the Department of Outer Space?"

"Sure he is." Martina smiled. "His predecessors were, so I doubt that's changed, and seeing how he appointed Clark the position at NASA, that only solidifies my theory."

"Charlotte, we need to meet with him," Waylen said.

"With the President." She rolled her eyes. "How do you presume I set that up?"

"You work at the White House," Gary said.

"Under the Press Secretary, not directly for Grant."

"Could you try?" Waylen asked.

"Fine, but I make no promises." Charlotte got up and muttered something about aliens while using her phone across the room.

It wasn't too late, only eight in the evening, and Waylen thought about dinner. "What are you guys into? Pizza? Burgers? Italian?"

Gary counted his points, grinning as he moved past Waylen. "I should say a salad, but a burger sounds better."

Martina seemed able to eat anything and drink all the beer she wanted, and never gained a pound. "Burger is good."

Charlotte came to the table with her phone. "What do

Shadows of the Earth

you know? It worked. I asked his assistant to mention the D.O.O.S., and he made time for me."

"You spoke to the President?"

"It was brief."

"And?" Waylen asked.

"He's coming."

"To Boston? When?"

"He'll be here in an hour," Charlotte said.

Waylen shoved the cribbage board aside. "We'll have to pause the game." He knocked on Rory's door, but no one responded.

"Rory? Silas?" Waylen opened it, expecting to find them staring at the Shadow in the dark. "They're gone!"

The room was completely empty. Not even the Delta remained on the bed, and he checked the table where he'd placed the second set earlier. It was no longer there.

―――――――

Cody watched the ocean as the waves swelled and crashed into the coastline. The sun was close to setting, and the brightness of it glared off the water on the horizon, keeping his gaze on the rocks near the shore.

He loved being home in California, but somehow missed the adventure back east.

Cody drank the rest of his soda in peace and waited for the last of the rays to crest the curvature, hiding until morning. Cody was a night owl, and preferred it to the daytime. He always did his best work in the late hours, coding until his fingers ached.

He went in and shut the balcony. Cody had filled the living room with space memorabilia. The walls were covered with signed photos, framed and mounted in order of landing dates. The last was from Helios 15, showcasing Swanson and Gunn as they posed near the American flag. Both of their signatures were scrawled on the bottom, and Cody gazed at them. This was likely taken before they stumbled into the Shadow, or they wouldn't have been smiling.

Cody often wondered what they'd seen through the Shadow, when they'd spent two hours on Planet D. He guessed that Brett Davis had known, but he was gone now too.

He stared at a different picture of Fred Trell. "Why didn't you say something? You did eventually mention the tokens, so you wanted me to find the Delta. But why?"

Cody had lost his functional replica of the original NASA spacesuit at Planetae, and it hadn't been offered back. He supposed if he requisitioned it from a bureaucratic government division, he might see it in... five or six years.

Cody never did tell the others how well he'd done in his career, opting to mention the IT part. What he hadn't divulged was that he'd sold his first tech company at twenty-three, and his second by thirty. Now he dabbled in friends' businesses, mostly consulting or dealing with fires when necessary.

Any time Cody mentioned his successful ventures, people looked at him differently, which was the reason he'd shown up in Loon Lake in his father's grimy old van. It had been something he was unwilling to part with for nostalgic reasons. A reminder of another era. Much like the NASA collectibles adorning his bookshelves.

Cody walked to the torn spacesuit, this version not functional. The fabric had breaches, and the hoses were

Shadows of the Earth

cracked. He set a palm to it, wishing he could view Planet D for himself, not just in the echo he'd braved by touching the token. Someone else had them in their possession now, and Cody wouldn't see the Delta again.

Maybe it was for the best.

He was about to flip the TV on, deciding to avoid the work emails that had piled up in his absence, when a text came through.

You in San Diego? It was from Silas.

He nearly ignored the message, going so far as to toss the cell onto the other end of the sofa. Then he stretched and retrieved it. *Yep.*

How quick can you get to Red Bluff?

Cody typed: *California?*

That's the one.

Cody did the math and checked his map program. *10 hours.*

That'll be too late. What about Sedona?

He wasn't sure where Sedona was until he typed it in. Cody realized these were the locations for the second and third unused Department of Outer Space bases. *Seven hours.*

His phone showed three dots while Silas composed a message. Cody nervously bounced his knee, wondering what this was all about.

Meet you there.

"Why?" he said as he hit send.

Just keep your phone on. We have to outrun Darren.

"Darren?" Cody asked aloud. *Do I have anything to worry about?*

Bring a gun.

He tried calling Silas, but no one answered.

Cody didn't have to leave. He could forget he'd ever

met Silas and Rory, and keep fighting the good fight from home. He was on his feet before he could talk himself out if it.

8

"How did you do that?" Rory asked Silas.

She was shocked he'd used the Shadow to travel through to the house on Loon Lake.

"It felt natural." Silas peered around the place after stowing his cell into his jeans. "I haven't spent as much time with the tokens as everyone else, remember? Also, I didn't go to the Moon with the others, and only touched the thing once. I guess I wasn't aware of the ability until we were alone with the Shadow in your bedroom."

"Why did you choose Peter's house?" Rory gestured to the home they were in. Silas looked at peace, and that worried her more than his latent talent for controlling the Delta. It was dismantled, and she was glad to breathe freely.

"Because you mentioned coming here when you were in the box in Kentucky." Silas walked past her, his finger brushing her arm. "You really came." He stared at the whiteboard on the fridge. *Rory was here.*

"Can you find the last pair?"

"Generally speaking. Once we get to Red Bluff, I'll figure it out."

"Are you planning on using the Shadow to drop us at a random street? Have you been there before?" Rory asked.

"No, but I think it's simple enough."

"How?" Rory had come to Loon Lake the first time because she knew it, and it was isolated from any witnesses.

"It's like how you connected to the Planetae Hex. We'll do that to the Department's facility in California."

"I don't love asking Cody to drive to Arizona alone," Rory said.

"He's a big boy. Remember, he's been dealing with the tokens longer than us. He managed to trick Leo Monroe's guys, then stole the entire Delta from under our noses. He's crafty," Silas told her.

"We're talking about aliens, Silas."

"I'm aware. I met them, remember?" he said, and the calm energy he'd been exuding vanished at the mention of aliens.

Silas's phone rang, then Rory's when he didn't answer it. "Why can't we tell Waylen?"

"Him, I trust. But if Darren changed teams and is working with them, how do we know Martina isn't? Or Gary Charles?"

Rory had thought the same thing, but refused to verbalize it. They needed allies, not more opponents. She gaped at the two sets of dismantled Deltas, wondering what would happen when they secured the third and final device.

She was exhausted after a few days with her parents, the demanding learning curve of her courses she taught, and the constant fear from her involvement in the Deltas' mystery. "I can't believe we're still searching for tokens."

"No kidding. I thought I could quit my job, hang out at the lake for a couple of months, and decide what to do next. Now…"

Rory hugged him tightly, wrapping her arms around his waist. "We'll get through it."

Silas kissed her on the lips. "We can move faster than Darren. With any luck, we'll be done soon."

"And I can keep my job," Rory said.

"Right. Shall we?" Silas motioned to the tokens.

"Sure." Rory paused. "I just have to use the washroom."

"Be quick."

She jogged through the living room to the hall, and glanced at Peter Gunn's office, where he'd hidden the token below the floorboards in a safe for years. Once inside the bathroom, she locked the door and typed a message to Waylen. *Go to Sedona*. Rory hesitated, then tapped the icon. She silenced the ringer. While she didn't enjoy going behind Silas' back, she thought he was being too rash, and Rory wouldn't allow a man to make all her decisions at this point in her life.

She used the facilities and returned to the living room, where the Shadow had already been established. Rory felt the draining energy of it and stepped into the fog to enter the room.

"Ready?" Silas reached for her hand.

"Ready." Rory hoped Waylen got the message, because her gut told her Darren and his alien allies wouldn't give up so easily.

She stepped into the black hole right after Silas departed from the property on Loon Lake, and they appeared in a dark room. It was different traveling while taking the contraption with them. With no return destination, the trip had a sense of finality it hadn't before.

Rory recognized the polymer walls, the scent of plastic and sterilized quarters. "We're in the Hex," she said.

"Yeah, I focused on the Department's Hex, since they built the facility near Red Bluff. Looks like these make easy travel targets." Silas undid the tokens, and the light from the triangle faded, along with the Shadow it created.

They pushed the hatch and stepped down the stairs to the laboratory floor. It was identical to the Planetae lab Leo Monroe had designed after constructing the three empty buildings for the secret government organization.

Rory imagined her caring and lovely grandfather being a member of the Department of Outer Space, and struggled to see it. "Waylen said the place near Hermon was empty too."

"They've never even used them," Silas said. When they reached the exit, Silas took off his light jacket and shoved it near the base, keeping the door from latching shut. The keypad flashed, then exuded a soft buzzing sound. "We don't have the code, and we might need to use the Hex again."

Rory didn't argue, and led Silas outside. It was earlier on the West Coast, and the sun continued to cover the region in a dusky glow. She held the door wide while Silas grabbed a decorative rock from the landscaping and propped it open.

The gate would be more of an issue. "I wish we had a car," she said.

Silas used his phone and shook his head. "No rideshares in the area."

"How far is the token?" Rory peered around the street. The Department's warehouse was the only structure in her sightlines. Across the road was a large snaking waterway. With a check on her phone, she saw it was the Sacramento River. There were also a few texts from Waylen, which she ignored.

Silas pointed to the west, into the setting sun. "I think it's this way."

———

"Still nothing?" Gary asked.

Waylen closed, then opened the app. "No. They're not responding."

"Why?" Charlotte peered at the screen.

"They think one of us has been infiltrated, like Darren Jones," Martina answered.

Waylen glanced at each of them, trying to assess if that might be possible.

"Don't look at me like that," Gary said.

"Like what?"

"Accusatorily."

"Darren *was* on our team. I know it," Waylen told them.

"Then the contact with the tokens did something to him." Charlotte moved away from Waylen, probably not even realizing she'd done it.

"I'm not under any type of alien mind control," Waylen declared.

"You viewed the echoes during a lot of sessions. None of us did." Martina checked the window again.

"I haven't been influenced by any outside forces." Waylen blinked, trying to think if he'd felt different since their time at the Planetae laboratory.

"Where is he?" Martina slid the drapes back.

Loud rotors whooshed overhead, the noise carrying through the brick walls and double pane windows. "I think our visitor has arrived."

Charlotte gestured to his phone. "What's in Sedona?"

"One of the D.O.O.S.'s buildings."

"Why tell us to go there?" Special Agent Charles slung his jacket on and cinched his tie up. Waylen did the same, not wanting to look like a slob in front of the President of the United States.

"They were searching for the tokens. Maybe one's nearby," Waylen said.

When they left her building, dozens of people were in the courtyard, filming the black helicopter.

"He better stay in it, or this story will be on the national news," Charlotte commented over the noise.

A man in a black suit exited the helicopter, and Waylen met the Secret Service agent halfway. He flipped his credentials, and the guy stopped Charlotte from joining their group.

"She's with me," Waylen said.

"No."

"Come on, Charlotte works at the White House."

"FBI only," the Secret Service agent said.

"Gary, can you stay with her?"

"Where should we go?"

Waylen considered the comment. The Department's laboratories seemed important and would be about as safe a place as they had to hide out. "Get to New York."

Gary nodded his understanding.

Waylen leaned into Charlotte's ear. "We'll stay in touch. You can trust Special Agent Charles."

Charlotte went with less of a fight than he'd expected, and he was grateful for it. Martina and Waylen jogged behind the agent, entering the helicopter before him.

They were ushered to a bench seat, facing a very fa-

Shadows of the Earth

miliar man, though Waylen hadn't met him in person.

President Hank Grant reached out, shaking Martina's, then Waylen's hand. "Special Agents," he said. "Tell me everything."

The rotors whooshed louder as they rose into the air. Waylen peered through the glass, finding Charlotte and Gary walking to the parking lot.

"Mr. President, do you know what the Department of Outer Space is?"

He nodded. "They were an old group from the Sixties. Kennedy arranged it when we started dreaming of conquering space."

"There's something I have to show you," Waylen said. He brought the footage from the Planetae lab onto his phone and passed it to the President. "This was taken a few days ago."

President Grant flinched while the Shadow in the Hex bloomed to life, and Darren stepped aside while three aliens came out. He grimaced as the red pulse erupted, killing an entire regiment of soldiers after they fired at the invincible Hex walls.

Waylen cringed when Jacob B. Plemmons was casually escorted past the mess of soldiers and outside.

"Where is Plemmons?"

"We tried to get in touch with you, sir," Martina said. "Clark Fallow is dead. Monroe's lead lab tech, Dr. Rita Singh, barely survived. Thanks to Waylen's quick action, she made it. She's recovering in the hospital, but we haven't been able to talk to her."

"How did you save her?"

Waylen gestured at the phone. "I traveled into the Shadow, onto the Moon, and brought her back."

"Plemmons told me about this insane venture, and I

didn't believe him. I've actually been planning on replacing him. When he stopped responding, I figured he'd realized what was happening, and needed private time with his family."

"We were under the impression you fully supported the operation. Leo Monroe wanted to…"

"Who is Monroe?"

"Leo Monroe, the owner of Planetae," Waylen said.

"I don't know anyone by that name."

"I…" Waylen changed tactics. "What about Theodore Belleville?"

"Of course I know Belleville. He's been a powerful and vocal lobbyist for ages," President Grant said.

"They were working together. Monroe manufactures weapons for the US, among others. He also constructed three buildings for the Department of Outer Space a few years ago," Martina told him.

"Wait, Belleville hired them?"

"Fallow and Plemmons were involved," Waylen added.

"Why? What were they trying to do?"

"There are three Deltas, sir," he said. "The first set was discovered on the Moon in 1972 by Peter Gunn and Colin Swanson."

"The astronauts?"

Waylen continued the story as the helicopter landed some distance away. He told the man everything, from Gunn's death at his home, to Fred Trell's loose lips and Cody Sanderson. It took a half hour to divulge the tale, and President Grant seemed to ponder the details before speaking. He had Waylen's phone in his lap. The screen paused on an image. "And these aliens are on the loose? In my country?"

Shadows of the Earth

"Yes, sir." Waylen paused. "Actually, Silas ran one over in North Carolina, so there might only be two."

"Right," Grant said. He let out a deep sigh and returned the phone. "What do you suggest we do?"

"Silas and Rory are trying to gather the last two pieces."

"So we'll possess three Deltas?"

"Yes."

"And then… what?"

Waylen glanced at Martina. "We don't know, sir."

"Good work. Special Agent Brooks, if you need to get to Sedona, whatever you require is at your disposal. How about a SEAL team?"

"Covert might be better," Waylen said.

"Take the helicopter," Grant told him.

"Thank you, sir."

"In your opinion, are we dealing with a potential alien invasion? I'll have to get my wife and kids to safety."

"Not if we can keep the Delta from being used," Martina said.

Waylen wasn't so confident.

"Take my number." Grant gave him a business card, black with white lettering and nothing else. "And God speed."

"Thank you, sir," Waylen said while the Secret Service agent opened the hatch. A black car waited in the parking lot.

"Contain this, Brooks. By any means necessary." He closed the door and patted the hull. The pilot passed them headsets, then rose into the air.

"*Sedona, Arizona?*" the female pilot asked.

"Roger that," Waylen answered.

9

"It has to be here somewhere," Silas said. They'd spent two hours scouring the grounds of the golf course, to no avail.

"Look." Rory uncurled a large poster from a cardboard tube. "It's the blueprints."

"What's the date?" he asked.

Rory's finger settled on the corner. "2003."

"They've renovated since my grandfather hid the token." Silas closed his eyes, picturing the echo he'd witnessed earlier. Peter Gunn had walked to the second hole in the middle of the night, and leaned a shovel on a large sequoia tree trunk. He scanned the sheet, which displayed the additional nine holes the course had added twenty years earlier. "I need the original." Silas scoured the general manager's desk using a flashlight, and eventually found what he sought. The old layout wasn't that different, with minor adjustments. Of course, hole two was the most changed. He laid them side by side, determining where the token might be in relation to the new version. "There."

"We're going to need tools," Rory said.

Silas grinned, and was glad for the cover of darkness as they exited the building. They'd waited until the last car

Shadows of the Earth

departed the lot an hour earlier, before venturing in. Lucky for them, no one had bothered locking up. The course was a couple of miles from town, and roughly the same distance from the Hex they'd arrived in.

They rounded the clubhouse, past the neat rows of clean golf carts, and reached the groundskeeper's shed. It was a giant structure with locked barn doors, but a smaller door was open on the edge.

"This'll be a piece of…" Silas stopped with a shovel in his hand as flashing lights bounced off the exterior.

"Damn it," Rory muttered.

Two police officers exited the car, one talking into his radio. The woman kept her palm on the gun holstered to her hip.

"Hands where we can see 'em." The guy gestured at them, and Silas dropped the spade.

"Be cool," he said, unsure what they were supposed to do.

Rory lowered her shovel too, and slowly raised her arms.

"Is there a reason you're skulking around in the dark?" the woman asked.

"My car got stuck a mile down the road, and we needed something to dig it out with. I almost hit a skunk, and…"

"Okay, sir. We'll escort you to your car."

Silas cursed himself for blurting the first lie that came to mind. "There's no car," he admitted, saving time.

"That's what I thought." The male came closer. "Turn around. Get to your knees, and put your hands behind…"

"We didn't do anything!" Rory exclaimed.

"Sure. Breaking and entering with the intent of property damage."

Silas felt the cold cuffs on his wrists. He'd been too cocky, too confident they could do this simply and quietly. He hadn't even considered that someone might notice his actions. Rory grunted when they hefted her up, and Silas hated that he'd dragged her into this.

"I'll make it up to you," he whispered.

Rory didn't respond while they were directed into the back of the cop car. It smelled like stale sweat and coffee.

Every bump made him even more uncomfortable, and apparently, the road was filled with them between the golf course and the police station. Luckily, it was on the north end of town, only a few minutes from where they'd been apprehended. Silas contemplated their options. If they weren't released soon, it might be too late. Darren Jones would win.

"Out," the man said, holding the door. The station's lights were bright, nearly blinding him after being in the dark for the last hour. Silas prayed they'd be thrown into the same cell and cursed when they were taken to the other ends of a hallway. Rory glanced at him before they were separated.

The male cop searched Silas' pockets after removing his cuffs. "Car or home keys?"

"Not on me."

"What are these?" The cop lifted the bag filled with two sets of the tokens.

"Bookmarks. I read a lot."

"Sure you do."

Someone knocked, taking the guy's attention. Silas grabbed them, sliding a single token out. He placed it into the pocket they'd already checked and tried to breathe evenly.

A minute later, the cop pulled out a breathalyzer.

"Blow."

Silas did without hesitation, hoping they'd just be released. "Happy?"

"What were you really doing out there?"

"Okay, I wanted a rose bush. My mom has been hounding me to get this"—Silas remembered the plans he'd scanned over in the office—"rare Pink Grootendorst variety for her garden, and I can't find them. I was only going to cut a sapling, I swear."

The officer narrowed his gaze. "Now I've heard it all. We'll put you in the cell and contact the golf course to ask if they want to press charges."

Silas reached into his pocket and slid the token free of the plastic case surrounding it. He touched the metal, seeing images floating in his mind. Black mist rose in the corner, but didn't catch him. "Officer…"

"Bates."

"Take this. You forgot it." Silas offered the token.

Bates mumbled and grasped the alien object. He huffed for air and fell to his seat. Silas dragged him behind bars, and took the keys on his belt, before slamming the cell door closed.

"I might need that." Silas unlocked the cell and snatched the flat piece of metal after a few seconds. The man remained on the ground, drool spilling from his lips. Silas spotted the fire alarm on the wall, and without hesitation, tugged on it, then gathered his few belongings.

Silas poked his head from the doorway as the female police officer who'd escorted Rory ran off. He rushed to find Rory in the other room. Silas dangled the keys, smiling at her look of disbelief.

"You'd better hurry!" she said. "I doubt they'll leave two prisoners behind if they think the building is on fire."

A minute later, they were in the hall, while the alarm turned off. Silas saw the rear exit, and they sped through, praying no one had found the unconscious officer on the floor of the locked cell.

"Will they check the golf course for us?" Rory asked as they ran across the parking lot.

"Why would two rosebush thieves return to the scene of the crime?" Silas jumped the short wooden fence and entered the forest butting up to the town's perimeter. According to his GPS, they were a mile from the course and the buried token.

The headlights bounced on the asphalt as Cody sped down the highway. In the darkness, the lines denoting the lane seemed to glow, keeping him from veering off the road.

He couldn't see more than ten yards in front of him, making the landscape past the highway impossible to view. All he noticed were black shapes as the hillsides lifted and fell.

It was nearly three in the morning, and the GPS showed him an hour out of Sedona. He peered at the incoming message icon on the SUV's dash, but he'd received no new texts.

"Where are you guys?" he asked. Silas was supposed to meet him there, which seemed highly improbable given the distance to Boston. Before leaving, he'd done his due diligence, checking flights. Nothing seemed plausible to Sedona from the Boston region, not until the afternoon, and that was only if they were willing to fly a tiny two-

Shadows of the Earth

seater aisled craft with a second-tier airline.

Cody had seen the maps of the Department's buildings and knew the structure was somewhere on the south side of Sedona, just out of the city limits. With that in mind, he slowed and manually adjusted the GPS destination to a water treatment plant along the freeway about ten minutes farther.

He tried to distract himself with an audio book, a fantasy volume from one of his favorite series. After twenty minutes, he rewound the chapter, realizing he hadn't heard a single word. He switched it to music instead and wondered if every man in the world ended up listening to folk music once they turned forty. The dubstep he'd blasted in headphones while working on his tech apps didn't do it for him anymore, so he'd shifted to something more contemporary.

Cody tapped his fingers on the steering wheel to the beat, singing the occasional line, though he wasn't positive of the words. It didn't matter, since he was alone and didn't care how off-key he sounded.

He drove slower within Sedona, cognizant of the police presence. The buildings were all covered in red stucco. San Diego had its share of clay roofs too, the Spanish style marketable, since they were also close to the Mexican border. He noticed a twenty-four-hour rest stop ahead, and pulled in to fill up the tank, then relieve himself. He walked out of the store at 2:49 A.M. with a huge plastic cup of cola.

Cody peered over his shoulder when he heard footsteps, but it was only a trucker coming from the bathroom. He nodded at Cody, then climbed into his semi, firing the engine on. It rumbled loudly, then the brakes squealed as he pulled from the parking lot, dragging a heavy load onto the street.

Once inside the SUV, he checked his messages again.

I'm here. What now? he texted Silas, but it didn't show read. "You better be on the way."

The roads were empty, with the occasional taxicab bringing people home from the bar. A girl rolled the window down as he passed one of them, and she thrust her hand into the air, clearly drunk. He honked once and changed lanes.

When he was free of the city, Cody opened the sunroof to let in a breeze of cool air. He sipped the cola, which barely fit into the cupholder, and heard something in the distance. He slowed, pulling to the shoulder, and turned the vehicle off. He noticed a low whooshing sound. Cody saw the blinking lights of the helicopter moving in the same direction as him.

Waylen asked the pilot to land within the government facility's fence line, and she obliged.

"It's empty," Martina said.

"Looks that way." Waylen hopped out. "Can you wait close by, but out of sight?"

The pilot gave him a nod and noisily departed. It was a good thing they were miles from town. The region was covered with desert landscape and not much else. The nearest residence he'd seen from above was a mansion about a mile to the north, with a gigantic swimming pool, and what appeared to be a miniature football field.

When the helicopter was gone, Waylen traversed the courtyard to the front doors. "Is the code the same?"

Shadows of the Earth

Martina reached for the pad. "Guess we'll find out." She entered the five-digit number and was granted access.

It was yet another duplicate of the familiar Planetae laboratory. These matching places were up around the country, with no one monitoring them, and that was alarming. What other secrets were scattered across the USA, with only a handful aware of their existence? Waylen was a member of the FBI, and he doubted even the CIA knew that the Department had constructed these labs.

They strolled to the secondary room, and Waylen drew his gun before entering, half-expecting Darren to be inside with three alien counterparts. Instead, it was dark and quiet.

"What are we even doing here?" he asked.

Martina paced to the Hex. "We're missing something. Think, Sanchez."

Waylen sat on the few steps connecting the platform to the floor and rested his elbows on knees. "Delta." He grabbed his phone, doing an internet search. "Delta resonances are subatomic particles and involve quarks."

"Does that help us?" Martina asked.

"Probably not." He closed the program and set it aside.

She finally stopped moving. "What's the deal with Charlotte?"

"There's no deal."

"Is she the one from…"

Waylen gave her a weak smile. "Yeah."

"Does she know about…" Martina wagged a finger between them.

"No. Not that I was trying to keep anything from her. We're not that young, and both had lives apart."

"Sure." Martina sat beside him. "You like her?"

"I think so."

"Your convictions are so resolute," she joked.

Waylen gazed at Martina. "You really pissed me off."

"Me? Why?"

"We're partners, and here I find out you're involved in some dead outer space organization. Not to mention, you accepted money from Monroe."

"I can explain," she said.

"I have time." Waylen tapped his foot.

"My biological father was larger than life." She spread her arms out, like a fisherman exaggerating her catch of the day. "When he died, Fallow approached me while I was still in school. He suggested the organization was stale and needed fresh blood. I accepted, but honestly, nothing really came of it. When Swanson died, the project turned dark, and no one talked to me. When Clark was introduced as the Director of NASA a few years ago, I presumed we were done."

"And Monroe?"

"He's a fool. Leo didn't know who I was, or that the D.O.O.S. even existed. I honestly wanted you to be safe and out of harm's way."

"Why?" Waylen asked.

"*Why?*" She glared at him. "God, men are stupid."

"I can't disagree."

"Because I'm in love with you, Brooks. There, you happy?"

Waylen froze, shocked that those words had escaped Martina's lips. "I had no idea."

"Which I concluded with the aforementioned comment."

"You… love me?"

Shadows of the Earth

"Don't get too excited. I've loved a few people in my life."

"I just didn't see it."

"Which part? Assistant Director Ben tried giving me my own cases, but I refused him. For an entire year! All those late nights, asking you to the bar, hoping you'd throw caution to the wind."

Waylen thought about it and nodded grimly. "I'm sorry."

"Don't be."

"I should have realized."

"It's not a big deal." Martina sighed and kicked her legs out long. "You're with Charlotte, and that's fine. I'm a big girl who drinks too much and gambles on sports, but really doesn't want to change."

Waylen stayed silent and looked around the laboratory, wondering why they'd even come. "Let's get out of here."

"Yeah?"

"I need to find out where Silas and Rory have gone."

"Okay." Martina stuck behind him, walking slower so they weren't matching strides. He figured she wasn't feeling at her prime after admitting her feelings, only for Waylen to mutter a brief apology. He couldn't face it at the moment, not with pressing matters taking priority.

The instant he stepped out, headlights shone through the front gates. "We have company."

Waylen reached for his gun and started forward.

10

Rory's palms had never been so sore. She tossed the shovel to the ground and sat on the bench while Silas continued digging. They were lucky the police hadn't stopped at the golf course again, because they would have been easy pickings, obsessively decimating the flowerbeds on hole two.

"Where is it?"

Silas didn't stop. "Cody must be in Sedona by now."

"Shouldn't we try to text him?"

"Not yet. Let's find the—" Silas shouted in surprise and crouched, clawing at the soil with his fingers. He pulled out a bag, another matching whiskey sack. He scrambled from the opening, covered in muck up to his chest.

Rory filled with a mixture of relief and tension. They were close.

Somewhere down the road, a car drove toward the golf course. "We have to leave."

Silas nodded and removed the Delta. They jogged to the tee box, opting for a flat location. As he clicked the tokens together, sirens sounded in the distance. Rory peered at the course's entrance, finding a steady stream of incoming police cars.

Shadows of the Earth

"Guess they finally checked here," she said while the Shadow billowed from the middle of the glowing triangle.

When Silas had all the alien segments in his pocket, he focused on her. "I don't have time to control our destination like before. Can you get us back to…"

Rory nodded, picturing the lab in New York. She pulled Silas into the portal, and the ringing sirens diminished.

The lab's emergency lights were on; otherwise, Leo Monroe's Hex was dark. Silas left the Shadow intact, and Rory stared at the lab's floor, where only a few days prior, the aliens had killed fifty soldiers without batting an eye. Someone had cleaned up the mess, but the shiny white tile was riddled with dents.

"One remains," Silas said, holding the last Delta's two pieces. He retrieved the token from the bag and made contact. His eyes pressed shut, and Rory noticed a sheen of sweat coat his brow. "I can see the final one."

"Where is it?"

"South of Sedona, on a trail." Silas dropped the token, and after a moment, stowed it.

"Peter Gunn didn't intend on these being found," Rory said.

"I'm not positive that's true."

"Explain that logic."

"He left the journal for me, and there are subtle clues, indicating he wanted me to find them. He mentions Beverly, who had files of the trip he took in ninety-seven. And last, he gave everything to me and Clare. Wouldn't he expect us to stumble on the safe and hidden token?"

Rory digested his theory and thought about finding Grandpa Swanson's token in an old Western paperback inside his nightstand in Rye, New Hampshire. "My grandfather didn't even attempt to hide his."

"Something's bothering me about the supposed Department of Outer Space," Silas said.

"Yeah, which part? Besides Brett ruthlessly running down Kevin, then casually putting two bullets in him."

"It was all too… sloppy." Silas opened the platform's exit. "What were they doing?"

"You're right. They were actively trying to find the third with the box in Kentucky."

"But that was when Colin was alive. Maybe they were just that unorganized?" Silas stepped to the floor. "But it doesn't explain the three facilities Monroe built. Those were completed after your grandfather passed. Meaning the Department had big plans still."

"There's a lot of missing information," Rory said.

"Being?"

"Darren Jones. You worked with him, right?"

"Yep."

"Was he… why would Darren bring aliens and leave with them?"

"He wouldn't. At least, not the man I shared dinner with for a week."

"Then…"

Silas held the tokens up. "It's these. They affected Darren."

"Have you seen or heard anything strange?" Even now, Rory saw pieces of the Shadow in the corner of her vision, besides the blatantly real portal centering the Hex ten feet from her position.

"No, but I wasn't using them like Waylen and Darren. They'd spend hours touching the different tokens, trying to learn what lay on the Moon or Planet D."

"We might not be able to trust Waylen," she said.

Shadows of the Earth

"Cody used the tokens all the time," Silas reminded her. "He could be affected."

The door opened across the lab, making Rory jump.

"It's Special Agent Charles," Silas said.

"And Charlotte," Rory added, squinting at the pair.

It wasn't until they were twenty yards away that Rory noticed the gun in Charlotte's grip, and the tense posture of the big government agent.

"Raise those arms," Charlotte ordered.

"What the hell are you doing?" Silas grunted and went rigid when she aimed the gun at him.

"Don't do anything heroic or I'll put you down like a dog." Charlotte grabbed her phone and dialed someone. "It's a go. I have them. Yes, at Monroe's place." She peered at Silas, then at the active Shadow. "We're only missing one. Bring it here, Jones, and we're done. Don't forget the champagne." Charlotte put the cell into her suit jacket pocket.

"You know Darren Jones?" Rory asked.

"Not until recently. We have … mutual friends."

"What do you want? Why are you working with *them*?"

Charlotte waved the barrel at Gary Charles, and he came to stand with Rory and Silas. "Give me the tokens."

Silas didn't budge.

"Don't make this harder than it has to be. We won, you lost. Peter Gunn screwed everything up, and now we're seeking our redemption. Just twenty years too late."

Rory figured Charlotte was only forty, so the math wasn't adding up. "Are you with the Department?"

"The Department of Outer Space?" She cackled and shook her head. "What a crock. Clark Fallow. They were clueless, but we managed to secure funding through the group nonetheless."

Rory considered the comment. "Three Deltas, three Hexes."

"Very good." Charlotte gestured at Silas. "Kick them over."

Charlotte smiled and pulled the trigger three times, shooting Gary. He tumbled and fell to the ground, clutching his bleeding neck. Rory instinctively lunged toward him, but Charlotte fired a warning shot.

Silas lowered the tokens, and he grabbed hold of Rory's wrist, dragging her from the various sections of Deltas. "Take them. Just don't hurt her."

Rory's chest ached at the selfless mention, and how he stood in front of her, acting as a shield.

"Don't worry, I need one of you," Charlotte said. "Waylen's a bleeding heart. He'll trade for living collateral."

"I thought you two were an item."

Charlotte's eyes gleamed, and Rory thought she almost saw a flicker of remorse, but it vanished quickly. "They can't be stopped."

"Who?"

"I think you know." Charlotte languidly walked to the tokens. She snapped the connected version apart, and the portal dissipated in the Hex. There went Rory's escape plan. "Brett Davis was with us, as was Theodore Belleville."

"And Leo?"

"That fool? Not a chance. He seriously thought he could mine the Moon," she said. "We let him perfect the technology and permitted him to duplicate it here at his own facility." Charlotte knocked on the Hex from the outside.

"And what do you hope to achieve with those?" Silas gestured at the tokens in her possession.

"This isn't a monologue at the end of a movie, kids." Charlotte's phone chimed, and she read a text, grinning the entire time. "They're close."

Rory had to alert Cody. They couldn't allow Darren Jones to get the final token, or they were doomed.

While Charlotte seemed occupied, Rory leaned toward Silas, whispering quietly. "Text Cody the location."

Silas didn't acknowledge the comment, and moved to Gary's dead body. He checked for a pulse that obviously wasn't there.

"You're wasting your time," Charlotte said, responding to Darren on her phone.

Silas' back was to the woman, and Rory saw his cell slip from his front pocket. He was fast, and it vanished as quickly as it appeared.

"Get away from him!" Charlotte ordered, flashing her gun again.

"Tell us what will happen when you open all three Shadows in the Hexes," Rory said, desperate to distract Waylen's ex-girlfriend.

"Enough talking. Shut up and stand still."

Rory sighed, then waited.

Cody Sanderson parked his SUV within the fence after Waylen opened the gate.

"Where's your ride?" he asked the duo.

Martina motioned to the west. "We had a helicopter."

"Must be nice," Cody mumbled. "I'm driving around

for hours like a chump."

His phone buzzed, and Cody snatched it out. "It's from Silas."

"What's it say?" Waylen rushed to his side.

"*DJ coming. Cathedral Rock Trailhead.*"

"Nothing else?" Martina said. "Ask him …"

"DJ's obviously Darren Jones." Waylen paced frantically. "Where's the trailhead?"

Cody found it on the map in a second. "Only a five-minute drive."

"Let's go." Waylen jumped into the SUV, taking the driver's seat.

"Come on, it's my car!" Cody shouted, but when it was clear Waylen wasn't relenting, he took the passenger side.

Martina climbed into the back without complaint, and they drove off, leaving the Department's test center behind. It was difficult to see the road in the dark, but Waylen made do, speeding faster than Cody would have dared on the narrow street. There was no shoulder, no center line, just a cracked old piece of highway connecting the hiking trails to the freeway.

"That has to be the monument." Cody gestured ahead of them, to a cluster of what he assumed was a natural formation of giant sandstone spires. He could see why they'd named it a cathedral. It resembled something out of medieval Europe in the middle of the Arizona desert.

The derelict road continued, but if they stayed on it, they'd go right past their destination, so Waylen slowed, pulling into an empty parking lot that faced the cathedral. It almost glowed beneath the Moon's shine. Cody reached into the glove box, removing a handgun.

"What are you doing?" Waylen asked.

"Protecting myself." Cody kept it gripped and went out. The air was crisp, and he wished he'd worn a jacket. Once Martina was on the dirt, he took a hoodie from the floor, shook it off, and slipped it over his head.

"Anything else from Silas?" Martina inquired.

Waylen and Cody both examined their phones. "Nothing," Cody answered.

"DJ is coming," Waylen muttered. "How would he know that?"

"You're not suggesting that they found Silas?" Cody balked at the idea.

"It's possible." Waylen stared at the trail's sign, then at the cathedral atop the hill. It was a mile to the crest of the hike, and they still wouldn't know where the token was. "Why choose a busy tourist attraction?"

"These old astronauts had minds of their own," Martina said.

Cody checked his pocket, finding the fake tokens. He never knew when they might come in handy, and perhaps tonight they would. If they could beat Darren to the piece of the third Delta, maybe he'd be able to switch it out.

Cody wasn't much of a hiker. Not that he didn't enjoy a pleasant walk, but he preferred even land, with comfortable sneakers and no risk of being bitten by a rattler in the dark. Martina progressed quickly, with Waylen keeping up. Cody had to pick up his pace a few times during the mile stroll to ensure they didn't lose him. He heard a howl and glanced at the desert surrounding them. "What the hell was that?"

"Bobcats," Waylen said.

"How can you be so calm?"

"In my experience, people are far worse of a threat

than a cat."

"What about aliens?"

"They take the top of the food chain," Waylen grunted.

The closer they got to the monument, the more impressive it seemed. From this angle, it blotted the sky's light, except for a spattering of stars breaking through a thin layer of clouds. They reached a wooden sign, advising them to go left for another trail, and straight to keep on to Cathedral Rock. Martina didn't even slow to read it, and started up the steeper incline. Shale and dust kicked up in her wake, and Cody waved it away as he stuck in the back of their three-person procession.

When they crested the top, Cody was winded, his body drenched in sweat, and he sat on the ground, trying to regain his composure. "The one-mile hike didn't sound so bad until you do it."

Even Waylen was breathless. Only Martina seemed unaffected by the arduous climb. She navigated the interior with flawless precision. "How are we supposed to find a token here?"

"We don't have a shovel," Cody said.

Waylen caught up to Martina, while Cody dusted his pants off, then joined them at the ledge overlooking the valley beyond. Cody peered down the road to an incoming set of headlights. "Guys, we have company."

"Where would Peter have placed it?" Cody tried to think like Silas' grandfather. He'd left one in a garden a thousand miles away. Another was supposed to be near Red Bluff, California. Cody couldn't understand the correlation, or perhaps the purpose of the random locations was to not have a correlation.

The car grew closer, and Cody felt the seconds ticking

Shadows of the Earth

down. "They'll notice our vehicle in the parking lot."

"That's true." Waylen puffed his cheeks out. "Even if we locate the token, it's not like we can run to the vehicle after, and wave at Darren and the aliens while we pass."

Cody shook his head, struggling with his plan, but had little choice. He pulled a fake token from his pocket.

"Not this again," Waylen said.

"It worked on you. Perhaps it'll trick them," Cody suggested.

Waylen took the replica and removed the bag. "Fine. We'll wait for them to find it, then return for the real one."

"What if these aliens can sense the actual tokens?" Martina asked.

"Then we lose." Waylen searched for somewhere to stow it, but struggled for a realistic location, since it had been secreted away twenty-five years ago.

The incoming vehicle, now obviously a white utility van, parked in the lot near the road. Cody couldn't see many details, but the sound of the slamming door carried through the valley and into the stone cathedral.

"They're coming," Martina cautioned. Cody made out three shapes, the lead smaller than the other two. "Looks like Silas killed the one he ran over."

"Good."

Cody watched as a flash of red pulsed near the original trail sign, and the next instant, his SUV exploded, booming loudly. The flames rose high, pushing in a fiery cloud, then it continued to burn as the tires struck down. "My car!"

Waylen shoved the token in a crack by the primary pillar. It stood apart from the others, but might not have been obvious enough for Darren to spot.

Cody scaled the back end of the rock formation, gashing his palms as he hurried lower. The bobcats howled with more ferocity, undoubtedly sensing a larger threat nearby.

11

"Now what?" Silas asked Charlotte, but she ignored him as usual. Special Agent Charles' corpse remained on the floor, and Silas stared at his lifeless body. He would die today. Rory would die. The aliens had won. "Can I move him?"

"Suit yourself," Charlotte said. She was inside the Hex, studying the interior of the platform.

"Let me help," Rory offered, but Silas didn't want to put that on her.

"Nah, I can handle it." Silas lowered next to Gary and set a hand on his shoulder. "I'm sorry it happened like this." The words of apology fell on deaf ears. When he slid Gary, blood streaked below him.

"Here." Rory offered her jacket and placed it beside the man. Together, they lifted him onto the article of clothing, creating a barrier between the sticky blood and white tile.

"Thanks," Silas said, and kept at it, bringing Gary behind the lockers. He found a tarp within one of the storage units and covered him.

They'd been waiting for two hours already, with Charlotte gaping at the thin air. Occasionally, she'd whisper to herself. Did the aliens talk to her? How did that work?

"Charlotte?"

She paused within the Hex and smiled at Silas. "Yes."

"Why would you possibly team up with someone from another world?"

"You wouldn't understand."

"Try me," Silas said.

She stepped clear of the Hex and joined them on the lab floor. "I heard them when I was three."

"You remember being three?" Rory asked.

"Of course, don't you?"

Rory shook her head, and Charlotte continued. "I later learned that my first encounter with them came the instant Colin, Brett, and Clark found the second Delta on the Moon. The precise second, if I can believe Brett."

"What did they say?"

"They didn't speak like us. They used energy. Vibrations. The connection grew every year, until I was certain of what I had to do," she said. "They were upset when Colin died, because he was supposed to find the last three tokens. Everything paused."

"Until Peter Gunn died," Silas said.

"Yes."

"What about Darren? How does he fit into this?"

"A byproduct. I saw him at my house, when Waylen met with him. Can you imagine my surprise when Waylen contacted *me,* of all people? Or maybe it's more than that. Waylen had touched the tokens, so I believe *they* put it into his mind. There's no reason for Waylen to reach out to me, not after our awful relationship. I was miserable, longing for communication with the Dreamers."

"Dreamers?"

"That's what I called them. I was a little girl and needed to give them a label."

Shadows of the Earth

"Was it always more than one?"

"It was a group presence, not a single entity. They were comforting, positive, and gave me direction throughout my entire life," she said, her smile growing with the memory.

If Silas hadn't seen the aliens with his own two eyes, he would have believed Charlotte desperately required medical help. "These Dreamers… what did they ask you to do?"

Charlotte's gaze snapped to Rory. "They were patient, but that's wearing thin. They needed someone close to the Deltas, and opted for Darren Jones. I thought he looked capable, and the Dreamers agreed. He'll be with the final token now."

She checked her phone. "They've destroyed your friend's car, and are heading to the location. Soon we'll have nine tokens and can complete the mission."

"You'll use the Deltas, a Shadow in each Hex." Silas gestured at the Hex behind them.

"Yes."

"Hermon, Red Bluff, and Sedona," Silas said.

"That's right."

"Then what? What happens when the Shadows are activated?"

Charlotte slapped her palms together, startling Silas. "The Dreamers come."

"You couldn't find them, so you waited for us to bring them to you." Silas glanced at the tokens he'd single-handedly delivered to the Dreamers' human puppet.

"And you did such an efficient job. Even the Dreamers are pleased."

"Does that mean you'll spare us?" Silas asked with a crooked grin.

"I believe you'd be better off dying tonight," Charlotte said, crushing his hopes.

Silas needed more answers. "Why did they leave any of the Deltas? It doesn't add up."

"They didn't."

"Then who?"

"Another. The Dreamers are just one of a thousand. They follow the trails from the Hub, taking each world over as they see fit."

"Planet D," Rory said.

"The field of Shadows..." Charlotte stopped and glared at them. The gun noticeably shifted to her dominant hand. "No more talking." Her eye twitched, and Silas had a feeling another entity was speaking to her.

Silas urged Cody to hurry and beat Darren to the last token.

Waylen would have traded a million bucks for a set of binoculars. They'd rushed down rough terrain, and all three of them were coated in bruises and abrasions. His pants were torn along the right calf, and Martina was limping. She was close, her breath on his ear while they hid from the aliens, trying to stay small in the scratchy shrubbery a mile deeper into the harsh landscape.

Sounds of insects, howling bobcats, and the occasional rattle noise surrounded them, and Cody shrank with every incident until Waylen could barely see him from five feet away.

"If we get out of here, I'm going to stop gambling," Martina said.

"Is this like someone swearing they'll go to church if

Shadows of the Earth

God helps them out of a precarious situation?" Waylen asked.

"I guess so." Martina's hand clutched his. "I meant what I said earlier."

Waylen thought about Charlotte. Had he really intended to make a go of it with her? He suddenly recalled their constant bickering, the fights late into the nights on each visit, which grew farther apart, thanks to the fact that neither wanted to be in a relationship with the other.

"You look pensive," Martina said.

"I made a mistake." The tokens had affected him. Waylen could almost feel his movements being guided by an outside force, and he pressed his eyes closed.

"Haven't we all?" Her grip was tight, her palm warm.

"Would you two keep it down?" Cody finally commented. "I'm right here. If you want to get it on, go do it on a cactus, far from my hiding spot."

Martina laughed, covering her mouth to stifle it. "Now that's a visual."

Waylen stared at Cathedral Rock, and held his breath when he noticed the figures leaving the formation. "They found it."

"Or they came across the real one," Cody mumbled.

Waylen couldn't make out any movement after a moment. "Where are they?"

They stayed out of sight for another ten minutes, not spying anything out of place at the rock monument.

"We go back," Waylen said.

Cody kept hidden. "Come on, give it another while."

"Nah, he's right. We have to find the real token, or at least learn if they took the bait."

Cody swore a few times, getting out of the bushes. From here, at this late hour, with the minor injuries, the mile hike up the incline seemed impossible.

When they returned to the flat top of Cathedral Rock, it was an hour later, and they all dropped to the ground, lying on their backs once they saw Darren's van wasn't there. Waylen stared at the stars, seeing bright clusters of distant solar systems. How was it possible that aliens from one of those stars were here on Earth?

He scrambled to his feet and checked the crevasse he'd dropped the fake token into. "It's gone."

This gave Cody the energy he required to stand. "Then the real token is nearby."

Waylen tried to figure out what the aliens intended to do with the Deltas, and was glad the others were safe with Silas and Rory. His legs were fatigued, but he couldn't give up, not when they were so close to being done. Once they had all three Deltas, they'd confer with President Grant and decide the best course of action. This spurred him on, and Waylen scoured every inch of the cathedral's ground, the base of each spire, and any visible fracture he could find on the walls.

"I think I found it!" Martina called, and Cody hurried over, beating Waylen. "Up there. Do you see the indentation?"

Waylen used his cell phone's flashlight and shone it where Martina was pointing. The corner of a token protruded a half inch. "It's eight feet high."

Cody placed a palm on the surface of the rising stone. "Martina, we'll support you." He got to a knee, and Martina stepped on his leg. Waylen helped, and she rose on her toes, grumbling while trying to pry it loose. Martina came tumbling down and landed on Waylen in a heap. She rolled off, smiling victoriously, holding the token up. It was covered in a clear coating, protecting Martina from

Shadows of the Earth

the echoes contained within.

"Now what?" Cody gazed at Waylen.

"We call for air support." Waylen removed the pilot's business card and dialed her number.

They waited for fifteen minutes under the darkness of the trail. Cathedral Rock was as obvious a marker as any, and the helicopter located it easily. The sound of the machine reached Waylen before he spotted the black vessel lowering toward their position.

He kept gazing to the parking lot where Cody's SUV continued to burn.

"What if they didn't leave?" Waylen asked as the helicopter descended.

"What?" Martina shouted above the noise.

"What if…" Waylen spied the loping creature zooming down the trail. Its long legs made quick work of the distance, eating it up with each stride. He pulled his gun as the first alien bashed into Martina. The token flew from her grip, landing on the earth. Waylen dove at the being, breaking it apart from Martina. They tussled, and his head slammed into the ground. Waylen's vision filled with red, and he realized it was coming from his opponent's wrist. Instead of attempting to best the much larger creature physically, he fired three rounds into the enemy's chest, and lastly at the non-human face.

It swung an arm, clobbering Waylen, but he kept hold of the gun as it toppled over, hitting the trail with a resounding thump.

"Waylen!" Cody called as the second approached. This one moved much more methodically, its steps calculated and sure.

Martina had recovered, but cradled her arm protectively. The helicopter lingered above, a bright shining floodlight turned straight onto the alien. It elevated a hand, blocking the brightness.

The alien's mouth opened, and it unleashed an anguished sound when it saw the token in the open. Cody crouched to pick it up, and thrust the flat metal shard into the air. "You want this, you ugly son of a bitch?"

Its triple nostrils flared and fluttered, and the alien stomped forward.

It met Waylen's gaze.

Glittering stars.

Feeling of weightlessness.

A field, filled with countless Shadows, all wavering and drawing his attention.

"Waylen, what are you doing?" Cody asked.

The alien bypassed the other man, shoving Cody to his seat with a meaty hand. He stood facing the special agent, and grabbed Waylen's head, squeezing it as he lifted Waylen from the ground. His feet dangled as he witnessed his future in the alien's black eyes.

Bang. Bang.

The tension released, and he fell, the air shooting from his lungs. The alien tripped backwards, Martina's gunshots ending its life.

"Is that it?" Cody and Martina each took one of his arms, heaving Waylen off the sandy trail while the pilot landed. She gaped at them, then at the dead aliens, her skin pale and sticky with sweat.

"What the hell are those?"

"Our demise, if we don't hurry."

The woman nodded slowly, not breaking her gaze on the huge corpses. "Where to?"

Waylen stepped over the unmoving creature. "New York."

12

Rory didn't remember falling asleep, but she woke nuzzled up to Silas. Charlotte was seated in the Hex, all the tokens spread out by her feet. Her eyes were closed.

Rory reached for her cell phone, but it was gone. She shook Silas gently, and he came to with a start. "Rory?"

"Shhhh." She touched his lips. "Do you have your phone?"

Silas was groggy, but his focus returned after a quick scan of the laboratory. He patted his pocket, then shook his head. "She must have taken them when we passed out."

Rory glanced at the exit. "We need to contact Waylen."

"Or we could leave?" Silas quietly stood and helped Rory to her feet.

Rory peered in both directions, weighing her options. Could she abandon the tokens? If she and Silas freed themselves, they'd be able to contact someone to stop Charlotte from accessing the Shadows. With her mind made up, Rory crept across the tiled floor. Her shoes seemed too loud, so she removed them, carrying the flats in her hand. Silas did the same, and they trotted in socked feet to the exit. She didn't know what time it was, but it had to be morning.

The doors opened with a little effort, and Silas slowly closed them, keeping the noise levels to a minimum. Once they were free of the lab, Rory slipped her shoes on again and ran down the hall.

Her heart banged loudly, and white dots shimmered in her view. With the sudden change in blood pressure, the ever-present Shadow threatened to consume her.

They dashed outside, and the cool morning air startled her. She reveled in the sudden bout of freedom while Silas searched for an escape vehicle. They'd only arrived through the Shadow from Red Bluff, and weren't prepared for this.

By instinct, Rory patted her pocket where the phone would normally be and sighed.

"Charlotte could wake at any moment," Silas said.

The darkness vanished as dawn spread throughout the industrial park.

Rory started for the gate as it swung wide.

"Maybe it's Waylen," she said, hopefully.

A truck's lights blinded her and she looked away.

At the same second, a helicopter was descending. Whatever they were caught up in seemed to come to a head.

Silas, with no weapon or means to protect Rory, planted himself between her and the incoming vehicle as it parked.

Above, the copter whooshed closer, the wind tossing her hair aside.

"Look what we have here." Charlotte emerged at the entrance, a maniacal grin on her face.

Shadows of the Earth

Waylen noticed Charlotte and wished he hadn't gotten her tied up in this disaster. She should have been safe at home, preparing for a normal day at the office. Because of him, she was below, about to participate in a shootout.

"Can you land?" Waylen asked, and the pilot nodded, probably praying they didn't encounter more aliens.

Martina was already unstrapped, clutching her gun. Cody seemed to hold his weapon reluctantly as they settled to the ground within the fence line.

The truck faced Silas and Rory, and Waylen was confused by Charlotte's behavior. She had a handgun, and it was aimed at Rory from five feet behind her.

He jumped free of the hatch and rushed into the fray, staying to the side of his friends for a clear view of the woman he'd only recently committed to.

"Waylen, they tried to kill me," she said, tears forming in her eyes.

He looked at Rory, then at Silas.

The truck door opened, and out walked Darren Jones, as expected. He held the fake token they'd left for him, and surely he knew it wasn't real by this point.

"Where is it?" Darren shouted as the rotors slowed. The wind ceased, and the courtyard grew silent.

"Would someone tell me what the hell is going on?" Waylen yelled.

Charlotte wiped her tears and walked to Darren. "I've been waiting for a long time." She grinned. "While I prefer to work alone, you've been a real asset."

Waylen couldn't believe that he was aiming a weapon at Charlotte, of all people. Rory and Silas had moved behind him and Martina, and even Cody stayed on the front lines, facing off against the woman he thought he knew better than most people.

Charlotte snapped together three tokens, and the light shone brightly as the Shadow emerged from the alien device, forming a hole in space.

A man stepped out of the mist.

"Brett Davis," Rory hissed. They'd watched him dramatically vanish into the Shadow in Kentucky.

"Are they coming?" Charlotte licked her lips and grabbed Brett by the collar. "Where are the Dreamers?"

Brett efficiently disarmed her, dropping the magazine to the concrete. "Sorry, doll. We're not doing that."

Waylen was about to begin negotiations when another figure pressed from the black fog, pieces of haze clinging to the guy's navy-blue jumpsuit.

Waylen knew the face, but it was impossible...

Rory shoved past Waylen, gritting her teeth. "Grandpa?"

The deterioration had been fast, but also a long time coming. It started out with small things. Colin forgetting where he put his keys or parked his car. He was always such a friendly man, rarely raising his voice, but Rory distinctly recalled a moment he'd snapped at her after she asked a simple question about his day. By the end, he was nothing like the man she'd loved for her entire childhood.

"He's not my husband," Rory whispered, remembering the exact phrase her grandma used to say.

Colin Swanson walked closer, and it wasn't the same version she'd watched wither until he died. This Colin looked to be in his fifties, with a strong jaw and a good hairline.

"As I live and breathe," Colin said. "Rory, is that you?"

Tears streamed down her cheeks, and everything ached in her body. She couldn't find air, as though it was the first time she'd touched the echo. "This isn't real."

Rory wished she could close her eyes and be back at Woodstock on the night she'd driven in from Boston to write a book at her parents' house.

When she opened them, the alternate version of her grandfather continued staring at her. "I'm sorry."

"For what?"

"For leaving you behind. I hope he didn't… I pray the other Colin lived up to expectations."

Rory couldn't understand what he said. "The other…"

"It was all necessary. Fred agreed, as did Peter. There was no choice, really."

Charlotte's expression contorted, her cheek twitching drastically. "You… we had a deal, Davis!"

"No." Brett grabbed her by the wrist. "They connected to you, but we were never going to concede our world to your Dreamers. You were a means to an end."

Waylen monitored Darren Jones. Martina circled the podcaster, and he lowered his weapon when he realized they'd lost.

Charlotte screamed while Brett clutched her arms, holding her tight as she attempted to thrash free. Young Colin stepped in, pressing a device to her shoulder. It hissed, and she flopped forward, and Brett brought her to the ground.

Waylen and Martina still had their guns aimed at Colin

and Brett, and Rory's grandfather motioned for them to lower them. "There's no need for that."

Darren feigned left and went right, jumping into the portal's opening.

"Should we go after..."

"We have it covered." Brett stepped aside, making room for two more men. They walked through, carrying Darren between them. He wriggled and fought for freedom, but Colin used the same device, knocking Darren out. He lowered Charlotte's accomplice beside her.

Rory recognized Peter Gunn, and knew the other to be the infamous pilot, Fred Trell. Like Colin, they appeared to be in their fifties, and very much ... not dead... as they were supposed to be.

Silas staggered forward, rubbing his eyes. "Grandpa Gunn. How can this be?"

"You'd be amazed at what our allies are capable of. Clones. We thought it was preposterous at first, but the more we discussed it, the more we realized we didn't have a choice." Peter's voice was strong.

Rory glanced at Charlotte, then at Darren's body. "Who are the Dreamers?"

"You've met a few of them. They want Earth, and were using this woman as a conduit. It seems they made a connection when we found the second Delta. She believed Brett was an ally, but we've been devising our own plan," Colin said.

"And what is that?" Waylen asked.

Colin gave Rory a paternal smile. "To stop the invasion."

Shadows of the Earth

They sat in the Planetae residence's common space, waiting to hear the entire story. Silas kept glancing at his grandfather, or this version of him. He couldn't tell if they were being messed with by an alien entity, but it sure looked like Peter Gunn. He noticed Peter peeling the label from his bottle of beer, and was certain he'd seen his own father do the same on many occasions. Had he picked up the trait from his dad?

They'd locked Darren and Charlotte into separate suites, with cameras on the doors, but the astronauts assured their group they'd be out for hours yet.

Silas took a drink, and everyone remained silent at the table, until Brett Davis finally returned with refills.

"Okay, will someone explain?" Waylen demanded after a quiet minute.

The trio glanced at each other, but it was Peter that spoke on their behalf.

"Colin and I were on the Moon together," he said.

"No kidding," Cody muttered. "We've all seen your echoes."

"Echoes?"

"It's what we call the memories stored into the tokens."

"Yes, it's a strange side effect, isn't it?" Fred Trell commented.

Martina motioned to Peter. "Please, go on."

"My colleague noticed the portal, and I followed him to another world. We walked for nearly an hour and encountered the meadow filled with them. It was then and there I vowed we keep it a secret."

"What changed?" Rory asked.

"We kept seeing things, visions, echoes from another

race. Much like you witnessed our experiences, we saw a different one, the beings who'd planted the Delta on our Moon. It was obvious we had to explore our options, so we got the old band together and made the Shadow. Colin was the best at bonding with it. Maybe you can explain."

Colin Swanson took another swig of his beer and leaned forward. Silas noted how Rory watched him. He'd already pinched himself to see if he was dreaming. "The first time we connected the pieces, I realized I shouldn't have separated it from the Moon. But what's done is done. When we learned there was a second, Peter considered using the Delta in our possession to gather it. But it was thousands of miles from Tranquility. Unless we had a rover and a whole bunch of air tanks, we couldn't make it. Our gang spent the next ten years figuring out how to return. That's when we brought it to Brett and Clark."

"You really flew an unsanctioned mission to the Moon?" Waylen asked, receiving a nod.

"Yes. The Delta was precisely where I'd guessed."

"And the third?"

"That was later," Fred said. "We activated both, but something came through."

Silas swallowed a lump in his throat, glancing at the tokens lying on the table. "Something?"

Fred lifted his shirt to reveal a long scar from his belly button to his collarbone. "I almost died. Thankfully, Brett was quick on the draw. We closed it up, and vowed to leave them shut."

"But you didn't," Silas said.

"No. Colin continued his quest to locate the rest, but Peter and I were out. We held on to the tokens for four years, until Colin convinced us there was a third Delta. We had to use the Shadows to keep our world safe."

Shadows of the Earth

"Where did you find it?" Martina asked.

"Your father was a good man," Colin said. "He came with me to Chile to get the Delta."

"Chile?" Silas finished his beer and noticed he was peeling the label as well. He stopped and slid the empty aside.

"It was in an extremely remote region of Patagonia. I'm only alive because Emmanuel Sanchez was there."

Martina smiled at the mention of her father, and former member of the Department.

"What transpired? You had all three Deltas. Why are you here, while the other astronauts grew old and died?" Waylen inquired.

"We activated them in a military base that Fallow had cleared out for our purposes."

"And?" Silas was on the edge of his seat.

"The Shadows connected," Peter whispered. "And out came a visitor. They offered us an exchange, and we took it."

"Who are they?" Rory's voice wavered slightly.

"Allies. We couldn't return to Earth, and our replicas would live out their days without the knowledge that they were… clones."

Brett Davis coughed and cracked another beer. "Peter Gunn's replacement was even more pig-headed than the original. He hid the tokens. All three were determined to keep the things contained. I held on to a Delta."

"So my grandpa wasn't you?" Rory asked.

"He was," Colin said. "They were created in a lab and brought to Earth with no recollection of ever meeting these distant allies. Everything they did was because of who we were. Imagine you were split off, and that version didn't know it, but they had your memories. Is it not you?"

"That's hard to…"

"Why are you here?" Waylen squinted. "You mentioned an alien invasion."

"These beings want to take Earth, and we must ensure that never happens," Colin said.

"How?" Silas asked.

"By destroying the Shadows forever," Peter answered grimly.

EPILOGUE

"Are you feeling better?" Marg Chambers asked when Rory entered the office.

"It was one of those twenty-four-hour things," she said. "Had some bad clams, I think."

"You sure you don't want to make it a long weekend? Garnet and I can cover for your classes. You look a little pale."

Well, I was arrested, and I found out my grandpa is alive, and only twenty years older than me. Oh, and we're trying to fend off an alien invasion with the astronauts from Helios 15. But I'm fine. "I'm fine."

"Have an excellent class, then." Marg walked off, leaving Rory alone in the foyer.

Since meeting Colin, the effects of the Shadow had vanished. The misty blackness had ceased to follow her everywhere she went, and Rory was eternally thankful.

Silas seemed happy, and returned to Loon Lake, showing Peter the house his clone had eventually moved to. Waylen and Cody were keeping an eye on Fred Trell for the moment. Martina escorted Darren Jones and Charlotte Halstead to the Kentucky D.O.O.S. facility for more interrogations.

Rory collected her books from her compact office

and walked to her first class. The students were bright-eyed, eager for a lesson before breaking for the week. She tried to recall what it was like to be that young, ready to let out some steam after working hard for five days.

"It's time for you to share your work." Rory gestured to Carmen, the student she'd met before the semester even began.

"Me?" Carmen gawked at her laptop and carried it to the front of the class.

"What's the piece called?" Rory asked, stepping aside.

"*Kolkata.*"

Rory listened as Carmen told a fictional tale, set in the bustling Indian city's black market.

The door opened, and in walked Colin Swanson. He wore a pair of jeans and a leather jacket. With black-rimmed reading glasses on, no one would recognize him as the deceased hero from decades ago. He sat in the back of the room without comment.

Rory didn't know what tomorrow would bring, but clung to the present with gratitude.

The cell door buzzed, and Leo nodded at the guards as he passed by. He went to the mess hall, stood in line for his turn at a serving of the mushy vegetable of the day, and glanced over his shoulder.

Reese, the pudgy guard with a limp, winked at him.

That was the sign.

Leo Monroe shuffled along and stared while the meal half-missed his plate, spilling onto the tray. He ate quickly, trying to look inconspicuous, but no one was watching him. Here, he was a nobody, a nameless man who'd bribed a few brutes with extra commissary cash for protection.

Reese tapped his foot impatiently, and Leo knew it was now or never. He walked past the guard, who slipped him a key. It pressed into his palm as he shuffled along, chin lowered until he reached the outer door. He glanced up, finding the camera lights off. Reese had come through after all.

Leo walked into the yard. He doubted anyone would notice he wasn't supposed to be there for another hour.

It had all been a front. Planetae. Making weapons for crime lords and governments.

What he'd required was capital, and the Department's backing to build the Hexes. Three of them, equally matched, plus one receiving end near Manhattan. They'd be hit first. Leo smiled as he imagined the destruction of their great city.

He'd been visited by them at the age of nine. Leo Monroe was a vessel for the coming war.

Leo stalked across the yard, reaching the fence, and made sure he was in the blind spot Reese had predicted. Getting out of Sing Sing would be far more difficult than his recent disappearing act, but it seemed to work.

He gripped the chain-link and slid the section free. Leo ducked under it and stepped out of the maximum-security prison. An alarm sounded as smoke billowed across the facility, hopefully drawing the attention of the tower guards. He waited, ensuring the patrol truck wasn't nearby, then he ran along the fence. The white van screeched to a halt, and the door slid wide.

Leo hurried inside, and the van sped off as the door slammed shut.

The musty alien scent filled his nostrils, and he stared at the pair of them, sitting near his partner. "Jacob B. Plemmons. Are you ready to make history?"

The Secretary of Defense nodded and tossed him a round device. "It's time."

Leo glanced at the nearest alien, sensing his thoughts like he'd always been able to do, and his vision filled with images of war and destruction.

The invasion had begun.

THE END

Printed in Great Britain
by Amazon